When We Grow Up

When We Grow Up

Angelica Baker

FLATIRON
BOOKS
NEW YORK

WHEN WE GROW UP. Copyright © 2025 by Angelica Baker. All rights reserved. Printed in the United States of America. For information, address Flatiron Books, 120 Broadway, New York, NY 10271.

www.flatironbooks.com

Library of Congress Cataloging-in-Publication Data

Names: Baker, Angelica, author.
Title: When we grow up / Angelica Baker.
Description: First edition. | New York : Flatiron Books, 2025.
Identifiers: LCCN 2024018039 | ISBN 9781250345776 (hardcover) |
　ISBN 9781250345783 (ebook)
Subjects: LCGFT: Novels.
Classification: LCC PS3602.A58415 W47 2025 | DDC 813/.6—dc23/eng/20240429
LC record available at https://lccn.loc.gov/2024018039

Our books may be purchased in bulk for promotional, educational, or business use. Please contact your local bookseller or the Macmillan Corporate and Premium Sales Department at 1-800-221-7945, extension 5442, or by email at MacmillanSpecialMarkets@macmillan.com.

First Edition: 2025

10　9　8　7　6　5　4　3　2　1

For my parents

SATURDAY

1

On the January morning in Hawaiʻi when they all think, for an hour, that they are about to die, they first sit together on the deck and look out toward the sea.

It's early Saturday morning, their second day on the island. Everyone is awake already and no one is hungover, a state of affairs that would have been unimaginable even five years ago.

Clare is here, on the island, because she's trying desperately to feel better. After the past year, after the past month, after the cluster of ill-advised decisions she made in Los Angeles a few weeks ago. She's here to sit in sunshine for the next six days with people who have known her since she was twelve years old. She has told herself that this will feel like healing.

And now it's eight o'clock in the morning, and everyone is up, and most of them have showered. The boys sit, stand, wander in and out of the house at lazy speeds. The sliding glass door remains open so that the lush air hits your skin no matter where you are. Clare sits at the table on the deck with Jessie, both of them scrolling the news on their phones. Everything is so aggressively peaceful that when she hears the insistent bleat of an emergency text advisory, she can't place the noise at first.

Jessie picks up her spasming phone.

"Ballistic missile threat inbound to Hawai'i," she reads. "Seek immediate shelter. This is not a drill."

She looks up, tilts her head like she's trying to shake one last drop of recalcitrant water from a clogged ear. Clare looks down at her own phone screen.

"I don't understand. It's a drill?"

Other phones begin to erupt. Kyle charges out from the kitchen, where he's been taking orders for breakfast sandwiches.

"Shit," he says. "Shit, shit, shit. Is this real?"

Renzo follows him.

"Kyle! Stop it. Just, stop."

Kyle stops. But there's nothing to replace it, his bellowing. So they all just stare at their screens in the breaking-news hunch they've perfected this past year, as synchronized as they would be on a dance floor.

Except for Mac, who flops down onto a couch, makes a point of crossing his arms, and turns his face up to the sun. He yawns.

"It's clearly not real," he says. No one reacts.

"Well." Renzo sighs. "We can't say we didn't see this coming. It's quite honestly a miracle it's taken a full year to get us all killed, no? We were promised 'carnage,' yes? So, *et voilà*. This is what we've been waiting for. To die as the world's most inane collateral damage. Happy 2018, baby."

"Oh, you're so fucking clever," Kyle says. "What do we do?"

He looks at Clare, as if it's a question with an answer.

She sits down on the edge of the hot tub, lurches forward and touches her nose to her knees. She can suddenly feel everything happening inside her body. Her stomach roiling and then ceasing the way it does right before she vomits, the saliva draining from her mouth like tides sucking at the sand. She looks down at her hands and they're shaking. Should she call Jamie? Does her husband know this is happening? She tries to remember where he is right now, if he's already home in Boston or if he's still in Hong Kong. Sydney? No, Hong Kong, she thinks.

But when she looks up at everyone else, they're in motion, flitting back and forth between the house and the deck. No one else is sitting still or even sitting down. She tries to refuse the terror any space to rampage, holding herself still the way you might hold a glass of water high in the air during an earthquake's initial lurch.

Because all the possibilities are laughable, right? The image of, what—of dying? The image doesn't exist in her brain, it's an unwelcome specter scorched from the edge of a future photograph. If the missile hits the ocean right now, then what? When will she be dead? How long will she sit here first, wondering exactly how much time she has left?

She looks up and Kyle is scrutinizing her, his arms crossed. He darts inside and returns with a glass of ice water.

"Drink the whole thing," he tells her. "Now."

Renzo rolls his eyes.

"Don't harangue her. Let her get sick! It may well not matter!"

"Ren, please, I beg you," Mac rumbles from his position on the couch. "Shut up."

"We need to turn on the news," Clare says.

She walks into the house and stands in front of the blank television. No one can find the remote. That's when Liam comes up behind her and puts his hands on her arms, cups her shoulders with his palms.

"Okay," he says. She can feel the lower tones of his voice in the base of her throat, the backs of her knees, along her scalp just behind her ears. "You need to calm down. There is absolutely zero chance that this isn't either a hoax or just plain human error."

She says nothing, thinks: *That's not what "zero chance" means.*

She cannot do any of the things she wants to do: cry, turn, put her lips to his collarbone, feel his hands circling her waist. Let him fold her into that aura, vague like smoke, that he carries with him everywhere: whatever this is, it will not touch him, it cannot compete with his life-long good luck. That's all she wants to feel.

Someone finds the remote, and the television blasts to life. It's so loud that they wince, but the volume is controlled by a different re-mote, which they also cannot find. The anchor's flat, nasal vowels are unavoidable everywhere, the kitchen, the deck. Clare and Liam stand there watching the lipsticked mouth move.

"Very little chance," he says finally. He takes his hands away from her and pushes past Renzo, who's suddenly standing at the sliding glass door, feet planted, hands on hips. Renzo follows Liam with his chin, then turns back to Clare. She refuses to meet his gaze. She stares at the television until her eyes burn.

Jessie is on the phone with her airline. She is, it seems, asking if they can get her on a flight that leaves in the next twenty minutes.

"Do you really want to be in the air?" Kyle mutters.

Is that possible? Clare thinks. Surely, planes aren't flying. If this is real. But Jessie periodically encounters a living voice on the other end of the call, hisses into the phone for a few seconds, and then returns to coiled silence while she sits on hold.

There is some comfort in that, maybe. She wouldn't be on hold if it was real. No one would have answered the call. *We're not just all going to sit around on hold with an airline until we're flattened*, Clare thinks.

Renzo bounces on the balls of his feet, offering increasingly crass jokes about their options for a ritual group suicide.

"Jessie," he calls over. "You're wasting time. Do we know anyone who has actual pull with an airline? *That's* what we should be doing. I hate to be gauche, but Liam—maybe we call your father?"

Liam doesn't respond. No one states the obvious: What, exactly, would even someone like Liam's father do? Is he going to airlift them out fast enough to, what? Outpace a missile?

They check Twitter, which, incredibly, seems like it might be the most efficient way to find out whether they're really in danger. Some girl they went to high school with is tweeting from Hawai'i; evidently she's become a reporter. Kyle says the name, but Clare cannot picture this person.

"I'm ninety percent sure," Renzo says, "that Kyle slept with her a few times. More than a few? Didn't we get a little bit competitive about her, sweetie? Wasn't I still trying to force it at that point? A square peg in a round hole, so to speak?"

Kyle flips him off without looking up from his phone.

"I don't know what he's so pissy about," Renzo stage-whispers. "He won, after all. I think she blew him once in an empty classroom. I was furious."

"This is what y'all are talking about right now?" Mac says, and Clare can hear his determination to be fearless already wavering.

"Maybe we should drive up to the club," Jessie offers. Her voice is brittle, and Clare realizes it's because of the reminder of Renzo pursuing other girls in high school. *Fifteen years ago, Jess*, she thinks. *Oh, honey.* Mac opens one eye and fixes it on Clare, and she can see he's heard the same thing. Well, he's one to talk. Look how closely he still monitors Jessie's moods.

"Up at the club," Jessie struggles on. "They might have a, you know? I mean, just in case."

"A bomb shelter?" Clare sputters. "Were you just about to say 'bomb shelter'?"

"Absolutely not." Emboldened by Clare's disbelief, Jessie nods vigorously, eager to be agreeable. "No! We are definitely not going to a bomb shelter."

"This is wild," Mac says. "I wish I had this on video, for later. We're fine. I'd put money down. The Black guy always dies first in the horror movie, and I'm telling you that, truly, he isn't worried. At all."

"The Black guy in the horror movie is *never* worried," Renzo spits. "That is precisely why he always dies first, moron."

"This isn't a horror movie!" Jessie shrieks. "It's about to be a disaster movie. How can you guys sit there making jokes?"

"More of a postapocalyptic drama, no?" Renzo says. "Nuclear winter?"

"Will everyone please, just," Clare says, closing her eyes again. Is she going to die today? Are they going to sit here, willing and frozen and frivolous, until the moment the missile hits? Is there some frenzied action they should take, or should have taken twenty minutes ago? Have they waited too long to *do* something? What were they supposed to do?

"I'll tell you what they *do* have up at the club," Kyle offers. "What they do have is, they have excellent mai tais. Maybe we should just go get drunk."

"Or start having sex!" Renzo brightens. Clare does not look at Liam. She tells herself that Renzo has not lobbed this intentionally in her direction.

"If this is real," Renzo continues, waving his hand in cavalier loops, "then, yes, I might indeed like a mai tai."

"Ditto," Liam says quietly.

If it's real, she thinks wildly, *we could tell the truth. I could walk across the room and touch him right now. I could take his hand and walk him inside and let him fuck me up against the bathroom sink.*

Just the thought of it rises in her throat, catches her. She coughs.

"You people are acting a whole-ass fool," Mac says, still pretending to be calm.

"I beg your pardon." Renzo draws himself up, elongating his spine from its usual seductive curl. "Might I ask what, sir, you mean when you say, 'you people'?"

Later, what Clare will remember is how little actually happens. No one exposes the soft underbelly that might allow anything to happen. They will always know, from now on, what they did when they thought they were going to die: absolutely nothing.

Renzo, with his unbearable snark, is the only one who seems to derive pleasure from the muted chaos. Mac remains on the couch, struggling to hold himself still. Kyle never stops his loping circles through the house, around the hot tub. Liam sinks into total silence. Jessie repeatedly takes the phone from her ear and stares at it, as if the elusive airline employees will see her frustration and snap to attention.

They just . . . dither. There's no other word for it. Maybe they're all promising some voice in their heads that they will change their lives. That even if this itself isn't real, they will nevertheless learn *something* from it that might be.

But mostly, they just insist repeatedly that it's hilarious. Then no one laughs.

Later, Clare will realize that another opportunity has been lost. If she could choose how to tell this story, from start to finish, she would frame the morning of the missile as something essentially disruptive. Something that left her mind jagged and unpleasant, a harsh space to be escaped no matter what.

If she could choose, she would say that she has sex with Liam then, in the immediate aftermath, or even in those brief, endless moments of thinking that she's maybe about to die. She risked it all, her husband, her marriage, because of this. The sizzling phones, lying on the table.

She would lie. She would shape the story to justify her own weakness. Is this what it will be like now, she wonders later that morning and so many times in the subsequent days they all spend together on that island. Will she be constantly preparing herself for some judge, some jury. Pleading righteously with no one, scheming and smiling her way through the secret and then still, eventually, begging to be let off the hook.

Nearly an hour after the first message, their phones erupt once more. It was human error. There was no missile. Their lives won't end, at least not because of this. They'll live to dither one more day.

They forget, so fast, whatever it was they vowed to change. They tell themselves that the dread, the panic they felt when they thought they would die together, has no significance beyond this morning. They forget those minutes when they expected clarity but felt only the settling weight of the knowledge that, for once, they were the ones in the cross hairs. They forget what they were waiting to learn. They forget the sense of terror that gripped them by their skulls, forget the haziness with which they stared and thought, *Is it you, then? Is yours the last face I'll ever see? Is there something I should tell you, right now, just in case?*

They remember instead only the details, the tiny flourishes that will color the novelty anecdote. They say again and again, *What a relief.* They laugh at one another. They tell demonstrable falsehoods, especially: *Fuck, we almost died!* They know it isn't true, but they say it anyway. They do not wish to feel embarrassed, and so they pretend that the most important parts of it, at least, were real. They claim for themselves that frisson of actual danger. They try it on for size.

2

In the end, they haven't spent so very long in limbo. But the sourness in the jaw lingers, the sensation of a sweaty fist clenched in the chest. The day has already lost its shape. It was going to be the last day, and now it's just another one.

Phones begin to ring, as if they've been granted permission. The room is airier now, the noisy tension has popped like a cork from a bottle. It happens almost in sequence: Kyle's parents call, then his older sister, then he leaves the room to conference in his brother as well. Mac's parents call twice until he answers, his mother's sobbing so loud it's audible to everyone else, and they insist that his brother will be calling, too. He steps out onto the patio, nodding regularly, one finger plugging the ear not pressed to the phone. Liam answers in the voice he only ever uses with his father: curt, efficient, close but not warm. He grimaces but listens intently, a beloved lieutenant confirming orders. Renzo said once that Liam's father could hit him with *Sorry, kid, you're out of the will, I just sold the story to* Variety, and Liam would at most bite his bottom lip and reply with *Got it, appreciate the clarity, let me know next steps.*

A mistake, Clare rebukes herself. To think about Liam biting his bottom lip.

She, Jessie, and Renzo remain where they are. They stare at their phones and not each other. They don't acknowledge that the phones re-main silent. Clare closes her eyes, hears her mother's voice. *Honey, by the time we even saw it the whole thing was over! What was I going to do, really? You were on vacation!*

Earlier there was talk of the club gym, a bike ride, possibly a yoga class on the beach at Shipwreck Beach. But now they all slide into some tacit agreement to just . . . sit outside for a while. Clare tries to figure out if anyone else is wondering whether to brim with gratitude. Or waiting for mania to manifest belatedly. Or hoping to forget everything every-one said.

The house sits on a parcel of land within a larger, still-unfinished de-velopment. After a morning at the beach, they spent yesterday up at the main clubhouse, competing on side-by-side treadmills and rubbing their elbows with salt scrubs and shooting pool during cocktail hour, mai tais on the lanai beneath the ceiling fans. They watched the sun set beyond the cliffs, past the pools and the rolling lawns. When Renzo first de-scribed this place, during the weeks he spent coaxing her into buying a plane ticket, he made it sound like some white-carpeted McMansion on a golf course. *I would have preferred you to experience the breakfast tacos in Austin or the ski condo in Mammoth,* he said, *but then you've skipped several years in a row, haven't you? And this is the big one. All the thirtieth birthdays.* She tried to mention money, that it would be irresponsible, but there was just a long and ragged silence on the line before he laughed at her.

So here she is. With Renzo, Kyle, Jessie, Mac. And Liam. Kyle's par-ents' second home, the Harmons' house on Kaua'i, is not at all what she expected. There is, to be fair, a golf course right across the road. But still, it feels like hushed seclusion, like the grounds of an elegant hotel aban-doned to its own lazy rhythms in the wake of some genteel disaster far away, elsewhere.

Jamie was due to spend most of the winter traveling for work, so she flew to LA early for Christmas and then bought this ticket on a whim. Their apartment in Boston has been sitting empty for weeks, the air-less kitchen appliances humming along fruitlessly without them. They somehow managed to speak on both his Christmas morning and hers without realizing, forgetting in two different time zones to say, *Merry Christmas, I love you*.

He did make a pro forma offer, at first. To come along. His hectic travel schedule saved her the need to clarify that he wasn't exactly invited, that no one has ever brought a partner along. Kyle proposed inviting a college roommate, once, and even though it never came to fruition, Renzo still mentions it darkly. This seems noteworthy to Clare in a way it didn't when she was younger. It can just be . . . hard. To see exactly where new strangers might try to fit themselves. It's not just Jamie.

In college, they all visited. But those weekends always devolved into cloistered reunions: downing shots cross-legged on the lint-fleeced floors of their dorm rooms, climbing statues together on darkened, icy quads. Not even the most performative interest in meeting friends or roommates. There were visits the year she met Jamie, but all she remembers now is a benign stiffness from him when he realized that Renzo and Mac weren't there to meet him, as if she were a divorcée and he the new boyfriend realizing that her weekend with the kids wasn't about him at all.

Kyle shakes off the torpor first, returns to the kitchen. He finishes the chattering bacon, scrambles some eggs, toasts six English muffins. Mac brews another pot of pour-over. Last night they were all quite virtuous, barely two bottles of wine between the six of them, but now Clare finds some Prosecco in the fridge and holds the bottles aloft like trophies, letting them pose their own question. Renzo nods decisively. He holds the glasses by their stems as she pours, intent as if he were helping her perform surgery, and then carries them outside with great ceremony.

Kyle passes her two empty plates.

"No eggs on mine," she reminds him.

"Excuse me?"

"I hate eggs. You know this."

"What? I've *seen* you eat eggs before."

She laughs, but he looks almost bereft.

"You're the story I always tell! The little speech I give whenever people try to force me to eat eggs. I told you once I didn't like them and you just could not comprehend it."

She falters. Because, of course, she's the one who's made that conversation an anecdote, who's burnished it across years. How many times has she conjured that memory, the boy gaping at her in blurred confusion? His hair was longer, whenever this happened, so shaggy, so greasy, he was always running his hands through it. He was thinner, too, his arms stringy and his shoulder blades sharp against worn cotton. Some morning they were playing house, trying to feel like grown-ups, waking up hungover and naked and deciding to make breakfast together. Kyle would never actually say anything out loud, in high school, about the money stuff, how anxious she was. But he was always, in tiny practical ways, taking care of her. Where were they that morning? Whose house, whose father's liquor seeping from their underslept, resilient pores? Those parts of the memory have vanished.

He must have these stories, too. The things she did long ago that have become tales he tells all the people in his life who have never heard her name.

"You were making me breakfast," she says. He smiles and shrugs, as difficult as ever to offend or unsettle.

"It was adorable. You kept asking, like, 'What about poached? I can see hardboiled, sure, but like—everyone eats scrambled, right? The fuck are you gonna order at a diner?'"

"Well," he replies. "Checks out. I believe that I was indeed adorable, whenever this allegedly occurred. But I'm sure I was horrified. It's . . . eggs. Who refuses to eat eggs?"

"Clare does, actually," Renzo calls, breezing back in to find the orange juice. "It is so deeply bizarre."

Kyle looks at her, delighted, and laughs. Renzo's head swivels between them in his desperation to interpret their shared glee.

"Oh, you two," Kyle says. "Little old married couple, as usual. No one else can compete."

"You never tried that hard to compete," Renzo shoots back seamlessly.

Kyle passes Clare her sandwich.

"I keep trying to tell her," Renzo continues, "that a few inexplicable quirks aren't going to be what magically turns her into a respected authoress."

This brief jolt of hostility, for which she is never prepared. This is familiar. Renzo hates to be shut out of even the most glancing, careless intimacies. Clare ignores him, simply because she knows it will derange him, and kisses Kyle's cheek with extravagant fondness.

"Thanks, baby."

As she leaves the kitchen she hears Renzo, still miffed.

"What the fuck was so funny?"

Eventually, everyone's breakfast is assembled. The air outside feels like a dream, drifting up off the ocean, toying with the ti plants. Clare sits with her bare feet up on the table and bites into her sandwich, the bacon crunching salt between her teeth.

She reminds herself, insists. This is it, what she was hoping for when she decided to come to Hawai'i. She didn't want to reward Renzo's canny manipulations, but she also knew that, in the end, it would just . . . feel good. To be somewhere warm and slow, to leave the whole year behind and with it the feeling of being crushed by degrees into submission to some amorphous authority, some acknowledgment about herself she'd hoped to evade for a few more years at least. She's sick of asking herself whether she's still on track to become someone who is actually good. She's sick of wondering if it's pathetic to cut herself that slack, *becoming*, when she's about to turn thirty. She's sick of sitting at tables with the wives of Jamie's colleagues and reassuring herself that she is aware and they are *not*, she is engaged and they are *not*. That she, at least, has made tangible efforts to change her life in the year since the election. Even if she can no longer tell which changes she's made because they are truly good, in some way that can't be discredited, and which ones she's made just because she wants everyone else to see them as good and admirable. Even if she can't parse that distinction, she's tried. Right? Hasn't she? She's tried to rise to the occasion, to meet this collective doom awaiting them all with something resembling real urgency. She's tried not to carry on as she would have before. They all seem to agree on this: they must not carry on as they would have before. Even if, in the meantime, that looks an awful lot like doing nothing at all.

Maybe that's the actual problem, she thinks now. The whole past year has felt like "in the meantime," but no one understands how they'll know when it's over. No one can judge whether all these little pats on your own back for (let's face it) the most minor efforts are, in the end, the sticky proof that you're obviously not a very good person at all.

She takes another bite of her sandwich. *That's* what she wants to focus on. Nothing about the past year and everything about the breeze, the old friends, the sandwich and the mimosa she's washing it down with. It feels good, she reminds herself. To be here.

But then Jessie squints at someone's copy of the *New Yorker*, the cover illustration of Colin Kaepernick kneeling alongside Martin Luther King, Jr.

"This strikes me as a bit much," she says. "I mean, athletes shouldn't be paid that much in the first place. It's so messed up. But so then, do we really need to be canonizing him as this great, like, revolutionary? Geoff was talking the other day, I mean—I do not follow football, obviously. But did he have a philanthropic bone in his body before all of . . . this? And now, suddenly, what? He's leading a movement?"

Geoff is Jessie's newish boyfriend. He is the source of much curiosity for everyone but Renzo, who has spent some time with him in Los Angeles. Clare cannot picture Jessie in what is, by Renzo's account, an actual adult relationship. But then, Geoff didn't know Jessie in high school. He met her so recently, is the thing. When you consider the whole sweep of time it's taken for their personalities to congeal. He doesn't know half of what Clare knows; he can't.

But he did recently move into Jessie's place in Mount Washington, and she has mentioned him every third minute since Clare arrived on the island.

"I'm sorry, but—" Clare begins, already regretting it. "Why does that . . . matter? Who cares what Colin Kaepernick was doing five years ago?"

She feels something in her stomach rebelling against the cold sludge left over from their earlier panic, and already she knows she's about to turn the full power of her bad mood in Jessie's direction.

"Come on," Jessie continues. "This is like when those undergrads threw the tantrum about racist Halloween costumes at Yale a few years ago. I was like, look. I've been there. That place is a paradise. I would *kill* to be twenty years old again and living on that campus. They're in for a rude awakening after graduation, when they'll have to face all the actual horror in the world. If we keep, just . . . if we're always in constant uproar about all these little things, whatever, everything's a, whatever, a *microaggression*, then people will just write us off! And I just . . . the stakes are too high. Aren't they? I mean, look at this morning! Is this professional athlete's career really our biggest problem?"

"This morning wasn't real," Renzo notes. Jessie blinks.

What a surprise, Clare thinks uncharitably, to hear Jessie mention the fact that she attended Yale. How unusual, for her to do that. *Babe*, Jamie will say sometimes when Clare FaceTimes him from a Los Angeles parking lot, leaving a bar where she's seen Jessie for the first time in a year and been reminded of this little habit. *You went to Dartmouth and Renzo went to Brown. I mean, come on.*

But I don't cram it down anyone's throat, she'll say. *Jessie just wants an excuse to mention that she was the third generation to attend.* And then Jamie will chuckle, shake his head. *Sometimes I forget that being "the poor one" was really just some whole other thing at your high school.*

"Guys," Kyle says, eager to deflate any possible argument before it gains the slightest momentum. "Can we not?"

"For you," Clare says, speaking only to Jessie, ignoring the boys, "Yale was a paradise. For you. Which, fine! No one is trying to take that away from you—Jess, come on. I'm really not. I just think that there is a possibility, maybe even a likelihood, that—I mean, it obviously wasn't a paradise for everyone. Right? Those kids aren't out there protesting on their quad for their own amusement. I don't think Black students at Yale are just . . . making it all up."

"Why are we presuming they wouldn't protest purely for their own amusement?" Renzo ponders. "They're teenagers." Clare can hear a bright, sharp warning in his voice.

"That video of the boy confronting, I don't remember," she tries again. "I think it was his professor? They both had tears in their eyes. I mean, when you say that 'we're in an uproar,' I guess it becomes a little bit for me, just. Who's the 'we' in that sentence? Right? Because actually we're just talking about other white girls. Usually."

"I have to tell you, I am so fucking tired of that," Jessie snaps. Kyle coughs down the last bite of his sandwich. Renzo curls himself into a pretzel, his legs crossed beneath him, and leans forward with his chin in his hands.

"I just, give me a break." Jessie has reined in the initial flash of anger. "If you're that miserable as a sophomore at *Yale*, of all places, then that's on you. Maybe you're a bit spoiled and a bit young and not yet prepared to participate in the adult world. I realize this sounds harsh, but I mean, Clare. *Come on.* Plenty of people would have given their right arm for my spot at that school."

Clare can feel Renzo willing her to make eye contact. If she looks at him, he will shake his head at her misguided belief that Jessie actually merits this argument. Which seems frankly more insulting than whatever it is Clare is trying to do. She tries to summon her husband's voice in her ear: *You're still upset, it's not about her, just let it go, why are you letting her goad you like this?* But her husband, after all, isn't here. And listening to her friends from high school debate whether Colin Kaepernick is allowed to protest is making her skin itch. And the truth is that she simply does not feel like letting it go.

"I don't . . ." She falters. "I'm not saying that—Quite obviously, the two of us sitting here debating this is idiotic. But don't you assume that we could ask—I mean, if that's our benchmark, plenty of people would kill for your spot now, too, right? But don't you think if you asked a Black woman our age at that firm, someone who trusted us enough to be brutally honest about what it's like to work there? She probably notices a million things every day that sail right past you. Right? I mean, it's going to be a very different place for someone else. The same thing goes for me, obviously. I'm including myself in this."

"Oh, yes," Renzo chimes in. "By all means, let's dig deeper. This is so fruitful, thus far, this piercing line of inquiry."

Jessie blinks again.

"I earned my spot at that firm. I worked my ass off in law school."

"That is so, *so* not what we are talking about right now."

"No? What are we talking about, Clare?"

Kyle stares down into his coffee as if it's administering him an eye exam, and Clare feels a pang of regret. He's been so sweet, taking such good care of them all, the consummate host. And she knows how distressing he finds even the faintest whisper of conflict.

"Ladies," Renzo tries again, striking a jollier tone this time.

"Clare, your husband probably makes more money than the rest of us combined, all right?" Jessie says. "So can we, just, maybe, lose the chip on your shoulder? You're not a better person than us just because you've decided to, like, I don't know. *Speak for* Colin Kaepernick? I mean, Jesus."

Then there is silence, for a smothering length of time. *Fuck the* New Yorker, Clare thinks.

"I don't think I'm a better person than anyone," she says feebly.

"Oh, please."

"If I may backtrack," Renzo says, putting down his sandwich. "I am just a bit insulted, Jess—quite hurt, actually—that you just *assume* that little Jameson makes more money than I do! I didn't sell my soul so you could all ignore my success! I demand some respect."

Jessie tries to smile at him. At this moment, predictably, Mac emerges from the house.

"Here," Jessie says with relish. "Clare, let's ask Mac. Mac, Clare has some incisive commentary, just some genuine life lessons to teach us all."

And of course, Clare is now caught out, deeply embarrassed by the prospect of lecturing Mac on the perils of clueless, well-meaning white women. She also has no idea what a conversation about this between

Jessie and Mac would look like and no interest in forcing him to do it in front of the entire group. Which Jessie surely knows.

"What's up?"

"Well," Clare begins. "We were just talking about Colin Kaepernick—"

"Nope," he replies, immediately turning back into the house.

"Indeed!" Renzo crows. Kyle chuckles, and Jessie looks, for some obscure reason, vindicated. She drops the magazine on the coffee table, follows Mac. After a moment, Kyle snorts, makes eye contact with Renzo, and mimes looking at his watch.

"Day two," he murmurs. "The Clare Campaign, TM, making friends but more importantly, truly *influencing* people, already gearing up."

"'Twas ever thus," Renzo warbles, extending a hand to her and pretending to do an exaggerated bow.

"How I've missed it," Kyle says. Clare turns to him.

"I have a question for you. Why is it that whatever has you so terrified at the tiniest hint of disagreement with anyone else, whatever it is that would probably convince you to sit here like a statue if someone started spouting off to defend the KKK—why does that impulse never, *never* seem to keep you from bitching at *me*?"

Kyle stands up, puts his hands in front of him as if to push her away, and walks into the house. Renzo eyes her over the rim of his coffee mug.

"Don't do that. You know he always defends you to her, always, especially when you aren't in the room. Don't kick out at him."

"She started it!"

"Well, be that as it may."

"Lovely," she says. "Good to know that you, evidently, don't defend me? She started it!"

"Mmm," he intones. "And I'm sure it has nothing, but nothing, to do with proving, for the five hundred eighty-third time since 2003, that you're smarter than she is."

"We should just let her sit there and wait for Mac to tell her she's full of shit? Because it has to be his job?"

"My love, I don't remember Mac asking you to fight this battle for him. Am I wrong? I would imagine that Mac is . . . shall we say, well versed in Jessie's views. I would imagine that, if he wants your help, he'll ask for it."

"I forgot that I'm meant to nod along politely and then roll my eyes and insult her intelligence as soon as she leaves the room."

"Believe me, darling, I was rolling my eyes at the both of you. But I do, you know, just tip my hat to you. So much valuable food for thought, so much for us all to mull tonight, lying sleepless in our beds. I think I'll change the subject, now?"

"Dear God, yes, please." Kyle reappears as suddenly as he exited, stepping back through the sliding glass door.

Jessie, too, returns to the patio without fanfare. She stretches out on a couch and picks up another magazine. Liam emerges from the house.

"It sounds like we're all having a lazy, hazy time out here? You've driven Mac straight into the shower."

"It's taken her less time than usual to decide that my very presence is an insult," Renzo says. He puts down his plate to rip a paper towel from a nearby roll, then folds it in quarters and passes it between his hands, cleaning hot sauce from his fingers. Clare watches him, says nothing.

"You know what?" Liam nearly shouts. He disappears briefly into the house and returns with the second bottle of Prosecco. "I'm topping everyone off. This is the last of it, though, so after this we'll have to start mixing our own mai tais. Or doing tequila shots. We don't have that many options in there, currently."

Renzo has reverted, on a dime, to his most charming mode. He curls up beside Kyle and Mac, who returns freshly showered, to discuss the boat excursion planned for tomorrow, the one particular fish they'll need to avoid. The blue something, whose organs can contain some dangerous chemical. Clare watches his honking laugh, always so at odds with the graceful elongation of his neck, the assumption that someone might at any minute (why wouldn't they?) want to take his picture.

There was a time in high school when he was so beautiful she couldn't keep her eyes off him, she would make up excuses to place his arm around her own waist and pull him closer, smell his neck. He was still having sex with girls back then, but not with Clare. He loved her, he loved Jessie, he wanted them both in his thrall, but Jessie could only ever exert any power over him by choosing, however intermittently, Mac. And Clare never touched Renzo because she could already see that he didn't care about any of it, and that intimacy—she was the first person he told, in high school, that he was gay—provided her the cover to catalogue worshipfully all the things about him that were so maddeningly attractive.

Even at fifteen, she understood his beauty to be precious *because* of the fact that it was so fleet, already breaking down before their eyes. *Everyone always says that teenagers don't understand how beautiful they are*, she thinks now. *That their appeal lies in their thoughtless inability to appreciate the skin, the hair, the plasticity of youth before it expires.* But Clare couldn't get enough of Renzo's beauty because she knew that, even if he grew up to be handsome, it would lessen with every passing year. They lived back then in perpetual fear that this was the most beautiful they'd ever be, that their future selves would be tired and gray and always looking back. Always missing the same memories of each other.

Renzo is indeed handsome now, and dashing, stylish and perpetually groomed, sculpted. His face has a chiseled shape it never had back then. But he isn't beautiful, not in the same way. Only his laugh, when it takes possession of his entire body like a seizure, returns him to his most familiar, scrappy, fifteen-year-old self.

Two nights ago, as her cab idled in the buzzing dark before a curving row of identical houses, as she scrolled through their effusive and ribald group email chain searching for an actual address, it was his laugh that she heard through an open window, distinct from all the other chirps and whispers of the nighttime island. His laugh that led her inside, finally confirmed she was in the right place.

If she says anything now, he'll insist that she misinterpreted his tone. That she's too sensitive, *so tetchy!*

"These fish can really fuck you up," Kyle is explaining. Evidently, your senses of smell and taste will scramble. Your tongue will detect bitter rather than sweet, flinch at cold water as if it were boiling.

Liam refills Clare's glass last. He kicks at Jessie's feet until she makes room for him on the couch, and then he sits down at the end closest to Clare. He sits so that their knees touch. Only when he holds his leg motionless next to hers does she register, for the first time, that she's been moving ever since the missile alert: her ankle twitching, her fingernails digging into the soft skin on her arms, her crooked canine teeth pinching the insides of her mouth until she can almost taste blood.

But Liam sits down and they both sit completely still, their legs touching. She can smell his hair, the sweat at his temples. She tells herself to stand up, to go back inside. She does not move as she tells herself twice, then a third time.

3

Looked at one way, Liam shouldn't even be here.

Clare is lying on a chair by one of the three different pools behind the club, the one that's essentially a series of cascading, shallow waterfalls. Kyle and Renzo have been jumping between levels, hurling themselves from rocks like children, and she represses the instinct to call to them, to point out that they're doing cannonballs in shallow water. Liam and Mac are splashing around in the last and fullest pool, cupping their hands to their mouths and whooping encouragement. Jessie is tanning, her wide-brimmed hat pulled low over her face. She's pointedly chosen a chair far enough away from Clare's to preclude all conversation.

Clare tries to look beyond the boys to the ocean in the distance, the layers of blue ringing the shore. She tries to ignore the manicured golf course that lies between her and this view, letting her gaze soften so that she sees only the ocean.

Her eye is drawn back when Liam pulls himself up out of the water, shakes out his hair. She reaches back to lower the chair with a sudden jolt, crashing onto her back and removing him from her sight line. She closes her eyes.

They all met in the seventh grade, even Liam. It took a few more years for them to realize they had already shaped themselves into a closed system, although Renzo and Kyle were a pair from the moment they met. She can't remember them as individuals before they were a duo, loitering outside the library and attempting to use cafeteria trays as skateboards. They were still such little, malleable humans, but already they had identified the things in each other that would need protecting, the innate qualities in each boy that the other sorely lacked. Kyle saw the terror behind Renzo's bravado, his lack of any bone-deep belief that his safety was guaranteed. Maybe as a thirteen-year-old Kyle didn't yet understand that this fear was about money, but he did see it. And Renzo, in turn, saw the softness in Kyle, a boy who never wanted for anything, saw the flexibility that could be so easily abused. And he appointed himself the one to stand behind Kyle in those moments, like the spine that holds the flopping pages of the book together.

They would career around campus, flirting with the concept of cutting class but never actually doing it, vandalizing various elements of school property. Renzo was the mastermind, Kyle was the one to intercede whenever an authority figure threatened to impose consequences. Jessie stood close by, applauding their misbehavior. Even if Renzo's focus hadn't settled on her yet, she was waiting for him. She was befriending Kyle as one way to get closer.

Back then, Clare noticed Renzo first. Kyle was the one who showed interest, seeking any excuse to tickle her, ambling around with his pigeon-toed sneakers and his sleepy eyelids, his slow grin. She knew, as soon as she could imagine herself one day having sex, that she would probably have it with him. But Renzo made jokes whose punchlines sailed past her, referenced films she thought only her parents had seen, carried dog-eared Martin Amis and Ian McEwan novels around in the back pocket of his skintight jeans. Made a habit of explaining to her what her taste in music should be. She could feel him waiting to discern his effects on her, and then his reluctant admiration when he realized that she was neither immune nor afflicted. That while she might obsessively chase his approval, she wouldn't fall in love with him. And that, as a result, he would be able to keep her close to him forever.

Mac came into things soon enough, first through Kyle—they were on the flag football team together—and then, of course, through Jessie, who was eager for any chance to make out with him in front of Renzo. It was only later, after everything with Renzo's mother, that Mac became as quick as the rest of them to protect Renzo, to excuse the vicious outbursts and the flagrant taste for self-destruction. Even when Mac was dating Jessie, somehow the boys never held it against each other. And by senior year, once Mac had established some well of resolve that was no longer vulnerable to Jessie, he and Renzo were, improbably, quite close.

But Liam? Liam wasn't a core member of the group, not really. Historically, he has never made these annual trips. He was around, in high school, but he was really Renzo's friend. Clare has tried this week to remember any significant time she and Liam ever spent alone. They didn't, and she feels sure of this. Nothing has been submerged, all this time. That's not the problem.

She rolls to her side, letting one leg flop across the other and savoring the fizz in her hamstring. Renzo laughed yesterday morning, took a photo of them all in the gym rolling out their IT bands, posted it to Instagram. The bodies may be breaking down, she thinks now, but they're all engaged in the exact same choreographed dances. Look where they all are at this very moment: Renzo and Kyle are performing physical feats for attention, Jessie is clapping, Mac is rolling his eyes, Clare is observing the rest of them.

And Liam, she notices, is watching her. She rolls onto her other side.

"Clare," Renzo calls to her. "You're going to tan like an old handbag. Get in here. Come splash around with me."

"Yeah, Clare," Liam echoes.

It feels forced, the way they're treating this week like some huge reunion. Still, a full week in Hawai'i, dug out and reanimated from the frozen death of a Boston winter. She would have been crazy to refuse. Her manager at the bookstore actually snorted when she asked if he was sure he could cover a full three weeks of her afternoon shifts: "Don't piss on my leg and tell me you'll consider canceling the trip either way."

Renzo heaves himself out of the pool, wanders over to shake water from his hair onto her legs. Clare yelps half-heartedly. Kyle materializes with two tall mai tais in his hand and Renzo takes both of them, places them on the table beside Clare's chair, and then noisily drags another chair over to sit beside her. Jessie comes to perch on the end of his lounger. Kyle groans and returns to the bar for more drinks.

Renzo hunches over the crossword in a disintegrating copy of the *Times Magazine* he's produced from Jessie's bag.

"Clare, come on. Help me, let's team up."

She still wants to resist him, which in turn makes him only looser, more affectionate. It's so familiar, the allure of his good favor settling on you like sunlight, just when you fear you've lost it. She can see Jessie noticing it too, drawn toward him by it. Clare feels suddenly exhausted. She thinks of how harsh he was this morning, how unwilling to admit that he was scared. Her limbs still feel too loose, like they'll float out and away from her torso without warning if she doesn't focus on keeping them steady. She just wants him to leave her alone.

"Come on," he wheedles. "Not devil, not Satan. Any ideas? Mephistopheles is *several* letters too long. Demon?"

"I'm thinking," Clare says. "I assume 'management consultant' won't fit?"

"Oh ho ho," he shoots back, but he's pleased. He'd much rather vicious banter than indifference. "Spicy talk from the Bride of Mephistopheles over here."

Clare would be surprised, in this moment, if Renzo could accurately summon Jamie's actual job title. Whenever any of them ask after Jamie, it's manners without curiosity, the stilted way you might ask an acquaintance about the daughter you heard was shipped off to the rehab camp in rural Oregon. Any and all significant others have, historically, been perplexed by the way they've all remained in one another's lives so deeply without really touching any outside part of those lives.

"It's not even that you're a worse version of yourself around them," Jamie said once, which led her to believe that this was, in fact, what he was trying to say. "It's more like . . . the whole thing is based on their memories of you, this personality that doesn't even really exist anymore.

You just talk past one another and pretend nothing has changed because you know that you loved them so much in the past."

They're all catching up to Clare, mostly. Renzo just bought a condo not far from the Koreatown bars where they once performed sloppy underage karaoke. Jessie lives with the oft-invoked Geoff, and Kyle is terminally single, and Mac is convinced he'll meet his future wife on the apps. The four years since Clare married Jamie have sluiced past so much more quickly than the previous five years, which felt endless, the years when the boys were all sneaking into hotel gyms with lax security or getting kicked out of bars in Atwater Village for slapping (or fucking) strangers they met in the bathroom line. Renzo used to call her on Friday evenings, pouring himself a vodka with only ice and lots of cold water. She would hear the ice cubes in his glass, cheerfully associating in anticipation of the night ahead. And he would be appalled to learn that in Boston she was brushing her teeth, turning off the light above her stove. He would hear Jamie grinding the next morning's coffee in the background and he would pretend to retch so loudly that Clare would carry the phone into the next room. Even though Renzo, of all people, should have understood how comforting it was for her to live in the same apartment for so long. The rent withdrawn from a joint account each month, the doorman in the lobby who signed for her packages. The gleaming dishwasher that never malfunctioned, the reliable central air. It was especially unkind for Renzo to tell her that her life was boring.

"What happened to my partner in crime?" Renzo asked her once, and from the slight imprecision of his plosives she knew that the current vodka wasn't his first. "There was once a girl, a complete vixen, who would just gleefully ingest any old thing I placed in the palm of her hand. Where is she, please? Put *her* on the phone."

She laughed, and they pretended he hadn't said anything too sharp, nothing meant to wound. It was true; when they were sixteen years old, that *was* her. Just for him, really, but still. Only he could have convinced her to tongue that tab of LSD before they sat through the spring musical, snickering at all the teenagers who somehow weren't afraid to display their naked hopes. It was Renzo who taught her that this was insufferable, letting other people see the things about you that rendered you most wistful. And it was Renzo with whom she would crawl up out of muggy sheets or sagging sectionals, whether they had slept curled together or in different rooms with other people, Renzo who drove her home. They might stop at some godforsaken IHOP in a hot, dry corner of the Valley, or Hugo's, or Du-par's. Coffee and pancakes and the Sunday crossword. For him, back then, she always had one more rally in her. She would never insist that the night was over. He was the one person she never wanted to see that she was afraid.

And here he is now, still doing the crossword, still reminding her how insufferable he finds her choices.

"Bride of Mephistopheles," she says to him. "How long have you been sitting on that one?"

"Private equity cannot compare, I'm sure, to the filthy lucre of consulting." He turns back to Jessie, who has been rubbing sunscreen into his shoulder blades. "Clare's lucre, we all know, comes from the purest source. Never would a mouth made unclean by amoral work touch *Clare's* lips. The horror! And all those poor little rich children who hired her to write their AP English essays for them? She was doing the Lord's work, there. I don't doubt it."

"I don't really do that anymore," Clare tries, but he's lobbed this at her precisely because he knows it's a sore spot.

"Because it bored you to tears! Hardly a case for sainthood."

Mac, Kyle, and Liam are pulling three more loungers across the limestone, sending horrendous screeching sounds echoing across the pool as they arrange themselves in a haphazard grouping. Two women in their forties, with a deflated look that indicates toddlers waiting for them somewhere nearby, approach the pool only to retreat immediately. Clare shrinks; those women surely deserve a peaceful hour by the pool more than she does.

"Are you two still fighting?" Liam asks in disbelief.

"It's a new fight," Jessie says.

"Oh, I doubt that," Kyle says. He looks over at Clare, noticing that she's watching the women move away down the path. "You okay? I feel like every five seconds this morning you look like you're about to faint."

She swallows, nods.

"Ren," Mac says. "Can we give it a rest? It's still very early."

"Are we sure that filthy lucre doesn't have . . . connotations?" Jessie wonders. "It seems like it's . . . anti-Semitic? Maybe? I feel like I've heard that."

"Jessie, my darling dearest, you are impossible this morning! I would appreciate a bit more support now that Clare's razor wit has destroyed me, drawn blood! I shan't soon recover."

"Give me that fucking crossword." Mac snatches the magazine from Renzo's hands. "I'm burning it. Either it goes or the two of you do."

"I thought we settled the great consulting debate, like, eight years ago." Kyle yawns. "Clare's disgusted and Renzo doesn't give a shit. Shouldn't near death have made the heart grow fonder, not driven you both back into your pissy little historic corners? This is allegedly vacation for the rest of us too, right? I'm not about to spend the next five days playing referee."

Renzo attempts to tackle Kyle, the sudden flail catching his mai tai and sending it to the ground. The glass doesn't break, and he ignores it.

It occurs to Clare what she should have done before they left the house, before tanning by the pool. She takes out her phone to text her parents, text Jamie, sketch the arc of the morning and its toothless conclusion. *Everything completely fine now*, she tells her husband. *I miss you*. She briefly considers relaying the Mephistopheles dig, which will actually make him laugh, but decides to save it for a call. She switches her phone to silent and places it facedown on the table beside her cocktail.

The past few days, for some reason, have been particularly thick with jokes about those early years of adulthood, the wayward late-, late-, later-youth period when they all more or less chose the career tracks they're still on. Those years, somehow, feel more alien and vague even than high school. Mac was teaching and completing his master's and staying out all night with Renzo, then vomiting into a trash can in front of his pet-rified second-graders the next morning. Renzo was a junior consultant reporting to a truly sadistic boss who was perhaps part of the last gener-ation fully permitted to hurl slurs and expletives at his underlings. Kyle wouldn't wash up in law school until a bit later, but Jessie went straight through, living in her parents' pool house and drinking with these boys every weekend.

They love dredging up the gory details from those years. The exploit-ative starting salaries, since talking money is so much easier when every digit remains firmly situated in the past. The light criminal activity of landlords who refused to fix gas leaks or repair crumbling exterior stair-cases. The roommates bringing home strangers from the bar who intro-duced themselves by chopping lines of Adderall on the coffee table. The twin mattresses propped on full bedframes because a mattress was a crip-pling expense that you couldn't purchase from a stranger online, unless of course you did exactly that, for the story.

Anecdotes describing dilemmas that were, for most of them, never more than a parental phone call away from a frictionless solution. But where was the fun in that?

But they were, at least, together. Except for Clare, the tourist dipping in and out of their lives. A blurry face on an iPhone, calling from Boston to see them all piled together in someone's backyard. Kyle carrying the phone into Renzo's room to surprise him and alarm his newest conquest; the girlfriend of Mac's who used to stand up when Clare called, her na-ked body fully visible as she stormed into the bathroom in annoyance.

Still, Clare tries to laugh as if these memories belong to her, too. She tries to imagine a world in which she never left Los Angeles. Never met Jamie.

"Here's the thing," Renzo muses, returning to his own chair, tiptoe-ing around the abandoned glass. "Someone needs to drive into town to buy beer. Among other provisions."

"I thought we were eating lunch up here?"

"Still, either way. We'll need things."

"Not it," Mac says, touching one fingertip to his nose.

"I'll go," Kyle says, standing with an air of noble resignation. "But you're coming with, Ren. I provided the house. I'm not going to be referee and chauffeur, too."

Liam catches Clare's eye again, raises an eyebrow. She does a quick calculation; he's probably right.

"I'll drive," she says. "I only had that one mimosa, back at the house."

Renzo whirls back on her.

"Oh, please. I can't get you to lift a finger to plan the tiniest part of this trip. You have yet to bother yourself with a single logistic. But now you're going to appoint yourself highway patrol?"

"She's right," Liam intervenes, pausing on his way inside to stand very close to Renzo. "You want to relax a little?"

Renzo's eyes dart between the two of them. Clare looks away, watches the pool softly calming itself after the boys' disruptions.

"Lucifer!" Jessie shouts. "I bet you it's Lucifer. That clue. Does it fit?"

Kyle hands Clare the car keys.

Los Angeles

She was at the restaurant on West Third, some place that served gour-
met versions of New England beachside snack bar food—fish sandwiches,
Old Bay fries, Caesar salad with impossibly creamy dressing—to meet a
woman she barely knew. Sofie was a friend of an acquaintance, not exactly
a high priority in the week between the holidays, but Clare had begun
to wilt under her mother's tactical scrutiny and her father's ill-concealed
dread over the status of her book deal, his peppering questions implying
that she was likely being taken advantage of, exposing herself to some
certain financial ruin. So she agreed to this dinner.

Sofie, who wanted to talk about potentially making a career swerve
from advertising into book publishing, sent a text that she was waiting at
a table on the back patio. Clare stood in the chaotic din of the restaurant,
unable to see how she was meant to access the patio, and then someone
tapped her shoulder. She turned around and it was Liam.

"You're here," she said. She hadn't seen him in so long. He smiled
down at her, touched the very ends of her hair with his fingertips and
then pulled back, clearly embarrassed by a gesture that was so intimate it
made absolutely no sense.

"Sorry," he said. "I just—last time I saw you, you still had such long hair."

"Oh," she said. "Well. Yeah."

Right away, even before he touched her, there was something going on she could not explain. Everyone always thought he was so handsome, in high school, but she never really got it. It was just that he was the child of a famous person, someone actually recognizable on the street. No one ever discussed it, the solid fact of his fame, but it was always in the air. In the way he held himself, not out of shyness or fear but out of a supreme, lifelong confidence. He wasn't like so many other powerful kids, he was never cruel or even just oblivious. Never snotty to waitresses or to the awkward kids whose pale vulnerability was so readily apparent on their faces, like the flesh of an orange exposed beneath the peel. He never picked on people, never peed into a Solo cup and told some freshman girl it was beer. When kids from another school approached him at two a.m. at the Mel's on Ventura and wanted to ask about his dad's new show, he put down his milkshake and thanked them. He wasn't protecting his own peeled-back vulnerability; he just didn't seem to have any. He already understood the exact currents that displaced themselves whenever he entered a room.

That was what Renzo had loved so much, she thought, that was the source of his tortured affinity for Liam back then. Liam made it seem that the identity he presented to the world operated in perfect harmony with whatever went on inside his own head, projected an untroubled, blissful unity. Within and without. Renzo, for all his bluster, knew early on that this could not be adopted. That Liam would always have it, that he never would. Renzo had been a scholarship student, which remained one of the most fiercely protected open secrets their group had ever collectively agreed to ignore. But even if he hadn't been. That's what you do, as a teenager. You look for those rare people who already feel utterly at home in the world, and you do everything you can to brush up against that feeling.

Liam was still smiling, almost inviting her to laugh at him, as if she had spoken this all aloud.

"You look great, too," she said, then immediately wanted to sit down on the floor of the restaurant. He had not actually told her she looked great.

"I heard about the novel," he said. "Unbelievable, Clare. Congratulations."

"Oh," she said. "No, well. I mean, I haven't finished it yet."

"Yeah, well, it takes time. How's it going? Do you want to come join us? We're in the other room, at a bar table, I'm with my editor, actually."

But he already had a hand at the small of her back, she was already letting herself be conveyed away from her dinner with Sofie, she needed it to feel like fate. Whatever was going on.

"How's the novel?" he repeated. She looked down at the phone in her hand, at the texts from this woman she suddenly could not have sat down to make conversation with in a million years. She texted apologetically, then looked up to smile apologetically. Liam was tugging at her jacket. She let him pull it from her shoulders.

"I'm sort of failing spectacularly, actually. I'm not even failing yet, I'm failing to begin to *try* to fail spectacularly, I would say—"

But she had overrated it, her ability to be flip about this, and she felt her voice get too thick too fast, and then Liam was giving her a look of such tender surprise that she almost had to step back, put some space between them.

"That's hard to imagine," he said. "You're talking to someone who knew you when you were a teenager, Clare. It's kind of impossible to imagine you failing. At anything."

She had no idea what he was talking about, what it was he saw when he looked at her, maybe she was hoping he'd tell her. Maybe that was why she sat down at his table.

His editor was a rangy and energetic man who hung on Liam's every word, seemingly to Liam's slight embarrassment. The man showed absolutely zero interest in Clare until Liam explained that she had a novel under contract, and then he peered at her over the rims of his Warby Parkers as if he hadn't previously registered anything about her.

"I'm sure you heard about it," Liam said. "It sold at auction. She had that short story that basically, like, went viral."

"Oh, fuck me. 'Unaccompanied Minor' was *you*? Oh, congratulations. You have no idea what a *boost* that was, coming when it did. Sales had been so sluggish, the frog march toward that cursed election all year. Everyone's glued to the news and then a short story devours Twitter all weekend! What a thrill. You must have been walking around in a dream for days."

She didn't mention: that Jamie was out of town the weekend the story published online. That it was one of those weekends she spent in lost hours along the river, speaking to no one and feeling like if she left the city no one would notice. The trip to New York a few weeks later, the train down from Boston and the eight different buildings and eight different humid elevators and eight different women across eight different conference tables hinting, with lavish abandon, at the fact that her life would never again be the same. The disorganized document currently lurking on her computer. The money that came not from her husband's job but from her own resources, her own efforts, even if "a lot of money" in publishing was barely a starting salary in her husband's field.

She didn't mention any of it. She just smiled. She tried to field the editor's questions about tour dates, launch events, publicity plans.

"I'm not . . ." she said finally. "I'm not really at that stage, yet. But I work in a bookshop, so. I've seen the process many times."

"I see," he said, his courtesy strained. She watched him count backward in his head. "Well, when was that story? Was that . . . more than a year ago, right?"

She could feel her mouth thinning on her face.

"Careful," he said, but his eyes were already strobing the room beyond her shoulder. "Strike while the iron is hot, and all that. You've got a window. You should pick this guy's brain, actually. He's been through the whole circus once already. I mean, essay collection, it's a different animal, but still. The basic rigamarole, he can walk you through it. God, I have to tell you both. I appreciate that this is your hometown, Liam, but

I fucking hate LA. We need to find you another lady friend in New York, I used to have no problem getting you back there all the time."

"You broke up with her?" Clare blurted, unwittingly revealing that she knew he'd been dating a woman who worked at *Bon Appétit*. Liam nodded once. A few minutes later, she was telling a story about high school, about a boy she'd pined for as a sophomore, and Liam immediately supplied the guy's name, Ethan Prince. And they both pretended they weren't learning anything, like two people in a blackout, dazed and unnerved to find their hands on one another's bodies when the lights judder back to life.

The editor paid and then they were on the street, watching him pop into an Uber.

"Clare, darling," he said. "Really lovely to meet you. Good luck with everything! And please, wherever you two are headed next, talk some sense into this one. Tell him that the essay collection was one thing, but he's not a reporter. This book-length criminal justice project, this is just . . . this is not the move. Tell him to write a goddamn memoir, okay? He's not a journalist. He shouldn't be cosplaying as one. You two have clearly known one another since you were, I don't know, running around in your little Vans and low-rise jeans, he'll listen to you. I'm begging you, Clare."

He made prayer hands and bowed, rolled up the car's window, and then he was gone. They were left there on the sidewalk.

"He seems great," she said flatly.

"He's not," Liam said. "I mean, he's an acquired taste. But he is loyal. He's gone to bat for me. More than once."

"Is that so rare for you, though?" This was, in retrospect, the moment at which it became clear that she was inadvisably drunk. Liam reached out to her again, fingered the sleeve of her jacket. He had helped her into it as they left the restaurant. She wondered, for a moment, if poor Sofie had seen them before she left. That, too, was another warning, had Clare been inclined to look for any. How little she cared about this selfish, rude thing she had just done to another person.

"Everyone goes to bat for you," she said. "I bet he'll even let you do the criminal justice reform project, in the end."

"I'm not trying to sound ungrateful," Liam said, a concession to someone like her, someone who couldn't even finish one book. "But I don't want to feel useless. I just feel like, if we don't change our lives this year, what are we doing?"

She changed her life, then, in one way. She went with him to a second location, to the whiskey bar in the mini mall. She asked him if he thought she was useless, if writing a novel was the stupidest possible way to spend this year. There was this part of her that felt sheer annoyance at his belief that he could just spelunk into another genre, another world, another role, but she also knew that he wasn't, probably, wrong. Who was to say he wouldn't produce something worthwhile?

"Why don't you want to talk about the book?" he asked at one point. "Why aren't you, like, proud? What's happening?"

She tried and failed to explain it, then, out loud to another person, for the first time. That being alone in her own mind was the only thing that felt like it returned her to any semblance of herself. Like even if nothing came of it, the writing she did alone in a dark room in her brain was the single glimmering thread that connected her to the girl she used to be and the adult life she once thought she would have. And now something impressive had, in theory, come of her writing, but it was just another piece of evidence that she was somehow unable to get a grip on the rhythms of adulthood.

"I think you have a pretty good grip on adulthood," he said. Which made her want to put her head in his lap and ask him to tell her all the things he knew and remembered about her, all the things he took to be self-evident and stable. Only a liar would pretend it's not intoxicating, to realize how closely someone has been paying attention, and for how long.

She didn't put her head in his lap. She just kept talking.

"I just, I used to love it so much. I used to hoard it for myself like this secret vice. And it was only for me, the way it felt when I was writing.

I never talked about it with anyone, not even when I was falling in love with Jamie and I would wake up in bed with him and for a second I couldn't tell our bodies apart."

She pretended she hadn't done this on purpose, just to see, and he pretended that it was a normal, sociable thing to say. She rushed, kept talking.

"Or when I was like, fifteen. And it felt like Renzo was the only other living human being who would ever understand me. I mean, you loved Renzo too, I know you did. But—"

"No," he said. "I remember. You two were so close, for a while."

"Yeah," she said. "Anyway. I just . . . I don't know. This was what I was supposedly working toward, and now, if I can't even actually do it, then what's the point? I don't even know what I want. It's not like I'm a mother, I don't have some great calling, I'm just . . . treading water."

She saw his brow furrow when she said that word, "mother," and thank fucking God he didn't ask, she probably would have told him everything. But he just reached out and put his palm on top of her hand and her mind went black, zapped like the spark from an electrical outlet.

"Do you talk about this with anyone?" he said, and she knew that he was asking about her husband, but he didn't say Jamie's name. She shook her head, and he went up to the bar for another round. She started tapping one foot to the floor beneath the table, every few seconds, to make sure she didn't have the spins.

"It's always useful, though," he said at some point later. "Once you figure out what you're supposed to do, then you do it. That's of use. You're meant to be a novelist. Right?"

"Isn't that argument dangerous, though? Then, no matter what, we can decide we're being of use. Can't we?"

He smiled at her. She did not say, *If that argument is correct, then this past year hasn't really required much from us, has it? Then our lives, our personal and specific lives, haven't actually been demolished in the way that, a year ago, we fretted they would be.*

"I just think," she said instead. She picked up her drink and took a sip, the whiskey no longer even burning as it went down. "That I spent a long time assuming that, once I wasn't petrified by the concept of going broke, I would become this, like. Engaged adult. I would actually do something to make the world around me better, however tiny the definition of 'around me,' however local, or whatever. But my husband has been making money faster than I can even comprehend it, ever since we graduated, and I'll be honest with you, I do not think that my new adult self has exactly come to pass."

"Clare," he said, "I'm going to ask you to come home with me in a little while. But I need you to—You have to stop mentioning your husband."

They sat rigid and upright in the Uber, and she walked carefully down the path to his bungalow in Beachwood Canyon, but when she tried to step out of her shoes in his foyer she almost toppled over. He reached out to help her and then he actually did fall over, and they remained there, him flat on his back and her kneeling above him, laughing so hard she couldn't breathe.

When she stood up, his living room looked like it had been designed by a dream abandoned somewhere in her brain. Everything placed to probe her homesickness, her nostalgia, urging her to find some door she'd forgotten she ever had the chance to choose.

There were shelves full of vinyl, all the music their parents once played for them on CDs, and books and expensive bottles of liquor abandoned on every surface. Little party-game curios and card decks from the seventies. Bizarre, kitschy paperbacks from 1963, the best playboy bars in Los Angeles or the best Big Sur ghost stories. Signed memorabilia everywhere, signed to Liam long ago by the original producers, by aging starlets. Prints of old photographs and magazine spreads with the grainy yet glossy finish of images from that era: houses in the Hills, glamorous women painting their toenails beside sparkling swimming pools. Framed set lists from the Wiltern and the Fonda, shows she had probably attended too. Pictures of Liam as a child, running amok on his father's sets, the world's most famous faces blurred in the background. Postcards sent from one of his dead relatives to another.

It was, she told herself, almost exculpatory. It wasn't just that it's easy to be held captive by every object in the house of someone you're dying to sleep with as soon as physically possible. It felt important to clarify—to whom?—that it wasn't only that.

"My parents are both only children," she told him. "I don't know if I've ever seen a family photograph taken before 1980. I feel like if we tried we could reconstruct the entire romantic history of, like, your grandmother's sister. Just using the materials in this room."

Liam smiled, disappeared down a dark hallway and returned with a few fingers of Blanton's in a tumbler rimmed with silver. She stared down at it and then looked up at him.

"I really need to leave," she said. "I'm sorry."

He waited until after her shoes were on, after he'd called her another Uber.

"I should probably tell you. Renzo has been trying to convince me to come to Hawai'i next month."

"Oh," she said.

"Do you want me to tell him I can't?"

"No," she said.

4

She walks away from the pool, crossing behind the off-duty bar and its cloying smells of limes and spilled simple syrup and flat soda, back toward the "bathhouse" that's really just a faux-wood hut fronting a row of open changing cubicles. She's thrown a light top over her bathing suit all morning, a concession to the sunburn that's her punishment for falling asleep on the beach yesterday, but it's sticky and starting to smell and she wants to change. She's already crossing her arms to wriggle out of it as she turns the corner, before she's even stepped into a cubicle. Then she's reaching back to unhook her suit and dropping her bag on the bench and when she turns she nearly screams because Liam is standing there, he's followed her.

She lets her hands fall to her sides, like she's been caught doing something wrong. Liam waits for her to meet his eye.

"He's jittery and doesn't want to admit it," he says. "It's not just you, he's being a dick to everyone. I can come along, if that would help."

"That's not necessary," she says. "It's just a grocery run. But thank you. I need to change, so."

She makes a fluttery, ineffectual gesture with one hand, but he doesn't move. *Fine*, she thinks. *Okay, fine.*

She reaches behind her again, her elbows jutting out, feeling extremely ungraceful. She unhooks her bathing suit and doesn't look at him, lets it fall from her shoulders. She reaches into her bag and pulls out a different tank top, places it gingerly over her head, tries to avoid all the places that hurt. She replaces the bathing suit and the sweaty shirt in her bag and then she slips it over one shoulder, winces, and looks back up at him. He's smiling. He swallows once, looks away and then looks back, but he's smiling the whole time.

She loses the upper hand, whatever that was, before she's even completed the little performance. There's something possessive about the fact that he followed her, that he's standing there, that he didn't duck back out when he realized she was changing. She resents it. That he wants her to feel rebuked, reminded. Her smeared virtue, or something.

And someone could have seen him, realized he was following her. But maybe that was the point.

"Sure." He nods. "Okay. Would you rather I fly home tonight, instead? So you don't have to work so hard to ignore me?"

She opens her mouth, makes a soft, ragged noise in her throat.

"I asked you," he says. "I don't know whatever this just was—" He looks down at her knees, looks back up at her face, skips everything else. "But I *asked* you if you wanted me not to come."

"I just want to be clear, I think," she says. "I didn't tell you not to come because that would have been absurd, to do that. Nothing happened. But I didn't—I didn't mean that if you came, we'd just pick up where we left off."

"Where we left off on the night nothing happened, you mean?"

"I apologize for drinking too much in Los Angeles," she says, trying to make her voice as icy as she can. He steps forward, closing the space between them, and she begins to panic.

"Believe me, I am extremely embarrassed. But it has—It has nothing to do with your being here. I'm not avoiding you. I'm not ignoring you."

"Okay," he says.

"Liam, look," she says.

"I don't know what you want me to say," he says. He's stepped closer again. "I, personally, do not regret anything that went on in Los Angeles last month."

"It's not that—"

"Listen," he says. "I think you're trying to pretend that you don't remember, what it was like in high school. When we would all jam in the back seat of Kyle's car, and you'd have to sit on my lap, and Renzo would give me endless shit for the whole next week. I used to practically start to shake."

"I don't remember that."

He takes a last step, close enough for her to touch him.

"I don't believe you," he says. "I don't think you just took your top off in front of me so that I would leave, Clare."

She looks beyond his shoulder, the open cubicle, the faint sounds from the pool.

"We're not," she says. "This isn't an enclosed area, at all."

He reaches out, touches her hair. She can smell his skin, he smells like vacation. Sunscreen and citrus and the slightest bite of alcohol beneath.

She thinks of leaving his house that night, when he stood in his doorway and put his hands on her shoulders, touched his lips to the top of her head before she left. His breath in her hair. *That's very hard to imagine, Clare. You're talking to someone who knew you when you were a teenager.* She wants him to do it again, surround her with that protective fog of absolution, the sense that there's nothing to explain away.

She tries not to think. She just reaches one hand to the place where he's forgotten a button on his linen shirt. She presses her thumb to the skin just below his navel, feels his breath quicken. She can tell that he's surprised, too. She grazes his shirt with her fingers, flattens her palm, and he comes closer. He touches his forehead to hers and she lets her chin float up, and then he kisses her.

An unfamiliar mouth, its unfamiliar heat. Like he's running at a much higher temperature than anyone can tell from just looking at him. Like he's on fire, she thinks, even lets herself think it earnestly for one second, but then she starts to giggle, smiles into his mouth. She can feel him smiling back, like they're both in on the joke, and then he runs his hands down the side of her body and her brain goes blank again. She struggles to form a thought, which is, dimly, that this is the first person she has kissed in nearly ten years who is not her husband. When was the last time her husband kissed her unexpectedly? She bites Liam's bottom lip and he wraps his arms around her and lifts her, briefly, off the ground, pressing his hips into hers. Then, just as abruptly as it began, he lets go. He steps back, staring down at her hand, still on his stomach. Then he grins.

"I'm not avoiding you," she says. "I just need to go."

"Don't," he says. "Wait."

She doesn't. But as she pushes past him, they reach for one another. He holds her hand for a half second before he lets go, releasing her back out to everyone else.

5

Clare drives them into town for groceries, Kyle and Renzo. They stop first at a small fish counter, really a shack, where they pick up lunch: rice bowls and a few different flavors of poke priced by the pound. Kyle jaws a little with the man behind the counter, who knows him well enough to ask after Mrs. Harmon, the grandchildren. Clare watches Kyle adjust his posture, the cadences of his voice, as if this man isn't fully aware of their respective roles. As if the decades of routine that have worn his paths around the island into familiar grooves, evenings at the club and high-fives with the teenagers driving the golf carts and the "Hang loose" gestures at other drivers on the small storybook bridges all over the island—as if any of it means that this man considers him an actual local.

But then, maybe this performance is mainly for her benefit, hers and Renzo's. Always, it's important that the two of them, especially Ren, grant some wordless approval. *When I complain about rich people, Kyle, I'm not talking about you. And I'm sure as hell not talking about me.*

She smiles uneasily at the fishmonger as they walk out, as if to communicate that he can mock them the second they're out the door. So, really, how different is she from Kyle? This insistence that this guy get it, that he see them as they wish to see themselves. As white people visiting the island, but not, you know. Not the ones who are *ruining* the island.

She hears Jamie's voice again: "Come on, babe. Does everyone who happens to meet you while you're with Kyle need to know that, actually, you were the poor one back then? Maybe, like—grow up."

She looks down at her phone with a sudden creeping terror, as if her husband has been watching her all morning, might call to demand an explanation.

"What do we owe you?" she asks as they cut across an empty parking lot toward the supermarket. Kyle paid for the food in cash.

"Oh, come on," Renzo says. "Kyle, you'll treat, no? Are you going to be so churlish as to charge me for lunch?"

Kyle shakes his head.

"I'm not indulging this," he says, and turns to Clare. "Did he tell you what he paid for the condo? Honestly, fuck it—you should be subsidizing this entire trip!"

"Oh, yes, darling. You'll be my first charitable cause." Renzo turns back to Clare. "He's not lying, though. I am indeed making fat stacks."

"Why the hell didn't I charge you rent for this week?" Kyle persists. "Do I get a cut? I don't know, the 'cost of doing Renzo' resort fee?"

Renzo rears back, performing a dramatic pose, shocked and scandalized.

"Wait one minute. Is *someone* hoping to *do* Renzo this week? Is *that* the price you'll be charging for these, let's just say it, absurdly lavish environs? Because, honey, if I've told you once I've told you a million times. You could have had this for free, so many times, just simply say the word—"

But they're off, now, scrapping like puppies. Renzo wails as Kyle traps his head with one elbow, and they move in jagged dashes toward the market entrance, bumping hips, poking at each other's ribs. Clare watches them career through the automatic doors.

"Save yourself!" Renzo shrieks. "Grab a cart! I'll distract him."

But Kyle has already sprinted off in the direction of the refrigerated dairy.

"Jesus," Clare says. "You two weren't this manic when you were actual prepubescents."

"God, that word always sounds so lewd," Renzo says, gathering himself, raking a hand through his hair. "Pubescent! Always good for a shudder. But look, look. I keep him young. And if we didn't perform this little theater every now and then, just to confirm that no latent homophobia is settling in as we age, we'd both get quite anxious."

"So you grope him every so often as an altruistic act," she says.

Renzo shrugs, but when Clare belly-laughs he looks utterly pleased with himself.

She pushes the cart. They grab beer and white wine and a few bottles of rum and vodka, in unspoken agreement that the group is likely to drink more each day. Sweet Maui onion potato chips and plastic tubs of flavored hummuses and some sundry, mismatched salad fixings. Radicchio, iceberg lettuce, wizened carrots and anemic celery the color of scallion ends.

"They don't have kale," Renzo observes. They stand shoulder to shoulder to inspect the greens. An old man in a golf visor passes just behind them, so close that she can feel air on her heels as his cart clatters past.

"Get over it!" he barks, and she startles. Renzo turns to face the guy, planting his body firmly in front of Clare's. He sticks out his tongue at the old man, who seems sufficiently spooked by this brazen violation of the social contract. They watch him shuffle, resigned, toward the checkout lanes.

"I assume it's your shirt," Renzo gestures. "Could also be the mention of kale, I suppose."

She's wearing a tank top emblazoned with the line A WOMAN'S PLACE IS IN THE WHITE HOUSE. She does not remember how she came to own it, and she chose it today while Liam was watching her, so nothing about that moment is at all clear in her mind.

"Really?" she says. "In Hawai'i?"

"And what do you want to bet he's a recent transplant, not an old-timer? Probably bought a house in our same development just last year. I think, if I may be so bold—I'd be willing to bet on Kyle's father, too. Well. Maybe he abstained. He certainly didn't cast a willing vote for her."

He's been scrutinizing the ingredients of a prepackaged salad, but now he catches her eye.

"Oh, get hold of yourself. Nobody yells at you in Boston?"

"Do you really think that? About the Harmons?"

"Clare." His voice is lethally soft. "Clare, don't tell me you've convinced yourself that someone with that kind of money will just . . . what, agree to have less? By choice? Please."

"You have money," she says. "Jamie and I do, too."

He glares at her.

"I'm going to ignore what I can only assume to be trolling, since you know full well that is quite a different state of affairs. Anyway. No such confrontations at home, I gather?"

They continue their ramble through the store. She tells him about the man she dialed in Montana last month, who angrily interrupted each of her prepared talking points, called her "little lady" repeatedly.

"I don't even know why I did it," she says. "I hate talking to strangers on the phone. I mean, I really hate it."

"I remember. The scripts, your father's legal pads."

She stops in her tracks.

"I cannot believe that you remember that."

He arches one eyebrow, something he's tried many times to teach her how to do.

"Please. I love when you reveal the chinks in your armor. You know that."

It is true that when she was little, and even well into her teenage years, she would write out scripts whenever she had to make a phone call. Her mother might ask her to phone a friend's mother to ask what time she should be dropped off, it didn't matter how simple the task, how perfunctory the conversation. Any telephone conversation with an unfamiliar adult made her feel such terror that she wrote out, before each call, a full script on one of the legal pads her father kept by the phone.

All of school felt like that, constantly. Like if only she could say it right, the perfect words with haphazard polish, then no one would look twice. No one would wonder why she never invited friends to her own house.

"I hate that you know that," she says to him.

"But you suffered! You worked the phones, for us. Our great democracy."

"Well," she says, "I did my best. It's not like I know enough about a Senate race in Montana to really, you know, stray from the bullet points they drill into you. If someone had tried to debate me on the merits, what would I have even come up with, you know?"

"My love," he says. "My darling. If we've learned one thing this year surely it is that no one, but no one, cares to debate on the *merits*. But. You must disagree? You've never been quite the cynic that I am. You don't see me dialing Montana, for example."

"I'm pretty cynical," she says.

"No," he says, without rancor. "You're not. You and Jamie have always believed in a potential rosy future. Maybe you're just now figuring out you'll need to work at it, but you're not like me. You didn't give up, basically, once we reached adulthood."

She feels puzzled by this. Does he actually see her this way?

"You're just saying that to let yourself off the hook."

"Probably," he agrees. "But keep going, tell me about Montana."

"My friend Celine badgered me into it. She's been hosting this working group, with her husband. And it started to feel awkward, whenever I saw her. They organized canvassing trips upstate, they were at protests every other week, she was at town halls for city council races, calling the district attorney's office. And she was a friend who, like—I had always thought of myself as the one of substance. Between the two of us. She has one of those media jobs that like, you can't even begin to describe what she actually does. It's, like, marketing adjacent. Chief content officer? Maybe?"

"Oh, the friendships we cling to because they make us feel intelligent," Renzo says. "I do so wish I had no idea what you meant."

"It just got annoying. We'd meet for brunch and she would talk about her latest 'action' and then there would be this silence before she asked what I'd been up to 'since the Women's March.' Just so I knew that we were not equivalent, just because we'd attended together. There was also always this latent, I don't know, criticism in the air? Like we shouldn't even be at brunch in the first place, what a waste of our time and resource capital, but how else was she going to spend time with me, the friend with no interest in the wider world? It just got exhausting. It was easier to just let her tell me where to go, what to do."

"Well, I actually think there's no shame in that. Literally. Do I mean 'literally,' is that proper usage? Or am I just being a gauche millennial. I guess there is some shame there. But so what? Shame, that very pointy social shame from someone you love? That can be a real, productive shove in the right direction, no? Or so I've found to be the case."

"Well, she hosts weekly meetings, and now I go. In their living room. Her husband literally bought a place in *Beacon Hill* a few years ago. With the money he earns, you know, representing Big Pharma, but. That's whatever, I guess. Doesn't come up at the meetings, obviously."

Renzo keeps one hand on the shopping cart, steering her with his other.

"That's great," he says. His voice is flat. "I mean, screw the husband, whatever. But if she kicked your ass into gear, then great. I'm intrigued, honestly. To hear you're doing this."

"Because it's so, so much."

"Well, no, but. It's more than nothing."

"You sound like Jamie. He acts like it's a hobby, something that will pass. Like I just learned to use a loom, or something. I told him last month that I was thinking of applying to be an observer, in the court system, because it's something I think I could actually be good at."

"You would be," Renzo says. She stops, presses her tongue to the roof of her mouth and tries not to smile, but he's already caught himself. "Something that allows you to empathize and to sit smoldering, passing judgment, without asking you to be confrontational in any productive way? Really playing to your strengths."

"I knew that couldn't be an actual compliment."

"I'm teasing you. I think it's a fabulous idea."

"But he acts like it's a hilarious concept, that we might try to learn something new before we're just, senior citizens. When I told him about the court watch application, he asked whether I didn't think they'd want someone who had 'at least considered law school.' And I've asked him to come with me. He's too busy, or he'll just write a check at the end of the year, or he's 'not sure that's where I want to focus my energy right now.' What does that even mean? It's bullshit."

She hears herself, she doesn't need to see Renzo's face. She knows it is unfair, despicable really, to complain about her husband to someone who doesn't already love or even really know him. Who doesn't understand his defensive crouch against a looming future when he'll realize he failed to make as much money as he possibly could while he was young. When they'll get the call that his mother finally drank herself into requiring around-the-clock care and needs her son to step in, to write the checks. But Renzo knows none of this, and even though he would understand it perfectly, Clare has always chosen not to elaborate. She knows that this is a good faith rule of marriage; this is the actual daily application of "for better or worse." Not to reveal your smallest, most cowardly selves to third parties every time you feel resentment or annoyance. She can feel herself violating the rule, edging up to some line, daring Renzo to ask her more. To ask what's shifted.

Renzo waits a moment before turning, lowering his sunglasses.

"To be entirely judicious," he begins, "to all involved. I have no idea whether I sound like Jamie. But I find it neither hilarious, nor pathetic, which seems like it would be your implication? That I'd agree with him? I'm simply surprised. Pleasantly and with absolute admiration."

"Okay," she says. "Somehow, that sounds worse."

"Then I give up," he muses, examining a yellowed lump of mozzarella before replacing it on its frosted shelf. "Everyone always says, 'Just buy the basics. Buy some breakfast staples.' But the truth is that no one can ever quite agree on what 'basics' are, can they? Kyle was talking about, like, some specialty omelet. Actually, wait a minute, hold the phone. Rewind."

He places one hand to his collarbone. "Jamie isn't . . . We're not talking, when you guys met, he wasn't the president of Dartmouth Baby Federalists, or something equally distasteful?"

"Bite me," she says. "He drove all over the state of New Hampshire with me."

"And what did that take? Fifteen minutes, end to end?"

"We knocked doors together. Both elections."

"And would have voted for the man a third time, I'm sure!"

She grimaces.

"Come on, you teed me right up for that one. Do you think if that poor screenwriter had known that the very people his movie skewered would be quoting that line for the next ten years, he might have cut it? Anyway. Very virtuous of our boy. Your boy. But I realized I didn't know, if he had bowtie-wearing skeletons in his closet. He's a self-made future millionaire, isn't he? You never know with those boys. You can't trust a bootstraps kid. He'll use the boots to kick back at anyone a few rungs below him. And you never know with you! I assume we would have discussed it at some point, but you always play your cards so very close to your chest, as it were."

"You're a bootstraps kid," she says quietly.

"Yes, but I'm a gay. And not a particularly self-loathing one, as you must know. I *do* contain multitudes, but let's be honest here. Whomst have I ever loved the way I love myself? I could never."

"You can be serious for a second," she says, still quiet.

"I tried sincerity a few moments ago, sweetheart, and you completely cut me off at the knees. You don't care for me in that mode! Never have."

Kyle reappears with all the practical supplies they've neglected—eggs, yogurt, cottage cheese, milk, fresh berries, cold cuts, sliced pepper jack, blocks of cheddar both sharp and mild. He unloads shrimp and avocados and jalapeños, for ceviche. Ground beef and chicken breasts and skewers and bell peppers and onions, for the grill. Everything tumbles into the grocery cart, along with the hummus and the alcohol and the solitary head of lettuce. Kyle peers down and then back up at her, expectant.

"Nice," she says. "Sorry. We haven't made much progress."

"Too busy debating the pressing issues of the day," Renzo quips. "May we live in wild times, or whatever the phrase is."

"Well, it's definitely not that," Kyle says. Renzo picks up a can of salsa.

"Why are so many random things here sold in cans?" he demands. "I was promised a luscious, verdant, rich man's paradise. I mean—why is this in a can?"

"We're on an island, asshole," Kyle says. "Flying in everything fresh is expensive. You guys didn't get enough beer."

Renzo steers them back to the refrigerated case, where Kyle picks out several six-packs.

"Do you find that these meetings help?" Renzo asks. "When you're making phone calls. Do you feel any less anxious?"

"I don't know. It's more like, if I'm going to feel so anxious, then I might as well be doing something useful?"

"Uh-oh," Kyle says, examining the label on a bottle of Vinho Verde. "Is she in AA now? Because that's really going to complicate my plans for the rest of the trip."

Renzo ignores him.

"I just can't imagine being this panicked all the time and feeling that I was actually still able to *do* anything useful."

"That's a rationalization, though," Clare tells him. "Right?"

He raises one eyebrow.

"Nothing wrong with those," Kyle says, jovially waiting for someone to clue him in.

"Can I clarify," Renzo replies. "Are you the sanctimonious friend, or was it . . . Celine, was her name?"

"I don't know, I just. Yeah, I do like it. It does feel useful. I think it's—I don't know, sometimes I think it's been a mistake, for me not to have a real job. Not to have a schedule and show my face in an office every day. And doing this a few times per week has kind of, like. Kept my brain in order."

"So you're doing it for *you*," Renzo says, but he's smiling again.

"Well."

"Who's Celine?" Kyle chirps. "I thought we were your only friends."

"We are," Renzo replies. "She clearly can't stand this chick, don't worry. You know Clare only cares about her little boyfriend! And sometimes us."

"Do you think you'll ever stop calling him my boyfriend," she says, trying to match their tone, trying not to count the multiple different stings from what he's just said.

"Dude," Kyle says. "That was extremely mean and for zero reason."

Renzo looks between them in what seems to be genuine chagrin.

"Oh," he says. "I was teasing. That was a joke. I just want to be the friend you love most, that's all."

"Anyway," Kyle drawls, letting the word last long enough to be sure they'll laugh. "Let's get out of here."

At the counter, Renzo puts down his credit card and then folds her into him, planting a kiss on her cheek.

"My treat," he says. "Unless I lose my temper later in the week. In which case I will be sending everyone a snarky Venmo."

"You are," she says, putting an arm around his shoulder and speaking directly into his ear, "the absolute worst."

"True."

"Also," she says. "I like you when you're sincere. I love you sincere."

"False."

"And wow, wow, wow, do I really hate that you remember that. The scripts on the legal pads."

He slides his credit card back into his wallet and nuzzles her neck again, his skin so warm even in this chilled supermarket.

"Someone has to know all your secrets, Clare. What's the fun of keeping them to yourself?"

She swallows so hard that she begins to cough. He cheerfully thumps her back with his fist.

6

"Just put it on my parents' tab," Kyle says. "I got a soft yes from my mother on whether that was allowed. Maybe not every night? But this would only be night two."

They're up at the club, after half-hearted efforts at mixing mai tais back at the house. As soon as a move was suggested, Renzo shouted in approval and swept one hand across the marble countertop, sending lime wedges flying. Still, they made enough of a dent in that first batch that they're already too drunk to shoot pool. Clare and Mac clown around, waving their cues in the air, until they're admonished by a club attendant, a crisp teenager in his khakis and white polo.

"Guys," Kyle attempts. "Please? My parents will still live here once you all fly back to the real world. Come on."

"They're all so young," Clare whispers noisily. Mac cackles. He's watching her make repeated, spectacular attempts to break. "Did you expect to be so much older than all the *employees*?"

"It'll just keep happening," he intones. "Soon we'll be older than everyone."

"Ha. Like, oh, okay, good one, Mr. McMillan. Very wise."

"That's me," he says. "The wise one."

She hasn't seen him speak to Jessie in a while. When they got back from the grocery store, Clare couldn't really see that Jessie's bubbliness was directed at Mac in any way, but Renzo's sense of threat still seemingly kicked into gear. If she's flirting, it should be with him. Everyone needs to remember who's adored and who's indifferent. Mac always retreats a little bit, when Renzo gets like this. Clare isn't sure what to do, how to let Mac know that she sees it. Did she used to know, instinctively, how to handle this? She can't remember.

She nearly falls over attempting to execute a shot, and Kyle whoops in spite of his own warnings.

"Clare Clare, what is happening right now?"

She peers down at her own hands. She can't remember how to hold the pool cue.

Kyle comes up behind her, lays his arms over hers.

"I know I taught you better than this," he says. She leans back into his chest.

"You smell yummy. What is that?"

"That's Hawai'i, baby. Also, my natural sex appeal. You remember these pheromones, I'm sure. Quit trying to distract me."

"Who's winning?"

Clare jumps, drops her cocktail glass to the carpet. Liam has appeared, his voice at her shoulder. Kyle leaps back, saving himself from a juice stain on what is clearly a new shirt.

"What is *with* you today," he says. "Liam, please, never again do something so terrifying as *speak* to Clare. She's a delicate flower."

They try to start over, but Clare's hand is shaking, Kyle keeps putting his thumb to the pulse in her wrist. When she whiffs the next shot, Liam laughs so hard he spits out his pineapple wedge. When he laughs, the sharpest parts of his face soften. The dimples in his cheek appear; the extremely lopsided smile takes over his face. His dirty-blond hair stands out from his head in random tufts, soft waves. He's wearing royal blue swim trunks and an untucked white Oxford shirt with ripped elbows and a torn hem. She keeps looking over at him and then immediately looking away and squeezing her eyes shut, like she's just gulped something too cold to drink.

She feels like she's watching it happen already. She feels like someone has helped her onto a train, she's realizing she has no way of speaking with the conductor, no say in the matter. She repeats to herself in her head: *What can you do? You can't tell yourself how to feel.*

She hits the white ball into the corner pocket for the third time. Mac curses loudly, pretends to snap his pool cue across his knee. Another employee, this one uncannily resembling a young Tom Cruise, approaches them.

"I'm sorry," Mac mutters, not to the kid but to Kyle. "I know they can't be used to loud Black men up in here."

"Be nice," Kyle says.

"Me? *Me* be nice? I *am* nice, baby. I've gotten fully on board with this whole plantation vibe, have you heard me complain once?"

Clare swallows an ice cube. It's undeniable. Entering the clubhouse with its sweeping lanai, the lethargic fans spinning overhead, the rattan chairs and the women fanning themselves. The sunset visible off beyond the porch, its sherbet hues receding across the rolling green to leave them all to their quiet dusk. It's impossible for the word "plantation" not to float up into your brain when you walk in, but Mac is the only one who's said it out loud.

The kid from the club is still hovering near them. Mac smiles at them all.

"I'm sorry, did I make a Black friends joke with the white friends? Did McMillan forget where he is this week?"

Clare tries to remember if they've seen a single other Black person anywhere at the club since they arrived. Mac shrugs; he knows he's right. The shrug is not a concession. Kyle looks miserable.

"Dude, take it easy," Mac croons, throwing an arm around Kyle's shoulders. "I dropped a pin the second we got here, so. Just, if I go missing. Let 'em know. Tell the Five O to check the metadata, run the tape. And so forth. Shit, man, Five O! I didn't even do that on purpose, I swear to you. Excellent pun not intended. Speaking of, though, when do we buy our puka shells? Where's my floral shirt? I didn't fly all the way out here to dress like an adult. I want to go full goddamn Tommy Bahama, get a whole new wardrobe, I'm ready to holler at some of these rich ladies, you see what I'm saying? Hook it up for us, Harmon."

"It's Reyn Spooner here," Kyle says. "That you want. Tommy Bahama would be in, like, Florida. Maybe."

Clare watches them tease one another back to equilibrium, away from the unpleasant edge they've pretended not to see. She perches on the lip of the pool table and once again hits the white ball into the corner pocket.

"It's actually kind of impressive," Liam says, not to her but near her. "How many times she's done that." He turns back to the kid who's so distressed by their rowdy behavior, gestures for him to come closer. Liam is suddenly quite chatty, which means he's drunk.

"You see this girl over here? We all told her to take her talents to South Beach, all those years ago. Too late now, though. Past her prime. Right? You get that reference? You guys watch basketball out here? Which team would you even root for, I guess. How old were you in the summer of 2010?"

"Leave him alone," Kyle pleads, turning to the kid. "Look, man, I really am sorry about—my guests. We'll be out of here soon. Don't worry, I'm on it."

"Sir," Liam tries again. "I wonder, have you ever seen the classic 1980s film *Cocktail*?"

"Oh my God, enough! Leave this man alone. I'm sure he deals with assholes and morons all day long." Clare takes one step closer to the kid. "Actually, honey. Maybe you can help us."

Honey? She, too, is drunker than she's previously understood.

"Where should we go, later? Like, if we want to go dancing. Where will you go after you get off tonight?"

"Um," he starts, cautiously cheerful. "There's not really, like, anywhere to go? I mean, sometimes they have live music. At Joe's? It's the pizza shack in town."

She laughs.

"No, that's great, thank you. We were just there last night."

Joe's did not seem like a bar that hosts dancing. Its primary patrons appeared to be elderly men in search of an amiable, collective solitude.

She plants a kiss on the kid's cheek, and he hurries off, tapping his empty tray frequently against his thigh as he lopes back over to the bar.

"We did not," Mac reminds her, "head to Joe's once we were already drunk. However. So it might look different tonight."

"How would we even get there?" she asks. The boys don't respond, so she asks and then answers something else.

"Another round? Another round. I'm buying."

"By which you mean, Kyle's parents will buy."

"We'll see. Maybe I'll feel especially magnanimous when I get up there."

"Great," Kyle replies. "Excellent. Let's not bet on *that* happening."

"Ouch," she says. "You sound like Renzo."

"Speaking of magnanimity," Mac says. "Are we still doing that beach yoga class on Monday morning? Has he deigned to tell anyone what it's going to cost?"

"I'm sure as hell not going to ask him," Kyle says. He resumes the game of pool by himself.

"That's dangerous, though. He'll have one of his brief spurts of generosity, and tell us he's covering it, and then—"

"Fly into a mood later and charge all of us some amount we never agreed to spend. I hear you. I mean, is this wrong? This is a fact, right?"

Kyle turns to her and holds out his hands, requesting approval of his thesis.

"Facts," Mac replies. "Facts, facts, facts."

They don't say anything else; Renzo's approach to his own finances is one of those topics that never really feel safe. Just before junior year, his parents walked into his bedroom and saw the AIM window on his computer screen, the graphic messages from an older man. He showed up at Kyle's front door in Hancock Park a few hours later. Kyle's frosty mother must have nearly collapsed, not too thrilled herself about an openly gay teenager living under her roof, but Renzo stayed for months. And by the time he moved back home, his mother had been laid off. Clare still doesn't know how he held it together, the first few years of college. But then he had the summer internship at McKinsey and a job offer and a signing bonus. And no one, least of all Kyle, ever wanted to make him discuss it.

"You idiots are drunk," she says. "Where are Renzo and Jess?"

"Don't look at me," Mac says. "Also, isn't the fishing trip allegedly tomorrow morning? We need to figure that one out, first. I have yet to pay anyone a solitary dime."

Liam looks at Clare, waves a thumb over his shoulder at a corner of the lanai, where Clare can just make out Jessie and Renzo deep in conversation, their silhouettes dark against the glowering ocean.

"Oh, Jesus."

She feels a quick twinge in her chest, a fist closing itself more tightly. She keeps forgetting the morning—everything before the pool seems too long ago to possibly bother with—but the general unpleasantness has lingered, the fitful spasms of remorse. It always feels like a concession, to be nice to Jess. And isn't that maybe Clare's fault? Maybe Renzo is right. Whichever objections Mac has swallowed to keep Jessie in his life, whatever is left of her operatic, decades-old relationship with Renzo—none of it is Clare's to untangle, is it? It doesn't matter whether she and Jessie feel any deep respect for one another. Is it maturity to know this, or the total opposite?

Either way. When you've known people this long, when you knew them in middle school, knew their mothers and their childhood bedrooms, you can always see the ghosts at their shoulders. You can always see where they've been carved into painful shapes.

She resolves not to start any more fights.

"Are you listening to me?" Kyle says, still trouncing himself at pool. "Ren got all pissy with me before. The bartender assumed we were a couple, and despite the fact that this has been happening on a monthly basis since we were fourteen, he's now taken offense."

"Because someone knew he was gay?" Mac asks. "Or because they paired him with you?"

"Dude, come on. First of all, ouch. And secondly, are you . . . are you asking me to interpret our little Lorenzo's moods?"

"Jeeesus," Clare repeats. Her phone buzzes for the second time since they left the house. She places it in her purse, leaves the purse with the boys, and walks back across the lobby.

In the bar, ruddy-faced men in golf shirts wait for their wives. Standing alone, swaying companionably, Clare watches them relax into the third beer, the second bourbon. She falls into conversation with the bartender, an older woman with a high blond ponytail and soft, feathery bangs.

"I saw you over there with all those adorable men circling you," the woman tells her. "What's your secret?"

"Let's see, I've known them since we were twelve? I've seen each and every one of them vomit in multiple public places? I think that's probably my secret. I know how bad their cystic acne used to be and what their feet smell like?"

The bartender laughs.

"Savage. I'm guessing they don't usually send you out as their wing-man?"

Clare looks back over at the boys, smiles.

"They're my favorite people in the world," she says, more or less truthfully.

"So what you're saying is, they've all had their shot, and they're bad in bed."

Clare feels a sudden need to make everything very clear.

"I'm married," she says.

The woman is absolutely thrilled to hear this. They crack a few jokes back and forth about men, husbands, the death of chivalry. Clare can feel herself getting fluid, performing with one hand on her hip, which means she can have at most one more cocktail before she is officially Too Drunk.

She orders drinks and leaves to find the bathroom, where everything is coral, lime, tangerine, gold. Soft Muzak floats in from hidden speakers, vaguely on theme, more an Elvis sort of interpretation of island music than anything authentic. But then, she thinks, as she waves her hands beneath the automatic faucet, what would she know from authentic? When she closes her eyes and thinks, *Hawai'ian music*, isn't she probably just humming that same old Elvis song?

A high window behind her opens to what she calculates must be the covered pathway behind the main clubhouse. She can smell cigarette smoke, which isn't entirely unpleasant. As she ponders whether her blood alcohol level is incompatible with the task of reapplying eyeliner, she hears a voice it takes a moment to recognize as belonging to their little Tom Cruise. Another voice replies, someone older but not old. She dries her hands on linen that she then tosses into a woven basket and moves beneath the window.

"I think that's actually worse," the older boy says. "Like dude, I would rather they just hand you their gross, snotted-up cocktail napkins and pretend you aren't there. It's not like they tip better when they think you're friends."

"The main guy has always seemed nice," the other says, the one Clare thinks of as "their" kid. "But he's always trying to say *Yo* when he sees me. Like, sir, you are a rich alcoholic and I'm the barback. I more or less work for your dad. We don't have to, like, *bond*."

"The friends are hilarious, too. Both chicks keep making such sincere eye contact whenever you bring them something. Like, 'Oh, thank you so, so much.' You're on vacation, lady. It doesn't have to feel like you're making the world a better place. It's . . . vacation. You don't have to be noble, or whatever."

"Yeah, but that's what they want, right," Tom says. "They don't want to pay to feel bad about it. They want us back here talking about how they're different from the usual. Not just tourists."

The other kid snorts.

"They're not paying for shit! His parents are for sure covering this tab tonight."

"Right, right. How old do you think they are?"

"I don't know, but that one lady definitely wants us to act like she's, what? A MILF? Like she's this forbidden babe. I mean, they're old, but they aren't that old."

"They were asking me where we go to get shitfaced. Like, yes, that's exactly what I want to see. Your drunk asses next time I walk into my favorite bar."

"Everybody acts like they come to Hawai'i to feel different, to focus on Hawai'i," the older boy says. "But they just act like it's boss level of the video game, they only want admin access if no one else has it. Nobody actually comes here for Hawai'i."

There are footsteps, their voices fading. She stands in front of the mirror for another minute, washes her hands again. Then she smiles brightly at her reflection and leaves. Back at the bar, her bartender is laughing uproariously, a customer leaning on his forearms for ballast as he looms into her space. Obviously this woman saw her with Kyle, knows Clare to be a guest of the Harmons. You never actually want to know, right, how a stranger would describe you based on a brief interaction. It's possible, Clare thinks, that there are very few people in her life whose opinions about her she'd wish to hear once she'd left the room.

It seems silly, not to pick up the drinks; she already ordered them. She resumes her position at one end of the bar. After a moment, Liam drifts into place beside her.

She remembers this so well from being a teenager: that old rush, the heat bloomed in every nerve ending. Felt it a million times, probably, when she was fifteen and didn't understand yet how to tell someone what she wanted from him, what she was so willing to do for him. She imagined she would figure it out, that eventually experience would accumulate as her hips broadened, as her face settled into itself. But what had she imagined, back then? That it would feel like reaching some steep summit? That one day she would just . . . be there. She would be someone who held power over another person. That it would feel incredible, to leave a room and will him to notice, to follow. And then, one day, when you've forgotten how badly you used to want it, he does.

Liam's hand brushes hers and she sees him this morning, his upper lip, his fingers so quickly knotted in her hair, gathered into a fist at the nape of her neck, pulling her head back to expose her throat. She's hit by a wave of desire so strong it feels like illness. And she's always been someone who can't buy junk food, who refuses to keep Doritos or Entenmann's in her house. She'll eat it all as soon as it crosses her threshold, she won't stop until it's crumbs.

"I like the dress, by the way," he says. "Don't get me wrong. Definitely a fan. But, I thought you needed, maybe. Delicate flower that you are."

He's picked a pink hibiscus, and he brandishes it now like a teenager taking her to prom. Who was his prom date, actually? It wasn't her. She went with Renzo, who abandoned her within five minutes of arriving at the hotel afterparty. How is it possible that this person occupied so little acreage in her brain just a few weeks ago?

Liam places the flower carefully, behind her ear. Then he smiles, his elbows on the bar. His forearm is warm against hers. He's tanned, which makes everything more noticeable—the wheat-colored hair on the backs of his arms, the thick veins running along the tops of his hands. He flexes his fingers, spreads them flat against the bar. Her skin immediately pebbles itself into gooseflesh.

The bartender has returned with four curvy cocktail glasses, their juicy triangles of pineapple already in place.

"Oh," she says. "Look at that." She forms a rectangle with her hands, pretending to snap their photograph. "God, I cannot remember the last time my husband brought me flowers. Even *a* flower."

Clare opens her mouth, and then she closes it.

"Well," Liam says. "I'm not looking to cause any trouble. Let's not tell him. But I can go snag you a flower right this minute."

Liam straightens up and Clare can almost see it settling on him like an article of clothing, the public persona. Even if this woman doesn't know who he is, even if it's not actually public. The ability to charm, the expectation that he must, has taken him over, which isn't surprising. The surprising part is how painful it is to watch him do it for someone else.

The bartender places three shot glasses on the black bar mat. When Liam protests, she tilts her cleavage toward him, rasps out another throaty laugh. She is, clearly, used to the men who frequent this bar finding themselves unable to pull away. She and Liam are perfectly matched, if only for these few minutes.

"Oh, come on. Live a little. We all could've died this morning!"

They talk about that for a while. The entire clubhouse was, apparently, bedlam. Their manager was adamant that no one leave the premises, but of course people wanted to go home, be with their loved ones, call family on the mainland. They did not want to die here, serving brunch to these retired old men.

"Did you grow up here?" Liam asks.

"No, honey. Almost none of us really did. But you see, right? You wash up here for a summer and you never want to leave. What do you two do?"

"He's a writer," Clare says, too quickly. "I work in a bookshop."

"She's a writer as well," Liam says.

"Oh, yeah? What do you write?"

He pitches his book, a curt and rehearsed speech he's clearly sick of. Clare almost interrupts to describe his new project, the reported piece, but she knows that it is one thing for her to find the idea interesting and quite another to tell this stranger that Liam is off on a crusade with no training and zero credentials. She feels reluctant to admit, even to herself, that it was a little embarrassing to hear his blasé confidence, the understood but unmentioned role his father certainly played in introducing him to whoever will make the whole thing possible.

"Well, maybe I'll order it on Amazon!" the woman says. "And hers, when it's ready. But back to this morning. How'd you guys handle it? The missile?" She forms extravagant quotation marks with her fingers as she mentions it, the purported threat that would have destroyed them all.

"We were going to go for a swim in the ocean."

"She's lying," Liam says. "We were thinking we'd all have sex. Some of us wanted to have sex."

"Well, look," the bartender tells Clare. "I know he's your husband, finders keepers. I'm well past the age of trying to break up a happy marriage. Hotsy totsy, who has the energy at my age, right? But if another 'mistake' heads our way in the morning, you put him in a golf cart and send him up here. Share the wealth."

Clare laughs as if it's the funniest thing she has ever heard. As if she is the gamest young trophy wife ever to glide through this place. The bartender's name, as they learn just after Clare realizes it's been rude not to ask, is Antoinette. They all take their tequila shot, and Antoinette is eventually pulled toward other customers, but Clare and Liam linger at the bar. Their cocktails are beginning to sweat, but they don't leave.

He watches her, that quiet look he's had ever since they were teenagers. She's never been able to tell if it's smug or observant. Probably observant. He's the writer, after all.

"You were always paying attention," she says out loud, in the same moment it's become clear to her. "You were paying attention, and I wasn't. Not really. That's why you kept pushing, and I gave up."

She steps closer to him, almost but not quite standing between his legs. Her dress flutters away from her body with a slight breeze, which is of course why she's chosen it. The straps sit lightly on her shoulders; she can feel how easy it would be to send them sliding down her arms. He'd just have to flick them, really, with one finger. Do men ever notice any of this shit? she wonders distractedly. Or do they just see the smile on your face, the sense that you know something more than they do. Is that what they're trying to twist out of a woman, that unexplained satisfaction, when they touch her clothes so thoughtlessly and send them falling away from her skin.

"I will be frank," he says. "I have absolutely no idea what you're talking about."

"Your book," she says. "I never called you, after I read it."

"You did not. You didn't read it."

"I—What? Of course I did. I absolutely did."

He looks away, signals for the bill even though Kyle has maintained that they can just charge it to the house account, figure it out later.

Every single thing about his face, his hair, his skin, feels like malicious taunting. She remembers touching his thigh under the table in Los Angeles, after he'd told her he was going to ask her to come home with him. Leaving her hand there and then slowly beginning to move it, drawing their bodies closer. It felt very effortless but surely, to the sober eye, she looked like a cartoon. She remembers it now and gives an involuntary shake of her head. That spear in your stomach each time you're reminded of your sloppy, inelegant desire. The recoil as she remembers what little she can of the end of that night, her behavior, the things she clearly made very obvious to Liam. She's forgotten how this feels. It's been so long since anyone saw her yearn this way.

There are very good reasons, she thinks, that you're only supposed to feel this when you're twenty years old, waking up in a frat house. Finding a tube of caked toothpaste and smearing it on a fingertip, peeing in a disgusting bathroom and wiggling your hips when you realize there's no toilet paper. That's the appropriate setting for this kind of dreamy, liquid-in-your-bones haze. There is something self-preserving about the impossibility of this happening with someone who's seen you naked hundreds of times. At a certain point, your bodies aren't buzzing anymore, you can't whisper completely nonsensical babble into his ear and call it some precursor to lust.

There are good reasons for this particular order of things.

Liam has paid for their drinks. He sighs.

"Who cares about the book?"

"Me," she says. "I do. I can't believe you thought I didn't read it."

"Clare," he says. "The book was a failure, by every metric. They want me to turn in the second book on the contract, and preferably make it a memoir, so they can push it out into the world and then wash their hands of me."

"I doubt that."

"They were counting on my last name," he says quietly. "They thought that would be enough. No one was more surprised than I was, believe me. That it wasn't."

"No," she says again.

"I mean, I can't entirely blame them. They felt like it was a bait and switch. They didn't want quirky essays about modern life. They wanted me to write a memoir about being 'the son of.' They wanted the headline for *Vulture*, you know? Like, you'll never guess whose kid wrote a book! But I thought I knew better than they did. So. My fault."

She sips at her drink.

"You didn't give up," he tells her. "You shouldn't act like you have. It's not finished yet. That doesn't mean you've given up. It takes however long it takes. Who gives a shit?"

There are very good reasons for this particular order of things. You're supposed to grow up, at some point.

But what if the person touching you remembers who you were when you were fifteen? Who would want to be a grown-up, then?

"I feel like . . ." he begins. "I feel like you want me to be the one to say this should stop here. I feel like you want me to pretend I got on that plane for some other reason. But that's not happening. If you tell me to leave you alone, of course I will. But, in my ideal world, that's not how this goes. And I feel like not in yours, either."

She plucks the umbrella from her drink and puts it behind her other ear. Then she takes the flower he brought her and tucks it firmly behind his.

"Who did you take to prom, again?"

"What is wrong with you?" he asks, but he's laughing.

This, she wants to say but doesn't. *This is what's wrong with me. I look at you and I think about prom.*

"All right," he says. He reaches up to touch the flower, to make sure it's really there. "You win."

"That seems pretty unlikely."

He smiles again. He squares his shoulders, as if that means no one can see them, and then he lets his finger trail along the side of her jaw, down to the skin just above her neckline, almost to her nipple. He turns his hand back and forth, touching her with the backs of his fingers and then with their very tips.

She's so close to leaning forward, to kissing him again, that she actually has to visualize something pulling her back, some physical force putting space between them.

"I'm going to be too drunk soon," she tells him.

"So am I," he says. "We're on vacation."

Los Angeles

Her mother had never actually seen Kyle's house. Clare herself had only been a few times, and she and Renzo usually either navigated the bus together from Westwood or else showed up in a group squeezed into the back of a cab. For all Clare knew, her mother had never even driven through this part of Hancock Park. The car was silent as they turned south from Third, as they coasted to a rolling stop at each tree-lined corner. Clare loved this neighborhood. All the houses looked so old. She'd never realized how bland they were, so many other houses she'd always thought of as gorgeous. How few places in Los Angeles felt old in this sort of honeyed way.

Her mother did not seem equally charmed. The ski trip itself was the problem, much more so than the fact that Clare was going to be sleeping over at a boy's house tonight in advance of an early-morning departure. Her mother had hardly seemed to notice that part of it, when Clare asked permission. Now she was peering through the windshield, murmuring house numbers under her breath. She pulled the car neatly to the curb in front of Kyle's house.

"I still maintain that you're going to freeze," she said. Her voice was somehow both cutting and vague, losing its bite somewhere in the air between them.

"I told you," Clare said. "He said his family has been skiing for years. He has older siblings and there's tons of gear I can borrow."

"Right," her mother said. "And he's covering your share of the condo. And he's paying for your lesson."

"Well, it's not—" Clare began, knowing that she'd already erred by engaging in the conversation. "I think the condo belongs to a friend of his family. I don't think he's paying that much for it. He might not be paying for it at all."

"But everyone else is paying *something*."

"I honestly don't know, Mom."

Kyle had, in fact, urged Clare to take a ski lesson, then offered to pay for it when he sensed her hesitation. She'd never been to Mammoth. Renzo had been invited by Kyle's family before; Jessie's family rented their own condo every year.

"All right, well," her mother said. Clare waited, and when nothing followed, she got out of the car to pull her suitcase from the back seat. The idea was to swim this afternoon; Kyle's parents were allegedly out of the house until at least ten o'clock that night. Clare hadn't mentioned that there were no adults inside.

Her mother rolled down the passenger window.

"Okay," she said. "Have fun. Swimming today and skiing tomorrow. Tough life!"

This time, though, Clare could tell that her mother was trying to sound sincere.

"I'll text you when we leave tomorrow," Clare said. "And once we get there."

And then she checked her purse for her wallet, and when she looked up her mother was scrutinizing her, almost squinting.

"Oh, honey. You're getting cellulite already. Just a little bit. We should do something about that."

There was something else, surely. They said that they loved one another, or the word "goodbye." Clare didn't remember, later. She only remembered watching her mother's car drive toward Sixth, remembered tugging at the hem of her terrycloth shorts. Remembered telling herself, as she had so often in the past year, that her mother was understandably wary of Clare's obsession with Kyle, of the weekends she had spent in his pool or, even worse, in Jessie's. That Renzo had grown up in circumstances somewhat similar to Clare's seemed to hold little weight for her mother, who would just say that he was in "even deeper than you" whenever Clare mentioned him.

Clare stood in Kyle's driveway for another minute. Beneath her shorts, she could feel the elastic of her old bikini bottoms gaping, stretched with age. She was wearing her smudged blue Converse, the ones Renzo had doodled all over. She considered wrapping her beach towel around her hips but decided that would look too strange, like some guy who'd just gotten out of a shower. She lingered there, probably looking to the neighbors like someone desperate for a reason not to go inside, and then she walked up the driveway and let herself in at the back gate.

There was a Sean Paul song blasting from the pool house speakers, which Kyle had dragged as close to the open windows as their extension cords would permit. The host himself was missing, but Clare could see one occupied lounger, angled away from her, two pairs of feet visible at its end. Jessie's, she assumed, and probably Mac, the new boyfriend. Of course he was here, and of course Jessie wouldn't miss the chance to canoodle with him in front of Renzo.

"Hi," she called over. Jessie didn't respond, but Mac strained until he could see her over the top of the chair, nodded in greeting. Clare always felt that he was waiting for her to prove herself to him. Whether this was because of Renzo or for some other reason was a question that drove her crazy if she thought about it for too long. It always felt like Mac was the only person who had noticed the sesame seed stuck between her teeth, or the twisted hem of her underwear visible through her tight jeans. This did not seem like it was his fault, or anything he cared about enough to do intentionally. But still.

"Oh, good," she heard. "Finally."

Renzo emerged from the pool house holding two highball glasses filled with drinks the color of a ripe peach. He held one out to her mid-stride, turning her gently toward the house, seizing her rolling suitcase with his newly free hand.

"Let's find Kyle," he said. "I've been so desperate for you to arrive. You should see how she's been parading this guy around in front of me. She also keeps talking about the trip, which I think is rude. Unless she's angling for him to come along? In which case, ask Kyle, don't keep dropping hints to me."

"It must be about you, though," Clare deadpanned. "No other explanation. Must be a performance solely for your benefit, right?"

"Well," he said. "Let's go with the odds, no? Come on, try your drink. It's a mai tai."

She took a sip.

"Is it?"

"I don't know," he said. "I didn't look up what's in a mai tai. We've got the blender set up in the kitchen and I just went with my gut."

He stopped for a moment, stood still, and shielded his eyes from the sun.

"Are you okay, love?"

She nodded, mute. He took her drink from her, placed both glasses carefully on the ground, and then stooped to hug her. He wrapped his arms under hers and lifted her almost to her tiptoes, let their cheeks touch, stood for several seconds without moving. Just long enough, she realized, until he could tell that she wouldn't start to cry.

"Whatever it is," he said. "You don't need to see anyone but us for, like, five days. Just, you know."

He stood back and let his shoulders ripple loosely, let his hips follow. He grinned at her.

"I don't think," she said, "that I fully realized until now how tall you've actually gotten."

"I know!" he yelped. "The much-awaited growth spurt. Anyway, come on. Kyle's inside."

And he was, standing in bafflement before the blender.

"What the hell did you put in here?" he said.

"Oh," Renzo said, putting his sunglasses back on. "Just try it first."

"Sup, ho," Kyle said to Clare. He loped over, dipped her backward and planted a wet kiss on her neck, then tossed her back to Renzo and raced out to the pool, executing a sloppy cannonball. Mac stood up, followed. Clare could see that Kyle's devotion to Renzo wouldn't extend this far. That he liked Mac, that Mac wasn't just here for Jessie.

"If I had to guess," she said. "Mac will be in the car tomorrow."

Renzo sipped his drink.

"Has anyone . . ." she said. "I just don't understand how we're getting there?"

"The nanny's driving us all up. I mean, you know Kyle drives all the time."

"Not *all* the time. He drives, like, five blocks to pick up pizza or do a Blockbuster run."

"Well, I guess an actual road trip is asking his mother to turn a bit more than her usual benevolent blind eye. I think they're also driving up next week? Monday? They'll be up at some point. But the place is huge, you'll see. We'll be fine."

"Sorry . . . the nanny?"

"Or, whatever. I don't really know who she is. Someone who's willing to drive an SUV full of, you know. Us."

"Well, I definitely think we should call her 'Kyle's nanny' as often as possible, at least when he's in the room."

"The *au pair*, perhaps?"

The day was perfect, quiet and slow, the sounds of leaf blowers echoing across the backyards down the block. Yesterday they'd been sitting in class, and now it was spring break, and tomorrow they'd be in the snow. She didn't swim. She kept her shorts on and stayed on a chair, flat on her back, for most of the day. At most she sat on the uneven stone edge of the hot tub, watched the rest of them floating and splashing. Renzo came over a few times, shook his wet hair across her legs, eased himself between her legs and pressed his back into her warm chest. She could feel him watching her, waiting for it to dissipate: the miasma of home clinging to her skin. But he didn't ask again. He just lay against her, rubbing at her shin absent-mindedly, and she kissed the top of his head gratefully. Besides, she thought, it gave him something to do. It was a problem to monitor that wasn't Jessie, and in this way everyone could get along.

It would be nice, Clare thought at one point, when she realized that Jessie had barely spoken to her. It would be nice if we could talk about something besides the guys, ever. She thought of a Saturday afternoon the previous fall that they'd been forced to spend at school, the Freshman Mother-Daughter Tea. When Jessie's mother had walked in gripping her daughter's arm, hissing into her ear. Clare had followed Jess into the bathroom near the cafeteria and they'd just stood at the sinks together, silent, passing one another lip gloss and mascara but never speaking, waiting until they were ready to walk back out to this event where none of the boys would be in attendance. That was, maybe, the closest they'd gotten. Maybe high school would be different from middle school, Clare thought. It hadn't been so far, but, whatever. Maybe.

She had two mai tais, or whatever they were, which was officially two more drinks than she'd ever consumed before in broad daylight. They ordered pizza from a place on Larchmont and stayed outside until it was chilly, then moved into the pool house and watched the first twenty minutes of a few different Academy screener DVDs Kyle's father had left stacked on the media console. The boys smoked weed, at some point, and Clare and Jessie abstained. Clare tried to ask Kyle about what she needed to wear on the slopes and he waved her off, promised that it was all packed already. When she kept asking, he tickled her until she gave up, let him pull her into his lap. She crawled into bed some time near midnight and congratulated herself for not dwelling on her mother's comment. Eventually Renzo crawled in with her, put his arm tightly to her waist and burrowed into the pillow, blew on the back of her neck a few times until she giggled. Kyle staggered in and let himself collapse onto the bed like a felled animal, pretending to snore. Renzo battered him with a decorative bolster pillow until he ceded the bed, crawled onto the floor, and scrounged two pillows and a quilt from beneath them.

"Enough!" Renzo cried, and they all fell asleep that way.

In the morning, Renzo kicked Kyle awake and shuffled him out the door. They walked up to the Starbucks on Larchmont, returning with drinks for everyone. The woman driving them up to Mammoth was a UCLA graduate student named Kimberly, and she waited patiently behind the wheel of the gigantic black SUV while they all straggled out. Kyle crawled into the very back row, and Mac followed. Jessie shook her head and climbed up into the front seat, to keep Kimberly company. Renzo beckoned Clare into the remaining row and built up a stack of blankets between them, leaned into her shoulder, placed his drink in the door's cup holder.

"Wake me up once we're out in the middle of nowhere," he told her. "Don't let me miss the whole drive."

"No," she said. "I would never."

7

Eventually, they all pile back into the golf cart. Kyle drives, as if his resident status makes him any less likely to career up onto someone's lawn. The attendants, cooling their heels near a discreet clump of greenery, look away tactfully when he nearly rams another cart on his way out.

But they make it home. Jessie planned ahead: the shrimp has been marinating all this time in lime juice. Renzo insists that he's fine to chop and is soon bent in concentration over small hills of diced avocado, diced tomato, diced jalapeño. He is very careful not to rub his eyes. Clare lingers at his side.

Liam crafts a playlist, all the explicit rap songs they found so tantalizing in middle school. They know the lyrics but they also know better, now, than to sing along. Mac delights in everyone's abashed silence during large chunks of each song, mocking them as he dances around the room. He wraps Clare in a bear hug, grinds against her. Acts like a teenager. *Y'all gonna make me lose my mind.*

"That hardly looks consensual," Renzo calls over, and when she pops her hip and surrenders to the vicious mockery her dancing will surely elicit, he throws up his hands.

"I tried to intervene," he says. "But you know what they say, can't rape the willing."

"Gross," she tells him.

Kyle sits down and pulls out his laptop, antically clicks between news sites. Every few minutes he'll read a tweet out loud, or a *Times* headline, a few times even one from Breitbart, and they'll all laugh but feel sick. Once they feel too sick, he puts the laptop away.

"Look," he says. "We really need to decide if we're in for that fishing trip tomorrow. I mean, at this point we'll still need to pay a cancellation fee, but. If we're doing it, I need to respond to this guy and send over the payment. It's six hundred for the four hours."

"What?" Clare chokes out.

"Not per person," he clarifies.

"Oh, I mean, I'm not sure—"

But Renzo immediately snaps his fingers in her face.

"Don't *even* start with me."

"I had the flight out from Boston, too, Renzo, the rest of you just—"

"Do, not, *begin* this with me."

Kyle noisily opens three beers, places them on the kitchen island, makes eye contact with Liam.

"Honey, look," Renzo continues. "I know you're not currently standing to inherit like our boy over here, but you do realize that you're actually allowed to *spend* your advance? It hasn't been earmarked for your retirement. That's not the last money you'll ever make."

Kyle casts his eyes heavenward at the mention of his inheritance, the accompanying elbow to his ribs. Otherwise, he pretends not to have heard.

"I didn't say I'm refusing to go, I just want to know how much we're expecting—"

"Our good friend Kyle has planned a lovely day for us," Renzo says. "He has done all of this in addition to hosting us here at the stunning, be it ever so humble, Harmon Family Second Homestead. We just spent our evening charging drinks to his family's tab. Would you like me to cover your share of the fishing trip, Clare?"

Mac appears behind her, wraps her in another bear hug. A warning, she knows. She has felt this since she got here, Renzo maneuvering, wanting to ask about the specifics of her book deal. He just wants her to say it, maybe. That even more than four years after her wedding, she doesn't quite think of Jamie's money as hers to spend.

He knows, too, that mentioning Kyle's largesse will make her fold. Any discussion of money makes Kyle so intensely uncomfortable that he resolves it by hastily involving more money. Even when they were teenagers, nothing sent his hand shooting into his pocket, frantic to withdraw his wallet, faster than Clare or Renzo expressing ambivalence about how to split a tab.

Or maybe Renzo just wants to fight. Start small fires, no matter the kindling. Torch all the painful places he knows about, press against every scar he can remember. It's not like this is new. She reminds herself that they have almost a full week left together in this house.

"No," she tells him. "I'm happy to pay my full share. Obviously."

And then it's over, immediately and without any lingering smoke. Everyone can be drunk again, they don't need to try anymore to sharpen themselves against the spreading blur.

"We really just need to sit down and *eat something*," Clare says at some point, but time has already grown elastic, it's reaching that stage when indoor lighting seems murky, when you swim through it. She's grabbing tortilla chips by the fistful. Renzo, Kyle, and Mac talk past her as she munches, arguing about yet another think piece, rehashing some crucial error a presidential candidate made more than a year ago. She hates that she is too drunk to chime in. They don't even *care* if she chimes in! Not really. They still don't think she's as smart as they are! They always acted like her brain was some bland, utilitarian object, like a high-end vacuum cleaner, maybe she could grind out straight As but she wasn't a thinker the way they were, she wasn't innovative or independent or a seeker. She was just the nerd; they were actually intelligent. She was just the girl; she wasn't a rebel. Well, she thinks, if only they knew. Who's the selfish, rebellious seeker now?

When will you outgrow this? she asks herself. The boys—mostly

Renzo, to be fair—convey that they don't see her as an equal, at which point she takes the bait and gets upset, at which point they perform their dismay that, as ever, she's been too quick to take offense.

She and Renzo went back and forth over email once, a few years ago. *Believe me*, he told her, *I'd be absolutely thrilled to move beyond this tiresome pattern of your excoriating me over various perceived insults*. That had been in response to a long email she sent him, pouring her heart out, telling him openly for once that he had hurt her feelings. She can't remember now what it was, the instigating offense. Only the feeling of exposing her underbelly so that even he would be compelled to, if not apologize, then, what? Acknowledge that sometimes he said things just to see if he could make her cry? But his response had been so much worse, one of the chilliest emails she could remember ever receiving from anyone she loved, anyone whose opinion actually mattered. And then they never spoke of it again. He texted her when she was next in Los Angeles—*Shall we find time for a colloquy, darling?*—and they simply met for lunch as if none of it had happened.

They all eat some sort of dinner, one way or another. Renzo stands over the glass baking dish, feeding himself ceviche with the serving spoon. She dances over to him now and embraces him from behind, nuzzling her face between his shoulder blades. When did he take his shirt off? Why? Well, she knows why. She runs her hands across his rippling torso.

"What's that for?" he asks.

"Just sitting over here, cataloguing your unforgivable faults and your innumerable virtues," she says, her cheek still pressed against his toasty skin.

"Oh, good! Your very favorite pastime," he says, but he sounds affectionate, it's warm. He steps away from her, disentangles himself from her arms, and then slaps her ass once for emphasis.

"Let's swim."

"I don't know where my suit is," Clare announces to no one. Liam reappears to hand her a pair of his boxers; where has he been? She's barely looked at him since they got home. She tries not to allow her body to track his as he moves around the room.

Outside, she's the only one who slides easily into the hot tub, submerging herself up to the neck. Everyone else perches on the tub's rim. She closes her eyes and listens.

"I just think we should each take a few more mints. Each. The last time you told me to try these ones, I didn't even really get high."

"I think you kind of have to ask yourself, right? You're sick of renting. I mean, we all are. And I hardly think my life as a renter is making Los Angeles a more equitable place to live, right? So then, do you buy? Are you comfortable getting in on the ground floor of the gentrification, literally? I mean, Boyle Heights, Highland Park, maybe parts of West Adams. These places are going to explode, nobody can afford fucking Echo Park anymore. Even Atwater Village."

"Listen, Renzo. Listen to me. We have had one mint *each*. The box says that two mints is *novice level*. We're not even hitting *novice* level!"

"Okay but, *that* whole thing was brutal, though. I mean, just so fucking idiotic. She opened a bar in Crown Heights and her entire marketing strategy was, like, how deeply can I disrespect the people of this community. Like, O-M-G, come order a cocktail with a long name that's a pun, bring your mom who's visiting Brooklyn for the first time, this totally used to be the ghetto, we're keeping the bullet holes in the wall, snap your drink and post it to Insta! It was just *brutal*."

"Madam, I will have you know that I, certainly, am no novice in this area."

"Yes, Renzo! Exactly! That is my exact point. Here, let's just take four. Anyway, what were you . . . Oh, right, my point is. Don't tell Clare, but—Clare, are you asleep? Kyle, don't let her slip into the water. Is she sleeping? Whatever, I would say this to her face. I'm just not ever, ever in a million years going to be someone who wants to knock on some stranger's door. Or call them on the phone. That is just . . . not going to be my thing. And that doesn't make me a bad person."

"Okay, but you realize that whole thing was bullshit to begin with, right? Those weren't bullet holes. That lady made it all up."

"Dude, you aren't worried about flying with these mints?"

"I didn't know you were so paranoid! I always thought of Clare as the one who's too terrified to fly with weed. She's like, a monk."

"That's not . . . You have greatly misunderstood what a monk is, my man."

"It was a former bodega. No bullet holes. Like, okay, yes. That lady was a moron. And racist as fuck, I think we all feel quite comfortable throwing that word around in her case, for sure. But that's what people think of when you say the word 'gentrification,' right? And I just think there has to be another way to do it. To be thoughtful."

"Sure, I mean, you can actually think about which local businesses get your money? I guess, right? Just the general idea of how you interact with these spaces other people have been living in for decades."

"Right, like, is that so hard?"

"Flying with *these*? You think TSA gives two shits about edibles? They absolutely do not."

"This sounds like one of those things you all can do, but I can't. Something tells me that if I roll up to TSA with contraband in my bag, I'm not making my flight."

"I don't know. It's very easy to say you'll do it, you'll be the enlightened gentrifier, when it's all a big hypothetical, right? Then you're actually living there and the Whole Foods is on your way home and most of us don't keep going to the established corner store for groceries. Correct?"

"I'm totally with you, by the way, Jess. You can give your money *or* your time. Both are equally necessary. The whole chat with a stranger thing, go knock on doors, I'm sure that's worthwhile. But it's not the only option."

"Maybe most of us don't walk the walk, but at a certain point, like . . . what can you do? You've gotta live somewhere. You can't necessarily afford to live in the place that's already been trashed by your white, gentrifying forebears. It's going to keep grinding along, with or without us. I don't see anyone here throwing their body across the gears of the machine."

"I don't think that's the quote."

"I think it is. But regardless. You know what I fucking mean."

"Well, tell that to her. Or I mean—not even Clare, specifically. But so many people who barely even knew what a midterm election *was* until this time two years ago. But suddenly they're out there acting like free-dom fighters, guilt-tripping the rest of us."

"That feels unfair. Clare, did you know what a midterm election was as of two years ago? Clare? Are you with us, darling?"

"What can you do? Some people would rather be out there, and some people would rather just write the goddamn check, at the end of the day. We need all hands on deck, man; that counts. Why wouldn't it?"

"TSA is not turning a blind eye on me trying to pass this little number through their scanner, I can guarantee you that."

"Look, Mac, my love. What do you want from me? Maybe you per-sonally cannot sneak edibles onto a commercial flight. Maybe you're right about that. Does that mean I shouldn't do it? Does that solve our bigger problem?"

"I don't know, Ren, does it? Please, by all means, explain to me how we solve the bigger problem."

"Okay, you two, calm down. We're supposed to be chilling out. That's the whole point. We're in someone else's hot tub in Hawai'i. Maybe we get to the bottom of that one in the morning?"

"He fucking started it."

"Here, love, take a few mints. A peace offering."

"Renzo loves giving me shit about this. I get it. I'm going to inherit a chunk of money. I hate even saying that word, *inherit*. It's not like that, it's not like . . . I mean, when my grandmother died, she left some money in a trust. The end. Like, I guarantee you my healthcare plan at work is no better than Renzo's, okay? It's not as different, on a day-in-and-day-out basis, than . . . I mean, of course it is. I know it is. But do you know what I mean? But whatever, maybe this is what we need. Eat the rich. Capital-ism is evil, we're all irredeemable."

"Yeah, everyone loves to say that lately. Everyone loves a slogan. No-body's sacrificing their time sitting here in this hot tub, though, so."

"I think somehow it's easier for the kids who are, like, five years behind us. Who didn't graduate into a fucking recession."

"No, I thought we were supposed to be more radical than they were. For that exact reason."

"Do any of the people who love retweeting their local DSA chapter even really know what the terminology means? This is my question. We have this friend who loves to say shit at dinner parties like 'Believing in capitalism is just as indefensible as believing in white supremacy.' I mean, just utterly absurd. Just to throw a bomb out there and derail the conversation."

"My sweet summer child, I hate to break it to you, but that is not an absurd thing to say. If you took the white supremacy out of the capitalism, the whole thing would crater. It's—You know what? No. I choose to enjoy my hot tub right now and not get caught up in white nonsense. You almost tricked me, dude. You almost got me to explain racism to you again. Not my fucking job, not on vacation."

"No, because we can still vaguely remember when things were good, dude. Generation Z—is that who we're talking about? When does Z start? Is there something between us and Z? Anyway, they can't remember a time pre-recession, I think that's the whole point. They knew from jump they weren't getting shit from us, let alone anyone older."

"No, Mac, but I just mean—that totally shuts down any meaningful dialogue, right? I mean, *whomst exactly* are you going to convince with that? What is the purpose of saying that to your friends, to people whose hearts are in the right place?"

"Christ, man. *In the right place.* All right, fine. Lemme get a few of those mints, man, hand them over. How about, reparations start right here. You sneak illegal drugs onto various airplanes and then give them to me for free. Let's fucking go. Jess, what's novice level? Fuck it, I'm taking four."

"I guess I would agree with him? I think we have to define 'right place.'"

"Dude, it's not even going to be illegal anywhere in another five years."

"Truly spoken like someone who's never left California. But sure, okay."

"We'll all bitch about capitalism for a few years, and then we'll elect a new president, and we'll all move on. Nobody's quitting their job. Have *you* seen anyone change their lives? It's all, like, fucking culture writers shitposting about no ethical consumption under capitalism to tee up the pictures of the 'little weekend cabin' they just bought upstate. While they're still paying rent on an apartment in Brooklyn that's nice enough to be photographed for a glossy print profile. Which, fine. But give me a break."

"That's what I did! I took four!"

"Do you remember that boss? How awful he was? I got reamed out in front of an entire conference room once because he wanted me to get 'Silk on the phone' and I couldn't intuit that there was indeed a person named Cylk on the callsheet. God, that was horrific."

"Dude, you don't know someone else's finances from their Instagram feed. Don't be playing hall monitor like that. That's a dangerous road to go down. That just leads nowhere good at all."

"Sorry . . . what is there to misunderstand about finances that allow you to buy a country home and still live well in gentrified Brooklyn? On a media salary? That's family money, honey! What am I missing?"

"Can we go get shaved ice tomorrow, by the way? We need to schedule out the rest of our treats. I want shaved ice."

"Dude, it's 'shave ice.' Do *not* call it shaved ice when we go into town, please. Don't embarrass me with the locals."

"We were such babies, though. Like, every job seemed awful, no? I still can't believe they never fired me. I threw up once in the bathroom and walked into a curriculum meeting with stains on my tie."

"Renzo used to come find me in the law library and make me do a shot before he left to meet you guys downtown."

"I did, proudly. And Kyle picked me up once when I realized I'd gone home with some guy who still lived with his parents. I had to crawl out onto the guest room balcony and drop down into the hydrangeas, ass first. So undignified."

"What did I do? I picked you up where?"

"Nothing, baby."

"I mean, none of these sanctimonious Silver Lake socialists are sending their kids to their local failing public school, right?"

"I don't know if that's true. I mean, I'll definitely think about that, down the road. At a certain point you have to live your values, right?"

"Oh, yeah? You feel confident you know what your values will be by then?"

Clare slides forward, floating her tailbone away from the step on which she'd perched. It has come back to her, unprompted. What she and Renzo were emailing about, years ago. He said something nasty to Jessie: "You know that, in the end, Clare will be perfectly content to just . . . live off her boyfriend."

And Jessie repeated it to Mac, who let something slip to Clare. Funny, she thinks now, that she allowed herself to forget the details, which still sting so sharply her eyes burn.

She sinks until her head is underwater. She waits down there for a moment and then surges back up, splashing them all.

"You people are *wired*," she says. "Did someone sneak cocaine past TSA too, and if so, will they share? Or have you all always loved the sounds of your own voices this much and I just forgot? I truly shudder to imagine what the deep gentrification conversation was at three a.m. on the Keep Austin Weird weekend."

"No one said you couldn't participate," Jessie shoots back.

"Come on, girl," Mac says, reaching over to tug at her wet ponytail. "You missed this. We certainly missed you, that weekend in Austin."

"Never fear," Renzo says. "I've just dosed them all with some high-quality edibles. How's the water? Is it nice? I'm coming in there with you."

But then, around one o'clock, he's the first domino to drop. He stands up in total silence and pads inside without any further announcement, his feet leaving wet crescents on the patio tile. Clues for a detective, wondering what has become of the revelers, Clare thinks, smiles. She's stoned now, too. A few minutes later, Kyle confirms that Renzo has passed out spread-eagle in the second bedroom.

"You and Jessie can take over two of the beds in the grandchildren's room," Liam tells Kyle. "I'm totally fine on the couch. I had to move out there last night anyway. Mac snores."

"No, you can have the big bedroom where I slept," Clare says quickly. "I mean, Kyle. It's your house."

He waves her off, wanders back inside with Mac.

She lets her feet float up in front of her in the water, like the tentacles of a jellyfish.

Jessie disappears quickly. Inside, Clare walks past Liam, who is pulling pillows from a high shelf in the linen closet.

Ten minutes later, doors are closed. She can hear Liam fill a glass of water from the kitchen tap. She cannot hear him gulp it down, but she imagines it, his throat contracting. When the door shudders, when he lies down behind her, she doesn't move.

Later, she will walk to the kitchen for her own glass of water. This will make no sense; there is a bathroom just off her bedroom, she could have gotten water from that tap. It will only register for her how deeply her decision made no sense, to walk out there in her underwear, her mouth swollen and stinging, when she hears the soft click of a door somewhere down the hall.

But that happens later. What happens now is that Liam lies down behind her and asks if he can stay. When she doesn't say anything, he curls into her so that their bodies zip together at the shoulders, the hipbone, the knee. This is easy because she's naked, she's been waiting there, on top of the duvet. He reaches down with one hand and slips out of his boxers, presses his dick against her. His other hand finds her breasts, her belly button, and he puts his lips to the back of her neck, then her spine. She tries so hard to lie still that it feels, in a way, like shivering. It occurs to her that he should have waited longer, that anyone might be awake. But she thinks about that for only another moment before she, what? She gives up. She rolls over and leans into him, their mouths meeting so quickly that she can't breathe.

SUNDAY

8

The next morning, they all return to the patio. They squabble over who will make the coffee. They agree that they should not, in fact physically cannot bear to, get that drunk again.

"We do have . . . a lot of alcohol lying around, though," Mac says, wary, as if the liquor will steal up and pour itself down their throats without warning. "Why did we charge all those cocktails? We could have just mixed drinks here, couldn't we?"

"Because," Renzo says, lifting his head with a certain quavering dignity. "Here, someone actually has to mix them."

He returns his head to his knees, where it's been resting. Jessie rubs his back.

"You know what?" she offers. "I'll do it. I will. I'll make a round of drinks right now. Maybe just a beer? Micheladas! I really do think it will help."

"Maybe a beer *would* work," Kyle concedes.

"I'm on it," Jessie says, already moving back into the house.

"Okay, but," Kyle calls after her. "That's it. We've got the boat trip at eleven. You all let me submit that payment last night, so we're definitely doing it. We need to meet them at the dock."

"Fucking thirties," Mac moans. "I don't even really feel like I drank that much."

"Please," Renzo says, "do not promote me to age thirty. That bell shan't toll until next month." He has noticeably brightened with the knowledge that a cold beer is en route.

They all sit together, listening to the throbbing of their own ear canals.

"Remember the time he threw up out my car window?" Kyle says. "On the 10? We got off at La Cienega and then sat at the light directly next to a cop car? Just, chunks of vomit fully oozing down the passenger door?"

"Why would you mention vomit," Clare whispers. Mac reaches out to Renzo with one arm, holds his hand. Clare pats Kyle's knee. They all sit there until Jessie returns with the beers, Liam close behind her.

"Wondering where you were," Renzo says. He touches one frosty bottle to his forehead, his temples.

"Well, I've been in the bathroom," Liam says. "I think. So technically, at least for a while, I slept on the bathroom floor. Thank you, Clare, for being very cool about the fact that I ran heaving through your bedroom at a rude hour. Sorry about that."

She smiles. Renzo watches her from behind his beer.

She looks at Liam and there's a flash of losing her balance as she climbed on top of him, the way he reached up to steady her, his hands on her shoulders like she was a steering wheel. They both laughed, but now she feels an embarrassment so consuming that she can feel her stomach muscles actually contract against her will. She tries to stop smiling.

They all drink the first beer together on the patio. Like a science experiment, after the first few sips, everyone's moving. Reaching their arms up above their heads, elongating their torsos and cracking their spines. Renzo does a cycle of stretches and then just stands there, stroking his obliques to check that they haven't melted away overnight. They prop their feet on the coffee table, pick at the bowls of fruit or at English muffins pulled straight from the package and torn into small, sloppy bites. Clare notes, without rancor but also without surprise, that it's she and Jessie who end up performing triage in the kitchen, which reeks of liquor and cilantro and the desiccated lime wedges and careless piles of dishes left from last night. Someone, mercifully, did toss the languishing pieces of shrimp.

She decides to load the dishwasher; that will be her contribution. She plugs her phone into Renzo's charger on the kitchen counter, turns it face down. There are texts she hasn't read yet. She feels a pestering awareness that she misses Jamie and an equal desperation to avoid his name on the screen. She rinses plates and thinks of the year she first met him, lying in his dark dorm room, asking questions about the house in Vermont. If you lived outside of town it was like someone had turned off the world around you, you couldn't see your hand in front of your face, it was so dark that it had auditory properties, it looked quiet and sounded dark.

"You think Hanover's quiet at night? Girl, you have no idea." He whispered a tour of the house into her ear, walking her through each room. When he got to the kitchen there was a glancing pause, almost imperceptible, as he mentioned that the dishwasher was broken.

"And we haven't fixed it because, I don't know, whatever," he mumbled. "That's just my mom, I guess." She still knew so little about his family but she recognized that instinct, to brush past anything too revealing. The same way she used to laugh about her father's car, whenever he picked her up from Kyle's house. Like he just loved the clunker so much, it was of *course* an option to replace it with an S-class but he just couldn't bear to give it up, who could say why?

Getting to know Jameson, all those little windows, the little boy peering out from behind the curtains. Jamie, the boy she met in a fraternity basement on College Street. They used to sleep together in his dorm bed and she can no longer summon even the slightest sensation of it, that closeness, how uncomfortable it must have been and how little they cared. One night, also very early on, Jamie woke up sweating. He had dreamt he was home, it was still unfinished, there was lumber stacked everywhere, and it was just him and his mother while some thick substance oozed down over all the windows, sludgy like mud, trapping them inside together. It wasn't exactly indecipherable. He apologized and she told him, don't worry, wake me up next time, wake me up whenever it happens. And he did. He made it her problem to fix, his insomnia. When they met, she was the steady one, she was excessively competent. Who would believe that, now?

She wills herself to summon the memories: the excitement, the thrill. She stares at her phone on the countertop and tells herself that, a long time ago, his name on her phone would have sent her into paroxysms of anticipation, desire plucking at her insides.

The truth is that she didn't think of him once last night. Even this morning, when she first opened her eyes after barely an hour of actual sleep and looked at the back of Liam's neck and remembered where she was. Even then, she didn't think of Jamie. That's the part she would never have believed, if she'd been warned.

She's only thinking of him now. After the fact.

She closes the dishwasher with unnecessary force, claps her hands with artificial efficiency. Renzo raises an eyebrow.

"One more?"

They all drink the second beers in their separate bedrooms, slipping into still-damp bathing suits. It is determined that among them there are at least two full bottles of sunscreen. They trade magazines, swap salt-ruffled paperbacks. Kyle stocks a cooler with the cold cuts and cheese, plus more beers. Renzo, at the last minute, throws in a bottle of tequila and a bottle of rosé. Then he removes the tequila and replaces it with a second bottle of wine.

Just before eleven, they pile into an old Chevy Tahoe that seems to live here on the island.

"Wait," Jessie says as she clambers into the back row. "This isn't your car from high school, is it?"

The car erupts in a chorus of disbelief.

"Jessie." Mac twists around in his seat. "This car is green."

She smiles at him, waiting.

"That car was black. Don't tell me you don't remember."

"Oh, Jesus, that's right," Renzo adds. "Talk about oblivious! That wouldn't fly for today's youth, now would it? Clare and Jessie would run me out of town on a *rail* if I made that joke today."

Jessie looks out her tinted triangle of window, smiles vaguely. Clare
sees that she has, in fact, forgotten that Kyle used to call his car the Black
Panther, that they all did.

Liam is sitting back with Jessie, directly behind Clare. At one point
Kyle slams the brakes at a stop sign and they're all thrown forward, straining against their seatbelts. Liam leaves his hands on her headrest for another moment, touches the back of her neck with his fingertips.

He kept asking her these nonsensical questions last night. Each time
his hands quieted at her lower back, each time she assumed he was
asleep, his voice would be there again in her ear, hoarse and thick. She
can't even remember what they talked about. Politics for a while, probably? That surly shadow looming over everything all year. The point
was just to stay awake, to stretch out the secret hours for as long as possible. Movies, maybe, and the sorry state of the Lakers. Which NBA stars
likely had the best sex lives, and which ones were too ascetic or single-
minded: *I don't think he wants the headache, frankly.*

She keeps her gaze steady, staring at the back of Renzo's head, until
Liam stops touching her.

At the dock, the fishing boat cruises into its slip to meet them. A short
man in a tank top and board shorts, his cheeks ruddy and the rest of him
deeply tanned, waves at them from the deck.

Clare hops out of the Tahoe with her Planned Parenthood tote slung
over one shoulder.

"I would leave that," Liam says.

"Why?"

"You're not going to be able to read," he says. "Way too choppy. When
was the last time you were out on a small boat like this?"

She pauses. He leans in, whispers against her earlobe, and her body
wants to fold in half, like crumpling paper.

"You might have to talk to me," he says. "Sorry."

"Come on, principessa," Renzo calls from the end of the dock. "You're
telling me the Boston finance bros never take you out on the water?"

She looks down at her phone. Jamie sent two messages last night, the
first an old picture of her on the crappy couch in their first apartment,

wearing a pair of his boxers and a silky demi-cup bra and standing up on her knees and tilting her breasts toward the camera, flipping him off with both hands. That photo must be eight years old. She's not sure she's ever seen it before. *God I miss you*, is the second text.

we're actually about to get on a boat (!) she types quickly. *service has been crazy spotty, sorry sorry try you before dinner promise. love you get some rest love you, Jameson, miss you too*

She tosses the phone into her bag, and Kyle locks it in the car along with everything but the beers and the two bottles of wine, cradled in the crook of his arm. She walks with Liam down the dock, and he lifts her into the boat. Everyone else is already on board, moving away from them. He holds on to her for one extra moment, kisses the top of her head.

Okay, so, what's the first condiment you buy? That had been another one, as the sun was already coming up, the room moving from concealed darkness to a cool blue wash that left them exposed. The secret hours only ever last so long. Sooner or later you have to watch each other come into focus, like two twinned Polaroid images.

What, when I moved in?

Always. Your first one, always.

Mustard? Mustard, I think. Even though I don't really use it that often.

Oh, he said, pulling the sheet over their heads and letting it float down around them, kiss their skin again, as if they could make the bed with themselves still in it and hide from the rest of the house waking up down the hall. *Oh, but that's the right answer.*

Each time she mentioned Boston she spoke in the first person singular, and they didn't otherwise acknowledge this.

She looks at him now, smiling at her like he knows exactly what she's thinking. The cruelty of it, the flashes of what it felt like to lie naked beside someone for the first time, is how freely you laughed at things no adult in daylight would find even mildly amusing. Those moments bubble up within you like uncorked champagne, and by the time you put them into words for yourself, they're flat. His voice crackling and low, his torso re-orienting toward yours in sleep, that lazy ballet of your bodies. You can't re-create any of it, it's impossible. Anything you said to one another in that darkness is useless, mundane. Humiliating and meager and surely some sort of trap.

Renzo has turned back to them, and they let their bodies drift apart.

"Is this a good idea?" she asks quietly. "Getting on this boat."

"I don't know," Liam says. "But we're already here, so. Let's find out."

9

Clare nestles into the ledge beneath the prow and tries to remember what "back of the boat," where everyone else is clumped, is even called. Port, maybe? Why is she allowed to be hungover on a boat if she knows so little about the basic mechanics of the thing?

"Fishing," it turns out, just means baiting the lines and letting them drag along in the boat's wake. This feels, to Clare, like cheating. Renzo, though, is suddenly determined. He wants to catch their dinner. He's buttonholed poor Kyle, who's slumped on the bench trying not to be sick. Renzo rubs his back in concentric circles, gesturing wildly at the water.

Her neck lolls back, a dizzying lift in her stomach as the boat rushes her backward. They're out on the open water now, and it's smoother, less violent, than it was at first.

Mac sits down beside her. She can smell his deodorant, the cologne he taps behind each ear before leaving the house.

"That shit was pretty intense," he says. "I'm serious. I was kind of picturing, like. A sailboat. I'm not trying to be lost at sea. How safe do we think this is?"

"I was literally just thinking about that."

No, "port" is left. She knows she had learned that by high school— something about the British navy seizing "our" ships. *Impressment.* This one she always remembers because she helped Kyle study that spring, after he'd barely attended class, and he kept wiggling his eyebrows and telling her that, to be quite frank, she was *impressing* him. They were having sex that semester, on a quasi-regular basis, and it made them both feel very adult and yet constantly wrong-footed, which might have been why they stopped soon thereafter.

At some point, she was taught the difference between port and starboard. There was an overnight trip in the fifth grade. Her class rode a bus up to Dana Point, where they were assigned jobs on a reconstructed vessel, pretending to be galley cooks or deck swabbers on a ship traveling from Boston to California. The whole thing was run by eccentric men—struggling actors, she now assumes, who were cashing a paycheck. There was a general scolding tone, wishing to remind forty children attending one of the city's most expensive private schools of their own luck. The rationing of toilet paper, the menial labor, such as it was. She was quickly realizing that tuition wasn't actually a ruinous expense for most of her classmates' families. That many of her classmates were not expected, at home, to wash their own dishes. That the roiling feeling she got sometimes, listening to them all talk about their lives, was actually something close to anger.

The entire group, faculty chaperones included, slept in a narrow room lined with wooden bunks. It took hours for everyone to fall asleep, their nerves giddy and popping in that way you really can only experience in preadolescence, then spend years experimenting with substances hoping to recapture. She remembers how illicit it felt that night, sleeping near so many boys. And only a few years after that it would be completely unremarkable, falling asleep in the same room or the same bed as several boys. And by then, she thinks, it was these boys, the ones sprawled around her today on this lurching boat. Something fundamental in her had changed, between the shy ten-year-old and the rowdy teenager, and whatever that was, it came from knowing these boys.

"It's a Yellowfin yacht that belongs to a resort community," she reminds Mac. "I think we're fine."

"Should we be wearing life jackets?"

"There's more than one lawyer on board, right? Just make sure one of them survives to sue. Because if anything goes wrong, we're total dead weight. They'll heave me over in, like, minute three of any genuine crisis."

"Jettison," he says. "That's where that word comes from, I think."

"I love that word."

"Let's try to grab a little nap, yeah? Maybe we can just sleep through the seasickness."

"You apply pressure," she tells him. "For the nausea." She puts her thumbs to his wrist. He slings an arm around her shoulder, and she snuggles back into his chest. The sun is clarifying, like it will slowly, given time, leach the alcohol from their blood.

"Let me ask you something."

"Yes, Renzo did try to crawl in with me this morning, and no, I didn't surrender. I told him for the hundredth time that he is simply just not my type."

"I have to say, this trip has made it quite clear to me that thirty won't be the magical age at which you or Kyle stop with the homophobic jokes," she says. "But hilarious, truly. Renzo's gay! I'd forgotten. Anyway, no. I was wondering. When you chaperone events, for school. Are you all just secretly drinking? I kind of assume you would be."

"I mean, now? No, absolutely not. When I was a new baby teacher? Sure. Do I assume that my protégés are pleasantly buzzed during the school dance? Yes. I mean, you know, it wouldn't fly if it's discovered, but. What I don't see can't hurt me. Why?"

"I was just thinking about this field trip from elementary school. We all slept below decks together and it just seems so obvious now—the teachers were passing around a flask, right? Did you guys go on the Pilgrim trip?"

"Girl, how are you actually going to ask me that? Did my mother send my Black ass on a weekend trip to cosplay the early 1800s with my class of entirely white children? No, Clare, she did not. I don't think my elementary school did that? I know I've heard some of you talk about it. They only let you use two squares of toilet paper, or whatever. I feel like I'd remember a sense of outrage if she'd straight up refused to let me go? But no, Lorna McMillan was sure as hell not going to send her child away to pretend be a Black man sailing the high seas *before the Civil War.*"

"Fair enough."

A shadow blocks the sun, and she opens her eyes.

"How you two holding up?"

One of the fishermen—is it accurate to call him that? Or captain?—has appeared above them.

"Ryden," the man says. "We didn't really get a chance to meet before."

He's tall, his muscles ropy, the kind of limbs built by accident rather than by hours sculpting them in a gym. He wears an ancient, tissue-thin shirt with its sleeves ripped off so that his nipples are visible each time he lifts his arms, one of which is sheathed in tattoos. The skin across his cheeks is so layered with sunburn it now exists in a permanent state of wear and tear. It's not really tanned, it's just weathered. His co-captain has the much more handsome face. But that guy is pudgier and somehow looks like a teenager who's never quite grown into his adult features. That one's name is Steve, she's pretty sure. They both introduced themselves back at the dock. She already knows Ryden's name. That's not why he came over.

Ryden will refer to himself as "questing" or "journeying." A real adventurer of the soul. He will absolutely wish to name and then discuss his own wanderlust. She can see this already.

"Hi, Ryden," Mac says loudly. "Nice to meet you again."

Ryden takes this in stride.

"Your buddy seems like he's struggling." He thumbs casually over one shoulder at Kyle, sitting in a position that you couldn't exactly call upright.

"We're not seasick," she says. "Hungover, maybe, yes."

"Maybe?" Ryden lets his mouth fall open, like he's anticipating her comeback.

As if cued by her comment, Liam staggers over, proffering the bottle of wine. She takes it, tilts her neck back to sip, and then hands it to Mac.

She doesn't speak to Liam or even acknowledge his presence. He waits a moment, then sits.

"What's the deal with the fish?" she says. "How will we know when we catch one?"

Ryden laughs at her.

"Oh, I think your buddy will make some noise." He squints at her. "Not a big fan of the open sea, I take it?"

"Sorry, how can you tell?"

Liam snorts, then stands. Mac watches him walk away. Ryden acts as if Liam was never there at all.

"So you guys are, what? College friends?" he asks, sitting down.

"High school."

"Middle school, actually," Mac corrects her. "This one and I were in the chorus together. And in ninth grade, we did a duet."

"Oh, Jesus, Mac. Don't."

"Cry me, cry me . . . Cry me, cry me . . ." he croons in his falsetto, tightening his grip around her shoulders.

"Is that your name? I heard her call you that earlier and thought it was maybe, just, you know. A nickname, Mac."

Mac laughs.

"My last name is McMillan," he says. "My first name is Jamal, and by the time I was thirteen I'd figured out that the white teachers at our school—so, the teachers at our school—would find me a little bit less intimidating if I took on a more, you know. A nickname with a bit less melanin involved."

"Sure, sure, I get it. Jamal, they're all going to treat you like a thug or something."

Clare winces.

"More or less. It was always fun to wait until, you know, a month or so into the school year, when my father showed up at Parent-Teacher Night wearing his scrubs."

"No shit, he's a doctor?"

Clare flinches again.

"He's a neurosurgeon," she blurts. Mac strokes the back of her arm as if to say, *Don't.*

"Oh man," Ryden says. "I always thought I would have loved being a doctor. I aced bio in high school. Not squeamish at all, not even a little bit. I think I would've been able to do the bloodiest, most intricate shit. Probably should've actually studied."

"Did you grow up on the island?" Mac asks.

"California."

"That's where we're from," Clare says.

"Right, of course. High school with Kyle. I'm guessing then you guys are also LA, right? I'm actually not far from there, the beach cities."

"My father grew up in Hermosa! Let me guess, Redondo Union High?"

Ryden smiles at her for a moment, running his tongue across his front teeth.

"Nope," he says. "Chadwick. Palos Verdes Estates."

She blushes, briefly, but he's already chuckling.

"No sweat. I get it, I'm not exactly dressed in my preppy PV uniform right now. You assumed I was some scrappy beach bum kid who blew off a bartending job in Redondo and fled to Hawai'i with ten bucks in the pocket of my board shorts, right? I mean, fair enough, there are plenty of lost boys on this island who did exactly that."

"No, it's just—" she begins. Mac is laughing, too. Chadwick is the wealthy private school in Palos Verdes; it is, arguably, every bit as bougie as their own high school.

"Where in PV?" Mac asks.

"Malaga Cove, right around there."

Mac whistles.

"Yeah, man, I know how lucky I was, I'm not an asshole. The view out my bedroom window as a kid? I mean, *this* place is otherworldly, don't get me wrong. But Malaga, man. I love it there. But I just couldn't work for my dad, inherit the business. Just could not do it."

He's shaking his head mournfully.

"I do this because I love it," he says. "I love being on the water, learning about the island, the people, the history of all these species coexisting. I've just got that wanderlust, man. I'm just one of those people."

Clare smiles to herself. In the end, it only took him a few minutes.

"Anyway," Ryden says, still shaking his head, sheepish and rueful. "Whereabouts did your dad grow up?"

"Near the public library," she says. "Like, fifteen blocks from the beach. Just the other side of PCH."

"But you ended up in LA," Ryden prompts. "Was it, like, everyone's parents worked in Hollywood, or what?"

Were Liam not on the boat, surely, one of them would mention his last name. Just to satisfy Ryden's hunger for something truly glamorous. That's what he wants to hear: everyone had famous parents, they served sashimi in the cafeteria, the first car was always a Mercedes. No one ever wants to hear that it was so much more mundane, so much less thrilling and more insidious. That it was just, for Clare, having no clue how many unpleasant things she'd never actually seen with her own eyes.

Ryden doesn't want to hear that. And to be fair, there *were* plenty of kids whose first car was a Mercedes or a BMW. There was the kid whose father bought him a Hummer with which he, unable to judge its size as he executed a turn, crunched another kid's Audi.

"Not everyone's parents," she says. "Right, Mac, what would you say? There were definitely people who worked in the industry, but it wasn't everyone."

"Yes," Mac says, refusing to play along.

Clare fights the urge to look for Liam, who's disappeared. In the end, last night, they both always looped back to high school. What else was there? Today, yesterday, the last five years, all off limits. What they did have were recitations of adjacent memories. Sketchy images of what it once felt like to live inside their own minds—all this time later, they could fill those in for one another. They'd both been spectators, once, at a legendary high school basketball game. Their team had lost, and the star of their rival school was now one of the most famous players in the world.

"I sat on the floor for the entire second half, under the basket," he told her. "One time he landed right at my feet."

She hadn't been able to remember Liam's presence at that basketball game. But she did remember herself up in the stands, their offensive cheers. Things she can't quite acknowledge, even in her own memory, because they were so cruel and clueless and so taken with their own malevolence. *That's all right, that's okay, you're gonna pump our gas someday.* They all remember it, but everyone probably remembers someone else doing it. Everyone has neatly rearranged themselves in the memory, like paper dolls moved around. Even now, she tells herself that it was awful but thinks—I watched other people say it. I watched other girls giggle at the lewd hand gestures, and maybe I should have taken a stand, but at least I didn't play along. She can almost picture it, their mouths moving and her own lips pursed. She can edit the tape even as she's winding it backward. On especially bad days she's fearful that this is, in fact, the animating principle of what it means to cobble together a set of political beliefs as a thirty-year-old white woman, even if you tell yourself it's something more sweeping. Just a vision of the world, and your own place in it, that might begin to redress the things you did when you still believed you had the excuse of being "only" a child.

And what about last night, she thinks. Where will you put the paper dolls in that memory?

"I like Kyle a lot," Ryden says. "Super genuine dude. But sometimes, when I'm around his siblings, the grandkids especially. Whatever, but I'm basically picturing, like, *The O.C.* Is that embarrassing to admit? I used to watch that show, and I was . . . not a teenager by then."

"Oh," she says. "We didn't dress like that, believe me. Not for school, at least."

"Oh, yeah? Well—that's a shame."

And then Kyle and Steve the co-captain are waving at them from the cockpit, cupping their hands, their words snuffed by the wind. Ryden makes his way back over.

Behind her, Mac shifts until she's forced to bend forward at the waist, away from him.

"Oh, no, we didn't dress like that, believe me." He's speaking in a breathy murmur.

"Excuse me? Is that supposed to be my voice? Come on, Big Mac. It's completely harmless."

"Don't get me wrong. You're perfectly entitled to a little flattery, and he's entitled to spend the night jerking it to images of himself bringing Marissa Cooper home to a Republican congressional fundraiser at the Palos Verdes Yacht Club, or whatever the fuck."

"Jesus," she says. "A bit graphic. Also, I think Palos Verdes has the same congressman as Santa Monica. Don't be a snob."

"Okay, please. I was waiting for you to stand up, adjust your bikini, and ask him to apply sunscreen to your tailbone. You put on a whole, like, voice for him. Plus, he's the snob. I'm a snob? Give me a break. His *wanderlust*? What do you want to bet that's sponsored by the poor, dull parents back in PV? His father who owns a hair salon or a real estate brokerage or a restaurant franchise? That's who's paying for this little nomadic lifestyle out here."

"I know," she says. "I called that one."

"Anyway, it's no crime. You get a little compliment, he gets a little thrill. You look great lately. Not just the tan. You've got your whole, you know, absent-minded, 'Oh I didn't even realize I was licking my lips,' come-hither thing going on this week."

She sits up, removes her sunglasses, puckers her lips at him in an exaggerated duck face, the face of a teenage girl performing for her mirror. "Like this?"

He laughs, skims her shoulder and hip with one hand.

"Don't act like I'm not just picking up what you already put down, idiot. You know exactly what I am *speaking* of. Always used to really slay with Kyle, as I recall."

"Oh, shut up."

"Prove me wrong. Which part of that is wrong?"

"Twice? I think? Fifteen years ago."

"Twice, my ass. That went on for years. Who do you think you're talking to, here?"

"It is truly, truly ancient history."

"Oh," he says. "Come on now. None of it's *ancient*."

"Do you want to open up a discussion of ancient history with me?" she purrs. He taps his sunglasses in surrender, lets them fall back into place.

"No harm in a little flirting," he repeats, contemplative. "Anyway, I'm just teasing. Other than that, how are things? I feel like I've barely gotten to talk to you beyond refereeing every fourth spat with Renzo. How's tricks? How is, like, work going?"

"Oh," she says. "Fine."

"Baby girl," he says. "I'm not Ren. I'm not asking so I can use it against you in future. I'm actually interested."

She thinks, then, what it would be like to tell him the truth. That the book is more than a year overdue, that her editor accidentally copied her on an email to her agent. An email with phrases like "come-to-Jesus moment" and "hard truths" and "gracefully bow out" and "separate visions" sprinkled liberally throughout its three pinched paragraphs.

She thinks, for a blissful few seconds, that she'll actually tell him. But he speaks first.

"I still remember that weekend. Four people sent me the story before I clicked the link and saw your name. And it was just like, *Yeah, fuckers. This is what I've always known about her, and now the rest of you get to bask in it, too.* I'm so proud of you. I know I have no idea what I'm talking about, I know it's probably annoying that the process takes so long. But I'm so proud of you, the life you've put together for yourself. I feel like I don't say that enough."

And then it's vanished, the narrow fissure through which she might have pushed it toward him, her fear and her misery and, whatever. Something honest.

"Work is great," she says. "My agent just wants to perfect the latest draft before we send it to my editor."

"I thought that's what an editor did," Mac says, not unkindly. "I mean, is that not how it works? Doesn't the editor turn it into a book?"

"Calling it a book," she says, "that's still, a little bit. Kind of a misnomer."

"Is it tough, like, do you worry that everyone will just assume it's about you?"

"It's not autobiographical," she says, too quickly.

"No, I know it's fiction, but I'm saying—"

"Mac," she says. "It's not based on me. None of it. Just because it's, like, a book about an unhappy family. Does not mean it's based on me."

He doesn't say anything at first.

"Okay, well," he offers eventually, "I would not say that you have ever exactly run your mouth about your family enough for me to assume that anything was autobiographical, but I can tell that you don't want to talk about this. I really was just asking. What the fuck do I know about writing, Clare. Sorry."

"Weren't we talking about you? Drinking on school grounds and flirting with the female teachers? How's all that going? Still on the apps?"

He sighs heavily.

"Okay, okay. Jesus, um. I guess so, yeah. Sort of? You would be completely floored by how much, just, *time* it sucks up. Like, if I message some woman on Sunday. It's probably not going anywhere before Wednesday at least. We'll move off the app and start texting once she feels reassured I won't send a dick pic or call her a cunt when she stops responding."

Clare's shoulders clench.

"Sorry," he says. "But you wouldn't believe what women deal with on there. Make sure you treat Jamie well, because trust me, you don't want to be out here."

She holds herself very still, but he doesn't even look at her.

"Anyway, eventually she's ready to meet. I'm sitting at school thinking I need a clean shirt, maybe even a shower, if I'm trying not to frighten this poor woman away. So I debate whether I should sit in traffic all the way home, then fight my way down to some brewery in the Arts District, plus parking? If I take an Uber, she might think I'm planning to get straight-up wasted, and I don't really need to look like a fuckup right from jump. And as we saw this morning, I am far too old to be showing up hungover at work at eight a.m. on a Thursday. So, after all that, I sit down and try to be funny for a stranger for at least two hours."

"Talking to strangers used to be so much more exciting," she says.

"There was so much potential. You were always worried you'd screw up something that could be so good. And now it's just like . . . *Leave me alone.*"

Mac laughs.

"Well," he says, "that approach doesn't get a lot of traction on the apps. But like, you're not wrong. There's a reason we all keep taking this same trip together year after year, right? We're all ready to commit homicide after the first forty-eight hours, yeah, but at least we don't need to, like. Get to know each other."

She nods.

"Anyway. So, I'll sit there at the brewery, or even worse it's some bar named, like, Thistle and Sprite, and I try to communicate to the waiter, nicely, that there is absolutely no point in trying to upsell me. And I try to remember what it was like to decide if you felt chemistry with someone. Before we put this whole system in place. Like, when I was twenty years old, I didn't decide shit, right? Either I got drunk enough to push her into a corner and kiss her and wait for her to tell me where to sleep, or she lost interest before I made my way over there. And that method has its problems, to be sure. But at least it was organic. I mean, I think it was?"

"Debatable," she says. "But I know what you're saying."

"And now I send these women these pithy little messages based on some misleading profile I wrote two years ago trying to make myself sound like a cross between James Baldwin and Ryan Gosling and, I don't know—Louis C.K., I guess? RIP? Renzo wrote most of it for me, actually. I think. And by the time she sits down across from me at a bar high-top, we've both had our teeth on edge for a week."

"Wow," Clare says when he pauses for air. "Are you really this miserable?"

"Oh, Clare Clare," he says without any bite. "You don't have to worry about this. Don't get me wrong, it's terrifying to imagine the girl who would have wanted me when I was nineteen. I mean, you remember. It was bleak. But this just gets, after a while. I don't know."

She holds his gaze, even though she can tell it's making him uncomfortable.

"You're lonely," she says, not a question. "It just gets lonely, doesn't it."
He smiles without teeth.

"I mean," she says, "I get it."

"No you don't," he says. "I just, you know. I want to get married. This dating thing, I'm over it."

"It's probably good, though. Flexing the muscle."

"The dating muscle?"

"I guess so."

"Oh, to be sure. I am *very* good at the actual mechanics of a first date. They don't know what hit them, these women. Smoothest evening you can imagine. I know not to order the truffle fries if I think I'll want to go in for a kiss later. I know to avoid sitting at the bar if possible, because I look gangly trying to fold up these daddy-longlegs-ass limbs of mine. I know to make at least two genuine offers to pay, but then to give in and split it if she insists. I've got all the details down cold, don't worry. It's a flawless choreography at this point, for sure."

"See? Good at first dates, a gentleman at the restaurant. Girls like that."

"But they're not girls anymore. It's never just a first date. That's why it's so exhausting. You pretend to be the same person you were when going on a first date meant absolutely nothing, but you're both just like, 'Don't waste my fucking time. Don't leave me out here running a fifty-yard dash and then realizing you straight-up turned around and walked off the track.'"

"At least you still get to *have* first dates," she says without thinking. She hears it, exhales a hiss. Nuzzles back into his arm and tries to pretend she didn't say it.

"I didn't mean, like, that I 'go in' for the kiss, by the way. I mean, I wait until I'm getting some pretty clear signals. That just sounded kind of off, I think, when I said it."

She pats his arm.

"The other thing," he says slowly. "The thing is that these apps already suck for me. It's just baked in. For Black guys. I mean, Black women on there *really* get screwed over, it's even worse. But for me, still, it's not great."

Neither one of them changes position, but they both harden their shoulders.

"Really?"

"Yeah, really."

"But, how do you——" she begins, then immediately falters. "It's not like you know why she swipes left, right? And everyone would just lie anyway, so like. You can't really know the actual reason, right? I mean, that sucks. That sounds awful."

He doesn't say a word.

"I'm sorry," she says immediately. "I didn't mean for that to sound, like——"

"Oh, come on," he says. "Sure you did."

"No, I really was just——"

"It's been studied, Clare. I'm not making it up. I'm not the one who's known for crafting sweeping analysis based on all my little personal grievances."

Already the best possible way to apologize, to convince him that this was idiocy and that she regrets it, has slipped through her fingers.

"I'm sorry," she says again. "Sorry. Is there anything else I can say?"

"I don't know," he says. "What do you think?"

And then Ryden and Kyle are walking over, with Liam close behind.

"Reports of my death have been greatly exaggerated!" Kyle says. "What are we talking about over here?"

"Work," Mac says.

"Oh, right. Dude, Renzo told me!" Liam claps Mac once on the back.

"What?" Clare asks.

"I have a job offer," Mac says. "Principal position. At a charter school in Oakland."

"Wow," she says. "Wow. Congratulations! You didn't tell me that."

"Principal McMillan," Kyle muses, writing the name in the air with his index finger. "Very, very hard to accept."

"You won't miss being in the classroom?"

"Dude, you're a teacher?" Ryden asks. "What age?"

"Fifth grade. But this would actually be a high school," Mac says. "And then, you know. Charter network. It would just . . . be a totally different kind of job."

"What's wrong with a charter network?" Kyle holds his beer bottle against the gunwale and bops it with the heel of his hand, popping off the cap. Ryden puts his hands in the air, a *Come on, man!* gesture, but he doesn't tell him, or even ask him, not to do it again.

"There's nothing wrong with a charter network," Mac says.

"Didn't you used to rail against charter schools?" Liam asks.

"Yeah, but then I got kind of sick of everyone telling poor women in Los Angeles where to send their kids," Mac says. "Telling them they have to go to the shitty, failing school on their block while the rest of us send our kids wherever we want, maybe I'm over that."

"Oh." Liam rears back. "I'm really sorry, I know absolutely nothing about this, I didn't mean—"

"It's okay," Clare says. "He's not mad at you."

Ryden looks back and forth between the four of them.

"Wait, what's wrong with charter schools?" Kyle asks again.

"Your school is not shitty, or failing," Clare says quietly. "You have done incredible work at that school."

"What do your other teacher friends say?" Kyle asks. "I mean, they're the ones you always figure this stuff out with, anyway. You never ask us about anything actually important. Which, reasonable."

"Oh God," Clare says, trying to keep her voice light. "Not his *real* friends. Not the actual adult acquaintances he keeps away from us like we're contagious! Are we even sure they really exist?"

Mac leans forward and runs his palms across the back of his neck, scratches his scalp.

"It is a fantastic job," he says, ignoring her. "More money, more freedom, a new city."

"You don't need the money, man," Liam begins, but Mac cuts him off.

"Maybe I want it, Liam. Maybe I'd like to make a little more money. For myself. Rather than let my father buy me a house."

They all get very quiet, then.

"So it's settled," Kyle says. "You guys have finally seen the light, you're listening to me. We're going to buy one of those amazing decrepit Victorians down near USC and live there, together, for the rest of our lives. No girls allowed! Except this one."

He pins Clare in a headlock.

"Jesus," she says. "I can't fucking breathe, you're going to suffocate me just to commit to the bit."

But he's already wrapped her in a bear hug, she's laughing. She could kiss him, for lightening the air they're all breathing. Mac is laughing too, his arm slung around Liam's shoulders. He's pulled it back, whatever he was ready to say to her, to the rest of them. Liam has stolen her seat.

Ryden stands with his legs planted wide on the deck, his arms crossed. He's still watching the four of them bounce off one another.

"This is cool. You can tell just by listening to you guys that you go way back."

"Yeah," Clare gasps. "For my sins."

Kyle finally lets go.

"Let's see," he says. "Let us see here. Stories, stories. What have we got for him, Clare Clare? Should we tell him about that time you blew a senior in my mother's upstairs guest bathroom while we all listened from the other side of the door, or shall we—"

"—tell him about the time *you* snuck your car off campus midday to go fuck your new girlfriend, got so stoned you couldn't get it up, and then got a flat tire on your way back into the campus parking lot and were suspended for a week," Liam interrupts. "Maybe we tell your stories too, Ky?"

But she was already launching herself at Kyle as soon as he opened his mouth, her hands scrabbling at his face.

Andrew Osterman, that was the guy's name. Kyle's wrong, though, he's conflating it with something else. It was some stranger's kickback, deep in the West Valley, the weekend of Homecoming. Hours of endlessly prolonging nonconversations as an excuse to haunt the kitchen, the central hub of activity. But in the end it was so simple: Renzo shoved her, hard, and she spilled a drink on Andy, who then led her to a folding table where some football players taught her how to play beer pong, something she'd never even heard of before. (But no, she remembers now, that's not what they called it in high school. They called it Beirut, and only later, in a humid basement in Hanover, would she refer to it that way and realize what she was saying when the boy next to her admonished her.)

The beer made her feel bilious, and she tugged on Andy's shirt and whispered in his ear, "What does it take to get a girl a vodka cranberry around here?" and he looked down at her and blinked as though she'd replaced herself with someone else, someone more appealing. It wasn't even a joke, it was just some dumb thing she said. But he made some vague comment about the backyard, led her down a hallway with ugly brown carpeting. It all happened in a series of quick steps, like keys fitting into a succession of locks. His hand pressed into her lower back, she stumbled into the bathroom, his fingers were at the waistband of her skirt and there was squirming, everything clumsy maneuvering, awful. *This cannot possibly be right*, she remembers thinking, and then eventually she tried not to think, tried to just wait it out. His hand pressed down on the top of her head, and very soon (that part, at least, was a blessing) she was gagging, pretending she wasn't. But already he was buttoning his jeans, and when she tried to hook her fingers through his belt loops and reach up to kiss him, he bobbed his head back, away from her.

"Whoa, okay," he said. "Come on." And then he was opening the door and letting light in, moving away from her, and Renzo and Kyle were on the floor in the hallway, their backs against the wall and their legs to their chests, laughing at her, clapping. Telling her they'd underestimated her, that she was right, she deserved to be taken seriously. All night Renzo told her that her cheeks were flushed, that she was bright red, even an hour later when it couldn't possibly be true.

What a fucking thing to bring up, she thinks now. But then, Kyle doesn't know anything about it. He didn't even remember it right. He thinks it's a story like any other, as funny as the time he lost a bet with Mac and jumped off his bedroom balcony and into the pool and grazed his chin on the edge of the hot tub. A madcap story, like the time Renzo stole the tiki torch from Kyle's mother's backyard and ran around the party waving it until some cooler head wrested it away.

She and Kyle have tackled one another to the deck, and she digs her elbow into his solar plexus.

"Okay, okay!" He puts up his hands, gasping.

"We've all got stories," Liam tells Ryden.

"I can see that," Ryden says, his eyes on her. Suddenly, though, she cannot stand to look at him. She's afraid to look at Liam.

"You people *should* live in a house together," she says. "No woman in her right goddamn mind is ever going to voluntarily shack up with any one of you."

"Anyway," Mac says.

Ryden laughs and moves away from them, shaking his head.

She still feels feathery motions in her stomach, burns on her knees. She is baffled by how angry it made her, Kyle telling that story. This is the whole basis of these friendships, she tells herself. Jessie is the girl who will always react, and you are the girl who will not. She is the one they can upset, and you are the girl they cannot. You never blush. You never stew. How is it possible this can still get so far under your skin?

The boat is grinding itself to an equilibrium, leaving them to float uncertainly. They have, she sees, turned into a small, quiet cove. Renzo appears, peeling his shirt up over his biceps, the tendons in his arms flinching. He whips the shirt in a loop above his head.

"Come on!" he exhorts. "Clare, jump with me."

Mac has turned away. He's taking off his watch, unbuttoning his shirt.

"I really am sorry," she says softly. "About before."

"You're sorry that you didn't just wait to say it behind my back?"

They stare at each other.

"It's fine," he says, unconvincing. She can see that he's lost interest in allowing the upkeep of her trembling lower lip to consume the rest of his afternoon. "I'm just fucking with you. Plus, you should have seen your face, rolling around on the ground with Kyle while he told some awful story about the first time you saw a penis. Very hard to stay mad at you after that."

"Great," she says.

"Let's just swim?"

Someone has hooked up the Bluetooth, and Lou Reed is blasting. "Suuuunday morning," he croons, which means it was Renzo's choice. He would destroy anyone else who was this unsubtle.

Mac runs past her and, in one leap, cannonballs off the side of the boat.

"Okay, a few ground rules," Ryden begins. Everyone ignores him.

They all know what to do now, she thinks. No more talking, no debates for the rest of the afternoon. This is the montage from the midway point in the heartfelt film about their reunion. This is when they splash, and swim, and sing together at the top of their lungs. They all know their moves.

Renzo is back, blocking out her sun. She's undressing too slowly. He cannot wait for the merriment to begin.

10

"Are we ready?" Renzo asks.

They're standing on the gunwale, their toes curled lightly around the edge. Jessie is behind them with the phone, waiting to film.

"Make sure it's in slow motion," Renzo barks. "I mean, you get it. You know these angles. You know what I want."

"Yes, Ren," Jessie says, and the exhaustion doesn't sound performative. "I know your angles quite well."

"Do it for the 'Gram, baby," Kyle says with a snort.

"Oh, shut up, you. You sound like a retiree. God forbid we make any lasting goddamn memories today. This trip? Never. This trip must be forgotten immediately."

"You!" Kyle yelps, rising to his feet in outrage. "You could give two shits about making memories! This photo is for your adoring hordes of InstaGays!"

"I'm with him," Jessie says. "I don't think you're being a photography tyrant because you want to preserve anything for the rest of us. Our opinions don't matter. Although, Kyle? I'm not sure that you're allowed to refer to his Instagram fans . . . that way."

"He's the prime offender! I am *quoting* him."

"Yes, but, again . . ." Mac calls up from the water. Jessie stamps her foot and mimes hurling Renzo's phone into the ocean.

"Agreed," Clare says.

"You two had better fucking jump, like, now," Mac yells. "Otherwise you're getting shoved in, and Renzo will lose his perfect shot."

"Oh, and what are you going to do to me from down there, exactly?" Renzo retorts, fleeing immediately when Mac feints at swimming to the ladder. "No! Do *not* touch me, you. I have the knees of a much older man."

He reaches out one hand without looking, and Clare takes it. They jump.

The water is so clear. So unbearably just as you imagined it could be. This entire island, she thinks, is such a studio backdrop version of its own cultural myth. The postcards, if anything, flatten it out and cheapen it. Reduce it to the most garish streaks of its own colors, like the product of an old desktop printer that's on the fritz.

Renzo sighs in appreciation. He flips onto his back. Behind them, she hears more splashing. She turns to see Kyle, Mac, and Liam swimming over.

Her swimsuit floats up into the water, the straps peeling away from her shoulders like string cheese. Renzo laughs at her.

"Shut up! I think it unhooked itself when we hit the water."

"Oh, sure. The suit 'unhooked' itself! The perfect excuse. Boys, I've already proposed this to her, but maybe you three give it a shot? I told her on the phone the day before we left—we should be skinny-dipping! We're perilously close to decrepitude, no? It's all sands through the hourglass, and so forth. Let's be an Italian sex comedy. *L'Avventura*, right? Or, well. Is that a comedy?"

He's practically shouting.

"We can all sketch her breasts from memory, can we not? Am I wrong? Who says that as we age, we must automatically grow prudish and ashamed? Not I, let me tell you. Take off your top, young lady! Let's get weird, let us strip down and be merry, for tomorrow—when the real missile surely arrives—we die!"

"Too soon," Kyle grumbles.

Renzo did, indeed, call her the day before they all flew out here. She stood in her childhood bedroom, turning in circles as he told her that Liam had agreed to come along on the trip. She was staring at her scuffed desk, her broken bookshelves, the plastic tub full of yearbooks and ephemera that her mother had dragged in from the garage and labeled with a Post-It that said WINNOW, OR ELSE! She stayed on the phone for ten minutes after Renzo mentioned Liam's name, trying not to project fear or guilt or anything else. Her skin became warm to the touch. The fear was like something creating an odor in the room, she was secreting it like sweat or blood, she convinced herself that Renzo would pause his chatter to ask, "Can you smell that?"

Now she watches him shout and grin and dive dramatically beneath the water's surface, kicking his feet in tandem like a mermaid. This was always her favorite selfish and giddy high, as a teenager. Keeping secrets, but always with Renzo. Never from him.

Kyle dives beneath Clare and comes up behind her knees, trying to flip her over his shoulder, which of course exposes her breasts to the group. Liam abruptly swims away.

"Your top's gone already?" Jessie has arrived, completing an elegant crawl that followed her noiseless dive from the boat. "That took . . . actually, that took a few days longer than I would have guessed."

"All right," Clare says. "So good to be here on this trip with all of you, bathed in the glow of our twenty years of friendship."

"Oh, enough," Jessie says. She swims over to grab at the swimsuit, clasping it shut between Clare's shoulder blades. She kisses Clare's left shoulder and pats her arm, treading water so they can stay close to one another just for that moment.

"Get a room," Renzo snaps.

"Yes, we know you'd love it," Jessie says. "It's not like you didn't try that, more than once."

But he's done it with so little effort, snapped the gossamer cord that was there, between them, just briefly. Clare turns in the water to mouth the words *Thank you*. But Jessie is squinting into the sun, looking away.

"Okay," Clare says to no one. She swims her timeworn, serviceable breaststroke, keeps her eyes closed until her toes strike sand, and then she sinks one more time, pushes her hair back from her face, adjusts her suit. She surfaces and walks up the beach to where Liam is stretched out on a rock in the sun. She lies down on the slab of rock just beside him.

Something she did not expect: to feel so proprietary. The desire to get closer and closer until the only option is to unhinge her jaw and swallow him whole. It makes sense, to feel this way sometimes about her husband. Right? There is some truth to it, however silly it sounds. In some real sense, Jamie belongs to her. They belong to one another. It makes sense to feel consuming pride and terror when she looks across a table at him.

It makes absolutely no sense to feel it right now, on a beach in Hawai'i, staring at a boy she has barely seen since high school.

She reaches out one fingertip, traces his hairline just to the temple, lingers in the seashell coil of his ear. He lets his chin nod vaguely in the air, as if to shake her off. Or else turn his head toward her, let her hand palm his cheek, allow her to bring their faces closer. She watches him lift his hips, adjust his posture against the rock.

"You left your admirer behind?"

It takes her a minute to understand that they're talking about Ryden.

"Oh, come on."

She withdraws her hand.

"You're right," she says, lowering her voice even though everyone else is still in the water. "Because I do this all the time, Liam."

"Okay," he says. "Because I'd have any way of knowing that."

She feels rage pinballing around inside her chest, a fury that singes everything it touches.

"What is it you want to hear? That I'm doing this with you when I've never even come close to doing it before? So that you can feel superior and shake your head and feel sorry for me?"

He shakes his head.

"I do not feel sorry for you, Clare."

"Yeah, fine. I'm awful. Except last night. I'm admirable enough when you're, at night."

Humiliatingly she fumbles, as if it's not the acts themselves but rather putting them into words, exposing them to the pitiless sun, that's revealing.

"When what, Clare? You're good enough when, exactly?"

Liam laughs, amused and aware of how angry it makes her. She feels suddenly so tired, the backs of her knees and inside creases of her elbows feel itchy and raw.

"When you're choking me with one hand and coming across my tits," she says in a rush, before she can change her mind.

She's already sitting up, looking away from him. She watches the water ferociously, her friends out there splashing like children. She hears him shift again and then he's sitting upright, too. She wraps her arms around her shins, fights the urge to dig her fingernails into the soft, crawling skin back there, the skin hidden from the sun. The air between their naked torsos seems so heavy, so unbearably full, that it seems impossible they won't just lie down again, submit to it.

He laughs again and she sees that this is all he wanted, for her to feel like shit. That he just wanted her to be thrown off, too.

"Everything I've imagined, and I really never thought you'd be such a prude."

"Fuck you."

"Sure," he says. "Fine by me. That was my end goal, actually. Is now good?"

She can feel herself twitching, her skin still feels miserable to sit in. She wants to take off the bathing suit again. It feels like having a fever. What is the point of talking about this?

"First of all," he says. "No one said you were awful. I am not feeling, I don't know. Tortured, about this. So don't put words in my mouth. And second of all, you get that this is happening to me, too, right? You've been acting like the only part that feels real is the part happening to you."

She doesn't know what to say. Of course the part that's happening to her is what feels real; of course she can't really tell what his end feels like. Isn't that sort of, unbearably, the definition of having a self? That your own emotions feel more real than those of anyone else? Of course it's selfish, of course it's cruel. *You can't tell yourself how to feel*, she repeats to herself again, like an incantation.

"I'm sorry," she says.

"No, stop it," he says, his lip curling with distaste. "I don't need you to *apologize*."

"Okay, well, sorry."

He picks up her hand and holds it loosely in the air between them. For a moment, she can feel his breath, its heat, at her neck, on her skin. If her hair weren't wet, his breath would be brushing it into motion, like soft weather.

She thinks again of Jamie, of the proprietary feeling she can still summon occasionally, when he's been gone, when they're reunited after time apart. But it doesn't feel like this. It can't, or at least she assumes it can't. Sometimes she'll see a woman respond to him, his sandy hair, his square jaw and his lingering athlete's limp, and she can't even force her stomach to turn over once. She'll watch the woman and think, *Go ahead, be my guest. He deserves the attention.* Because anyone can be cavalier about a loss that won't happen. If she ever actually thought she might lose Jamie, perhaps she'd be able to feel this again and realize how foolish she's been. But it would be out of fear. She'd think back on this week, this exact moment, on the beach, and she'd ask herself how she could have been so blissfully unconcerned. You can't tell yourself how to feel.

"Let's go swim some more," Liam says.

"Why?"

"Because that way I can take your suit off without anyone seeing. I want to feel you up," he says. "So sue me."

He clambers off the rock, running headlong down the sand, and meets Renzo where the water is still just shallow enough for them to stand. She watches five heads bobbing happily in the sparkling afternoon, spread out across the cove. They all look perfect. She doesn't want to run toward them, doesn't want to disrupt that glassy surface.

Boston

She realized, too late, that she'd come out here because she wanted a cigarette. But of course she didn't have one. She was wearing a fucking wedding dress, after all. She didn't even know where her cellphone was. Probably in Caro's purse? But that would be because of foresight on Caro's part, not because of anything Clare had kept in mind. Caro was, much as she had been throughout the four years they lived together at Dartmouth, the engine driving this entire milestone event of Clare's life. She had arranged the hotel suite, booked hair appointments for the two of them and for Clare's mother, designated herself the point person for any day-of inquiries from the venue.

"Don't people usually pay for this level of service?" Clare had asked a few weeks ago. "Or at least split it between bridesmaids?"

But Caro had taken advantage of the fact that it was a phone call to steamroll directly over the question. And there *were* no other bridesmaids. And tonight, she had clocked Clare's every movement, including her departure from the table a few minutes ago. She'd kept an eye on Clare's wine intake and gently urged her to eat from the plate of food Jamie brought over just before his mother stood for her speech.

"Not on an empty stomach," he'd breathed into her ear.

But in the end his mother had been fine. She was disjointed but not yet slurring. She'd talked about what a good boy he was and had said essentially nothing about Clare, true. But unlike Clare's father's speech, there had been no barbed comments about what this waterfront winery wedding must have cost.

When both speeches were done, Jamie slid his arm around the back of Clare's chair and drew them closer together.

"Made it," he'd whispered. And she'd reached out to hold his face in both her hands and kiss him. His former teammates, several of whom were at their table, cheered, mistaking it for performance, for display.

The patio was, technically, a different venue than the barrel room, which was the tiniest and most "affordable" part of the winery in which you could hold a wedding. It seemed like there had been something earlier in the afternoon out here, there were high appetizer tables scattered around at intervals, but the event had clearly been over for hours. Every now and then a server raced through carrying tubs of used dishes or crates of wineglasses, but no one seemed to mind that Clare was standing just where the tent lighting bled back into darkness. Or, if they minded, the fact that she was wearing a wedding dress made them think better of asking a question, of assuming that she was unintentionally lost.

The building's side door opened, light spilling out onto the ornamental cobblestones.

"Well, shit," she heard. She felt a sudden flood of relief. It was Mac and Renzo.

"We've been chased all over the goddamn place," Renzo said. "How rare can it actually be, that two wedding guests want to enjoy a quiet cigarette?"

"Oh god," she said. "Please, yes. Do you have some?"

"Not this again," Mac said cheerfully. "Not this charade that you're a hardened addict like Renzo over here."

"I'm not an addict," Renzo said through clenched jaw, lighting two cigarettes and passing one to Clare. "I'm an aficionado. And come on, you come to her on the day of her wedding and deny her this little bit of stress relief?"

Mac was right, though. It was true that Clare had only ever really smoked at parties, usually at Renzo's goading. In college it was just an excuse to stay out on the porch talking to some boy, to stand closer in the cold. And then she met Jamie, and she no longer needed excuses.

Renzo blew a smoke ring in her direction.

"How are we holding up out here? Happiest day of your life, hands down?"

"It's been kind of shockingly smooth, right? People seem like they're having fun?"

"Oh, for sure." Mac nodded.

"Trick question," Clare said. "You two haven't spoken to anyone but each other."

"False," Renzo said, holding up one finger in the air. "I spent a lovely half hour talking to two gentlemen from the Dartmouth hockey team."

"I can vouch for that," Mac said. "It was bleak. You should have heard him vibing with these guys about his 'job.' He's suddenly *building out his toolkit*. He's discussing *cadence* and *deliverables*."

"It's all top-down." Renzo exhaled. "Impact-focused. We're driving impact, is the important thing to remember."

Mac turned to her, jutting his chin out and bugging his eyes.

"You see? I had plans to keep it light this evening, but I've switched to Scotch. Excellent selection in there, by the way."

"One of the only places we refused to cut corners," she said. "So, to be clear, you spoke to our friends just long enough to gather material to mock them?"

"Excuse me, but I was mocking him," Mac said. Renzo held his cigarette in his mouth long enough to flip them both off at once. "But come on, babe. We're here for you."

"And Jamie," Renzo said, and there was a brief silence. Clare slipped out of her shoes, placed them on one of the abandoned cocktail tables.

"Kyle texted, by the way," he continued. "Sent his love. He wouldn't have come, you know. You could have invited him. Just the gesture."

"It wasn't about that," she said. "I realize that you have this story you've written in your own mind, but I don't even think of that, whatever. That part of it. I just—I can't remember the last time I talked to him, Ren. We're both kind of your friend, now. It's not hostile, I just—You see how few people we invited. It's tiny."

"Let's not start this, you two," Mac said gently.

"Oh, she's already smoothed it over," Renzo said. "She's admitted that I'm the only one any of you like. It's all I wanted to hear."

"And Jessie?" Clare said. "Did she text?"

They all laughed, and it passed. Mac took off his jacket and put it over her shoulders. Renzo wrapped her in a bear hug.

"I should go back in," she said, letting her cigarette butt fall to the ground and gesturing for Renzo to stamp it out. She slid her fingers into the straps of her heels, didn't put them back on. When she went back in, Caro would give her speech, and then it would be time for dancing, anyway.

"I'm happy for you," Mac said. "He's a good guy. And you two, you're kind of in your own world all night. In a good way. Weddings are always such a bummer, the couple's always performing for everyone else. But I've been watching you both, and it's like no one else can touch you."

"Yes," Renzo said. "You're very us against the world, the two of you."

"Okay," Mac said. "I meant mine to sound actually nice."

"I know," Clare said. "Thank you."

They stood for another minute, reluctant to move, lost without the cigarettes to ground them and keep their hands busy.

"Do you feel different?" Renzo asked.

"No," she said. "Not at all. Happy?"

"If you are," he said. "I was just wondering. You know this is quite foreign to me, this level of maturity."

She slid her arm through his, and they turned back toward the main building.

"Thank you for coming," she said. "Both of you."

"Thank you for inviting us," Renzo said. "The first of the gang to bite the dust."

"Those," Mac said, "are two different songs."

"Well, I was never quite the little eighties enthusiast that you were."

"Excuse me?" Mac said. "Are you thinking of Kyle? I know you're not implying that I listened to white boys from the 1980s more often than you did?"

"Only one of those songs is from the eighties," Clare said.

"You've both utterly ruined the moment," Renzo said. "I was being sincere."

"Footage not found," Mac said. "But, Clare Clare, I promise. We'll go make friends. Honestly, I won't speak a word to Renzo for the rest of the night. It'll be a refreshing change of pace."

"You guys could talk to Caro," Clare said. "She misses you both."

"I already told her she owes me a dance," Renzo agreed. "And I'll go flirt with some hockey player's mother. Push myself beyond my comfort zone, and all that."

He held the door for her and then Mac closed it carefully behind them. They walked back down the warmly lit hallway and pushed open the door that led to Jamie and Caro and a few dozen other people who had only known Clare as someone who lived on the East Coast, as someone who was Jamie's girlfriend. She looked for her husband and found him right where she'd left him. He held up her wineglass, which he'd refilled. He saw who she was with and smiled at her, as if he could have guessed. She shrugged, and he shrugged back. She left the boys behind, still holding her shoes in one hand, and walked back over to her husband.

11

Back at the house, everyone needs a break. Perhaps a nap before dinner. Their hangovers were muffled by the midday sunshine and the reasonable doses of wine and beer, but foreheads are still tender, lower guts are still roiling. Clare's stomach feels like the colorless, mealy innards of an unripe tomato.

It seemed, briefly, that their swim had lulled them all into laziness, that they'd spend the ride back feeling their bodies reach a salty equilibrium with their surroundings. But Kyle spent twenty minutes crumpled against the boat's hull, spewing bile into the water and then lying there like damp laundry, and when Ryden suggested tacking closer to shore for a smoother ride even if it meant abandoning the hope of fish, Renzo threw a fit.

"You do realize that we're the ones paying today," he said at one point, before Liam belatedly snapped to attention and began to whisper soothingly into his ear. "This isn't a Harmon family trip. We're the ones paying you."

Ultimately, though, he got his way. There is a gorgeous fish, snagged only minutes before they arrived back at the dock.

Now, everyone just wants to be alone for an hour. That most peaceful, undemanding of places: a quiet, dozing house on an afternoon in the middle of a vacation. They can all read it in one another, the desire for a darkened bedroom or a soundproofed bathroom or, just for a little while, no other person attempting to talk to you.

All of them can read this in one another, that is, except Renzo, who has paid attention to no one else since he caught the fish. The last leg of the boat trip was spent photographing him dozens of times from several different angles, so that he might later select the shot that best flattered both the girth of the fish and the cut of his abs. He then talked about it incessantly, the enormous blue trevally. How scrumptious it would be when served as ceviche. Only one photo was deemed worthy: Renzo with his leg bent and his foot resting on the gunwale, one hand braced against his knee and the other holding the fish triumphantly above his head. It had been posted to the grid by the time they docked.

Now the fish needs to be descaled, deboned, and he has no idea what to do. Kyle, who still looks shiny and vulnerable, his skin like peeled garlic, says it's complicated. That they should ride up to the club and ask someone from the restaurant kitchen to do it.

Inside, Liam slices into a grapefruit. Clare stands at the kitchen island and watches him separate one sparkling piece, offer it to her. She pops it into her mouth, wipes its juice from her chin with the back of her hand.

"They're still bickering out there. He's got the fish all spread out."

Liam nods.

"I'm going to make one last attempt to keep them from killing one another, and then I'm going to shower," she announces. Jessie must be around here somewhere. Mac appears, raises his eyebrows. But she hasn't said anything significant, there was nothing to overhear. She hasn't said anything at all.

"Shower?" Mac echoes. "Can I come?"

"Always," she replies. He grins, sticks out his tongue, and disappears into his room.

Liam has turned back to the open refrigerator. His shoulder blades seemingly have nothing to say to her.

"Or, I might take a nap," she continues to inform him. She goes back outside, feeling the afternoon warmth in the terra-cotta tiles against her bare feet.

Renzo is squatting on his heels, watching some YouTube video, purportedly an explainer. Two Australian men sit on a beach, slurring instructions at a camera operated by an equally clueless, blasted friend.

"Okay, but how can you possibly believe that this is really our best bet," Kyle entreats him. "Just, logically. How can this be the solution?"

The fish and its innards are glittering in the sun. It has already been dispersed into small chunks, although the bones and the skin also seem to be still entirely wedded to the actual meat. The fish looks like it suddenly, mourning its own capture, began to dissociate from itself.

"Renzo," Kyle says again, stern this time. Clare can see that he's already tried various degrees of condescension or cajolery.

"Ren, come on," she says.

"Oh, you! You can piss right off. You didn't have my back with that guy at all. He just assumed that the Harmons were paying. That we're all just little freeloaders. I couldn't possibly have the deep pockets, so what I think doesn't matter at all."

"I don't think that was it," Clare says gently. "I think he thought you were being obnoxious. I don't think it's more complicated than that."

"You never think it's more complicated," Renzo says. Kyle has gotten very quiet.

"Well, I'm sure I'm always wrong," Clare says. "I'm sure Ryden meant to insult you deeply. In the meantime, the whole idea with the fish, I think, is that we need to be careful. We can't eat the dangerous part. And frankly, this is looking like you're going to end up wasting anything that's actually edible."

"He's not doing such a terrible job, actually," Kyle says. This seems a dubious claim. "Or, I mean. I think he started off pretty well?"

"I'll accept yah praise," Renzo growls, adopting the accent of his new YouTube friends.

Kyle looks at her imploringly. She crosses to him and touches her hand to his forehead, his clammy cheeks.

"Leave this," she tells him. "It's his little passion project, and he's going to be the only one poisoned. Given that this looks like an actual crime scene, no one else is going to eat it. Go lie down, all right? You still look awful."

"You will all be sure to devouhr this 'ere mackerel," Renzo mutters darkly.

Kyle looks at her with dismay, his palms to the sky in supplication.

"I know," she says. "I get it. But he's not going to do any lasting damage. It's not like we're letting him drive the golf cart or rinse the stemware. You can force him to hose everything down after. Just let him stay out here, playing around in his *sandbox*—"

Renzo pauses his surgical pursuits to set down his knife and, without glancing up, flip her a double bird.

"Until he loses interest," she finishes. "Until he decides to come inside, spend time with his friends, and maybe, I don't know, apologize to his host, whose spectacular vomit session he basically ignored."

At this, Renzo stands, wiping his hands across his swim trunks and leaving fish entrails in their wake, viscous smears against the bright floral print of the swimsuit.

"Baby boy," he says to Kyle, reaching out his arms stiffly. Kyle darts back and Renzo begins to pursue him, scampering off down the driveway. "Let me make it up to you, my darling! Hug it out! You'll get used to the smell, I promise!"

She goes inside. Liam is no longer in the kitchen. In her bedroom, she lies down and curls in on herself. She pretends she isn't waiting. She does not pick up a magazine, or a book, or her phone, because that would be an admission, this wouldn't then resemble anything like a nap. She has forgotten that this is torture. She has forgotten how heady it can be to torture yourself this way, so willingly.

Finally, she gives up. She goes into the bathroom and steps out of her bathing suit.

It's only a few minutes later that she hears tapping at the door. It's soft, barely perceptible above the tumbling water from the lavish shower head above her. She has been rubbing shampoo into her scalp, the suds flowing down her neck and shoulders and frothing around her feet. She waits, motionless, her whole body drawing itself into the unbearable simmer at its core.

He grabs her hips first, backing her up until she's pressed against the wall. She shivers, forced beyond the corona of hot water, and he laughs, reaching up to adjust the shower so that it envelops them again like rain, like steam.

He bites her collarbone, her neck, kisses her breasts, and then he lowers himself to his knees. She gasps without thinking and he reaches up with one flailing hand, cups at her chin, trying to cover her mouth. At first she doesn't think this is going to work, really. He's too aggressive, too harsh. You forget how simply two people can misunderstand the most basic mechanics, when the bodies involved are still so unfamiliar, so new. But then, suddenly, she's wrong, it's working. She was wrong to worry, wrong to doubt him. It's working really, really well. She knocks her head gently against the shower tile three times. She feels everything go liquid, like she's going to disappear down the drain with all the other water.

He stands up and spins her around, presses himself against her back, one arm tight like a vise against her breasts. She reaches up and puts her palms flat against the wall. He fucks her this way and she forgets again and he clamps a hand across her mouth. His own groan buries itself in her wet hair. When she bites into the fleshy side of his palm and then they step away from each other, she is amazed that she hasn't drawn blood.

They both stand there facing the wall, the small open window high above them. The birds are loud again, the floral scents stickier and harder to ignore, everything popping at the corners of her vision like she's held her breath for too long. Everything rushes back into this room, this enormous shower, the water slapping without cease at the tiles beneath their feet.

He pulls her back into his chest. He kisses the nape of her neck, right there beneath the streaming water. It's almost ordinary. It's almost something that's already habit.

12

That evening, she makes herself a deal.

She's standing before the mirror in Kyle's mother's bathroom. It's a weird, sideways intimacy, using another woman's things in a house only sporadically lived in. A closet opens off this room, full of sheath dresses and scarves that smell like a spa, like dinner outdoors, like hibiscus and mangoes and a little bit of salt, of sweat. There is a small shelf in the closet holding dozens of DVDs, presumably for when the grandchildren visit, except it's an odd assortment of titles drawn from an era long before those children were born: *The Bodyguard; Broadcast News; The Sandlot; Honey, I Shrunk the Kids; The Land Before Time; Look Who's Talking.*

This is a house, after all, that was built to host grandchildren. And yet Kyle never mentions them. Other than a few initial jokes about who should most appropriately sleep in the kiddie beds, it's barely remembered that they exist.

The deal she makes with herself is that she will stay sober tonight. She will not be tempted to misbehave. She gets ready for dinner, and she makes herself this deal.

She sheepishly explores the bathroom drawers, searching for tweezers. They're strewn with items either deemed inessential for Los Angeles or else so essential that their doubles live here: undereye cream that retails at more than two hundred dollars per half ounce, Clinique lipstick looking like it dried to chalk during the Clinton administration, a single Bakelite bracelet. A photograph, its colors smeared where water droplets have left it stuck to the drawer's liner, of Kyle's parents together at what appears to be a poolside barbecue in the seventies. Her hair is teased into stiff feathered waves despite the heat; he's wearing aviators. They look almost breakably young. Clare touches the photograph, closes the drawer.

She finds an old, heavy hair dryer beneath the sink. She applies a light sheen of creamy eye makeup and a smear of pale, golden lipstick and nothing else, no jewelry, nothing.

Kyle drives them all to a Mexican restaurant, a place with high, airy ceilings and a bar opening out onto an expansive bricked patio. There are only two other occupied tables in the entire place. Desultory ceiling fans rotate high above them like sleepy teenagers flipping their bodies in the sun.

Pitchers of beer and margaritas appear, then tiny wooden bowls of salsa and red plastic buckets of tortilla chips. Platters of burritos and rice and beans and tacos and ceviche. And through it all, Clare does not drink. She pours herself a margarita, just so the boys won't give her any shit, and toys with its straw.

When the kitchen closes, they ignore the undisguised displays of hope from the waitstaff and wander over to a round booth in the empty bar. Everyone else is loud already, shouting past one another. The missile alert is mentioned again.

"I just . . . How wild would that have been? To fly out to this island and then, we all die here? Together?"

"But we didn't, and now I'll tell my kids that story."

"Sure, dude. Absolutely. Our grandfathers were, you know, battling Panzer assaults in the Ardennes or pulling dead bodies out of the water at Coral Sea, but, yes. We have this."

"Don't be a dick. Yesterday morning was terrifying."

Clare laughs, though. That joke, she thinks, would have made her husband laugh. He has called twice today, and she feels a sudden pang for him now, for the husband who effectively quit drinking a year ago. Jameson, the man you could never convince to leave the party, close the tab, direct the taxi home rather than to a fourth bar where the night's actual destiny, he promised, would take shape. He could never believe that he now had access to the private rooms, the back entrances, the corporate tabs, and he never wanted to waste that access. They went out a lot, his first few years in Boston. They had to: he had to prove he could hang with the older guys. And if he was going to bring the girlfriend, then she'd have to prove herself, too. That specific taste of the hangover after a night of vodka tonics, which was what the older partners assumed the young girlfriend would want. And then they would spend Sunday in bed together, both wearing his old Dartmouth hockey shirts. An NBA game on TV and junk food massed on the bed between them, beer bottles clustered on the floor. Maybe they'd have sex twice, once in the morning when they were still sleepy enough not to feel their hangovers and then again in the heavy afternoon, to fight off their headaches.

He wasn't even her fiancé yet. By the time they got married they never really went out anymore, and she was getting those transcontinental Saturday night phone calls from Renzo. And then, one morning, Jameson just woke up and decided he had aged out of binge-drinking. And turned it off immediately, like a faucet.

Each time she raises her voice after a second drink, now, simply to make herself heard inside a cacophonous restaurant, she sees him roll his eyes. She once found herself in an argument with his coworker that pitched dangerously close to yelling, over a television show about young wayward women in Brooklyn that Clare thought was overrated and indulgent, and on their walk to the T station after dinner Jameson was absolutely silent. But he has never asked her to stop drinking, and he's only ever framed his own choice as a matter of health, sleep rhythms, a growing paunch. And still she resents it.

Tonight, though, has revealed the full extent of her ignorance. What's been picking at the weekends of her marriage isn't so complex. It's just the plain fact that sitting sober at a table full of drunk people is a virtually intolerable experience. It would be worse if they were all stoned, maybe, but at least then they'd be saying things that, by virtue of their inscrutability, were somewhat funny. As it is, everyone is just combative, inarticulate, touchy, and very, very loud.

My poor husband, Clare thinks, watching Jessie nod like a metronome at something Renzo is saying, her eyes slightly crossed and her lips chapped.

Clare misses him, then, misses him acutely. Her friends are exhausting, the memories they keep poking one another to unearth, the endless recitations of the same stories and the way they all perform them for one another. Whatever her complaints about Jamie, whatever her fears about how boring they've become, she knows this much: they don't perform for one another.

When Mac catches her eye, Clare realizes how thoroughly she's dropped out of the conversation. Renzo and Liam are back at the bar, Jessie is pointing Kyle to the jukebox.

"They're doing another round?" she asks.

"Don't blame me. I tapped out once we ran out of chips to soak it all up."

"Shouldn't we call it a night? We've got yoga in the morning."

"Then I suggest you take a disco nap, my child. These clowns aren't going anywhere anytime soon. You okay, by the way? You're downright morose compared to last night, your little routine at the pool table. What's wrong? You can tell Uncle Big Mac. You missing your little enterpriser?"

"Did someone binge the entire Cruise back catalog recently? That's, like, the third or fourth Tom reference since yesterday."

"Maybe Renzo's going clear. But no, that's what I've always called Jamie, for real. Maybe never to your face? But it's meant as a compliment. I know how hard that guy works. I know how smart he is. Deadass, I'm not being snide. You could've picked some idiot, so that you got to be the little genius. I love that you didn't."

"You're being suspiciously nice," she says.

He laughs.

"I don't know. Maybe leading by example? Trying to get you to be nicer to Jessie and ignore Renzo when he refuses to be nice to you?"

She stiffens, sits up.

"I haven't said *anything* to Jessie since yesterday morning."

"Yeah, you acted like she wasn't even on the boat today. That was kind of my point."

She breathes in, deeply.

"I'm just saying. You know she's constantly reading you like tea leaves, convinced that whatever you do is actually a signal from Renzo. You can have a little compassion. You know she's fragile."

"I don't have any more insight into Renzo than she does. Than you do."

"That's what we all always tell one another. Everyone acts like he's this black box, but come on. We know him. You think anyone else knows him like we do? All his little party people in LA? I doubt any of them have ever even met his parents. And the guys from college, I don't even know if he's still in touch with the roommates, at this point."

"I can't believe you still do this," she says after a pause. "Protect her like this."

He stares for a moment, too, like he's deciding how harsh he can be.

"I'm sorry," he says. "For asking you to show some baseline courtesy."

"Okay," she says, backing off as if he's convinced her. "Okay, okay. Regardless. They haven't dated since they were seventeen, and Renzo no longer dates women at all, which I believe she's aware of. How is this my problem?"

"Well, yeah, but," he says. "You know as well as I do that, you know. He kept her on a string for a long time. Like, until she met Geoff, long time. Why are you looking at me like that?"

"What do you mean," Clare says slowly. "Kept her on a string."

"What, like, do you need me to draw a diagram of how it works? When a woman loves a man very much, and the man loves keeping said woman distraught and under his thumb . . ."

He trails off, squints at her.

"Are you genuinely telling me you didn't know this still went on sometimes? How is that possible?"

"I don't know," Clare says, holding her face very still. "I don't know,

I—I don't know. I didn't, I mean. I didn't know exactly what the end date was, but yes, I thought there had been one."

"Sorry," he says. "I wouldn't have brought it up so casually, I thought—I mean, I thought we all knew about this. It's not like—I don't just know about it because, whatever. Because of me and her. I thought we all knew."

"Mac," she begins, "doesn't it, I mean—"

But he puts one hand in front of his face and begins to shake his head rapidly from side to side.

"Don't."

"Okay," she says again. "Okay. Okay, but, still. She's an adult."

He bunches his shoulders toward his ears, looks up at the ceiling fans.

"Right. We all are, technically. But what does that matter? You could try a little harder, with her. Just while we're here."

"Can we go back to you complimenting me?"

She reaches out to play with his beer bottle, tilting it as far to one side as she can manage without spilling a drop. She crooks her thumb and catches a rivulet of condensation right where it's beginning to shrivel the label, which she picks at with one fingernail.

"Where was I? Talking about how you married an even bigger brain?"

She smiles at him, grateful.

"You only think I'm the smart one because I got good grades in high school."

"Uh, yes. Shortlisted for valedictorian, but still made time to get shit-faced regularly with the rest of us slackers. I wasn't aware that this opinion was controversial."

"But you've never revised it," she says. "High school was fifteen years ago. And the way I'm smart has been worth absolutely fuck-all since then."

He whistles.

"Sobriety does *not* agree with you, my love. Can I get you a drink? I cannot reach this stage of the dark night of the soul with you here if I'm mostly sober and you're stone cold."

But she's already reaching for her purse.

"Just a joke," she says. "Wasn't supposed to sound bitter. But you're actually right, I should call Jamie. He tried me earlier."

She walks back through the restaurant, the plastic chairs overturned on tabletops, their legs thrust up with an air of uniform indignity. She locks herself in the bathroom and takes her phone out of her purse and does not call her husband.

Jamie always tells her that, too. That she's the smart one. But the line blurs in the same way it does with these guys, somehow; she is the one who feels insulted more easily, and this seems to translate as intellectual inferiority. At least, it feels that way to her.

He took her to a client dinner, once, and somehow they were talking about Dr. Seuss. The client had toddlers, maybe twins? The wife was older than Clare. And Jamie told a story from Clare's childhood, that for years her father had woken her each morning by saying, "Pup is up!" And that Clare had believed this to be her family's little joke, something meaningful only to them, instead of a line cribbed from one of the most famous children's books of all time.

The other wife clapped in delight. It wasn't that funny, but they were on the table's third bottle of wine. *That's not the story*, Clare thought blindly. She knew she'd told Jameson that her father said that each morning. That everything about his parenting had essentially been formed against the concavity of his own father's behavior, a man who had allegedly not understood his children until they could return his handshake, who'd spent his afternoons at the local legion hall. And once, when she'd begun to tell the story of how he always said that, when he woke her up, Jameson had interrupted: "I already know this one. Remember?"

It had been such a warm surprise to be reminded that this one person knows you so well, has mastered every phoneme of your interior dialect. That you can lose sight of your own memories, because they're utterly familiar to him. It was a nice moment, and now he'd reimagined it as an embarrassing story to repeat for a florid client and his drunk wife.

Clare fumed for the rest of the evening, stonewalling the wife's intrusive questions about Clare's potential fertility, angry at Jamie far beyond what was probably justified.

It was only later, while he lay sleeping beside her, that she wondered if he had purposefully edited the story. Or did he actually believe that she was someone who went about with her head so far up her own ass that she thought a quote from Dr. Seuss was something known only to her family? Or had he understood her perfectly well at the time but somehow let the anecdote deform itself in memory? Did it matter? They were all variations on a theme. Either he wanted to make her sound silly or he thought she was, a little bit.

She never mentioned this to him. She was icy for a few days, and if he noticed he did not ask, and then eventually it was in the past. Which she thought, in darker moments, was maybe what marriage was. Endless calcified grievances that you told yourself were the same thing as forgiveness.

None of the grievances seem permanent, not at first. Moving to Boston with her boyfriend didn't seem, when she was twenty-two, to preclude later choices that would send her off in wildly different, potentially promising directions.

She puts the phone back into her purse and takes out her lipstick, so that she'll have something to show for this time in the bathroom. She applies it and then washes her hands very slowly. She walks back through the dining room and comes into the bar and sees that Liam is now sitting with Mac. He looks at ease, his arm stretched out across the back of the booth, cradling the empty space next to him. She allows herself to sink into the way it will feel when he doesn't adjust at all for her return. She allows herself to imagine that he'll leave his arm where it is.

It is time, she thinks, *for you to get off this fucking island. Just, fly home. Go.*

Three hours later, as he's moving on top of her, he gathers her arms above her head and layers them over with his own. Their arms stretch into twinned diamond shapes. She could be with anyone, if she focuses on their bodies and nothing else. The shapes they're making against one another. She could even be with her husband. She thinks dreamily of those paper fortune-tellers her friends used to make in elementary school. She can see them, their corners, floating in the black fuzz behind her closed eyes, printing themselves on her eyelids, expanding and spinning like the images seen through a kaleidoscope.

She could never get it right back then, but if you folded it properly it looked like a little paper mouth, and you operated it with your hands. It was a diamond shape, but when you slid it over your fingers and moved it back and forth, it was a mouth. To tell the fortune, you asked a question and then gnashed the paper jaws together. The mouth would emit its little, dry, papery sounds. Back and forth, back and forth. You kept gnashing, of course, until you got the answer you wanted. Until that hungry mouth produced the right answer.

The right answer was always, always yes.

Los Angeles

They went out to celebrate, on the Saturday before Christmas. It was kind of delicate. They'd all applied early, and the results had come in on Friday. Clare and Renzo and Kyle were all accepted, Jessie and Mac were wait-listed. All of it, both technically and literally, good news, so Renzo muscled them through any awkwardness and insisted that it had been a shitty fall, college applications were now firmly in the rearview, senior year could now, finally, begin. That they were going to do it up properly, that everyone would just say they were crashing at Kyle's or Jessie's and effectively be released into the city on their own recognizance for the rest of the night.

They all had new IDs, courtesy of a kid who lived on Kyle's street, and they bar-hopped around West Hollywood for a few hours before Clare had the idea.

"Guys," she said, "I want to go to the Body Shop."

"Oh good," Mac said. "That sounds suuuuper fun for us. Taking you and Jessie to watch naked ladies dance. I'm sure that won't produce any exhausting philosophical debate."

"Excuse me? You guys are always going there without us," Jessie said.

"It's always like, oh, Clare and Jessie would be such buzzkills, but you never even give us a chance! Come on, I want to go. I'm intrigued!"

"Hold up," Mac interjected. "We are not 'always' going there. I think I've been there, like, once."

"You know what?" Renzo said. "Fuck it, let's take them. They're begging for it! Liam wanted to come meet us, I'll text him."

"Oh no." Jessie pouted, sticking her tongue out at him. "Not your boyyyyyfriend, not Liam, the world's most perfect man."

Kyle blinked, looked over at Clare.

"Not touching this one," he stage-whispered. "I doubt he'll come, anyway. I don't think a trip to a strip club with Renzo would appeal to literally anyone on earth but you and Jess, babe."

But the truth was that the second they arrived, it was unpleasant. Clare had always imagined something kind of glamorous, if louche—she later realized she was picturing, essentially, the VIP tables at a high-end casino in Vegas—but this was just a dive bar with fuchsia backlights and naked women. From the moment they arrived until Renzo offered to split a cab with her, Jessie remained in motion. She was up and headed to the bathrooms, she was buying a round of shots for the table, she was darting outside to make a phone call (to whom?) and then returning to their table and announcing another round of drinks. She was clearly miserable, and if Clare was being honest, so was she. The guys were just rolling their eyes and the whole place smelled like unaddressed vomit and it wasn't sexy or fun, maybe it would have been if Clare had come alone with Jessie (or, she thought, a different type of girl) but with Mac and Kyle and Renzo it was kind of just a fucking bummer. Eventually, Renzo and Jessie left. Clare saw Mac's chin sharpen ever so slightly, but then he shook out his shoulders and turned back to the stage, clapping. Clare chugged what was left of her beer.

The dancers themselves, though, were absolutely incredible. She couldn't stop talking about their bodies, the muscles in their arms popping as they spun themselves around the pole, their abs, just how strong they looked, how confident in their own appeal.

"I mean, look at her nipples," Clare said. She didn't realize she was actually pointing until Kyle put his hand on hers, returned it to the table. "Hers are so cute and tiny. What I wouldn't give for those."

"Okay." Kyle sighed. "So that's another round, then."

When she and Mac were left alone, she reached for him.

"Are you upset that they left together?"

"Clare, come on. Not tonight, okay? We're allegedly celebrating. At a strip club."

"I just meant—I don't think they like, *left* together. I think he's just making sure she gets home."

"Yes," Mac said. "That's certainly what Renzo is known for. His chivalry with Jess."

"Can I ask you something?"

"I'm sure you're going to regardless, so let's get this done before Kyle comes back over."

"It's been a while, right? Since you two slept together?"

He nodded, once.

"Why do you still let her do this? I mean, what is it, like—I just don't know why you let her do this to you, again and again. I feel like, you know, you can maybe leave her to her misery with Ren. You're so much better than whatever they keep dragging you into."

He looked up from his beer then and she saw something so hardened and hopeless in his face that she felt ashamed for asking, ashamed for saying any of it out loud. She saw it, somehow, then. That he just wanted Jessie to admit to him, to all of them, that it wasn't only about making Renzo jealous. That whatever went on when she and Mac were alone, whatever it was that had been so obvious even back in ninth grade, before they ever touched one another, wasn't entirely fake. That even if Renzo did have some sort of power over her, fine. But Mac had it, too. There was a deeper reason, somewhere, that Jessie couldn't resist bouncing back and forth between them in this endless, chaotic loop.

"Look," he said. "I'm not trying to be, whatever. But I just don't think I'll be able to explain this to you. You've never been in love, right? I mean, I'm not trying to be hurtful, but. You haven't. Correct?"

She felt suddenly naked, unspeakably embarrassed by Kyle's return to the table.

"Here you go, you filthy animals," he said, passing them the cold beers.

But that beer turned out to be the tipping point, literally, she tried to nap while sitting upright on her barstool and fell off, which was when Kyle announced they were taking her home. Besides, he had to be up early. His parents had already left for Hawai'i, but he was due to meet his siblings at LAX the next morning.

They split a cab to Hancock Park, Clare wedged between the two of them, burrowing into Mac's shoulder because she knew that burrowing into Kyle's would send a signal she wasn't interested in sending. Since Renzo had moved home for good, Kyle had gradually relocated to the pool house, sleeping there most nights. Even though the house itself was huge and dark that night, they all walked down the carport and back behind the pool without even asking.

Inside, no one felt like sleeping. Kyle and Mac dug into a six-pack from the mini fridge, attacked the liquor cabinet. Renzo would have insisted on a stronger substance and convinced Kyle. *Come on come on come on just send the text, I know you have the cash, stay up with me, just crash on the plane, you simpleton! It's the first night of the rest of our lives! Do it do it do it!* But Kyle and Mac were perfectly content to sprawl out with a shot and a few beers.

Clare passed out in the bedroom, listening to the rise and fall of their chatter through an open door. She knew she was too drunk, that falling asleep without swallowing a few glasses of water would later prove unwise. But she was so happy, that night, just to lie there in darkness listening to the boys, their voices. For the first time, she knew where she would be next year. She knew where she'd be flying back from, landing at LAX and dropping her bags at home and sailing out the door to meet these same boys. The little crooked house in Santa Monica didn't need to be the pained locus of her father's resentment anymore, of her mother's ambivalence. It could become, soon enough, just the place where she'd been a child.

She woke a few hours later, sandwiched between them, Kyle's phone angrily informing them that he'd slept through his alarm. He answered and she heard his brother's voice, noisy and livid. Kyle rolled out of bed and out of the house. Mac nuzzled into Clare and she went back to sleep, rousing two hours later when he lightly punched her shoulder.

"We should get out of here."

"Come on," she said. "Nobody's even home."

"Still," he said. "Call Renzo. We'll get breakfast. My treat. Let's just get out of here."

Clare lifted her tongue to the roof of her mouth, felt it stick. She fumbled for the bedside table, felt for her rings and found a beer can instead, tried to drink from it and gagged.

"Okay," she said. "But I want, like, pasta. Or maybe a bagel."

Mac nodded, kneeling to find her shoes under the bed, holding out her ratty fur coat so she could slip into it easily.

"You name it. Let's go."

They soon discovered, though, that the mini fridge was empty, and she tried to impress upon him that she would not make it much of anywhere without something cold to drink—a seltzer, a ginger ale.

"Mac, I know where she keeps the key," she told him. "It's, like, under a rose bush or something. I can find it. Can we just call a cab and wait for it inside? I don't understand why this is such an emergency."

They walked up through the garden, Mac close at her heels. Inside the house, he called a taxi while she raided the fridge. His eyes followed her as she snagged a few string cheeses, stole an apple.

"What?" she said, her mouth full. He shook his head.

"Mac," she said. "Do you think they care that we're here? I mean, they know that Kyle was here alone. He could have thrown a fucking party, or something. This is nothing."

"It's different," he said softly. "When Kyle's not here."

"I don't know," she said, chewing her string cheese. "I think it's fun. It's like playing dress-up. I'm guessing you're not willing to let me go peek through Sherry's closet?"

She remembered the first few times she'd been in this house, in middle school, her awe at the pervasive sense that everything was perpetually staged for some public event. The artful clusters of candles or fruit bowls on tables, the magazines and vases placed in color-coordinated groupings. As if, were she to pick up a book from a coffee table, there might be a blue-taped outline showing her the exact angle at which to replace it. She had mentioned this, once, to her mother, who had told her not to touch Sherry's things.

"Clare," Mac said. "I'm asking you to do me this favor. Can we please just wait out front?"

"Jesus," she said, but she followed him.

They paused in the foyer, beside the fragrant golden Christmas tree, and Clare caught a glimpse of herself in a mirror. Beneath her coat, she wore a tiny black dress with thin straps. Makeup smeared itself across her cheekbones and formed dark clumps along the pale, puffed skin beneath her eyes, which had that special quality of a hangover, the ability to appear both sunken and bulging. Outside, they stood on the front steps together and she was about to make a joke at her own expense when she felt Mac's body tense beside her, looked down to see his hands slide from his pockets. She followed his gaze and saw a blond woman in yoga pants and a zipped velour hoodie approaching them warily, walking a tiny fluffy dog on a long leash. She was still nearly half a block away, but Clare could see that her steps had slowed, that she was trying to stare at them without fully turning her head.

"Great," Mac said. "This lady will love this. The Black kid skulking around with a tiny, clearly intoxicated white girl. The visible bruises are a nice touch, too. Cool, coolcoolcool where's our fucking cab at?"

Clare looked dumbly between him and the woman, who was no longer pretending not to stare. Mac appeared, after all, clean and groomed and well rested. Clare was the one who was half-naked, who had bruises all down her legs and thighs, he was right. She was clumsy, an explanation that probably wouldn't satisfy a concerned stranger. Mac had mentioned the bruises so disdainfully, and now they felt inculpatory. As if Clare had applied them purposefully, with stage makeup, colluding with this woman to frame Mac for a salacious crime. But Clare was the one broadcasting her own dissolute drunkenness, the one who looked like the smell of her skin would hit you in rancid waves if you got too close. Not him.

"I'm sure it's fine," she told him. "We can just tell her we know Sherry. We'll mention Kyle, or something. Just ignore her. It's fine."

The woman did, eventually, keep walking, and Clare made a great show of waving at the little dog. Mac smiled, kept his feet flat on the ground, didn't move until the woman had reached the opposite corner.

"It's okay," Clare said. "I think it's fine. I don't think you need to be worried about this."

She tried to think what to say, what to apologize for. She tried to make a joke, to feign outrage and inform him that, *please*, she hadn't been intoxicated for a few hours at least. But for the remaining ten minutes they waited, she couldn't shake the way he had looked at her exposed skin and her greasy hair, the bruises. He didn't speak for most of the cab ride and only periodically cracked a smile over breakfast at the Farmers' Market, where they met Renzo and eventually Jessie.

The interaction lingered at the edges of her vision, retreating when she tried to examine it. How nervous he'd been, his certainty that her own messiness would expand outward, like a poisonous cloud, to include him. She told herself that it was the right thing, to let him say what he was feeling and then move on, rather than forcing him to dwell on it. Because if not, then she had missed some chance he'd offered. Some way that he'd tried, maybe, to ask her for more.

Eventually, at breakfast, she caught his eye. Resigned, he passed her the remainder of his breakfast tacos, but she waved them off.

"You feeling better?"

"Oh," he replied. "I feel fantastic, Clare. You know me."

MONDAY

13

Clare and Jessie are sitting in the sand at Shipwreck Beach. They're far from the water, just where the dunes fade back into dirt beneath the sparse shade thrown from a few straggling kiawe trees. Behind them, a heritage trail leads back up into the cliffs. Renzo lobbied everyone, on the drive over, for a hike to follow their yoga session. He was outvoted.

Both girls are comfortably, annihilatingly stoned. The yoga teacher is late. Clare stretches her legs in the direction of the shoreline and sinks back into her elbows. Gritty sand rubs against the heels of her hands and she lets her neck slacken, peers up into the trees. Behind them, everything is so lush. As long as they don't look left, don't look right. Ignore the hotel, its parking lot clotted with SUVs belching out sunburned children in rash guards yanking their watery, exhausted parents toward the ocean.

If they had just agreed to follow him up the hiking trail, Renzo insisted, get some cardio for a change, they could have expected untold rewards: stunning limestone cliffs, dramatic petrified sand dunes. The tallest promontories jut out over the far end of the cove. The water looks too shallow, but every few minutes Clare sees another tourist dash along the cliff and throw himself, legs akimbo, into the waves.

Untold rewards. He kept saying that.

So much of the island's flora, the flowers and creeping vines streaming past the Tahoe's windows every morning, look like creations sprung from the pages of an illustrated children's book—their waxy leaves reaching out to breach the barrier of the page, touch their thick, glossy tips to your skin. Just like every other aspect of this island, the most vibrant version of whatever you imagined. We all want to insist that it isn't mere leisure, not just vacation, Clare thinks. We want to insist that the gravitational pull is something so much more mysterious than what it is: the plain fact of the island's almost pornographically lush beauty, its wet air and its nighttime clicks and hums and all the ambient fragrances hitting you with each shift of the winds.

"Nobody comes here for Hawai'i," that kid said the other night.

She readjusts her hands in the cool sand. *Just stop doing it.* She remembers all the women she's dismissed by whispering, as they left rooms or stood up from tables, *She's just so self-destructive.* All the mistreatment tolerated, the objectively ill-advised sex, the powders snorted at unwise hours of blurred early mornings. The grasping text messages sent to exes or professors or married colleagues, the relationships sabotaged in pursuit of some ill-defined, childish desire. To all of this, Clare would just murmur, knowingly and with distaste, *She just can't help herself. It's like she can't stop.*

And she always found them so maddening, these flagrant, unrepentant obliterators of the self. She has always assumed that any woman who truly loathes herself should apply (at the very least!) a little patience. A bit of, you know, delayed gratification. But to watch someone fling herself at it so publicly? Shouldn't self-destruction be muted, gradual disintegration rather than violent explosion?

As it turns out, though, self-destruction is remarkably easy. It generates almost no friction whatsoever. All these years she's refused to slip up, wrapped herself in the most reliable man she could find and wordlessly promised her parents that they'll never be asked to scramble their limited resources to protect her from the consequences of her own judgments. All these years she thought she knew what was required to be happy:

never to lose what she'd already gained. Flail all you want, stall out, achieve nothing new. Just don't lose what you already have.

She sees now how smoothly it begins, the exact pattern that will lead to that exact loss. All along it's been such a thin membrane laid over her daily life, keeping her from the things that might destroy the fragile peace permitting her to imagine a cluster of traits as "the sort of person" she really is. We can all be very aware of our own efforts to be good people, can treat them as insurance policies against becoming truly terrible. But all of that, it turns out, is ephemeral. *That*, maybe, was the sort of person you were in the last moments right before *this* happened. But you can be someone else again before the next rupture occurs. In the past week, Clare has become an entirely different "sort of person," actually, without expending very much effort at all.

If anyone was honest about this, the effortlessness with which someone might simply choose not to carry the guilt or disgust or even the fear? The ease with which she has been aware of what she should feel, has even sensed the dark edges of those feelings at the very corners of her vision, but has still avoided any stimuli that might bring them squarely into view?

Like her husband's voice on the telephone, for example.

If anyone were honest about this? It would be anarchy.

You do one selfish thing. You slam your brain down on any revulsion, like the blade of a paper cutter. And you're not obliterated, you're still there in the mirror. And every morning, the part of you that has always analyzed your own life so closely is simply, just . . . no longer present.

The whole past year has felt this way already, she thinks, as though tiny, pivotal parts of her are absented from the daily roll call. Best to focus on the hypothetical efforts you might make in future, to be better, rather than to look for the parts of yourself that are no longer there. And this particular loss feels so simple, so explicable. She's just someone who cheats. It's easy to understand.

Every morning she wakes up here, in Hawai'i, and she is both people. The one doing it and the one who might never do it again. That was part of the simple slip of it, that was why you fell into it like sliding off a rock into the ocean. You never have to admit to yourself that it will happen again. Even while it is, in fact, happening again. You're already glancing ahead to the next day, to the next time you'll see him, to the possibility that you will resist the compulsion. The need to do something, anything really, to break his gaze, to break your sense of your own desperation. You feel it like a fever, so you reach out and touch him and it begins one more time.

But maybe not tonight, she thinks. *Maybe not.*

Beside her, Jessie stirs.

"What are you thinking about?"

"I don't know, really," Clare says. It's not a lie. "High school, probably."

Jessie giggles, slowly and then gaining steam.

"Right?" Clare says. "What else?"

"Uggh, yeah."

"I miss swimming at your house," Clare says. "At night, in the summer."

"My parents' house."

"Well, yeah."

"But I guess that's why I loved it, when you would all show up and stay for, like, days at a time. I liked feeling like it was mine. Like I was taking care of everyone."

Jessie peers up at the cliffs.

"What does that mean, petrified sand dunes? Like, how can that be a thing?"

Clare sifts her childhood for clues, all the exotic worlds she once read about.

"Like the people at Pompeii," she says. "Or, like, fossils."

"There's that ghost forest in Japan," Jessie joins in. "The trees were just, like, consumed by the water."

"The people in peat bogs!" Clare tries. She thinks of a picture she saw once, the features melted but never completely rotted. The motionless swimming centuries suspended, waiting. And Pompeii, now that she thinks about it, seems merciful, even. At least it was quick. They were alive and aware and hurting and then they weren't. There was no limping along, wondering whether the world had ended without their noticing, whether they were planning for an evaporated future. Living out the series of hacking coughs that precede the final cessation of breath.

"These are not vacation topics." Jessie giggles. "Where is this yoga teacher? And why were you thinking about my house?"

"I don't know. I mean, we're all together. The memories pop up."

"I was always so jealous. You'd get there and then he wouldn't pay attention to me again until it was time to go to bed. And they'd all be making such a mess, I'd be so paranoid that my mother would come home and find the kitchen sink busted or something. But you always helped, right? We always cleaned up after them. It's so frustrating, still. We're still the ones doing the dishes, even here. We stamp our feet about their little sexist comments, but."

Clare peers over at Jessie. She's always assumed that Jess saw this as an appropriate tax for the chivalrous hands guiding her by the hip, the tabs picked up without discussion, the arms reaching to pry her from the clutches of a predatory guy in the bathroom line.

But then she steps away from the thought, as if distancing herself from a painting too chaotic to view at close range. Because whose thoughts is she describing, Jessie's or her own? And look at their parents. Every single husband of that generation loves to hold court over an audience of younger couples, insisting that even back in the eighties his wife knew that her mother's way wouldn't be for her. That his marriage was going to be straight down the middle or nothing, that his wife, believe it, takes absolutely zero shit! Every single roommate's father who ever treated Clare to this speech—whether over dinner at the Hanover Inn or at his estate in Westport, whether he was the primary earner or functionally unemployed—barely knew how to launder his own shirts. Often, as he expounded on the novelty of his equal marriage, his wife was clearing the meal she'd prepared, plated, and served.

"It's just what they all learned," Clare says. "We did too, right?"

"Even Jamie?"

"Well, he grew up alone with his mother, Jess."

"But what about now?"

"I mean, he literally has the job that supports us. I don't, I mean—it feels like it would be kind of fucked. To demand that he, like, vacuum when he gets home. He would probably just want to hire someone, anyway."

Jessie smiles, ruefully. "Right, exactly, though."

She lowers her round, oversized sunglasses, fixes her eyes on Clare. Those glasses are outdated, they look like holdovers from 2005. The Olsen twins, Lindsay Lohan, other girls who grew up to be women who aren't really famous anymore. All the tiny, emaciated girls with heads too big for their shoulders, photographed with giant handbags resting in the crook of one arm and cups of branded coffee in one hand. The huge sunglasses hiding their faces from the cameras. Those are the images embossed in her brain. She and Jessie both wore the bulbous sunglasses, looking like little precursors to the alien emoji. They've got all the same signifiers slotted into all the same spaces in the attic corners of their brains, too many shared memories that cannot be disowned. Isn't that its own kind of intimacy, whatever its limitations?

Clare looks away, buries her fingers in the sand—the sand that's not yet petrified, still breathing beneath her palms—and is loopily amazed to feel that each grain remains chilled even in the late morning, even buried only inches beneath the layer baked through by the sun. She arches her back and hears her neck pop, crisp sounds like those little snap closures on baby clothes.

She shivers.

Out in the waves, Liam stands huddled with Renzo and Kyle, their necks crunched over someone's phone. Looking at Liam, his sweatpants rolled up to his knees, she feels such a storm of affection that she wants to stick her face directly down into the sand, bury her own incriminating grin.

"Hey," Mac calls, jogging up from the water. He stands shirtless above them with his hands on his hips. "I assume this is her?"

A royal blue Prius has spun into the parking lot. Hopping out of the car, the yoga teacher is one of those frazzled and bright women Clare always views with disdain but then cannot look away from. She is slap-dash in the details but endlessly captivating in the aggregate. Everything about her spills over, like a bowl of cherries or chocolates your hand continually strays toward, despite each attempt to lick your fingertips clean in some decisive way.

A faded black sweatshirt slips from the woman's browned shoulders, where tanned skin strips off like tape unfurling. Her dark hair, tinged slightly with henna red, is piled high and held together with several plastic clips. She looks nothing like what Clare pictured when Renzo described the influencer teaching beach yoga. Her black pants somehow manage to emphasize both that her stomach is not flat and that her entire lower body curves from her waist in perfect proportion, like she was poured into the plaster mold for a cartoon temptress. Clare just wants to be drawn close, wants the airy, distracted sloppiness to envelop her, too.

The woman catches Clare's eye as she enters the circle. There is an obligatory roundelay discussion of Saturday morning. Olive—this is her name—was on the road when the missile alert came through, and she had to pull her car onto the shoulder. She felt, she says, sheer terror. It was completely out of character for her; she is someone who has spent her entire adult life unlearning such impulses, she really tries not to let herself be buffeted so violently by every little dip in her fortunes. She had to remain there, other traffic passing her by, until she was able to drive the car. She uses the word "hysterics" without couching it in irony or apology, as if unaware of the fact that women should never, really must never, refer to themselves as "hysterical."

She turns to Clare last. She doesn't shake Clare's hand so much as clasp it and then joyfully reintroduce it to Clare, like some precious bauble whose owner, she feels certain, has forgotten its value.

"Thanks so much for coming, we're so excited," Clare says.

"Well. You've paid for my time, haven't you?"

Clare is momentarily rocked back by this, which seems to please Olive.

The yoga class, in the end, mostly sluices past Clare. She moves her limbs this way and that, trying not to stare at the sweat gathering in the small of Liam's back. He's a star student, flexible and steady, but he rolls his eyes, tosses off comments to Olive about his hip flexors. He's clearly endeared himself to her immediately; she lingers often to stroke his spine, drumming her fingers as if he were a tabletop. He's the only one who seems to be trying not at all, who doesn't care if he improves his technique or if his body realigns itself one degree from where it began the morning. He simply wants to be adored. Clare resists drawing any conclusions from his seeming indifference to the source of the adoration.

Each time his arms extend above his head, his shirt lifts to expose the thumbprint dimples just above his tailbone. Clare touches the tip of her tongue to her own upper lip and imagines that it's him, his skin, she can fill each divot with her tongue. She loses her balance repeatedly and eventually forces herself to stare down at the sand.

They all compete with one another, of course, and so the class isn't even slightly relaxing. It's a total lost cause until the very end, when Olive forces them all to close their eyes and lie back in the deep sink of corpse pose. Clare knows that this is the standard way to end a yoga class. But it still feels, somehow, as if Olive has their number. As if she's figured out no one will listen to her at all unless they can't see each other.

She pads back and forth in the sand, between their bodies. Her voice moves over them like fog, shapeless and drifting. She talks about Nevada, where she's from. "Ne-VA-da, please, never Ne-vah-da," she says with an airy laugh. She's been on Kaua'i, though, for twenty years, and she pronounces that properly, too. She tells them all about Shipwreck Beach.

"It's a difficult balance, as you might imagine," she says. "To love this island so much, even as you know that in a world that was truly at peace, you would never have settled here at all. This beach is just one reminder. It used to be so hidden, secluded, accessible only by dirt roads cut through sugarcane. Now, there's a hotel."

First the sugar, she describes, sounding bewildered. Then, the developers.

"You see, I do it too. I talk about this possessively, as if I knew it in its first form, because the island is already so different from when I first came here. But by the time I got here there were already so many things that had been taken from the island. This is a pattern, no? For people like us. We come crashing in once a path has been cleared, wreak havoc, and then begrudge the havoc that follows behind us."

Clare has a strong urge, then, to open her eyes, find out if Renzo is smirking. But the instinct not to break the spell, and not to be seen as an asshole by Olive, is even stronger.

"I understand that you all grew up in Los Angeles, so I'm sure you see this there as well, in many contexts, many neighborhoods, I don't need to explain it. Although of course this island is not Los Angeles, I'm not suggesting that. But the idea that we take greedily, with both hands, and tell ourselves that it's permissible so long as we don't leave actual trash strewn around at the end of the day. For a brief moment, this morning, I simply ask that we reflect on what this really means and how we might change our behavior going forward. It's true, I hope, that you'll gather any physical detritus before you leave the beach today. Only your footprints will remain. But is that the best we can do?"

Clare hears one of the boys murmur, another clear his throat. She can almost feel Jessie vibrating with anxiety.

"What about tonight, tomorrow, later this week, when you all leave this gorgeous place and fly back into your own lives? What impression will you retain of this island, and the people for whom it is home? I hope you'll remember this hour that we spent together today."

She tells them to open their eyes. She tells them that the light in her sees, honors, and adores the light in each and every one of them.

And then everything proceeds as it would have anyway. Renzo pays her promptly and sends the rest of them a Venmo charge to cover the total. They accept his requests for payment, standing in their little clump on the beach. He posts a photo of them all in tree pose, the ocean as backdrop. Jessie comments, shares it to her own Stories. *The only antidote to a brush with death? Beachside asanas . . . truly hashtag blessed #islandtime #thebigchill*

Renzo leads the charge, running gracelessly into the water. Jessie follows, while Kyle and Mac linger with Olive, who stands with an arm on the open door of her little blue car, one leg bent carelessly, her foot tucked against her other knee. Liam is closer to the water, sprawled on the packed wet sand, and Clare goes to sit beside him. She can smell him beneath the ocean air, beneath his deodorant, a smell so sharp that in the early mornings it has woken her. A smell she found unpleasant at first, too acrid, but now craves. She can smell it beneath his arms, behind his knees, in the dark wiry hair on his chest or the softer hair beneath his belly button. It might not even be extreme, for all she knows. But how long has it been since she smelled another man's skin in the morning? She's thinking of Jamie, using him as the benchmark against which any other man must be measured.

"That was kind of a bit much," she says. "A little overblown, right?"

He shrugs, his eyes still closed.

"I mean, I liked it, actually. I respect the hustle. Charge groups of guilty vacationing millennials for the hour but then sneak in a little lecture, harsh but fair, before you go."

She's not just saying this; she did, actually, enjoy the tartness of that final, rebuking speech. *I'm not a complete moron*, Clare thinks, *I get it*. Manipulation, when it corresponds to however you best enjoy being manipulated, is never really unwelcome. The softer and hazier the terminology, the better. That moment, lying there, when the inside of Clare's eyelids grew eggplant-dark and she knew that Olive was leaning over her, she wanted to laugh but feared she would cry.

Maybe it was all just hushed little koans, the same ones offered to every other group of navel-gazers visiting from southern California. But still Clare wanted to ask: Seriously, if you ever tell a story about us, what will it be? Are we any more obviously spoiled or useless than your typical clients? Would you say that you're a spiritual person, not just an unhappy person in search of a distraction but someone who is actually, truly, spiritual? Do you think that's why you ended up living on an island far from your previous life and do you think there is any actual way to become a more spiritual person that isn't just, excuse my language but, a crock of shit? Do you think there is a way to become something less hideous to yourself without immediately looking around to see who's watched you make the decision to start to *try*?

Liam sits up, takes out his phone.

"Where's the shipwreck? Shouldn't we be able to see it?"

"A hurricane destroyed it," she says. "For a long time it would come and go, it was buried in the sand but you could see it at low tide. And people kept stripping parts of the hull for firewood. But there was a hurricane, like, thirty years ago. More. Before we were born. And no one's ever seen it again."

"What, did you just check Wikipedia?"

"Yes," she says.

They look at one another.

"So it's probably still there, part of it," he says. "It's under the sand, but it's still there somewhere."

"Maybe."

"Well, didn't it say?"

"I don't know, Liam, why don't you go ask her?"

He looks past her to the parking lot, where Olive is pulling Kyle into an embrace.

"You know what, Clare? I will."

He stands up and jogs over just as Mac and Kyle return.

"So," Kyle says. "Our girl says there's, like, a party, tonight. Up at the main pool. I don't know, it's one of the employees' birthdays, or something. Maybe our little Tom."

"Oh, I'm sure they really want us crashing their party," Clare snaps.

"Well, she just invited us."

"What is he doing over there?" she asks. Mac follows her gaze.

"Probably perhaps discussing the party he just mentioned?"

Clare exhales through her nostrils.

"Sorry," she says. "Yes. A party. Let's do it."

14

It's a twenty-first birthday. It is actually a twenty-first birthday that they, despite Olive's alleged invitation, are more or less crashing.

Clare sits with her jeans rolled to her knees, her feet in the pool. She has planted herself here while the boys drift back and forth. Kyle and Mac found a folding table that a friend of the birthday boy had left propped against a deck chair, and they've set up a makeshift bar.

"It's the least we can do," Mac kept reassuring the kids, but none of them have objected, generally, to the presence of these strange adults. It isn't little Tom's birthday, but he is here. As she and Jessie made their way down the path from the clubhouse, he spotted them and gave a brief wave before slugging a shot of tequila.

Mac and Kyle return to sit with her. Jessie and Renzo have ingratiated themselves with the main cluster of boys, or Renzo has, and Jessie has followed in his wake to soak up the attention. She looks beautiful; she's wearing a slinky dress the color of coral that manages to look both like a nightgown and like perfect vacation wear, like it's a swath of fabric she picked up locally and just twisted around her body to form a dress. As they all boarded the golf cart back at the house, she looked down at Clare's outfit.

"I guess they call those boyfriend jeans, right?" And then she smiled to herself without ever making eye contact. It was the first thing she'd said to Clare since the conversation about whether Clare's husband does his share of housework and somehow it felt related, Clare spent the entire ride up to the clubhouse pissed without being able to explain to herself why. She feels, not for the first time, like a sexless tomboy next to Jessie. Nine times out of ten she is confident that Jessie is trying too hard, and then the tenth time Jessie's efforts look perfect and Clare feels like the little sister invited along on an older brother's date, or something.

Olive was already here when they arrived. She is curled on a pool chair, her hair piled on top of her head, her eyes rimmed and their whites glinting when they're caught by the pool lights. She's wearing harem pants and a soft, flowing top that exposes one shoulder. She hasn't moved since they arrived; the kids have kept her drink steadily refreshed, and two or three of them can always be found on the recliner across from hers. Clare has heard a few of them calling her O. She seems to play a warm, den mother role for all of them, like they know she won't report this party to management.

Liam sits now at the foot of Olive's chair, close enough to touch the heel of her right foot. He made a beeline over there as soon as they arrived. First he stood over her, then he sat down on the other chair with the kids, and now he's sitting on Olive's chair. He has not spoken to Clare all night, and what's worse, he's given no indication that this is intentional, that he even cares if Clare notices. She cannot understand what's different.

She decides she can either go home or else get much, much drunker than she is currently. She's been nursing something one of the resort boys handed her, rum and lime juice and soda, but that will need to change.

Kyle puts his feet in the pool and Mac lies down on his stomach, rests his chin on his hands, gazes at the water.

"How long are we planning to stay?" she asks Kyle.

"Come on," he says. "This is fun. Don't you feel young?"

"No, I feel like an ancient crone, actually."

"Okay, well, there are exactly two other women here, and you are technically younger than both of them. Go flirt! Jessie's having the time of her life over there."

As if on cue, Renzo comes over. He sits down and drapes his arm around her shoulders.

"Oh no," he says. "Is she not getting enough attention?"

"We were just telling her," Mac says. "She can go make someone's whole night."

"Yeah," Kyle says. "Lean over, give him a nice shot of the twins. Why not?"

"Thanks, guys," Clare says. She leans into Renzo's shoulder. "All I want is a little more attention from *you*, babe. Is that so much to ask?"

"Oh," he says softly. "No, I wasn't talking about me."

She stiffens, swirls her drink.

Someone upgrades the speakers, the music now loud and tinny against the limestone. A few boys are standing over there, one of them holding an iPhone in his hand, scrolling idly. Some of them are shirtless, including the birthday boy, who scratches the back of his head with one hand and the taut expanse of his stomach with the other. They all stand with their shoulders broad and their spines curved, their necks and tailbones arced away from one another like they're comparing belly buttons. There is something so guarded and yet naked about them, how unsure and yet supremely comfortable they are in their bodies, that makes Clare want to cry. They just look so young. One of them selected this song, Jay-Z rapping over a bhangra beat, and it must be nearly as old as he is. What were the equivalents for us, Clare wonders. Madonna songs? Prince? The idea that this song might seem as remote, as frozen in amber, to these boys as "Lucky Star" once seemed to Clare is obvious but still, in a glancing way, painful.

"I hope they keep doing this," she says. "They should play all our middle school stuff. I want to hear, like, Ja Rule."

She takes the bottle of rum from Kyle and sloshes more of it into her pint glass. The ice cubes have melted. He snatches the bottle back from her.

"All right," he says. "All right."

"Let's do a shot, too," she says to Renzo. He obediently takes the bottle back from Kyle.

"If she wants a shot, let her do a shot," Renzo says. "Why are we here if we're not going to get drunk with these children? We're certainly not here to flirt with them. Would it kill this resort to hire some hot cabana boys who are actually of legal age?"

Mac laughs. "I'm so sorry that you're forced to hang out with us all week instead of seducing some hot employee."

A torrent of protest begins: Renzo has spotted, on Grindr, several "absolute confections" among the local talent, men whose messages he's ignored simply because his time, these precious hours spent with the un-grateful Mac, is so limited. He cannot bear to abandon them all for even one night! And does Mac doubt it, that these snacks aren't clamoring after the glamorous visitor from the coast, a man at least twenty years younger than most other options around here?

"You happy?" Clare grumbles.

"'From the coast,'" Mac says. "That always sounds so retro, to me. Like, the Didion-Dunnes are flying into Idlewild this afternoon from the coast. What was that movie where the agent murders everyone? Or maybe he's murdered?"

"Why are you encouraging him?" Clare demands. "You know he'd love for an innocent bystander to assume that he's 'in the business.'"

Mac snaps in agreement, points his index finger in her direction.

"Facts."

"Why *are* we here?" Clare says. She shifts her weight, the stone harsh against her sit bones. She looks over, again, and she can't quite tell in the dark but she thinks Liam is touching Olive's ankle. Just with one hand. They're not any closer together but they somehow keep isolating them-selves, in conversation, the other boys drifting away as if to respect their privacy. This feels like a violation of some agreement Olive made with all of them this afternoon. She would teach her class, give her weighty speech, and then they would never see her again. She would not flirt with Clare's friends. She would not be reaching out and holding, for one mo-ment too long, Liam's fucking arm.

"What is the bug you have up your ass about being here tonight?" Mac says, yawning. He rolls over onto his back and looks up at her. "You know you can go home. You can walk it if you're so miserable."

"I'm not miserable. I just don't, like—What if they get in trouble? They're definitely not supposed to be drinking down here, right?"

"Oh, Clare. Leave them alone!" Renzo chides.

"And why is Olive here? She's older than we are. It's weird, isn't it?"

"Sorry," Kyle says mildly. "But you're making a little bit of a 'stay in your place' argument here, no? About the hired help? This is sounding a little bit 'get off my lawn.'"

"And it's not even her lawn." Mac smiles, closing his eyes. "She's your guest just like we are."

"That isn't what I meant," Clare says. She drinks directly from the bottle this time.

"The rest of us are filthy capitalist pigs until Clare is in a bad mood and we're asking her to socialize with the little people," Renzo murmurs.

"Stop it," she says.

"Hey man, is it cool if we put a few of your beers in the cooler?" one of the kids yells over from his post by the speakers.

"Yeah, dude," Kyle yells back.

"Actually," Mac says, sitting up. "Can we make a music request?"

"Oh, for sure."

"So, like, we'd love to hear some nostalgia tracks, keep them coming. My friend Clare here was actually hoping to hear some Ja Rule, if that's cool?"

"Jesus Christ." Clare stands up and splashes Mac, who protests. She hands the bottle back to Kyle and then she's crossed the patio, she's standing above Olive's chair.

Liam has his back to her, and Clare thinks she can see Olive, in the moments just before Clare is within earshot, whispering to him. His shoulders sharpen, but he doesn't otherwise acknowledge Clare's presence. Olive gazes up, her face expectant but not entirely inviting. Clare hesitates, then sits down on an empty chair.

"Hello again," Olive purrs.

"I just wanted to thank you," Clare says. "We all did, we really enjoyed today."

"Oh, no, thank you," Olive says. One of her delicate feet is actually, more or less, in Liam's lap. Her toenails are painted the pale pink of strawberry ice cream, of baby blankets. Clare forces herself to look away.

"I always feel that I get as much from my students as they get from me," Olive continues. "More. Seeing all of you learn the poses, watching how the atmosphere we create may linger."

"Sure," Clare says. Olive inclines her head.

"Liam was just telling me about his work. It sounds like a real period of transition for him, real creative ignition."

"Clare is a novelist," Liam says.

"Well," Clare says. "I wouldn't say that. I haven't finished my first book."

"You can't let that dictate whether you call yourself an artist," Olive says. "The recognition of an industry doesn't make you an artist."

"Oh no," Clare says. "I have the recognition of the industry. I just haven't finished writing it. I haven't actually made the art, so I think calling myself an artist would actually be kind of pretentious, still. Don't you agree?"

Olive nods graciously. Liam looks over his shoulder, then fixes Clare with a stare so intense and inscrutable that she begins to fidget.

"Liam, however," Clare says. "Liam can write anything he puts his mind to, apparently. He's moving from thing to thing without giving it a second thought."

He doesn't reply right away.

"Clare," he says finally, "is known for being quite deliberate. She never hops from thing to thing. She really thinks through each and every decision."

Olive looks back and forth between them, but her face shows no discomfort, not even any surprise at the sudden shift in Liam's tone. She flexes her foot, a gesture so warm and so possessive that Clare looks away.

"I'm sorry," Liam says, his voice low. "Is there no one else willing to pay you the attention you're craving?"

"It can be hard," Olive says, pretending not to have heard, "to negotiate the things we want, to see them clearly against the things we already have. And of course, you know, that's one of the great horrors of this time in your lives, all of you. That you'll misjudge. I'm a bit older, but you're all really in the thick of it. Your twenties are for being cavalier with what you have, and perhaps realizing too late that some of those things are more fragile than you took them to be."

"I think everyone has realized that the world is a bit more fragile than we took it to be," Clare says. "I think that's been the lesson of the past year. That's why it's felt like such an emergency."

"Has it felt like an emergency for you?" Olive asks, tilting her head again. "I think it's easy sometimes for people in our positions—"

She waves one hand, clearly meant to encompass everyone at the pool.

"Do you feel that your life has changed irrevocably?" she asks. "In the day to day, I mean. Of course we're not immune to the larger story. But do you feel that you've lost something? The word 'emergency' . . . it's a big word, no?"

Liam looks down at his lap, smiles. Clare waits a moment, then lifts her glass and drains it again.

"You could have just asked me not to interrupt," she says to him then. He doesn't protest when she walks away, finds the teenagers and their cooler, grabs a beer.

She puts one arm around the birthday boy, a ruddy-faced kid in a backward baseball cap, kisses his cheek. She calls Renzo over and they do another shot. When Mac tries to bundle her up and carry her over to a more distant chair, she shakes him off. Kyle tackles her and they fall into the pool, but that's later. Even later than that, she's underwater. She crosses her legs and sinks to the bottom of the shallow end and stares up at the water's surface, the pool lights. She tries to remember when she last replied to a text from her husband.

Los Angeles

"I don't know," Mac said. "We should go somewhere, though. Let's just go to Westwood and walk around, I don't care. We've gotta break the orbit of this house, man."

"Westwood?" Jessie squawked. "With all the eighth graders? No thank you."

They were in the hot tub at Kyle's house. It was August, and the steady stream of departures would begin soon, so much sooner than anyone wanted to discuss. Everyone kept showing up at Kyle's house because his parents were in Ojai. Renzo wasn't living there anymore, but Sherry had remained noticeably lax about rules, as if her sudden and unrequested responsibility for the additional child last year had counterintuitively released her from playing any sort of in loco parentis role for the rest of them. She'd never warmed up, really, at least not to anyone but Renzo. Still, she had more frequently absented herself, and so they were always here. They got stoned and walked to Larchmont Pizza, got stoned and drove to see movies at the Grove. No one wanted to talk about roommate assignments, about the trips to Target or Bed Bath. Everyone was desperate to avoid as many dinners alone with their parents as they could.

Clare wasn't stoned; it was becoming too much, too regular. She didn't want to stay over. That was becoming too much, too. It felt like she had to draw some line in the chronology, had to bring stuff with Kyle to a conclusive end when she left. If not now, if not college, then when?

It was unseasonably chilly, and Renzo kept springing up out of the water to dart inside, bring them all hot drinks in chipped coffee mugs. Mulled wine, hot toddies.

"No glass in the pool," Kyle kept reminding him.

It was getting late, close to midnight, and the wine had a soothing, soporific quality. Clare had never had warm wine before; it would never in a thousand years have occurred to her to heat up wine.

After another half hour, she stood up. Kyle's eyes followed her as she emerged from the water.

"Quit while you're ahead," she said.

"What did I do?"

"I'm going home, I just need to shower first. I'm freezing."

He didn't knock, five minutes later, when he barged in on her shower. She had expected this, had kept her suit on.

"Come on come on come on," he said, over her protests. "It's my house! I'm freezing, too!"

He started cupping his hands, letting them fill with water, splashing her. Then he was tickling her. This was the problem, always. She could turn off her brain and watch them from outside her body and it looked, actually, really fun, like they were in some movie montage. He was an extremely good flirt. It was when it moved past that point that she started to kind of hate what was happening, usually. And then the way he would act later, as if she'd pursued him and smothered him and forced him to pay attention to her. She hated that, obviously.

"Can you not? Can we, like, turn the lights off?"

He pulled back, made a face of genuine puzzlement.

"Sorry, did I not just see your entire body in the pool?"

But of course she was so good at being in the pool, making sure they never really saw her full bare stomach, making sure that her bathing suit covered any problem spots with her bikini wax. This felt different.

"Just, stop."

"Clare," Kyle said, and then something shifted, she could feel him quieting down. He took a step forward and put his hands to her hips. Water kept streaming in her eyes, and he tipped her toward his chest, rested his chin on her head. "Don't be an idiot."

She smiled into his chest, but she didn't pull away. And then something else shifted, the longer they were touching one another. Their wet skin, standing there. Something started to feel possible, or at least, different. She let her hand trace along the top of his swim trunks, felt him growing hard against her stomach. Well, harder. He was kind of always hard, always ready to respond to her.

It felt extremely adult, was the only way she could think to describe it later. Not that she would ever admit this to Renzo, or to anyone. But she felt like . . . Oh, this is why people do this. This is why it's worth it, if you can remember feeling *this* then who cares how he's going to treat you next week. She lifted her face to his and he started kissing her impatiently, staggered backward and tried to step out of his wet, clinging trunks.

And then someone was knocking at the door, insistently.

"Get out of there, you two," Renzo yelled. "I'm starving and Clare's for sure the only one who can drive right now."

Kyle buried his face in her neck, blew a loud raspberry.

"Dude!" he yelled at the door. "What the fuck?"

"Oh, like you two care," Renzo said. "Like whatever is happening can't be delayed an hour? Have you both forgotten that I'm your joint confessor? Don't pretend you've been swept away by passion in there."

Kyle looked down at her.

"I can get rid of him," he said. "Clare, look at me. You can stay over. Don't, like—"

He was always inarticulate, unable to explain himself in any deeper way, but this was the first time she'd ever seen him frustrated by it.

"Don't let him, whatever," he finished.

"Let's . . ." she began. She brushed her fingers against his shoulders, his chest. As she grazed his nipple, he bit the inside of his cheek.

"Let's just go get something to eat," she said. "I'm just—I don't know, I'm exhausted. I would love to, like. Eat three tacos and then go to sleep."

"Right," he said. "Fine." He reached past her, roughly, to turn off the shower. It was, for Kyle, the equivalent of blind rage.

Still, she went with them. She felt like she had no choice. At Cactus, up on Beverly, they sat down at a picnic table. Kyle, who in spite of Renzo's rationale had insisted on driving, stalked to the window to order. Renzo slid onto the bench across from Clare.

"I'm really sorry," he said. "I didn't think this would be such a problem."

"It's not," she said. "He's just—I don't know why he's pretending to be, like. Every time we've ever had sex he's ignored me for weeks afterward, so."

"Well, but," Renzo said. "You can't remind him that you don't really care either way. He can't have you be the indifferent one. Allow himself to be insulted like that, and risk ruining his little 'chillest bro alive' persona? How humiliating. He needs to hold the power over you and me, you know that."

But immediately his face drained of color, he looked at her with pain.

"I don't know why I said that. That's not true at all. You know as well as anyone, he's—I mean, whatever this is, I don't know, but. I shouldn't—"

He tried to laugh, briefly.

"I sound super fucking ungrateful, don't I?"

"Honey," she said, her voice soft, her eyes fixed on Kyle, who still stood in the harsh yellow light of the taco stand. "You know he's not like that. I mean, this"—she gestured at the night around them—"this is Kyle losing his temper. This is his big swing at starting the conflict. Like, basically just pouting."

"Yeah," Renzo said.

They let it sit there, heavy between them. She couldn't tell if he wanted her to ask him about his mother, to say out loud what none of them had said since the night he'd first showed up on Kyle's front steps almost two years earlier.

"When I was little," she said. She kept an eye on Kyle, reassuring herself that he wasn't yet heading their way. "I would be in the back seat, driving somewhere, and she would yell at me in the car. My mother," she added, but he nodded, it was assumed.

"And everything felt bigger, somehow. You're trapped in the car with that anger, there's nowhere you can go to let it slowly dissipate. And I had this thing I would do in my head. I was sort of too old even by the time I started doing it, I always knew it was silly. It's extremely silly. But I'd just close my eyes and imagine building a brick wall. Like, a literal wall. Actually stacking bricks on top of one another, one by one, crouching behind it. And then, once it was tall enough, I could hide behind it, and I wouldn't be able to feel each word anymore."

Renzo smiled ruefully.

"It's not—I don't know, I'm not comparing anyone," she said. But then he reached for her hand, tossed it between his own. "Even if Kyle gets upset with you, he's not going to, like—It has nothing to do with the bigger situation. You don't need to live in fear that he'll get actually angry, for the first time in recorded history, now of all times. It's not— You can take it at face value, that you're safe with him. You'll always be able to come home to him. Or not home, but, you know. He's there. Whatever happens elsewhere. You know that."

Renzo held her hand, stopped playing with it, stared at the cars slashing past on Beverly.

"Do I?" he said.

"Ren, come on."

"Yeah," he said. "You're probably right."

And then Kyle was back, unceremoniously tossing down their tacos. He stormed off, returned with three different types of hot sauce, placed them neatly in a row. Renzo snickered.

"Okay," Kyle said. "Whatever, let's eat."

She hadn't realized how hungry she was, but mostly she watched the boys. The way they tore into the food without concern, sauce on their faces, licking the wax paper. Kyle reached across the table with a crumpled napkin to swipe a diced onion from the corner of Renzo's mouth. Renzo gathered their detritus and funneled it over to the trash can.

Back at the car, Renzo dove into the back seat and buckled himself firmly in the middle, so that he could lean forward with one hand on each headrest.

"Come on, let's not go back yet. Take us on a Better Homes and Gardens of Hancock Park tour! Remember when you used to drive me around and show me all the Christmas lights? This may be the last time we ever drive together at night, after all. At least until you two aren't mad? I'll simply feel terrible until we reach some kind of détente. Let's just stay in this little sports car together until we do."

They both smiled, avoiding one another's eyes. Renzo made a low noise of satisfaction, and Kyle kept driving, west and then down into the dark, quiet streets south of Beverly. He put on the Broken Social Scene album they'd been listening to for three years straight. Without warning, he coasted to a stop in front of one house, its enormous camphor tree strung with white lights. Soon, he said, immediately after Halloween, they would be replaced with red and green ones, with an animatronic Santa waving from an angled sleigh.

"Sounds subtle," Renzo said. "Understated and elegant."

"Shut up, dude."

"No, no, I love it, baby. If you loved it as a little boy, then I love it."

Kyle drove in repeating loops while he told them stories about who lived where, which homeowners were currently feuding with his mother. The houses were all dark, the sweeping façades frozen in some forgotten golden age.

"I don't know," Renzo said sleepily from the back seat. "Don't you feel like we're wasting all of it? Like, even us, Clare. We were handed all these frivolities at birth and so we're frivolous now in all the wrong ways. We don't appreciate that we could always swim in January, or the ocean, and now we act like we know that it was so beautiful. Because we're leaving. But we never just drive out to the ocean, just to look at it! We barely ever go at all. We're wasteful in all the wrong ways."

"You," Kyle said, his hands gliding across the steering wheel as he finally turned back onto his own street, "are too high."

"Doesn't make me wrong."

"No, but it does make you difficult to converse with."

They parked in front of Kyle's house. They were facing north and Clare could see, suddenly, that the Hollywood sign was framed perfectly between two rows of supplicant palm trees, as if you could lay one long carpet straight from Kyle's car to the hills beneath the white letters.

"How have I never noticed this view?" she said to him. "This is, like, the perfect postcard view."

"Really?" Kyle said. "I mean, yeah."

"This is exactly what I was talking about," Renzo said.

TUESDAY

15

She wakes up and must gather, one by one, the clues. She's in her bra, her underwear is damp, she's wrapped in a towel, and the overhead lights are repulsively ablaze. The bed is made; they're both lying on top of it. Her tongue feels enormous and the place where it meets her throat tastes like curdled yogurt.

She goes into the bathroom and splashes her face with cold water, letting it stream down her nose and into her gaping mouth. She folds toilet paper and rubs violently at the makeup all over her face. She puts on shorts and a bathing suit. Then she goes into the kitchen and, for a second, Jamie is standing there.

She nearly gives up and sits down on the floor.

But it's not Jamie. The man is too tall, too rangy, his hair darker and thicker. Still, for a horrifying moment she's hollowed out. It feels obvious, terrifying, but also logical, finally. There is a new person in the house, so it must be her husband. He will show up this morning, when anyone with a brain will look at her and understand what's been going on. And now it will all unfold. She won't have to worry, she won't be able to make decisions or mistakes. The rest will be easy. Her hand will be forced.

Anyway, there is a man in the kitchen, but it isn't Jamie. He stands at the counter, his hands cupped lovingly around a NutriBullet. He seems to be weighing whether it's permissible to use it. Clare stares at the digital readout on the oven display. It is only eight o'clock.

"Hi," he says calmly and without explanation. He squints a bit, even though he's wearing squarish tortoiseshell glasses with thick rims. Classic pair of Warbys, she assumes.

"Renzo let me in right before he took off for his jog. I hope this is okay? It's just that I'm ravenous."

"Sure," she agrees. "Who are you?"

"Oh, right. Duh. Of course—I'm Geoff? I live with Jess. I'd offer to shake, but."

He indicates his gestating smoothie and then, after one more moment of hesitation, detonates the blender.

So this, she thinks, is Geoff. Definitely *not* Warbys, then. He's dressed for cocktail hour at the family compound on the Old Saybrook waterfront rather than a sticky tropical getaway. The Patagonia vest; the striped button-down that's faded but not tattered; wrinkled and soft-looking Nantucket reds. Very odd that this man lives in Los Angeles, allegedly. But then, isn't that perfect? Jess can live in LA, firmly within her lifelong comfort zone, and still end up with the WASPy future patriarch she felt she was destined to meet at Yale.

Immediately, Clare chastises herself. There is every possibility that Jessie's boyfriend will be someone witty, and warm, and amiable. Thoughtful, even. A fun addition to the house for the rest of this week. *Your husband is also, technically, a finance bro*, she reminds herself.

"So, does she—"

But the door down the hallway has already opened, footsteps are padding into the kitchen, and then an ecstatic shriek has answered Clare's question. Jessie leaps at Geoff, wrapping her legs around his waist. His arms cord with muscle, it's clearly no effort at all for him to lift Jessie to the counter just as cleanly as you'd place a vase of cut flowers in that same spot. Another guy who would have just been skinny, she thinks, except that after graduation he hired a trainer to make him feel strong.

Jessie dislodged the Bullet from its base when she jumped him, and Geoff pretends to admonish her for this. He does, though, seem genuinely eager to finish blending the smoothie, proceeding even as Jessie drapes herself across his body, burrows into his neck. She keeps darting looks back at Clare, who shoots a stiff-armed thumbs-up. Clare has never seen Jessie this unguarded and goofy, this unashamed of her own need.

As soon as the smoothie has been poured, though, they're sucking face again, straining Clare's benevolence.

"Could I just," Clare tries. They hear nothing. She desperately needs a glass of water, but she doesn't want to squeeze past them to get to the refrigerator.

He wrenches himself away, finally, to sip at his smoothie.

"I didn't realize this house had a NutriBullet," Clare offers.

"Oh," he says. "No, this is just my travel setup. I've got the Vitamix at home, obviously, but, you know. Not as practical to just toss that one in the carry-on."

Clare smiles. At least they don't seem to care that she's standing there watching them nibble at one another's bottom lips. No one is curious. Liam's blankets and pillow are on the sofa, exactly where they should be.

And then she hears the screen door snap at the front of the house, and he and Renzo are tumbling into the kitchen.

"Look who I found suspiciously vagranting around outside," Renzo announces. "I can only imagine how many power-walking resort doyennes he frightened before I rounded him up."

"I was looking for *you*, Lorenzo. Forgive my friendliness, I forgot that you prefer outright hostility."

"Oh, of course! You were merely seeking the pleasure of my eight o'clock company. The plan was to join me for a barefoot mile?" Renzo stares pointedly at the loose sweatpants hanging off Liam's hips, his exposed toes.

Staring at Liam's feet feels like an intimacy somehow beyond what they've done, what Clare desires. She thinks of Olive's toes curled against his thigh last night. She looks away.

"I woke up, couldn't sleep, decided to go for a walk. Figured I might as well seek out the one person whose rigorous vanity guaranteed he'd already be up and in action. Also, isn't running barefoot, like, the thing to do? Isn't that what all the actual fitness heads are recommending these days? I'm surprised at you, bro. Such a blinkered perspective from such a proud heterodox thinker! Still out there pounding the pavement in actual shoes, like some sad misguided suburban father of two? What would Goop say if GP could see you now?"

Renzo shakes his head in wonderment, sucks his teeth.

"Oh, you. I cannot *believe* you. You are simply, let's say it, *beyond* belief. How dare you! I resent that, deeply. I told you about the coffee enema colonic business, whatever it was, in confidence."

He turns to the rest of them to make his case, but Jessie interrupts.

"Boys? Hi! If we're not even going to acknowledge Geoff's presence, can we at least refrain from talking about Goop for, like, the first ten minutes? Just so, you know, we're not immediately parodying ourselves?"

"Renzo is beyond parody," Liam says, shrugging happily. "Sorry, Jess." He pours himself a glass of orange juice and waves uncertainly at Geoff.

"It was an *adventure*!" Renzo hisses. He had clapped Geoff's shoulder, to say hello, but now he spins back on Liam, advancing on him with his brows knitted. "It was an *ironolonic*, okay? You know this. I suppose all would be forgiven if I'd let you write about it, if you'd gotten one of your little essays out of it? Why did I ever tell you about that? Why do I tell you anything?"

"Hey! Low blow." Liam raises both hands in surrender. They're laughing, but Clare saw it, at the mention of the "little essay"—a slight softening of Liam's features, like winds blowing patterns in the sand. But it disappeared just as quickly; he let it go. *How does he do that so easily?* she wonders. *Can he teach me?*

"Oh, hello, Clare," Renzo says brightly. "I'm pleased to see you're still with us. Have you thanked Liam?"

They all turn to look at her except for Liam, who opens the refrigerator again and peers into its corners. Clare's headache expands, compressing her skull.

"He essentially had to carry you back," Renzo says. "No one wanted to tear him away from his ravishing older woman, but he did ultimately fall on his sword and bring you back so that the rest of us could stay out.

And then, evidently, checked on you this morning to make sure you weren't aspirating your own vomit, or whatever. Quite the little party animal."

"I don't think Olive is really all that much older than us," Jessie says. "I was looking at her last night, like around the eyes and her neck. I think she's probably not even forty."

"Irrelevant to her future with our boy!" Renzo says.

Liam looks over at Clare, finally.

"Thank you," Clare croaks. Something fragile hangs in the air, an eggshell just before it's brought down against the bowl's rim.

"I think your jeans are probably still sitting by the pool," Renzo says.

"No, I grabbed them for her," Jessie says. They're all talking as though Clare isn't in the room.

Her headache is the kind that generates its own heat, like brain cells are boiling. She thinks of that novel Renzo loved so much in high school, the whole thing in the second person, the party boy doing cocaine in lower Manhattan. *It's four a.m., do you know where you are?* This is that kind of hangover. She has not blacked out like that in years.

You should read, Renzo said in high school, when he gave her that book. Everyone always described it, he said, as a book about rich young things in the city. But the main character wasn't actually rich; he was just some rando from Kansas who surrounded himself with rich party kids, and everyone who read it really only remembered that. *This could be constructive for us, right?* he'd said. *Something to consider.*

"You know," Jessie muses, "I have to say. I think it's really nice, truly a sign of growth, that Renzo just mentioned his colonic without anyone making some insane homophobic joke. I really think that says a lot about how far you've all come. Maturity!"

"Jess," Geoff stage-whispers, trying for a certain archness but clearly unable to gauge the tone of the conversation, "I think that maybe calling our attention to that fact is, you know, maybe that counts? As offensive? I know I'm new here, but—"

"Yes, trust me, you'd assume so. Until you heard what they normally sound like."

"She's right, I'm quite inured," Renzo confirms. "Don't worry. Years, decades of scar tissue. Nothing pierces the skin at this point. And you haven't even met Kyle or Mac—just wait until they all get going as a group. This started long before I'd even actually slept with a man, mind you. *Question*: What's Ren's favorite position, really his only position? *Answer*: Sitting on a nice, firm, pointy rock, holding the girl's head down with one hand and popping a Cialis with the other. I mean, this is what passed for a punchline, back then. So hilarious, that a friend might be questioning his sexuality. God forbid. They would say this publicly, mind you. At parties, to the girl's face as I took her upstairs! So, you know, a little passing homophobia in adulthood, it's hardly going to, whatever. It's their tragedy if they've never aged past this shocking revelation, that I have sex with men."

There is a silence then that rips right through the fabric of their previous banter. Clare looks at Jessie and Liam and knows that they must have heard it too, the dormant pain, the searing indictment of all the former selves they've never really repudiated. She forgets all of that, she thinks. She never remembers, because it's unpleasant to do so. But of course Renzo remembers.

"You make it sound so ugly," Liam jokes weakly. "Come on, not in front of the new guy, Ren."

Geoff is at sea. He has absolutely no idea what he's meant to say here, whether Liam and Renzo are excavating something poisonous or just running their mouths.

"Look," Liam continues. "Far be it from me to stand here defending the juvenile shit we said back then. But he did in fact use to steal Kyle's father's Cialis. On, like, a regular basis. We wouldn't even have known if he didn't pop the pills in front of us."

"They were always pissed," Renzo tells Geoff. "Let's face it, I had a kill count that these pimply malcontents could only dream of."

"Lovely," Jessie says. "Clearly, I spoke too soon. Babe, as you can see, not a lot has changed since high school. Welcome to Hawai'i, honey."

She grabs Geoff and plants another long, dewy kiss on his mouth.

Renzo claps his hands.

"Were you surprised, chica?"

"Hey, man, seriously, welcome. Sorry to hurl you into the deep end with all the Cialis talk." Liam offers Geoff a hand that's treated with the same gusto previously applied to the NutriBullet.

"I just cannot believe the two of you!" Jessie says this more than once. "Co-conspirators! I'm so impressed."

"Wait," Clare begins. Liam shakes his head, warning her. "You knew?"

"Duh," Renzo says. "Someone had to guide the poor man to our location. I masterminded the whole shebang."

"Wow," Clare says. "Big surprise!"

"Oh, don't pout. You would never have kept the secret."

Renzo scampers over, tickling her ribs and then turning to pull supplies from the refrigerator, all things he'll have little interest in consuming once he's convinced someone else to prepare them: bacon, English muffins, eggs.

"Well," Clare says to Geoff, because she cannot help herself, "I really hope you appreciate the historic nature of this visit. Every other time anyone has so much as mentioned inviting an outsider, Renzo has threatened to cancel the trip."

Geoff puts a hand to his chest, feigning outrage.

"Ouch! Guess I didn't realize I still qualified as an outsider."

"You don't," Jessie says with a glare, just as Clare replies, "You'll always be an outsider."

She has meant it to be light, self-mocking, but the room doesn't seem to hear it that way.

"I thought he was Jamie," she flails. "When I first came out and saw him."

Renzo holds a plastic clamshell of strawberries, passing it back and forth between his hands for a moment as if it's hot to the touch.

"Well," he says, "that must have been a bit of a shock for you, especially emerging from your little Lohan circa 2005 performance last night. The last thing anyone wants to see the next morning is the husband."

Clare stares at him, and even Jessie tears her eyes away from Geoff to glance back and forth. Liam closes his eyes, runs a hand roughly over his face.

"I think Lohan in 2005 is too harsh," Jessie says, unsure how to align herself. "She had too much to drink, Renzo. Everyone's allowed to be the embarrassing one, we can rotate every night. Give her a break."

"Good point," he says, and then it's like he's never said anything, he's smiling at Clare with a complete lack of guile. "Anyway, Clare darling, a little help? People must be starved."

"Bad hangover?" Geoff asks Clare brightly. She smiles with effort.

"Is Jamie . . . her husband?" he murmurs. No one replies.

Renzo hands Clare the cutting board and she draws a knife from the block. They all move stiffly around the kitchen. They have no idea, she realizes, how to be around one another in the presence of this new, unknown quantity. They're posturing for Geoff—*Look, this is exactly how Renzo always teases Clare, this is how crass our jokes always are. Look how well we know one another.*

She slices the strawberries. The cutting board immediately filigrees itself with watery, blood-red stains. Her stomach vacillates between rumblings of acute hunger and the rush of saliva, the suspicion that she may never wish to eat again.

Renzo babbles at Geoff about the flight, the airport and its outdoor baggage claim with vines everywhere, *which, to be honest, it's just showing off, right?* The little plastic cup of grapefruit juice they serve on the shorter hop, with its foil cover and saccharine promise of the island that awaits. It becomes clear, to Clare, why Renzo brought Geoff here. She can see it happening, like one of those bank robbery paint-bombs erupting in slow motion. He's spreading himself all over Geoff, the one part of Jessie's life that she's probably kept at least a little bit separate. He's splashing his approval, his camaraderie with Geoff, all over the place, and he's doing it for his oldest and most loyal audience.

It could be Jameson watching Renzo grind the coffee. She could be catching her husband's eye, watching him suppress a smile each time Renzo says something condescending or passive-aggressive.

Liam has quietly sidestepped his way around the kitchen island, drifting to her side. He places his hand idly on the countertop, just beside
hers, and she feels a wave of utter wretchedness move through her body.
You wouldn't be sweetly making eyes at your husband if he appeared in this kitchen,
she thinks. *What the fuck are you even talking about.*

"Sorry I ruined your night," she mumbles.

He fixes her with his gaze, unsmiling. She shakes her head. She feels
like a dramatic adolescent, it's embarrassing, but truthfully every single
thing that has happened since she got out of bed has made her want to die.

"Anyway. You went out the window, I assume?"

No one is listening to them.

"Yeah," he says. "We're in genuine French farce territory now."

"That's not funny."

"It wasn't supposed to be, I don't think. And it was dumb, he obviously already knew I was in there anyway. I just said you were sick and I
wanted to keep an eye on you. It's obviously fine, Clare, he has no idea,
but even if it wasn't? You understand that—you get that I don't care,
right? I would just kiss you right now. You made it clear last night that
you want me to be available to you, no matter what. Which is fucked,
but you know what? Fine. I'm available to you, Clare. I can't really pretend otherwise at this point. And I don't care who figures it out. If it
were up to me, I'd say fly back to LA with me and stay. Just for a few
weeks. Just take some time. I'm not the one who needs it to be a secret."

She barely moves. They're both barely moving. He takes the knife
from her hand and puts his hand over hers, stroking his thumb slowly
along the length of her index finger. No one is looking at them.

"Don't," she says.

"Nah," he breathes. "I think you like it." He takes his hand away,
returns the knife.

Mac appears behind them without any warning, placing one hand on
Clare's shoulder and one on Liam's. He's shirtless, wearing only boxers.
Liam grimaces.

"Go put some clothes on! Everyone in this house who's in better
shape than I am needs to stop rubbing it in my face."

"Not a chance. Now, who we mad at?" Mac wobbles his chin into Clare's shoulder. "You two look like you're plotting. Co-conspirators."

"Well, lots of that going on this morning. Evidently."

"Clare's offended," Liam says. "Renzo invited Jessie's boyfriend instead of hers and she's pissed about it."

The air between them cleaves. Mac is sleepy but not totally oblivious, not clueless. He shakes his head.

"Okay?"

"How is Kyle the only one still sleeping through all of this?" Liam shouts. His voice has a burbling sound to it, like he needs to clear his throat.

Belatedly, Mac notices that there's a new person standing in the kitchen. Clare watches him find Geoff, then look for Jessie and Renzo. A swirl of something she can't even begin to parse moves across his face before he puts one hand to his head and scratches at his scalp like he's physically trying to shake his thoughts loose. He looks up again, smiles brightly at Geoff.

"Oh," he says. "Shit, man. Hello."

16

Two hours later, she and Jessie are up at the spa. They move in overlapping loops through the steam rooms, the ice baths. Eventually, when Clare is lying wrapped in a towel on the highest bench in the sauna, the door whispers. When she opens her eyes, Jessie is hovering.

"It's fine, Jess. Come sweat it out with me. That was a good call, that we shouldn't do the mints beforehand."

Jessie picks up the ladle, drizzles the rocks with water. She climbs onto the step just below Clare's and breathes deeply, letting the knot of her towel loosen just where it's nestled in her cleavage. Clare rolls her eyes.

They've come up here, just the two of them, because it's easier here than it would have been at the house to avoid one another in pleasant ways.

The boys are playing golf. It took them an hour to get dressed and out of the house, during which time Jessie and Geoff conspicuously disappeared. When Geoff reemerged in his golf outfit, only a nominal adjustment from his travel outfit, Renzo and Liam did a round of catcalls. They pelted him with the blueberries they were eating in fistfuls, while Kyle begged them, with the same thin effort he's summoned all week, not to throw food near his mother's rug. Clare saw Geoff's sheepish grin and her stomach churned, and there were so many possible sources. This was how they would all react to conquests in the next room when they were sixteen, those moments of frenzied, stolen semiprivacy that she and Jamie won't ever experience again, that they never even experienced in front of this group to begin with. She missed him, in spite of everything. And she worried that it was written all over her stupid, obvious face. Her sick longing, her guilt, her jealousy.

And then Renzo was making lewd jokes, and Mac, mouth full of English muffin, admonished him not to be a jerk just because he hadn't gotten *his* dick wet all week, and Clare was muttering that she hated that phrase, and Mac was turning to her with flared nostrils and shouting, "Good morning! I'd love to introduce you to the concept of picking your goddamn battles." And Kyle was pleading again, "What is it with everyone this morning?" And Renzo was insisting that he would dress Liam for the golf course, that Liam couldn't wear his "emotionally tortured little Mediterranean linens" today, and Liam was looking at her helplessly, and Kyle was stooping to rescue the last few abandoned blueberries, and then they were all gone. Jessie emerged from her room and kept running her hands through her hair, gathering it up and then letting it fall shining across her shoulders again. She looked—what other word was there?—happy. And when she said, "Should we take some mints and go hang out at the spa? They'll be gone for hours, they've probably already picked up a thirty rack," Clare said only, "God, yeah, let's."

And now, here they are.

"It's so odd to me," Jessie says. Clare peers down at her. Jessie is, of course, sweating prettily, rivulets trapping tendrils of escaped hair against her cheeks. "Flying all the way to this beautiful island to play golf."

"If it makes you feel better, we've got that massive hike planned for tomorrow, right? So we have an island-appropriate activity on the books."

"God, tomorrow's already Wednesday." Jessie yawns. "And then Friday, we fly home."

"Yep. Anyway, how does it feel? Still basking in the surprise?"

Even without seeing Jessie's face Clare can sense her beaming, her body melting into the cedar.

"It'll be so hilarious, watching Geoff get used to these guys. He's met them all before, I think? Maybe not Liam. But even with Renzo it's usually, like. A quick drink. Not three days in a house together."

"I'm still shocked Renzo allowed it," Clare says. "Actually, made it happen! Must be a good sign, he must approve."

"Right, because I so need his approval." Jessie attempts to toss it off, but she can't do so with any real force.

Clare tries to be kind, says nothing.

"You could have brought him, you know. Just because Renzo wouldn't have wanted to share you doesn't mean your husband couldn't come."

"He had to work."

"Plus, he doesn't like us," Jessie says without rancor.

"Oh, that's not true. He doesn't really . . . know any of you that well."

"Right, but. He's been in your life for, like, ten years. It's okay, I'm not—It wasn't a question. And I get it, totally. I think it's easier because Geoff and I met as adults. I mean, he knows. Obviously. About me and Renzo. He could care less, but he did make a joke right away when they first met, I think Renzo loved it. And Mac, obviously, but."

Clare wonders how this will go.

"Jess, it was such a long time ago. We've now been alive for almost twice that long."

Jessie's nose pokes at the air, as if she's tracing patterns with its tip. But that's her only tell.

"You know what I mean, though. Like, does Jameson know you've slept with Kyle?"

"Even I forget about that sometimes."

"But you know what I'm saying. Although you and Kyle, that wasn't the same thing."

"Nope."

There is a curt silence, not really adversarial in shape. They haven't disagreed on anything. A few fumbles at intimacy and the eventual realization that it wasn't going to be romantic, that even Kyle would, in this context, find a way to make her feel like shit. A period once memorably and offhandedly described by Mac as "when she practiced on Kyle." It hadn't, in any way, been the same thing.

"I don't think Geoff really gets it. Our whole thing, all of us. His friends are from college mostly, and he thinks it's weird I don't keep in better touch with law school people. He barely talks to anyone from high school at all."

"It tends to be one or the other," Clare says. "That's been my experience."

"Which one is Jameson?"

"Oh, college. I mean, he still checks in on his mother, but otherwise he couldn't get out of his hometown fast enough."

"Right, I always forget that he had this pseudo-Dickensian childhood."

This seems callous at best, but Clare lets it pass.

"Do you think that's why . . ." Jessie says. "Like, I don't know. I don't know why you make things so difficult for yourself, but being with someone who's always had to kind of, deal with actual difficulty. He must have never really felt at ease, right? At Dartmouth. Like maybe you couldn't actually be with someone who felt *that* comfortable in the world. Do you think that's why you fell in love with him?"

Clare stares at Jessie, whose eyes are closed. It is, to put it mildly, unpleasant to consider whether her husband would, in fact, agree with this exact summary of their bond. She tries and fails to keep the hard edge out of her voice.

"Why did you fall in love with Geoff?"

"Oh," Jessie says airily, "you can never identify it yourself, you always need other people to point it out for you."

"Like who? Renzo?"

Jessie twists over her shoulder to look up at Clare.

"Sorry," she says. "Did I say something rude?"

"No, I'm just—Sorry. No, you didn't. Can we get out of here, though? Maybe go sit in the pool? I feel like I'm going to faint."

They retrieve the mints from Clare's locker and place an order for a pitcher of mai tais that's waiting for them by the time they make it outside, delivered by yet another fresh-faced teenager uninterested in them, in conversation.

They both ease into the water at the shallow end, groaning as if the spa morning has already been such a grind, and Jessie pours the drinks. Clare shakes five mints into her own palm and then passes the box.

"Anyway," she says. "It will be fun, I assume? For Geoff to see us all together. Plus, I'm always suspicious of women who have no close male friends."

Jessie laughs, a sudden sound like it's surprised even her, her mouth open and her molars visible.

"What?"

"Just, hearing you say that. I remember how important that used to feel. Right? To convince everyone you were one of those girls who just found it *so* much easier to be friends with guys. What was that? What were we proving?"

"Why is that so funny?"

"Because you still feel that way! Right? You think it says something about you, that you surround yourself with them."

"I do not *surround* myself with them. They're my oldest friends, Jess."

Jessie doesn't reply.

"I have female friends."

"You never had very many, though. Right? I feel like you've only ever mentioned, like, one girl from college. Caro, right? Renzo always loved her."

"All I meant was that it's odd, these women who by age thirty have slid themselves into this role where they only ever spend time with men who are friends of the husband, and then only with all the husbands in the room. Like, who gives a shit."

"But that's not what you're saying. That's not what you're noticing. You think you have something they don't have. You can say that this is why, they don't get it because they aren't friends with men. But you just like being around guys."

"My oldest friends? Yeah, Jess, I enjoy their company."

"Guys who flirt with you, who pay you that attention."

"I wasn't the one flirting with college kids last night!"

Jessie starts to say something, bites her lip.

"Well, you, I mean, sure. All I'm saying is, you just want someone to have a crush, even if it's totally harmless. It's like the guy on the boat."

Clare recoils. Two seconds more and she'd be able to keep her next impulse in check, but she doesn't wait.

"Well, talk to me when you've been married for a while," Clare says.

Jessie smiles then, but it's more of a wince, and so of course Clare regrets it. Why is it always so difficult to just let it all go? What is it about Jessie that leaves her so uncertain of what it is she's even *trying* to let go?

"That's always what it comes down to, right? I'm not married."

"I didn't mean anything by that, Jess, I just—you're what, a year in with this guy? Sometimes it feels good to be reminded that your nerve endings remember the concept. Flirting with someone who wants to flirt with you."

"You sound so bitter! I've met your husband. He's crazy about you."

"I'm not bitter. I'm just, you know. Marriage is a different thing."

"So you've reminded me," Jessie says in a singsong. "But I was so jealous, then. When you got married."

Clare is surprised by how deeply wistful this sounds. Jessie, of course, wasn't at her wedding. Only Renzo and Mac were. And on the morning after Jamie proposed on an unremarkable street corner in Back Bay, his Adam's apple straining each time he swallowed, on the morning after she'd said yes even though what she was thinking was *Already?*, on the morning she had tried to find a way to ask him that and his only response had been laughter and "Come on, Clare! What are we waiting for?"—on that morning, when they took a bottle of champagne into bed and started calling people, her high school friends were some of the last people she called. Because the truth was that they knew her better than Jamie did, but they also no longer really knew her at all. And they'd never figured out how to explain that to one another, out loud or otherwise.

"I was . . ." she starts, almost losing her nerve. "I was feeling so jealous, earlier. When you guys were mooning around the kitchen. That swoon feeling, like teenagers."

"Oh," Jessie says, as if she actually cannot conceive of Clare feeling openly and casually covetous of something she has. "Well, but, when you got married. I was barely out of law school. And you were already, you were just, done."

"I don't really think of it as 'done.'"

"Sorry, that didn't sound—"

"No, I mean, I don't really think of it as anything. It's idiotic, I know, but I think my mind didn't fully understand that now we can never break up. We had been together five years and we lived together but now we're married. We will never be able to, just, go our separate ways. It would be getting divorced, which is different. I don't know why, but I didn't fully understand that. I don't think I did. It's so obvious."

"Your mother or someone didn't warn you?"

"My mother and I don't really talk about, I don't know. Marriage."

Maybe, Clare thinks, she should keep talking. Maybe saying some of it will break the spell. She just fucking wants someone to admit it, out loud. That there's always going to be panic beneath the clarity, that planning for the future does not eliminate that white-hot, rudderless feeling of wanting to look not forward but off to the margins. To the edges of your peripheral vision, right where your present bleeds back into your past.

She sucks on her mints until they're wafer thin, until she can swallow the shards. She flattens her palms just beneath the water.

"I sometimes wonder, though," she finally says. "I just look at Jamie and think—we will never be able to surprise one another ever again. I will never wonder if he's about to kiss me. We have the potential to hurt each other, and to be surprised by that, I guess. But that's about it. Don't you feel that way? Sometimes?"

"*You* don't actually feel that way," Jessie says mildly. "You're not re-membering what it felt like. Taking your clothes off in front of someone who would later text his friends about whether your wax met his standards. Sitting at dinner with two guys you consider friends and listening to them just rip apart some girl from your seminar, how there were too many teeth involved when she went down on their teammate the night before. You're not remembering what it feels like to spend an hour crafting an explicit text to someone who ignores it until he's sure that his first choice isn't interested."

No, Clare thinks, she's not remembering those things. She's remembering the opposite, when you sent someone an explicit text and he immediately stood up from wherever he was and walked to the bar to find you and shoved you up against a wall in the bathroom. Pushed your underwear to one side and left a trail of saliva from the nape of your neck all down along your spine. Held himself at an odd angle the next day because he'd torqued his neck but had been unwilling to stop.

"Well," Jessie says, as if she's listening in. "Maybe every guy was just always obsessed with you, Clare. But Jameson can't stay some huge mystery forever, right? You're building a life and are, like. *Married.*"

"Right, sure."

"I mean I guess at some point we can all just decide to be selfish monsters," Jessie says again. "But that doesn't seem realistic."

No, Clare thinks. *It is not realistic to be a monster.*

"You're sounding awfully wise," she says. "About marriage."

"You mean, for some girl who's still not married?"

"No, Jess. That wasn't what I meant at all."

"It's okay, I'm just teasing."

"Is that where this is headed, presumably? You're thinking you'll marry Geoff?"

"I think so. I mean, we want the same things. And I want to have kids, so. In the next few years that should probably happen."

Clare nods, pours herself a second mai tai. She wasn't even conscious of swallowing the first one, actually. Jessie sips at hers.

"Here's the thing I think about," Jessie says. "Are you telling me that all women are just totally cool with not being able to drink at all for nine months during which you're more anxious and physically uncomfortable than you've ever been before?"

She's holding her hands in front of her face now, inspecting a nonexistent manicure. She peers at Clare.

"Do I sound like an alcoholic?"

"Not *all* women," Clare says.

"Excuse me?"

"Not all women want to have children. Also, I think that's been re-vealed to be bullshit. That pregnant women, like, mustn't touch a drop. I think that's just women being infantilized by the medical establishment at every turn. Supposedly women in Australia drink throughout their pregnancies, so."

"Right, but who wants to test that theory? Actually." Jessie piles her hair on top of her head, the ends wet, water running down her neck. "Here's a question. Do you think your mother . . . do you think she really wanted children? Like, actually wanted them. I always wonder if mine was turning thirty now, instead of the late eighties. If she would have chil-dren."

Clare repositions herself, settling onto a lower step. Her mother had always expressed disdain for the obsessive nature of Clare's friendships. It began as a distaste for the casual opulence of Jessie's world, of Kyle's, but it had spread to include everything, Clare's devotion to them all. Her parents had made some bargain with each other, some agreement that if they were never again going to occupy the same social class that Clare's grandparents had, then fine, but then they also weren't really going to need *anyone* socially, no one beyond each other. They were not going to compete, not going to compare themselves. And then, suddenly, that was all Clare ever did.

By the time Clare was in high school, her mother seemed to operate under the assumption that if they weren't going to be supporting her *beyond* her teenage years, then they didn't have standing to impose es-pecially stringent restrictions on her *during* her teenage years. Why not trust Clare to come and go on her own recognizance? If Clare was in the house by ten a.m. on Sunday, safe, intact, and self-possessed, why pry into where she'd been? Clearly Clare would follow these boys all over the West Valley every weekend no matter what.

Clare had not understood until she met Jameson that this was, in fact, an unusual approach for most mothers who worried about money. That Clare's view of the world, when she arrived at Dartmouth—her slapdash mix of constant, looming fear and aggressive, casual disregard for her own safety—was an uncommon one among girls who had grown up as she had, with the perpetual awareness that while there was plenty available to her, any part of it could well evaporate within the month.

Then again: most women in her mother's position were not raising their daughters in close proximity to children like Kyle or Mac, Jessie or Liam.

"I think that my mother . . . I think she married my father without really articulating, at least for herself, what that meant. That she was kind of falling off the bottom rung of something she'd been clinging to, maybe. I mean, she grew up with practically nothing, but—"

Jessie bristles and Clare knows immediately what she's thinking. It's terrible, to know so much more about one another than they would if they'd met as adults. *But then, everything was so secretive in high school*, Clare thinks. *I would never have talked openly with her about any of this. We only knew what we could piece together, whatever we hated ourselves for revealing.*

"I don't mean—Nothing. Sorry. I know that the way your mom grew up was—I mean, my mother, it was. Things were modest, but it was like—I understand that my grandfather was once, like, wealthy, my mother didn't have 'nothing,' that was a dumb thing to say. Anyway. I think she'd always had a sense that she had to make up for all her father's losses in her own life. So she married my dad thinking they'd keep scheming, they'd figure it out. But they never did. And then they have me, but she has trouble getting pregnant again."

"I didn't know your mom had fertility issues."

Clare says nothing, just feels it building in her sinuses, across the bridge of her nose.

"Sorry," Jessie says. "Continue."

"No, it's just that—I don't know. I don't think she ever really wrapped her mind around what her life ultimately looked like, and I think, you know. I reminded her of that."

Clare lets herself drift until her lower lip touches the water, then resurfaces.

"My mother had these, pajamas," she says. "This is stupid."

"No, tell me."

Clare can see, on Jessie's face, the same tentative eagerness she's feeling. The sense that this is their one chance to get along.

"She had these beautiful pajamas some distant relatives gave her for Christmas one year, like silk, or maybe linen? They were cobalt blue, but striped, sheer, and they just kind of floated against her skin. They were so soft, I loved them. But the fabric was so thin and delicate that they had holes, after a few years, and she was going to get rid of them. So I begged her to let me keep them."

Jessie nods uncertainly.

"I folded them so carefully, put them in my drawer. And they smelled like her. But she kept saying they were in tatters. And I kept saying, 'But why do you care, let me have them.' And she took them out of the drawer and was holding them up, thrusting them at my face, like, *look*—they have holes in them, what will people think of you. This is how you behave if you're *poor*. She actually said that. And I kept saying, 'Just let me have them, why does this bother you?' And then finally she just held them up and fully ripped them in front of me. Just ripped them into these long shreds, so that I wouldn't be able to wear them at all."

Jessie blinks.

"And I remember thinking, *She's always telling me I'm ungrateful, that I have no idea what she gave up for me.* But it felt like that was actually sweet, wanting to keep these pajamas because I associated them with her? And it made her so angry, for some reason. And if it was about the luxury, whatever the pajamas cost, then why had she happily worn them for so long? And who was it, exactly, who was going to see me and deduce, from the state of my pajamas, that I was poor? I just remember standing there in tears, feeling pretty sure that it wasn't my fault but not understanding what had happened, like, at all."

"Sure," Jessie says slowly. "None of that is about whether she wanted to be a mother, though."

Clare exhales with a childish breezy noise, *pffff*.

"I don't know. Sometimes it's like, you can see how unhappy they are, but you can't figure out which parts of that have to do with you. I knew there was some line drawn between my grandparents and then my father and then me, like we were insulting her as a collective, but I couldn't figure out how to erase it, I guess? And I was always just . . . not the hypothetical child she might have had, I'm the one she got. And then I come home from this school she can barely afford and act like I'm ashamed that we don't have a guest house, you know? That we never went skiing."

"That sounds kind of brutal," Jessie says.

"Yeah, well. It's just a theory."

When the pitcher is mostly empty, they stand up and pad inside, leaving their wet footprints as they go. They stand side by side beneath a rain showerhead in a giant tiled room with a garden planted beside the shower and rafters left open to the sky above. They wring out their bathing suits, slip into the robes left for them on hooks, dress in silence. The mints have taken effect, and it feels so easy, suddenly, to be quiet together.

Jessie comes to stand beside her at the mirror, the warm lights bathing their skin in a flattering glow.

"What now?" Clare asks.

"Let's go for a walk."

They wander the paths that lead through the resort, emerging near the edges of the property, the cultivated lawns with sweeping vistas of the beaches below. As they walk in silence, Clare looks up at the sky, slips off her sandals and carries them so she can feel the grass beneath her feet. *Why not?* she asks herself eventually. Why not Jessie? Who cares? What if the problem is just that they never talk about anything important when the boys aren't in the room? If they've known one another this long, there must be something there. She thinks of the cord she imagined between them in the water the other day, the way Renzo snapped it without trying. But there are other cords. There must be.

"There's this other thing," she says abruptly.

"I'm actually kind of worried that we're wandering into the golf course?" Jessie says. "I don't know. What if we literally ran into the boys? How funny would that be. Let's sit down?"

She drops, immediately, into a perfect lotus position. Clare sits beside her.

"I got pregnant last year," she says. "I had a miscarriage."

She holds up a hand, to get out in front of Jessie's instincts.

"You don't have to say anything, Jess. I realize that even just telling you that, it makes it awkward."

"Jesus, Clare. Something can be sad without being an embarrassment."

They're both silent again.

"I'm so sorry. I really am. I'm so sorry to hear that."

Clare adjusts her sunglasses.

"Thank you."

"How far along?"

"Ten weeks, about."

"Have you tried again, since?"

"I wasn't actually trying then," she says. "It was kind of a surprise."

"Oh, wow. That must have been such a mindfuck for Jamie, too. You've just barely processed it."

She's told Jessie something so naked, so personal, but even now she can't tell the rest. Clare lets her assume what anyone might: Jamie knew, he waited with her for the digital test readout, they made a little game of switching their wineglasses in public for a month. He was there for the ultrasound. He was beside her in bed that weekend, while she bent in half and cried so hard it felt like her throat was shredding, like eventually she would heave up all her smashed, useless organs.

"Yeah," she says instead. "I hadn't really—I hadn't processed it yet, either. That I was actually pregnant. And then I was lying there with my feet in the stirrups looking at, you know. Effectively a blank screen. They say something dystopian that is I guess supposed to sound less harsh? Like, 'There's blood flow here and here but we don't see any blood flow circulating to this specific spot.'"

Jessie shudders.

"Was it—I'm sorry if this isn't my business. But physically, was it awful?"

Clare is still, improbably, carrying her bulbous cocktail glass. She pulls out two pineapple wedges and passes one to Jessie.

"I mean, there was a lot of blood. Sorry."

Jessie's mouth has drawn thin at the corners, her cheeks pale.

"Well, anyway, I don't have to go into it. But no, it was painful, but not so graphic. They gave me fucking Percocet, which seems like a little cautionary American parable I made up but is actually what happened. They gave me, like, a lot of Percocet."

"Is it something where you find out and then you can do it that same day?"

"No, you have to go back two days later, just to be sure. But the second day it was a different doctor, a dude this time, and he was immediately like, 'Why don't you wait, let's get another day of hormone levels, maybe your math is off, I have to tell you, if you were my wife, I wouldn't want to do anything yet—'"

"Jesus, Geoff would have cold-cocked him, I think."

There is something almost rancid about the pride on Jessie's face when she says this, her rich, creamy belief that this man she hasn't even known that long would commit sudden and pointless violence on her behalf, that it would be proof of his love. Clare opens her mouth but then thinks, *I don't know, maybe let's just leave it?* Is this personal growth, her ability to decline to nettle Jessie? For a moment, she wishes Renzo was here to see it.

"He's lucky that Jamie is so even-tempered!"

Jamie had not been there. Clare tries not to think about the fact that, after today, Jessie will know about this and Jamie still won't.

"Anyway, I got him to sit down and read the chart. Something he could have maybe done before he walked in, but. I explained again that it was abundantly obvious to me exactly which week I got pregnant. He listened to me, and I think he felt bad, honestly. Maybe that's why he threw in the Percocet. But I took the pills at home the next day."

"And then you just have to wait? What did you guys do?"

Again, she thinks about whether she wants to say any of this to Jessie. But why not? In six months, she has not wanted to tell anyone else. What if it's possible to craft intimacy this way, by abandoning your own secrets? Besides, she's rolled the words around in her mouth like marbles for so long that they've lost all luster, they sound like nothing at all finally spilling out.

Abandoning *some* secrets, she cautions herself. No matter how many mai tais you suck down, only some secrets.

"I just kind of drifted around the apartment. I'd sit on the couch and watch fifteen minutes of a movie, then turn it off and go into the bedroom and start a different one. And then I realized I could drink again—"

She already expects Jessie's raised eyebrows, the sweet-and-sour smile on her face.

"Yeah, yeah."

"Sorry, I—Was that funny? I thought it was funny."

"And then at some point I realized I had this packet of Gauloises in my bathroom cabinet? That I bought when I was, like, nineteen years old. In Paris. And I'd never opened them. And I was like, yep. That sounds perfect, honestly. And I found a lighter and a huge hoodie of Jamie's and bundled up like the Abominable Snowman in summer and went out looking like an actual crazy person, and just walked around in a loop and smoked a cigarette."

Jessie nods, crunching on an ice cube.

Clare can feel that she's going to cry. She knows there is nothing, at this point, she can do to make it otherwise. "It was just, I hadn't even planned for any of it to happen to my body. I wasn't that excited about it. But then once it was no longer happening, I just felt so fucking wretched."

Clare almost spits the word, and Jessie, surprised, begins to rub one palm in obsessive circles with the thumb of her other hand, as if she'll be able to transmit some sense of calm to Clare without touching her.

"Sorry," Clare says. "But it just felt like—what the fuck is the point of my body now? I just walked around feeling like a husk, because for a few weeks, for once in my life, I had known exactly what my body was for. I felt, like, anchored. I wasn't drifting around anymore, I was anchored in place, I had a job to do, and I had a reason to take care of it. My body. I always assumed I would hate that part, that you're a bad mother if you can't at least pretend to love the idea of being fully subsumed. And then I got pregnant and I don't know if it was really, like, being subsumed exactly. But it just felt like such a relief. I would look at the berries I was washing three times, and the flax seeds I was pouring over yogurt in the morning, and the vitamins. And it felt like—I fucking hate even saying this. I hate it so much."

She pauses, but she can tell that Jessie is afraid to open her mouth, afraid to interrupt.

"It felt like my body was, like, holy. There was this divine purpose for it, it made sense now to keep it alive. And then I walked around smoking that cigarette and getting drunk and thought, What's the use of my body now? It feels like it has no purpose anymore. It doesn't matter what I put inside it, where I drag it, how awful I feel tomorrow, if my tongue tastes like I licked a fireplace. It's not mine anymore. For a while it felt so . . . purposeful. But now it doesn't even feel like it's mine."

She chokes in the middle of the last sentence.

Jessie, for once, knows exactly what to do. She just waits.

"That was what I hated," Clare says. "Not the feeling itself, but the idea that I would be someone who felt that way. That I only felt useful if I could, like. *Gestate*. I didn't know if I wanted to have kids. And then suddenly I don't think I'm living up to some feminine ideal or being a good wife or, whatever. Just because I'm not pregnant anymore? And why have I never in my life felt like my body was something holy on its own? And when I've always felt such disdain for women who decide that this makes them more special than women who can't or won't? That was the embarrassing part."

Because it would have made up for the past few years, she thinks and does not say. *Because I would have told Jamie, eventually, that I was pregnant. And the scales would have righted themselves again. I wouldn't be this dead weight anymore, I'd be someone with a purpose, someone who resembles the girl he met in the fraternity basement in New Hampshire.*

"None of it's embarrassing," Jessie says softly. She looks genuinely sad, unsure if she should come closer to Clare, who shifts away slightly, just in case.

Clare rubs one hand across her streaming nose. She stares out across the lawns, to the view they're now too low to the ground to see. All of it, the ocean, the roads below, the entire view, has disappeared as if it's fallen off an edge.

"I have to tell you," Jessie says. "It sounds like, even before you had a miscarriage. You sound like you are maybe a tiny bit depressed."

Clare laughs again.

"If it makes you feel any better," Jessie continues, "I've never felt that way, either. My body has never once felt like it's, I mean. Holy? Never in my entire life. I just, I don't know. I find it hard, sometimes. Being around them all in a group like this. I mean, it's hard to forget what it used to be like. That I only ever evaluated my body according to what they said about it, or something? I don't know. You couldn't fucking pay me to be sixteen again."

Clare stares at her. "Yeah. I actually—I mean, yes. I have been thinking along those same lines all week. The other day, on the boat, Kyle was—"

"I felt bad about that," Jessie interrupts. "I feel like I should have intervened. That was gross. You're talking about the blowjob story, right?"

Again it's unnerving, how cleanly she has intuited what Clare is thinking.

"It was just . . ." Clare says. "I was thinking about what it felt like, walking down that hallway with that boy. And it seems like it should feel more distant, maybe? Like I can't imagine myself being so desperate now, I feel like I know at least a little bit about who I am, compared to when I was sixteen. But it feels too close, sometimes, still."

Jessie smiles.

"It doesn't feel distant to me at all."

Clare thinks again about the boy in that house, the way he pushed her away from him in the dark bathroom when it was all over. The way she understood in that moment that she would have to get very, very good at it, that the twinned miseries of thick saltiness at the back of her throat *and* the knowledge that she had probably screwed it up were just too much, taken together.

"It brings a lot of stuff to the surface, I guess," she says finally. "I think that's probably normal. We know a little too much about each other, maybe. I just—I mean. You still feel it, right? That need for his approval."

"Yes," Jessie says, for once unoffended. She doesn't ask who "he" is. "But that's only when I'm with them. The rest of my life is so separate.

This isn't our real life at this point, right? Like, Jamie doesn't care about any of this, I'm sure. So this is just the place we all get to act like children again for a while. Because it's kind of irrelevant."

Clare can hear the hope, how much Jessie wants her to say, "Yes, of course."

"My real life is elsewhere," Jessie says firmly. "Isn't yours?"

They watch each other. Clare nods.

"We aren't actually near the golf course, are we?" she says. "I mean, if we are, we should probably stand up."

"Also, not to be a pill," Jessie says, ignoring her. "But maybe you need more friends who aren't boys we met when we were thirteen, Clare. Just a thought."

Clare smiles. They both sit where they are; they don't move yet.

"And I won't tell anyone," Jessie says. "You know that."

Los Angeles

The third text came through around six o'clock, at which point the line of customers had already wrapped around the corner and down Santa Monica Boulevard. Clare could only see a dozen people from behind the cash register, but Josh, one of the managers, kept trotting outside to jog around the block and report back. They fed into the tiny yogurt shop in an endless stream, ordered their swirls of plain or green tea, funneled back out. One actor always brought a girl to wait in his place so he could buy one yogurt, eat it greedily in the sun, and then slide back into line to buy another almost immediately. He had done this twice already today.

ur coming, right? Clare shoved her phone back into her apron pocket, aware that the owner watched them on closed-circuit cameras. She'd told Jessie she would be there. Jessie, who also worked here, knew Clare's shift wouldn't end much before midnight.

It was unclear what the urgency was until the fourth text arrived, just as evening finally tipped into night. Clare loved how late this happened in the summertime, how endless the days felt even though she spent them indoors, listening to Korean pop and ringing up yogurt purchases.

ren invited, like, fifteen sophomores??? not even anyone we know??? i am now
officially the only girl here not born in the NINETIES pls don't change your mind

Clare had been working here since May, desperate to pad out her bank account before senior year began. Jessie visited one afternoon in June and abruptly realized she didn't need to spend the summer lying by her pool, waiting for Renzo to call so she could inform him that she'd already made plans with Mac. Who was actually dating another girl, finally, a junior at Archer whose father was also a doctor. Which didn't really render him any less useful for Jessie's purposes, that Clare could tell.

The shop was in the heart of Boys' Town and, besides Clare and Jessie, staffed entirely by gay men in their twenties. The one straight guy, Matt, had called out so often he'd finally been fired without ceremony the week before, and Clare missed the inherent thrill of working a shift with him. Nothing ever happened, of course, Clare knew it wouldn't. That was a story about another, more interesting girl. But something could have happened, in theory, which was enough.

He was older, probably close to thirty. His otherwise standard scruffy appeal was heightened by just the right amount of menace, like still-glowing embers hastily covered over with dirt and ash. Clare had spent hours imagining his dark, close apartment. Being undressed on crumb-strewn, unwashed sheets. Other women's underwear surfacing from the tangle at the foot of the bed like plastic flotsam washing ashore at the beach. She wasn't a virgin, and however feverish her fantasy life in moments of boredom, she was aware that this guy wouldn't have much to offer her if she ever saw him naked, beyond the brute fact of his body. But, still. That body! He used to stretch as he stood behind his register, his store-issued polo riding up to expose his belly, its thicket of dark hair. She was realizing, that summer, that she'd had sex but maybe never felt desire, because that was what happened every time she saw that part of his stomach. She *desired* him. She wanted to kneel on the floor in front of him and run her tongue along his tanned skin. On the days he didn't show up, she imagined him smoking a cigarette on some scuzzy stretch of beach in Venice, ashing into the sand as his body slowly darkened.

Sometimes Clare would watch Jessie behind the yogurt counter, crafting a text message, and wonder. One night last December they'd been at Jessie's parents' place in Malibu, driven golf carts down to the beach and drunk Jäger from the bottle, and Mac and Jessie had stood making out in the moonlight and for a second it had really looked so romantic Clare had wanted to scream. But, still. Was it possible that Jess felt for either Mac or Renzo—Mac! Renzo!—what Clare felt when she looked at this guy, Matt? What she'd never once felt with Kyle, with anyone?

"Dude," Josh said, hustling back through the glass front door with polite apologies to their flushed customers. It was nearly ninety outside. "I think Leonardo DiCaprio's out there, no joke. Clare. Did you hear me?"

Anyway. Matt had been fired for never calling out properly, and now work was dull. The late-afternoon sun glinted, unforgiving, through the glass storefront. Clare shifted her weight between her feet, snuck mouthfuls of carob chips or coconut shavings with her back to the camera. She got free yogurt whenever she wanted it. Leo wouldn't be the first celebrity to show up, if he was indeed outside. The yogurt was a serious trend, all summer. Just a few weeks earlier, the rumpled star of an HBO bro comedy had sauntered in, his green eyes so vivid they looked like they'd been colored in with crayons. Draped himself over the sneeze guard and peered at Clare through dark curls. It felt like time stood still in that shop, lazy and dreamy, every afternoon stalked with the potential that something might happen. By this time next year, she'd be preparing to leave Los Angeles for good. Sometimes she wondered if, when she tried one day to remember how it had felt to be a teenager, all she'd be able to retain with any clarity would be this: the jazzed, pinpricked boredom, the hot afternoons when the sun baked the glass windows of a yogurt shop in Boys' Town.

Once Josh was occupied with a malfunctioning yogurt machine, she slid her phone out of her back pocket. *i think one of them brought smirnoff ice???? also mac is bringing his gf which like fine but would really love to have like one girl here who doesn't make me want to murder*

Clare smiled at that one. It had actually been nice, this summer. She and Jessie were kind of friends, on their own. They had spent, in two months as colleagues, more time alone together than they had in five years of school.

as you know, she typed furiously, *i will be there prob like midnight, will bring yogurt don't hate me, susan probably watching me type this right now phone's about to ring telling me she can see everything on the camera feed, see you soon x*

"I don't want to see that phone again," Josh muttered as he passed behind her, on his way to tame a dispute brewing in the line.

Three hours later, after she'd wiped the tablecloths with a fetid cloth and pressed Saran Wrap to the metal toppings tubs, she drove west to Jessie's, where everyone was still buzzed and swimming in the summertime dark. She cut north through the flats of Beverly Hills, wound her way up into the streets behind the enormous pink hotel, parked her car on the street downhill from Jessie's house, and sent a text from the front gate. This road curved directly behind their middle school campus, a proximity she still found jarring whenever she was here. She'd changed shirts in the car, but her jeans and at this point probably her skin still smelled like twelve summer hours of liquefied strawberries and cleaning fluids. She was too tired to be here, but she felt she should display some solidarity. In the past year, it had become a real bummer to spend time with the boys when younger girls were there, too. Even if you didn't care, it was still harsh. To be reminded of how little these boys were interested, these boys who had once spent whole nights driving you around the city, trying to find a party, trying to make you laugh.

The gate opened with a mechanical thud and Jessie texted. *can you just come find me? i'm in my mom's room*

Clare walked up the long, curving driveway, sidestepped the front entrance with its portico and skirted the garden, came out on the wide lawn and walked down to the pool.

Right away, it was strange. There was, indeed, a gaggle of younger girls swimming. Mac was nowhere in evidence. Kyle lay by himself on a lounger, shirtless, missing a shoe.

"Hi," she said, standing over him. He opened one eye, squinting up at her, and she could see that he was uncomfortably high. "Long night already?"

"Hey babe," he said. "Didn't think you'd make it."

"Here," she said, handing him a gigantic tub of yogurt and a plastic spoon. He yelped.

"Oh," he said. "You're so good to me."

"Whatever," she said. "Have you seen Jessie? She sent me a weird text?"

"Yeah, no," he mumbled. "I'm trying to stay out of it."

"Shocking." She looked over at the pool, waved at the girls, most of whom waved back. "Do you even know any of these people?"

"Not my house, not my plan, it was Renzo's plan," he slurred. "And he took off."

"Are you going to need me to drive you home?"

He waggled his eyebrows and then shoved a heaped spoonful of yogurt into his mouth.

"You'd love that, wouldn't you, Clare Bear."

"Please don't call me that and do not flatter yourself. I'm going to find Jess, but if you need a ride home, come find me. Is your car here? Do not drive home. Kyle?"

But he was up, invigorated by his snack, using his bare foot to wedge off his remaining shoe.

"Ladies!" he shouted. "Chicken fight?"

"Wait," she called. "Where's Mac?"

He thumbed over his shoulder, nodding at the pool house.

"Someone should tell them to turn the lights off."

Clare looked over and saw the warm glow from one window, the last bedroom at the end. Jessie's pool house was, of course, roughly the size of Clare's actual home. Whatever Mac and his girlfriend had been doing would have been fully visible from the pool. She wondered if Mac already knew that.

"You're disgusting!" she yelled, but Kyle was up on the diving board, balanced on one leg, pretending to fall. The girls were clapping. One of them was topless. Clare watched for a moment, ambivalent. Then she walked back up toward the main house.

Upstairs, she tried to remember which room belonged to Jessie's mother. It was intriguing, that Jessie had identified it not as her parents' room but as her mother's, but that was likely an issue to be explored another night. Renzo was apparently gone, and it was when he treated Jessie with the most villainous lack of feeling, when he was really an absolute dick, that Clare felt obscurely responsible for his behavior. As though her very willingness to be his friend was just another slap in the face to the girl whose heart he broke so frequently.

There was a door ajar at the end of one hallway, so Clare gave it a shot. She knocked, twice, and then pushed it open. A bedside lamp was on, and the sheets on the bed were wrinkled but undisturbed, like people had been lying on top of them. Jessie's ballet flats were at the foot of the bed, kicked off at strange angles. A pack of Marlboro Reds lay on the bed, too. So Ren had been here at some point.

She knocked on the door of the en suite bathroom.

"Jess?"

There was a sniffle, a clattering of glass.

"It's open."

She walked in.

At the far end of the bathroom, past the vanity, Jessie was curled in the Jacuzzi tub. She was barefoot, in Soffe shorts and a Yale sweatshirt, polka-dot bikini straps visible around her neck. She put one hand to her face with a jerking motion, swiping at her eyes, and when she brought it away her thumb was black with wet mascara. She looked fucking awful.

"Hi," Clare said uncertainly. She held out the yogurt. Jessie took it, stared at it like she had never seen such a thing before, placed it down neatly beside her. Clare sat down on the gleaming steps that led to the tub, resting her chin on her hands.

"I met those girls downstairs," she said. "Kyle's clearly loving the attention."

"Is Mac still here?" Jessie said, her voice tilting up at the end of the sentence.

Clare nodded.

"I think he's—I think they're maybe in the pool house."

Jessie nodded vaguely.

"Sure," she said. "Of course. How was work, though?"

Clare shrugged.

"Without Matt," she said, trying to sound jaded, trying to make Jessie laugh, "there's not much to live for, is there."

Jessie looked blank, as if she could recognize the rhythms of a joke but couldn't decipher the words.

"Did you . . ." Clare tried. "Was there a fight, or something? You and Ren and Mac? It's been a while, I know things have been more, I don't know. Peaceful. But did something happen?"

Jessie shook her head.

"Why did Renzo leave, then?"

Jessie laughed, once, but it sounded like it cost her something to make the noise.

"Why do you think," she said. "Any time I'm not willing to just, like, lie back and let him completely control me. Any time I try to stand up for myself at all. He loses his mind."

Clare felt something cold seep through her in that moment, something more than fear but less than comprehension. She couldn't just stand up and leave the room. She couldn't just ask Jessie to talk to someone else about it. Someone else, like who? Mac? Kyle?

"What do you mean," she said. "What do you mean, lie back."

Jessie looked at her with sudden hatred, her eyes so red she looked like an animal.

"He thinks he can just insult me all night," she said. "Rub my face in it. I mean, he is more or less openly dating a boy right now! We all know about it, the guy from Silver Lake. And then all night, he . . . he actually did a body shot off one of those girls! And then he told me he wanted to talk and we come up here and he thinks it's just going to be, like, a given? Like of course I would want to have sex with him?"

Clare felt her shoulder blades draw toward one another, her weight shifting back onto her heels to prepare for escape.

"Well," she said. "Jess, I mean. You usually do want to."

"Thank you, Clare. Thanks. Jesus. I am trying to, like. Set some new patterns for myself. And I told him, repeatedly, that I *did not want to have sex with him tonight*. Every time he told me he'd be my puppy dog, every time he told me he'd follow me around for the rest of the summer, that he wouldn't be able to get me off his mind, that we'd be together. I told him that I *was not interested*."

Clare felt it again, the chill. Freezing her fingers, closing off her throat. She couldn't believe Renzo still spoke to Jessie this way. If he actually had. If he'd said any of it in reality, or if it was just what Jessie wanted to believe she'd heard.

"Jess," she said slowly. "Did he—Is what you're telling me that he had sex with you anyway?"

Jessie put the heels of her hands to her eyes, swiped them violently under her lashes again. Her cheeks were blotchy, swollen, like she was having an allergic reaction to the air.

"No," she said. "He started trying to take my bathing suit off anyway and I had to literally, like, punch him. So I put on a sweatshirt and told him to leave, and then he told me I was still desperate and pathetic, and a total bitch, and that whoever he fucks isn't my business. And he left."

"Did you let him drive, though?"

"Clare." Jessie's voice rang out against the marble. The room suddenly felt cavernous all around them. "I was supposed to follow him downstairs and ask him to be careful getting home? It was—It was bad, Clare, okay? It was like fifty fucking pairs of hands, fighting—I just wanted him to leave. Why is it my job to make sure he gets home?"

"Because if he gets a fucking DUI it will be a very big deal. You *know* his situation isn't like yours, Jess. You know that his parents will kill him if something happens this year. I mean, his mother—Do I need to explain this to you? He's so close to getting away."

"Fuck," Jessie said. She stood up, stepped out of the tub, and padded over to the vanity. She turned on the faucet and plunged down, cupping water in her hands and drenching her eyes, then buried her face in a pillowy cotton towel. When she brought it away it was smeared with mascara, foundation, eye shadow. The stains would never come out, Clare thought.

"You're right," Jessie said. "I should have just let him, and then tucked him in for the night. Brought him fresh-squeezed juice in the morning. My mistake. What was I thinking."

"That isn't what I said."

"Isn't it?"

There was silence until Clare finally spoke.

"I'm sorry, I just—You can't tell me this story and pretend like there's no history, Jess. I'm not trying to be an asshole. It sounds like he was really out of control, tonight, I'm sorry I couldn't get here earlier. But he's acted like this, for, you know. For years at this point. And I kind of think you both enjoy it."

Jessie fixed Clare with a stare so blank it felt like it turned in on itself, like some essential part of Jessie's brain had retreated from the conversation.

"I don't know why I thought you'd get it," she said. "You'll never stand up to him. Not really. You'll bicker with them, but you care just as much as I do. And you think you're the mature one, that because you never ask for *anything* from them, they'll somehow respect you more. I feel bad for you."

"You feel bad for me," Clare said, flexing both hands to avoid saying more. "Okay, well, Jess, I had a really long shift tonight and I have another one tomorrow, and this job isn't a novelty adventure for me, I need the money. So, if this is all you wanted to say to me, then I'll probably head home."

"Great," Jessie said. She stormed out of the bathroom. By the time Clare followed, the bedroom was empty. She stared at the bed, at the cigarettes. She knew she'd handled this wrong but the contours of what was happening felt obscured, a shape she could feel with her fingertips but couldn't see. More than anything, she just didn't want to know any of it.

She sat down on the bed, fingered the edge of a linen pillowcase. It only now occurred to her to wonder where Jessie's parents were. She thought absently of an afternoon last winter, when she'd run into Jessie and her mother at the Century City mall. Jessie's mother had insisted Clare accompany them shopping for the winter semiformal, and something in Jessie's glance had indicated, to Clare, that she was trying to the best of her own clipped abilities to ask for help. So Clare went along, even though she felt dread—surely Jessie's mother wasn't offering to buy her a dress? And if she was, was it rude to accept?

Of course, she wasn't. She was inviting Clare to watch Jessie try on dresses in a very expensive boutique aimed at the thickening, uninterested wives of the lawyers who worked nearby, a place Clare had never been inside before. And the first time Jessie stepped out, her mother glanced up from her BlackBerry long enough to say, "Oh, sweetheart, not that one. You'll have to suck in your gut all night. That's no fun." Clare felt her jaw actually drop. Not that it mattered, she kept thinking, but Jessie was the thin one! She always had been!

Clare had stood up wordlessly—Jessie's mother having forgotten she was there—and knocked on the fitting room door, slipped in so that they could stand shoulder to shoulder. Jessie's cheeks were pink but mottled, rubbed raw; she'd looked not so different from tonight, in the bathtub. And Clare had reached out to touch her fingertips to Jessie's, testing, before taking her hand and squeezing twice. The salesgirl had knocked behind them, her head floating up in the mirror between their shoulders.

"Honey, you just need the right bra. It's just not quite hanging right. But I can convince your mom, I really think it's stunning!"

But Jessie had chosen, instead, a different dress. Something four times more expensive than anything Clare had ever owned. And when Clare told her mother that story, she'd said only, "That woman is such a piece of work. People like that really think that money is the solution, not an accessory."

Jessie's mother had not grown up the way Clare's mother had, the first generation after the money ran out. Jessie's mother had grown up, to quote Clare's mother, "quite blue-collar." But then she married Jessie's father, and Clare's mother married Clare's father.

"That woman," Clare's mother had repeated. Clare thought of the phone calls she was trained not to answer, her father's fury when she suggested applying for financial aid in the ninth grade. The three times they'd moved houses in Clare's childhood, and his refusal to throw out the cardboard moving boxes in the trunk of his car until they'd lived at the house in Santa Monica for four years. *Wouldn't money be part of the solution for us, though*, she had not said to her mother that day. She'd just nodded when her mother asked if she wanted to borrow an old dress, something from the eighties, for semiformal.

She tried to smooth the sheets on the bed before she left, closing the door behind her. She fought the brief temptation to look for Jessie, walked downstairs instead.

In the driveway, Mac was hopping into a cab. Clare craned her neck, waved at his girlfriend.

"Hey," he said. "Didn't know you were here. Do you know where Jess is? Tried to find her to say goodbye."

"Don't go up there," Clare said, viciously enough that he put up his hands.

"Whoa, what's up?"

"She's just being a fucking drama queen."

"Great," he said. "Well, that's not my problem anymore, so. I'll take your advice."

"Yes," Clare said, gesturing at the cab's back seat. "Clearly, you've totally moved on."

Mac cocked his head. "You have a problem with me, Clare?"

She shook her head.

"Are you okay?" he said, this time with more concern. She looked down the driveway toward the gate, closed her eyes.

It smelled amazing up here, like cut grass and flowers and chlorine and scented candles. The whole neighborhood somehow fragranced, the second you turned up off Sunset. It wasn't the clean brine of the ocean air in the South Bay, wasn't the peppery dust of a hike through Temescal or Griffith. This was jasmine, heliotrope, plumeria and moonflower and hyacinth, flowers that would smell delicious anywhere but that up here smelled like something quite specific: seclusion. You could close your eyes and understand that Beverly Hills had once been just a bucolic, woodsy village populated by the richest people in California. You could remember that there was no grocery store or fast-food outpost or DMV office within walking distance, that the closest place to buy lunch wasn't a supermarket but, in fact, the Polo Lounge. Tomorrow, this reverie would be shattered by the constant jackhammering of new annexes being built, new swimming pools being dug out of the ground. Tonight, though, it was just very dark and very quiet.

Like everything else in LA, this was misleading, it was all a myth. It might feel like you could just pretend you were on some Mediterranean hillside villa, ships bobbing in a twinkling harbor somewhere far below. But on that very block one night forty years earlier, the night of the Manson murders, girls who were camped out in sleeping bags on their middle school's athletic fields could hear the screams. The way noise traveled through the canyons was eerie and unpredictable. It felt wild, like you were in the middle of a forest. You could actually see the stars up here. It did not feel like it existed in the same temporal wedge of existence as the 405 or even just the bars of West Hollywood, the yogurt store.

She hated how much she loved it up here. There was absolutely nothing real to love about this neighborhood, nothing of any cultural salience or topographical interest. Nothing except the money. And she hated that she knew this and loved it anyway.

She opened her eyes and turned back to Mac, who was touching her shoulder now with genuine alarm.

"I have to go," she said. "They were all watching you, by the way. Having sex in the pool house or whatever. They could all see you guys. Not sure if you knew that."

She didn't wait for his reaction. She all but ran down the driveway, pumping her arms, so eager to make it back down the hill to her crappy little car.

WEDNESDAY

17

Renzo forces everyone to agree not to eat lunch until the summit.

They park at the Waimea Canyon trailhead and peer down into the gash of the canyon. All the obvious things are true: she feels small, and insignificant, and intrusive. She can almost grasp what it might be like to view the world in geologic time, to watch the land crumble and shift as if she were blinking her eyes in a sluggish daze. She sees the landscape as it will appear one day soon, after everyone she loves has destroyed themselves and their legacies. That the island will be fine once they've all finally left it alone. But standing here, staring out at the canyon, it feels so silly. To be planning all their little activities, nursing all their little wounds. The striations of color in each cliff face, all the moss greens and bloody reds, the layers almost like cake, so luscious you want to grab hold of them in heedless chunks, smear them across your face.

There is no real way, she thinks, to have a sufficient or even a unique reaction to beauty like this. Kauaʻi, the great unifier: it makes us all boring in the exact same ways.

"Take a picture," Renzo demands of Kyle. "Of me with Jessie and Geoff."

"Okay, so you're not even going to pretend to include anyone else? Is this one of those days?"

"Jesus," Renzo says. "Don't be a bitch about it, you're welcome to jump in. Mac or Clare will take it."

Mac looks at Clare, smiles with phony brightness.

"Of course they will!"

Clare can feel them all gearing up, but Geoff reaches out to snatch the phone from Renzo's hand.

"Wow," he says. "Nothing's too small to get you all going, is it? I'll take it. I am, after all, as we discussed. The outsider."

Eventually, Renzo summons everyone to the trailhead. The hike sends them scrambling down an incline of sand-colored rock formations packed tightly into the dried mud of the hillside. They stagger along sideways, knees bent in a protective crouch. Renzo seems irked by the plodding pace and mostly ignores everyone but Geoff. Jessie and Clare have treated one another with exaggerated courtesy ever since the boys came noisily home from the golf course yesterday, snapping that fragile cord again. At dinner in town, they barely spoke, although to be fair anyone who wasn't Geoff barely spoke. He listened with such poised interest that it took a while to notice what he was actually doing: peppering you with questions, digesting your replies and slotting them into the appropriate categories of his own opinions, then grandiosely explaining whatever you'd said right back to you, this time as a clear reinforcement of his existing worldview.

"I'm just curious," he said to Clare at one point. "Is this really a viable business model? If they paid you more than a year ago and you still haven't produced your deliverable? Is this how the industry operates?"

"Geoff," Jessie admonished him, but without any real rebuke. He was just asking, Clare knew, what more or less everyone, and certainly her parents, was wondering.

"Oh," Clare replied, trying to sound airy, "I don't think industry recognition is what makes me an artist." She said it without looking at Liam, but when she glanced over moments later, he was smiling.

"If it's art, it might take a while," Mac said, tactfully, squeezing her hand under the table. Which was a risk he'd taken, since they were then treated to a few solid minutes of Geoff's meditations on the nature of art.

It seems like his arrival should have helped; he should be a lightning rod, someone who can receive all their ambient annoyances, but it's not working. Maybe it's because he's here with Jessie, and Renzo has always felt that no one else is allowed to question Jessie's choices. *Maybe*, Clare thinks miserably, *no one else finds Geoff that annoying.* Whatever it is, he's added himself to the group like an unnecessary and ill-placed table leg: wherever they press down, the surface refuses to steady.

And of course, it's not his fault that she told Jessie everything yesterday. He isn't the one trying to imagine how it would make Jamie feel, to find out that Jessie knows this thing he doesn't.

At some point, they cross into Kōkeʻe State Park and pick up a different trail. Clare just lets herself stumble wherever she's directed. Her every movement feels like cutting through custard, her eyeballs like they've been rubbed vigorously against the grainy rock beneath her feet.

The sleeping arrangements, naturally, shifted last night. Everyone agreed that Geoff and Jessie deserved the big bedroom, and while they were on this topic, why had Clare been allowed to claim the best room for herself all week?

"He's up and out of here every night anyway," Mac said through a yawn as she set up in the grandchildren's room with him and Liam. "Allegedly I'm snoring; he'll end up on the couch regardless."

Mac then fell asleep in the middle of the movie they put on after dinner, woke up long enough to brush his teeth in total silence, and saluted them both as he crawled into his twin bed. Liam looked over at her, briefly, before climbing into the top bunk above hers.

She lay awake all night wondering if he would climb down, wondering how deeply Mac would really sleep, wondering what was wrong with her. Pretending that her frantic sense of urgency had nothing to do with the looming end to this trip, pretending that she wasn't always giving herself permission well before the actual moments of transgression.

The trail becomes suddenly vertical, a narrow dirt path thrashed out of the underbrush with little more than random outcroppings of rock to use as handholds. When it levels out again, Clare finds Renzo sitting alone on a boulder, skulking like some peevish park ranger.

"You okay?"

He smiles blankly, doesn't remove his AirPods.

"Just waiting for Jess."

Liam and Mac clamber up behind her.

"I'll wait with you," Liam says. "That last part was murderous on my shoulder."

Mac looks at Clare, makes a twirling motion in the air with his index finger. The implication is clear. *Leave it alone, let's get out of here.*

He stays close to her side for as long as possible, until they come upon wooden planks driven into the hillside like stairs. The planks, set at uneven and perilous heights—more bad news for their knees—lead them down across a stream. And then they're in a new landscape. No more boulders, no more caked mud that feels safer than what it really is: a substance that will suck you down and in.

The trail is swampy and uneven now, all mud or boggish pools, and Clare loses interest. By now she and Mac have left the others completely behind, holding back ferns and mossy branches, catching one another by the elbows whenever a plank rolls beneath their feet. The air is thick and gray, fog drifting from the direction she assumes they're heading, the coast, although it occurs to her that they've now been at this for well more than two hours. Birds circle above them, birds whose calls she would recognize if she were a more curious person, a better traveler. If she had actual interests or hobbies beyond excoriating herself for the lack thereof.

"So," she says. "What do we think of Geoff? Have you spent any time with him?"

Mac chuckles behind her, their steps thudding in tandem. They can't see one another's faces.

"Not a lot," he says. "I've been out with them a few times."

"Renzo always up his ass like this?"

"Kind of? It's an odd . . . I don't really know the deal. Or, I don't care enough to ask. But yes, Renzo's very big on them being, you know. Besties."

"Don't get me wrong, I did enjoy being told that crypto will lift millions out of poverty," she says. "Also, the land he's purchased in Wyoming for when 'things get really grim.' That was charming. But, whatever. It's not like I haven't met that type before. Is he ever not wearing that vest?"

"Who, Mr. Frat-agonia?"

"I thought it was Prada-gonia."

"Girl, I think you know that it's both."

"Jessie seems really happy with him, though. Like, calmer."

Mac exhales noisily.

"Well, he seems like a moron to me, but a perfectly ordinary moron. Nothing but gracious always, very smooth. Randomly pays the tab when no one's looking, remembers the details of my job each time. Shit like that. I don't have some burning desire to be best friends with the guy Jessie ends up marrying, you know? If she's all set, then great, I'm happy for her."

She can't tell if he's trying purposely to give her an opening. The trail is still too narrow for them to walk side by side.

"It must be weird, though," she tries. "To see her with someone else."

He sighs.

"I've seen her with someone else all along, Clare Clare. All I ever *did* was, you know. See her with Renzo."

"But I mean, someone *else*."

"Clare, is it—Is this what you've been hinting at all week? Are you under the impression that I'm still longing for Jess to choose me?"

"That's not what I meant, I just—"

"Honey, oh, wow. Let's get this cleared up right quick. I can't even—I cannot even *access* the person who used to think he was in love with her, Clare. It's embarrassing, for me. To remember that it happened. I mean, truly, God help me if, in the year of our Lord twenty eighteen, I'm chasing around a . . . a girl like Jessie."

"Oh," she says. "Oh, well. Okay. Sorry."

"Don't apologize," he says. She can hear how close he is to losing patience with her, but she decides to push once more, while they're alone.

"Well, actually, I did want to," she says. "Apologize again. For what I said the other day. About the dating apps."

"Jesus, Clare, anything else? You've got me alone here as a captive audience, so we have to run through the whole list? Okay, here we are, then. You've been chewing on this one for the past two days? Go ahead."

"I don't—I don't have a go-ahead; that was all. I just wanted to apologize. I mean, I *am* apologizing. I'm sorry. It was a stupid fucking thing to say."

They walk in silence again, thrashing at the swamp around them. The air keeps getting thicker, louder, buzzing and rustling.

"Do you remember," he says. "This was a while ago. And some celebrity did some interview, I can't remember who. Black celebrity. Talking about the elevator in his luxury building in Chelsea, or whatever. His neighbor got in with him, a little white lady. And he could see her start to reach out and then do the little stutter movement with her arm. Then make up her mind, press her floor. And then they rode up together in silence, and she told him to have a good night?"

"Yeah," she says. "I remember that. Or, whatever, something similar."

"And you were talking to me about it, like—'Oh, you know, this is something I'd never think about in a million years, I'm sure you've thought about it even though'—I don't remember how you said it, exactly, do you?"

"No," she lies, miserable.

"But basically, you were like, 'I'm sure it's on your mind a lot, even though obviously nothing like that would ever happen to *you*.' Said it with total confidence. Just breezed right past it. Like, well, 'Mac never gets these reactions, but after all he is Black, he probably is at least aware that it happens.'

"And I was just sitting there nodding, like 'What is it she thinks is going on when I'm by myself? When she's not around? Does she think I carry fatheads of each of them around with me, proof that I've got white friends, some of them are even lawyers? Maybe a picture of my dad in his surgical scrubs to reassure the lady in the elevator? Does Clare think that she and Renzo give me, what? Protection? When they're not around? Because *they* know I'm not a threat?'"

She keeps walking. Each time she reaches out to grasp a branch, she holds it away from her body and lets her arm extend back until he catches it from her. Their hands touch each time.

"I'm sorry," she says. "I don't really know if there's anything else I can say. I'm really sorry. That sounds—I must have made you feel really lonely. That conversation."

"No," he says, and what feels most damning is how calm he is, how little his voice quavers. "I used to feel lonely. In high school. You guys said much worse shit back then, I won't lie. But that felt lonelier, because somehow, it surprised me every time."

She nods again.

"We'd be sitting at a table on the quad, or I'd be in Kyle's backyard, and then someone would say, whatever. 'Well, obviously Mac will go to college wherever he wants.' Or, like, 'He's not even ghetto like that, so-and-so is Blacker than you are, dude.' Or worse, obviously. And I just suddenly would be on the other side of the yard. It would feel like I could scream and nobody would hear me, I could chuck my beer bottle right at Kyle's head and it would just glance off, roll away. I'd be far away and I would know that I'd always been all the way over there, I'd just forgotten for a few minutes. And I'd think, *What did you fucking expect, you idiot.*"

"I mean," she says. "You could have expected more. It wasn't idiotic."

"I don't know. I thought for a long time that maybe it was my fault. That I never told all y'all what my life was like. Not that part of my life, at least. So you took me at face value, which is incredibly naïve, but then, you know. I never asked you *not* to do that."

"This could be construed as asking me not to," she said. "This conversation we're having right now."

"Sure, baby," he says, and there is simultaneously such tenderness and such dismay in his voice that she shrinks from it. "But we sure as hell weren't having this conversation back when we were kids. It's kind of, you know. I'm kind of over it, you know what I mean?"

They're both quiet for a moment.

"Like," he tries again, "I do appreciate your apology. It's not nothing, but it also doesn't really do anything for me in the long run, right?

It doesn't make me feel like you'll think first, next time. Or, like, oh good, now there won't *be* a next time. All my college friends, my work friends, my Black friends—you guys are always making your bitchy little comments, because I don't really introduce any of you. But they always make fun of me, like, 'How bad can they be, J? They're not as racist as you are, at least they all had *one* Black friend in high school. *You* sure as hell didn't.'"

"But you did," she says, only now remembering. The two girls he used to sequester himself with, reluctantly dragging himself away to return to the table where Renzo held court. One of them was named the head of the Black Leadership Club senior year, and she was always trying to convince Mac to attend meetings. But whenever he did, Renzo and Kyle teased him mercilessly.

Belatedly, Clare realizes the other thing he's said: that his adult friends, evidently, don't call him Mac.

"We just always acted like there was something weird going on if you wanted to spend any time away from us. That you would specifically choose something that didn't include us. Why would you need anyone else, I guess. It felt like an insult."

"It was," Mac says.

They've reached a flatter, drier part of the trail, and he comes up next to her.

"Look," he says. "Most of this happened such a long time ago. This is what I'm saying, about Jess—I just hate thinking about it, I hate having to remember. When I say I was in love with her, I mean, I was sixteen, what does that even mean, right? She liked having sex with me and she needed to make Renzo jealous. We all knew the situation. But every other white girl at that school treated me like a fucking mascot, like this sexless teddy bear they kept around to listen to their problems and protect them from whichever white boy was upsetting them. I think I was just, like . . . grateful. That she at least saw me as someone she wanted to fuck, someone she would consider dating. I mean, Jessie was never really going to date me, but still. That she wanted me at all. And when I think about that, my heart breaks for that kid. I hate remembering that. But when we're all together, it's kind of like . . ."

Clare nods.

"'Remember when' is kind of all we have," he says. "And I don't think any of you really ever think about, like, if I really *want* to remember. Like, I love you guys, and it's fun to tell the stories, right? We knew each other when we were such babies. But like, sorry, my adult friendships are . . . different. I don't really know what to say about that."

"How?" she says, tentative, worried that any interruption will remind him that he doesn't usually talk to her like this.

"How what? How are they different?"

"Yeah."

"I mean, I don't know. I don't, like, I'm not having to think about any of this. Certainly wouldn't be putting it into words, no offense. You wouldn't ever ask that question. I can just kind of . . . *be*. I don't know if that makes sense to you. But I can never really just be when I'm with you all, and there's other good stuff, obviously, but it's still . . . there."

"Oh," she says. "You really don't feel like you can be yourself? Around me?"

"I mean, Clare, come on. With them, I mean, I'm not the Black friend. Obviously."

"You're not the Black friend here." He sucks his breath in. "No, but you know what I mean. You're not."

"Oh," he says, tartly. "Okay, then."

"Sorry," she says.

"Please, God, please stop apologizing."

She stops.

"Even, like, the morning of the missile," he says. "I sat there watching all of you, like, you get it, right, that I actually have felt this way before? You guys couldn't stand to feel that way for forty-five fucking minutes. All year, you've been avoiding this feeling, you're all talking about how you're gonna change your lives and be, like, *radicalized*. But never once have you been curious about the fact that I maybe felt this way long before last year. Or felt this way the whole time you knew me. But again, I never really demand that of you guys. So, that's on me, too. Maybe."

"Well," she says. "I mean, you're kind of demanding something right now, right?"

"Oh," he says, grabbing her hand and swinging it through the air between them. "No, no, please don't misunderstand me. You asked about this, so I'm telling you. And I love you, you know that. But I am not terribly interested in doing, like, consciousness-raising about the past. You know there's an Instagram account, now, run by Black kids at our school, the current kids? It came up at a party in LA, before the holidays, and everyone thought they were *making it up*. These children. Manufacturing stories to post anonymously to an Instagram account. And I called my Uber. I just peaced out. I just get sick of having to swallow everything, sometimes."

"I'm not," she tries, but she can already see that this has died on the vine, that every movement of his body right now—his arms swinging, his neck cracking from side to side—is calibrated to show her that he isn't upset, does not wish to be. "I don't want you to have to swallow stuff with me, though. You don't have to walk on eggshells. Maybe with Renzo, but not with me."

"Clare," he drawls. "You gunning for that 'good white person' badge again? You know those are pretty hard to get."

"Stop," she says, but she tries to laugh, too. "I don't know. I know you want me to stop apologizing, but I am sorry. That I was so totally unaware of this stuff when we were younger. Of how you felt."

"Well, now," he says. "I don't know if that's really true. I don't know if you—I mean, you were aware. At least, sometimes."

But I wasn't, she thinks. *If he's saying that, he's saying that I knew and just didn't care. Isn't he?* But before she can ask, he's talking again.

"It's not—The fact that I don't pick you, for this stuff. We don't have to get every single thing from each other, you know? It's just—I have a life beyond you guys now. There's a big part of it you're not going to understand."

"I guess you're just basically saying that you're leaving us behind," she says. "Leaving me behind. That makes me sad."

He looks at her, for a moment.

"Clare, this all happened in, like, college. This is old news. For you too, no? You don't—I mean, being together this week makes it easy to fall back into the pattern, but. You left these boys behind, too. A long time ago. Not in every way, but in most ways?"

They're leaving the swampland and the trees are growing thicker around them. He doesn't wait for an answer to something that, evidently, wasn't a question.

And then they've suddenly emerged on a small wedge of land hanging over the bay. They're at the overlook.

"About fucking time," Renzo says, bouncing on the balls of his feet, incandescently annoyed. Tucked to one side of the little clearing are three log benches, so low to the ground that Liam, Kyle, Geoff, and Jessie are practically squatting. Improbably, Clare's phone buzzes from its berth deep inside her backpack. Up here, for the first time all day, she has service. She ignores it.

"Where the fuck have you been?" Renzo pushes. "You must have taken the wrong route through the swamp, or something. We've been here for, like, forty-five minutes."

"Maybe ten," Liam mumbles into his rice.

"We were worried! For all we knew you'd fallen off the path and were lying at the bottom of a ravine."

Clare does a quick survey of the other four, hunched over their poke bowls, shoveling food at their faces. Kyle waves a hand as he chews, disavowing whatever Renzo's said.

"Yes," she said, "you all appear to be in quite a lather."

Mac steps in front of her.

"Dude, relax. We didn't even realize we got lost, okay? We're here. I know you're jealous when anyone gets alone time with anyone else, but back off."

They all freeze, the delay between slicing your finger and seeing the bloom of blood. But Renzo merely pouts.

Clare and Mac take pictures while everyone else eats, their heads bulbous in the bottom third of the frame, the green hills of the valley and its horseshoe-shaped turquoise bay looming beyond their shoulders. Geoff stands up, wiping his hands on his thighs and gesturing gallantly at his bench, and they sit down, ravenous.

"I would exercise caution," Kyle says, even as he scrapes his spoon against foam to chase down the last few grains of rice. "Ours was, just. Food poisoning is not impossible, let's say that. The mayo had been, like, cooking in my backpack this whole time."

"Excellent," Clare says. "Thanks for that."

By the time they've all finished eating, the sun is fading.

"Let's take a last picture," Clare says. "Everyone."

"No," Renzo says. "I'll take it."

"But then you won't be in it."

"Clare," Mac says. "Just let him."

Mac hands over his phone, and Clare gestures for him to stand beside her. He rolls his eyes, but he reaches for her hand.

18

The thing that brings the weeklong simmer to full boil, incredibly, is some dumb argument on a subject none of them know anything about.

The point is that no one at that table can reasonably claim to give two fucks about the issue itself. Not if they're honest. They might be able to generate an eloquent panic about the general stakes, take the long view, but to what purpose? The very concept of a "long view" exists in some other sphere, one that only rarely taps up against their own. The long view scrolls past them every few hours in a headline, creating caverns in their chests until they decide to think about something else instead. A brief silence while they wonder what to say, then acknowledge that, really, there *is* nothing to say. What are they going to do in the moment, come up with a solution? Absolutely not.

Jessie starts it. Clare can admit later that it cannot be laid entirely at Jessie's feet or even at Geoff's. But Jessie definitely starts it.

It's Wednesday night. Friday will be one long parade of Ubers to the airport, staggered flights out of the islands. Other than their drunken attempt at ceviche, they haven't cooked, and Renzo's dismantled trevally is still sitting abandoned in a salad bowl in the refrigerator. So they decide to rent the development's outdoor pavilion for a few hours: long communal table, wooden benches, enormous grill, limited outdoor kitchen facilities. A firepit overlooking yet another tangerine vista of rolling lawns and distant beach and the sun dropping into a flaming ocean.

Everyone has a job. Liam prepares the skewers, Mac and Clare chop the vegetables. Jessie mixes drinks, Geoff pontificates. Kyle preps the meat and Renzo hovers at his shoulder critiquing his methods.

After the food is served and demolished, there's a lull. The fire has reached impressive heights and Clare wants to suggest they all sit over there until their cheeks get too warm, but she never does. Jessie takes out her phone and scrolls, her fingers playing idly at the nape of Geoff's neck.

Dinner was easy enough. The food itself, messy and eaten with their hands, required lots of attention. The conversation was mostly chatter, punctuated every so often by something sharper. A museum sit-in to protest Big Pharma donors. A comedian saying something disgusting about trans women. A march on Gracie Mansion demanding urgency in climate policy. Each one mentioned only briefly; no one wants to be a bummer, not here, not tonight.

Anyway, Jessie mentions it first: a protest on a university quad in New York, divestment from fossil fuels.

"Good God," Geoff says. "That is just so idiotic. Just absolutely pointless."

He doesn't even look up. He's not spoiling for a fight; this isn't Renzo, coiled like a spring. Geoff is wholly engrossed in his phone, his other hand lovingly cupped around the "skinny" margarita he mixed separately.

"Wait, what?" Clare says. Jessie looks up, alert. She might as well have tiny, sensitive doe ears on the top of her head.

"I just find it hilarious that anyone thinks this will matter. That they'll affect a university endowment by one iota. But, sure, they can all feel special. Breathless coverage and soothing pats on the back. By all means. This isn't so different, you know, from our annual DEI workshop, where they ask us to sit there for eight hours and hear everything that's wrong with us and then walk out with a few catchphrases and absolutely no intention of voicing a single qualm with our existing systems of professional merit or reward. We can certainly indulge this, but let's not pretend it's real."

"Sorry," Clare says. "Which part is idiotic?"

Mac slouches against the table, his feet in Clare's lap. She begins to knead the tendons between ball and heel.

"Ouch," he hisses, but she steadies her grip and keeps her eyes on Geoff, who's shaking the ice in his glass, trying to free up the dregs. She can feel Renzo on Mac's other flank, holding himself very still, marshaling his resources.

"No one gives a shit about this protest, if we can even call it that," Geoff says. "A university corporation is hardly susceptible to these sorts of public shaming campaigns."

He reaches across Kyle, who's on his left, to grab a knife and the last few lime wedges. Kyle fixates with great concentration on the firepit, then the limes, then the fire again.

"Okay, I understand that it's not some startup where you can tank the IPO, or whatever."

Geoff smirks, which Clare ignores.

"But the school is padding its endowment, in theory, on behalf of its students. So why shouldn't they try to shift public opinion? Isn't that essentially what happened with Big Tobacco? Executives got sick of being humiliated at, like, cocktail hour at the golf club?"

Geoff liberates a cutting board from its few last pieces of grilled peppers, shaking them onto his plate beside the limes. He holds the serrated knife to the fruit and then smiles at her with irritated benevolence.

"That was a lawsuit," he says. "Divestment is not a lawsuit."

She can't help herself. This might be where it goes off the rails, in retrospect. She tries to summon Jamie's voice in her ear, his fingertips at the small of her back. *Sweetheart. Who gives a shit what he thinks? You can't get so worked up over the blared opinions of people you don't respect.* But of course, she hasn't actually heard her husband's voice in days.

"Yeah, I'm aware of that," she says. "I appreciate that I didn't go to HBS, but I do in fact know what a lawsuit is."

He shrugs, performing his amiability with great care.

"If this school agrees to divest," he says slowly, squeezing the lime over his cocktail, "what then? What's the plan? These are publicly traded companies. Someone else who's an equally bad actor, worse, will snap up those shares. Bet on that. So what exactly does divestment achieve?"

"Fair enough," Clare says. She can be just as amiable as he can. "But in the meantime, their school is profiting from shit that's evil, and these kids want it to stop."

"Better their school than some shadowy Chinese investor, though."

This seems like it almost certainly must be racist, but she lets it go.

Kyle's body has drifted until he's on the very edge of his chair, hands on his knees and palms flat as if to ground him there.

"Does that argument really work, though, Geoff?" he says. "I mean, can't you use that argument to justify . . . anything? Like, sure this company uses slave labor, which I am against. But at least I take the morally defensible position that slavery is wrong, and let the slavers know that I disapprove?"

"Do I need to clarify that I do not support slave labor?" Geoff asks, as Jessie simultaneously trills that this is *not* what he means.

"Sorry, that was—" Kyle says softly, nodding in Mac's direction. Mac laughs out loud. He sits up and pulls his feet from Clare's lap.

"Let's not start with this," he says. "I am not the judge of when you're allowed to reference slavery. Don't look at me, Jesus."

"Sorry," Kyle says again, his face reddening.

"Look," Geoff says. He's now waving his knife in the air, and Kyle's eyes follow it with concern. "Their university waded into those waters long ago, and it's too late to really stop them. A little campus teach-in is hardly going to move the needle. The students should be using their time there to learn to engage with the world as it is, surely."

"I actually agree with you there," Renzo says, finally. Liam, at the table's head, is still silent. "We've made our beds, so to speak."

"Great," Clare sputters. "Then, what? What would you two do?"

Geoff picks up another lime and begins carefully segmenting it into small wedges.

"Look, guys, I am not the enemy here. I read some Marx this year too, all right? I'm quasi-literate in all the same ideas, I've looked at all the same options. But I'm not interested in abstract theory. I'm not interested in whining about capitalism while reaching out to it with both hands for everything I need. I'm interested in improving the system we have. I don't see the point in stamping my feet and complaining that the sky is blue just because that stance is currently, what? Chic?"

"I have not read any Marx this year," Kyle says.

"We know, baby," Renzo murmurs.

"Have any of us taken any steps to dismantle this system we find so abhorrent?" Geoff asks, carefully squeezing his lime. No one answers.

"This is the bigger problem," Jessie insists. "People refuse to engage with anyone who disagrees. No one wants to listen, everyone has to be right. Everything has to be clear-cut, with one easy villain."

"Some people *are* villains," Mac says. "Who's defending Big Oil? Why am I going to listen to them?"

"Yeah, I'm with him," Kyle says. "We can't sit around smiling at the people who are joyfully screwing us for generations to come."

"Of course not," Jessie snaps. "No one is saying that. But *this*"—and she holds her phone up, shaking it as if it's a rattle—"this is not the way to go about it."

"And I'll ask again," Clare says. "How would you go about it instead?"

Jessie stares at her.

"Look," she says. "I get that this is not your thing, Clare, to try to take a second before, you know, *demonizing* someone—"

"Yes," Renzo says. "Spare a thought for the poor, demonized, most powerful institutions in the world."

"But," Jessie continues, and Clare can see her breath speed up, can see what it takes from her to ignore him. "I feel like . . . okay, I'm just going to say something. I already know who's going to jump down my throat about this. But one of my best friends at the firm, he's been such a mentor to me, we love his wife and his toddler, they come for dinner all the time. We just think the world of them. He has the office next to mine. He is *whip* smart. An incredible mind. And not just, like, *lawyer* smart, but also so thoughtful. And he's a supporter of the president. Big supporter!"

Clare drops her head into her hands, tightening them around her skull like a vise.

"Well!" Geoff says. "That one was hard to predict. You don't approve of friendship with Republicans, I take it."

"No, continue, please,'" Clare says. "What's his argument?"

Jessie shrugs.

"He thinks both parties are colossal tire fires, totally incompetent, and that we needed something new. An actual champion for the working man."

"This is your fellow corporate lawyer, yes?" Renzo says.

"Yup," Mac chimes in. "A champion of the worker, for sure."

There is something almost delicious about watching Renzo and Mac align themselves against Jessie, against the man she's sleeping with. Clare cannot be the only one thinking this.

"He prides himself," Jesse continues, louder. "On, like—I mean, this is not a Fox News addict. Not by any stretch. No Fox, no CNN. He just really values, you know. Reaching his own independent conclusions. He isn't easy to classify! But no, he really doesn't trust, like, most mainstream news outlets."

"You asked about the corporate tax cut last month?" Renzo says in a very low voice.

"Of course I did," Jessie retorts. "I mean, keep in mind, I only learned all of this recently. We've only known him socially for, like, a year."

"But you're an expert on his worldview," Clare says. "You know him to be a very thoughtful person."

"He's our friend," Geoff says.

"Sorry, but. The tax cut?" Renzo presses.

"He said he needed to do his own research," Jessie falters. "He hadn't followed it closely."

"How's he going to do that," Clare nearly whispers, "without reading the news?"

"Let me guess." Mac rubs his eyes with both fists. "He'll wait to see how it affects his family's investment portfolio and then go from there."

"Ding ding ding!" Renzo chirps.

"That's actually a good question," Liam says, finally. "He's, what, our age? I get that he's a real intellectual renegade, but was his vote ever actually up for grabs, or was he raised Republican and just keeps humming along?"

"Nice of you to participate," Renzo says, reaching out to pinch the soft skin at Liam's elbow.

Jessie doesn't initially respond.

"Well?" Clare says.

"His family is Republican, yes. His father is a—I mean, they're all . . . His father served in the Bush administration. He was, I mean. I think he was pretty high up."

There's a brief silence before Liam fails to contain his laughter.

"I'm sorry, but. Come on, you both have to admit it, that's funny."

Jessie rests her head on Geoff's shoulder.

"You see, right?" she stage-whispers. "They're impossible."

"No, baby, go ahead," Mac says, leaning in with his hands flat on the table. "What are you trying to say? Go ahead."

Clare is almost positive there is the tiniest flinch, a knot somewhere in Geoff's shoulder contracting, when he hears that. *Baby.* But he's not too perturbed to reply on his girlfriend's behalf.

"I just think people are *so* complicated. People are so much more complicated than any of you seem willing to allow."

"People are complicated is, like, the simplest observation you can possibly make," Clare says. "It's a literally meaningless statement. He might be the most complicated fellow in greater Los Angeles, but no, it does not sound like his actual reasons for voting the way he did are all that complicated, actually."

"I'm complicated too, bitches," Renzo says sotto voce. "And yet, somehow, I didn't vote for the man who hates me. I'm the middle hour of a David Lynch film. I'm a fucking Thomas Pynchon novel. You'll never plumb my bottomless depths."

"We're not defending him—" Jessie begins, but Clare interrupts.

"That is very much exactly what you're doing."

"We're just saying that, even if the guy has some abhorrent views, they aren't the whole story of who he is!"

"I do not think he necessarily has abhorrent views," Geoff says.

"For fuck's sake," Mac says, almost under his breath.

"Look, I don't know him that well. I'm just saying. I guess I just prefer to allow for a bit more nuance."

"Yeah, I don't really have that luxury," Mac says. "Fun game, but I don't have that option, actually."

"Nor do I," Renzo says.

"Well, it's certainly efficient to write someone off after a single vote in a single election."

Mac waves one hand in the air.

"You know what? I don't need to explain this to anyone. Or maybe I do, but I choose not to. Not today. You can all sit here committing white-on-white crime all night, I'm not your confessor. It's my vacation, too."

Clare looks over at Kyle, who's staring intently into the distance.

"You have anything you want to say, here?"

"Of course he doesn't," Renzo says. "God forbid we ever need his support, loves. God forbid anyone ask you to raise your voice, Kyle."

"Ren," Liam begins. "I think he, like me, just maybe thinks this is not the most productive conversation, and—"

"Forgive me," Renzo interrupts, and that's when something begins to shift. Somewhere in the air above them, an unmistakable pressure system deepens and then pops.

"Forgive me," he repeats. "If I've lost my taste for people who could not be more protected, in every single sense of the word, talking about how *un*dangerous it is for them to handwave someone's tasteful fascism because they happen to like having him over for a glass of Pet fucking Nat on Sunday afternoons. As if that isn't the oldest story in the known universe. Forgiving someone for the way they treat faceless strangers because you happen to like the way they treat you? This is heart-wrenching nuance? I mean, come on."

There's another silence.

"We've wandered off topic," Clare attempts. "Geoff, you were going to tell us your plan for the climate that won't piss off any fossil fuel companies."

He's eating again, somehow, cutting a bell pepper into tiny pieces and using his knife to gather them onto his fork. He smiles without looking up.

"So," he says. "You're a nascent novelist. Yes? How much do you know about the CEO of whichever conglomerate it is that owns your publisher?"

"Absolutely," Clare says evenly, ignoring that "nascent." "Unless you're going to completely isolate yourself outside the system, there's always something disgusting you've bought into. I don't feel good about it. But I am also not a multibillion-dollar university endowment."

"I see," he says. "Insignificance as absolution. Interesting. But if you were the face of these billions, you'd potentially achieve a much greater good by working to effect change from within, no?"

"'Potentially' is doing a lot of work over there, isn't it."

"All right, Clare, enough," Jessie says.

"No," Geoff says. "Let her tell us how she's going to return her advance and apply to law school and become a public defender. Or travel the country chaining herself to bulldozers and blowing up pipelines. Or move to the border. Or cure a single devastating disease without holding her nose and accepting funding from some unsavory source."

"There are ways to help people that aren't being a public defender," Clare mutters. "That aren't working with refugees."

"There are?" Renzo snaps. "I don't believe I've ever heard you say anything to that effect. You can't mean that there are ways to be virtuous that aren't just . . . whatever it is, exactly, that Clare does? That's a first. We've all grown so accustomed to your little digs at *our* choices, so this comes as quite a shock."

"Come on, man," Kyle says. "She was just defending you."

"No, she wasn't. She changed the subject so she could talk about what she wanted to talk about again. No one is listening to me at all. You're all sitting here like it's an intellectual exercise. None of this matters to any of you."

Clare shakes her head, once, as if to clear it of a heavy fog. *We skipped a scene*, she thinks. *We're talking about something else now and I don't remember why*. Too late, she thinks, *Oh, right, we're all drunk. We should not be discussing any of this right now.*

"I have to say," Renzo says, his voice so quiet that her stomach contracts, actually convulses in fear. "I get so sick of being told, by people who have never in their lives been truly fearful about a single monetary concern, that I'm not doing enough to be a good little global citizen."

"No one is telling you that," Kyle tries, but Renzo holds up one hand.

"None of you have any idea what it is to be actually afraid. Not even Clare, despite her passion for casting herself as some poor little match girl. And yes, McMillan, I'm including you in this."

"Oh, so you don't want me on your side anymore?" Mac says, his voice sharp and ragged like a steak knife. "It's no longer convenient to count me as your fellow disenfranchisee? I never know when you'll decide to claim me."

"Oh, I think you know well enough what I mean," Renzo says. "We can leave it there."

"With due respect," Jessie says, "it's been a long time since you had to worry about your bank balance, Renzo."

"With due respect," he replies, "fuck you. You're asking me to sit here listening to how unpleasant it is for you to hear us call your friend selfish because, what, he's *nice* to you? I have an observation that will blow your mind, Jess. Rich, powerful people are *always* nice to each other. They're *always* willing to overlook little peccadilloes like voting for the fascist who will give their father a job and keep their taxes low. Guess what? Your parents' neighborhood was the only one that broke for that idiot in the entire fucking city of Los Angeles, wasn't it? And now it strikes you as an indescribable novelty that you enjoy this man's company because you have never for one second thought about how it might feel to understand that the world simply does not give a shit if you're alive. I mean, I don't ask you to think about me very often, not really, but please don't sit here telling me that I'm the small one. That I'm not complicated enough. Me, someone you've known for twenty years. Compared to some man you've just met."

The silence this time lasts. Renzo exhales so harshly it sounds like a cough.

"Honestly, sometimes I just want to tell all of you to fuck off," he says. "You have no idea how clueless you actually are. You have no idea what it was like to be a teenager around you people. And you're not *interested* in knowing."

"Yes we are," Kyle tries to say, but Mac talks over him.

"All right, but you are not exactly known for putting yourself in anyone else's shoes, Ren. I mean, I appreciate that you're saying something true here. But, you know. Come on."

"Can everyone please stop interrupting me, maybe?" Kyle says. "Renzo's trying to be honest. We can't always ding him for being so flip and then ignore him when he's trying to tell us something real."

Mac breathes deeply.

"Guys," he says. "I was trying to say this to Clare earlier. But, we are thirty years old. I think the time may have come to admit that, you know, we are old friends but not, maybe, friends who need to fulfill every single function for one another? Like, when was the last time any of you relied on me, truly? I'm not that person in your lives anymore. But then we've got to stop pretending otherwise. Isn't this, just, enough? Can't I just . . . love y'all, without it being this whole undertaking? You guys are so greedy sometimes. You want so much from me."

Jessie makes a brief noise, almost a whimper.

"Who's pretending?" Renzo says, his voice icy. "We were very close to one another for a few years, as children, a long time ago. Who claims otherwise? I don't *need* any of you to be *anything* to me."

"Okay," Mac says. "I didn't ask you to go scorched earth, Ren."

"I'm agreeing with you, you imbecile."

"Um," Kyle says. "I think of you guys as true friends. I mean, I wouldn't invite you here for a week if I didn't."

"I think," Clare says, slowly. "I think, this week, some of this stuff has come up more than once. About how often we've all, sort of. Ignored one another's feelings. And I think Renzo is just trying to ask us to be more aware?"

Renzo flicks at the dampness on his cheeks with annoyed fingertips.

"Sweet Christ," he says. "At least Jessie and Kyle are oblivious. But you, you're so proud of your own self-awareness. Why are you even here? You only keep the rest of us close so you can feel like you aren't so bad. So you can feel reassured or virtuous or engaged or truly whatever the fuck. I liked you better, frankly, when you spent your days tap-dancing to avoid anyone realizing that your house didn't have a swimming pool. At least you weren't constantly keeping score. And what kills me is— this week, of all weeks? You're going to lecture us on being selfish or delusional? Because you're so good. You've performed such a ruthless self-accounting, right? You're not engaging in any questionable behavior this week, after all. Unlike your selfish, myopic friends. This week of all weeks, when you've been lying to everyone every single day, you're still acting like a sanctimonious cunt. Even for you, Clare, it's a ballsy move."

Finally, everything stops.

The panic comes as such a shock that it manifests as inaction. After Renzo tells her what he's told her, in front of everyone, she's frozen. She can see that he's surprised even himself. That he expected a returned volley, eruptions of protest. When he gets only withheld tears, he looks somehow abandoned. But it's too late. He'll never retreat. She knows this about him. It is one thing they have always known about each other.

"Look," he says, almost faltering. "I didn't—Was this really a secret? Did you really think you were fooling us? Of all people? You love to act like we're the ones you can be open and honest with, we're the dirtbags who won't judge you. But you aren't open with us. You're just so careful, so attuned. Checking on what we think so you can clock whether we're even shittier than you are. I know you think we're parts of your hopelessly distant past, I know every fifth sentence you've uttered all week is a reminder that you never come on these trips anymore, but. Come on."

She doesn't bother to say that this isn't true. She can feel Mac beside her, trying to keep himself calm. Kyle stares down at the table. Geoff looks confused but unmistakably gratified. Jessie looks alarmed, like a toddler too stunned to scream. Clare doesn't look at Liam.

She thinks of that first morning, of the minutes before they knew, for sure, that the missile didn't exist. She had been genuinely eager to see them all, these people with whom she hadn't spent two consecutive days in so long. But what was clear, Saturday morning, was that they no longer know one another well enough to see anything poetic in the act of dying together.

She brushes the crumbs from her lap and rises.

"He's right," she says.

"Come on, guys," Kyle says. "This has gotten completely out of hand."

"It's fine. I'm going to walk back."

"No," Kyle says. "Wait. I'll drive you. Don't storm off."

Clare laughs.

"He called me a cunt," she says. "I think I'm all set."

She looks one last time at Renzo.

"Can I ask you something, though? If that's all true, then why are we all here? Why did you beg me to come along?"

He looks at her.

"I don't know," he says, not unkindly. She knows, suddenly, that they're thinking the same thing in this moment. It makes her sad, that she can't joke with him about this, their proudly matched, soulmate brains. But she lets him keep talking.

"I have no idea. We act like a long history is the same thing as enjoying one another's company, as feeling good when we're together. I don't know why we do that. We're so obsessed with elevating something that was, let's face it, perfectly mundane. It wasn't this halcyon era. It was just being young. I mean, Saturday morning."

He pauses, then, but she wants him to finish it, say it.

"What about it?"

"Well," he says. "You weren't the only one. Right? None of us wanted to die here together, did we? We all felt burdened by each other's very presence. We would have rather just been alone."

19

A few hours later, Clare sits in the hot tub. Everyone has scattered, but there's only so much space in which to do so. They're all circling each other like billiard balls ricocheting across the same green felt.

Jessie and Geoff retreated to their bedroom, though he keeps popping into the kitchen to retrieve fruit or seltzer or handfuls of almonds. Mac and Kyle sprawl on the couch watching an impenetrable action film set on a submarine. Renzo, after a tipsy attempt at a nighttime jog, joins them. Liam is at large.

The sliding glass door eventually whispers. Kyle lowers himself to the lip of the hot tub, dunks his feet, and brandishes the box of mints.

She takes four, places them under her tongue. He tilts his head back, pops several.

"It had been so long," she observes. "Until this week."

"Jameson doesn't approve?"

"No, he's suddenly the poster boy for clean living, this past year. I think he also genuinely believes that if I didn't drink or smoke or distract myself, and if I exercised every single morning, I would have finished the book by now."

Kyle says nothing, and she feels horrible. She edges herself closer to him, leans into his leg.

"I have no clue why I said that. Sorry. He's not like that. I don't know why I'm trying to pretend to you that he is. He's completely supportive and he literally has a job he hates so I can have a life where I'm able to write and if I ever finish my book it will one hundred percent be because I married him."

"Kiddo," Kyle soothes, "I believe you. I'm not about to call and read him a transcript of our conversation. Relax."

"He also would *not* have approved of that back there," she says. "Taking Geoff's bait."

"I mean, I assume Jameson is the kind of person who refuses to get worked up by . . . that," Kyle says diplomatically. "He couldn't be like you. It would be perpetual chaos, right?"

"Right."

"Remember that period of college when Renzo was really doing way too much coke?" he asks suddenly. "When we were worried that it was becoming an actual problem."

"I remember how much he punished us for worrying. He didn't speak to me again until we were all home in December and it was too hard *not* to speak to me. And he threatened to evict you, right? The summer in New York? I remember finding that a bit . . . audacious. Even for him."

"He's threatened a lot of things. And that was—I mean, that fight, I couldn't mention that he'd lived with my family for a while. I never would have used that against him."

"I know," she says. "But that's . . . you. I do remember the time I visited when he called his dealer three times in one night."

Once, years after the fact, Kyle got very drunk and told her that Renzo had had a busted lip the night he showed up at Kyle's front door. Not his father; his mother. It made sense: Why else would Kyle's parents swallow their objections, let Renzo move in? She doesn't think Kyle has any memory of telling her that, and she has never asked him about it.

"He hated us visiting," Kyle says. "And seeing everything. Remember how he used to pretend like it wasn't happening?"

His hand is very close to her shoulder. They're talking into the darkness, not looking at each other. He's worrying at the box of mints with his other hand.

"Because he was ashamed."

"Right, but there are lots of ways to be ashamed. Sometimes he wouldn't even go on the defensive, he wouldn't even throw his usual tantrums or whatever. He would just—pretend. He'd pay the dealer an extra fifty to come faster. And then when he blew through it in a few hours, he pretended like he'd never bought any. If you said anything the next morning, he'd look at you like you were crazy."

Beyond them, somewhere between the hot tub and the ocean, frogs are going wild. The first night, she didn't believe the sounds were real. She was convinced it was a tape playing on a loop, some ambient noise Kyle's mother piped in for atmosphere.

"Is there something you want to say to me?"

"It's none of my business, Clare. But it was absurd, even back then. For him to act like I wouldn't be able to see what was going on."

She shakes her head vigorously.

"I'm not sure he understands," he says, more gentle. "Where you're coming from."

"Renzo never understands where I'm coming from. That would involve giving me the benefit of the doubt."

"Right; we both know I'm not talking about Renzo, though."

She stares at her feet in the water. If he turns on the lights her skin will be washed a pale, lifeless color in the green spill.

"Sometimes I think you make everything so hard because then you never have to figure it out," he says. "You just send yourself careening between these exhausting extremes and then you're allowed to throw up your hands. Either you and Renzo are inseparable, or you can't stand the sight of each other. Either Mac needs to absolve us for every single past cruelty, or we obviously mean nothing to him. We're either the fundamental, like, forces in each other's lives, or it's all a total sham."

"I don't think I'm like that," she says. "I don't think—I mean, I don't see myself as a cold person at all. You're making me sound like I don't actually feel anything."

"Oh," he says. "No, you feel things, believe me. But it's tiring, right? Either your marriage is perfect, and you never admit the tiniest flaw, and the rest of us can't possibly understand a *real, mature* relationship. Or . . . I don't know. And either we all blow up our lives this year in reaction to the world around us, or we're evil? I mean, maybe you're right about the last one. But not the other stuff."

"I'm not blowing up my life."

"Um," he says. "Okay."

"What?"

"I mean, no one ever gives me credit for understanding all of you pretty well. Just because I don't throw it in your faces at the first hint of conflict. Just because I'll let you all talk over me."

She wants to tell him he's wrong, that actually she is one way and not another. But how would she describe herself? The core of what she means to do, at any given moment, of how she's trying to live? All she knows, really, is that she finds so many other people's purported self-analyses to be laughably dubious. You'll sit across from someone with a volcanic temper, who just drove six blocks out of his way to blare his horn at a careless driver, and he'll happily insist that he rarely gets "short" with strangers. Who wants to be like that? Isn't it better to avoid the embarrassment, to make sure you're never the least self-aware person in the room, by avoiding these sweeping summaries of your own belief system? Deflect what you can, focus the conversation on some vague and lofty collective action that *we* should all be taking, acknowledge that *we* are horribly flawed without ever subjecting *your* flaws to the pitiless exposure of actual honesty?

But here she is, still convinced that if only she can strike the right pose, it will all come together. Pose long enough as a novelist, as an engaged and devoted citizen of some wider community, as the sort of woman who acts. Pose long enough as a wife and eventually it will mean something in her bones, it will become her identity on a molecular level, she will not conveniently forget she's married one night when she's had too much to drink and feels lonely.

Pose, for a few weeks at least, as someone's mother.

She tries not to say the next part, even in her head, but the very effort means, of course, that she already has. *And look how that turned out.*

"Hey," Kyle says. "Hello? I didn't mean it like that. I know you have feelings. I just—I don't know what's going on, okay? There's no judgment here, you know me. But Liam is a human being. Not an open window."

She and Kyle have never been that close, not really. Mostly they're just two people who love Renzo, who have known one another for twenty years, who as teenagers fell asleep in bathtubs together at houses on the beach. She once gave him a blowjob in the shower stall of a Holiday Inn; when a girl he was hoping to sleep with burned cigarette holes into the back seat of Clare's car, he wordlessly paid to have it replaced so her parents would never know. Maybe, if she'd been someone different, they would have fallen in love. *Is that how it works?* she wonders now. She always assumes that her emotions are weather systems, that the best she can do is remain standing as she's buffeted by them. What if that's just another way to absolve herself of her own behavior? What if she could have just . . . chosen to fall in love with Kyle? Would they have grown into their adult selves together instead of as two separate people who remember how it used to feel, once upon a time, to be close?

Maybe if the part of him that so deeply believes that his own place in the world, safety and sumptuousness in equal measure, is perhaps not deserved but nevertheless unimpeachable—maybe if that part of him had made her feel secure, included. Maybe Jessie was right that Clare could only ever have fallen in love with someone like Jamie instead. Either way, she knows she is no longer someone Kyle would ever come to in panic or distress. She wouldn't be his first emergency phone call, maybe not even his tenth.

"Do you ever think about it?" she asks him. "Why it never really worked between the two of us? Like, what if we had actually tried it?"

"Ha," he says. "Very funny."

She clears her throat.

"Oh, wait, I—Really? I'm sorry. I really thought you were teasing. But no, Clare, I mean . . . never. You know that I love you, but. I don't really think you do either, do you?"

"I just . . ." she says. "I don't think I'd really want to be married to me, honestly."

The few times in their marriage that Jameson has been truly angry, has raised his voice to her, have all been because of her high school friends. Once, a few days after a dinner with Renzo, he lost it. *Your high school friends are allowed to be awful to you*, he said. *You treat Renzo like your beloved, wayward child no matter how vicious he gets, or how rude he is to me. But I come home after a shit day of work and snap at you once and you're practically out the door. You're all fucking grown around each other like twisted little tree roots, and I guess I just wish you ever wanted to be as careful with me as you are with them.*

She was so frightened, by Jameson blowing up at her for once. She was such a good wife for months after that. It felt like the moment of revelation: someone told the truth about her, and now she had to grow up, get serious, take herself in hand and become a better person. It briefly seemed plausible that this was how maturity might implement itself inside her brain: as a series of desperate responses to dire moments of crisis. There was something about making him that angry that somehow felt like an accomplishment, like proof of something.

She swallows, hard. Of course, she may have finally found a way to make Jamie so angry that he'll never stop. And why? For what? Whatever the source of her unhappiness, it's not really her husband. It's no secret, that it's easier to be happier while on vacation, screwing someone new and living in a borrowed house on a Hawai'ian island. There's nothing radical about seizing it for yourself, that kind of happiness, however much it might feel better to call this a rebellion.

"I'm sorry about dinner," she tells Kyle. "I know you hate a fight. It's just, my telling Geoff that he's full of shit isn't the apocalypse."

"Let's hope not."

"Do you not feel any panic at all?" she asks Kyle. "Even if I'm an asshole, I'm smug and unbearable and I'm obsessed with proving that I'm the girl you all like best. Even if I grant you that, all of it. I'm not wrong. It's not . . . melodrama, to feel bottomless despair. We're all talking about having kids in the next few years? Are we just going to . . . proceed? Shouldn't we all be quitting our jobs and giving you shit until you liquidate your trust fund and just . . . doing *something*? What are we doing? We thought we were going to die on Saturday and all we did was get our little jokes off?"

"What are you really upset about?"

"Because I'm a woman, it can't possibly be the world that's upsetting me? It must be my husband or my stupid fucking book?"

"You're right," he says. "You sound utterly at peace about both."

She groans.

"I think you know me," he says, "so I'm going to ignore the implication that I think 'the girls' can't worry about the fires in Sonoma, or the travel ban, or no one being allowed to vote in two years, or *Roe* falling, or, I don't know. We can play catastrophe Mad Libs all you want. The missile that almost killed us. You can admit that you're also upset about something close to home, Clare. It's not useless to be depressed about your marriage instead of the Supreme Court, I think. It's not really an either/ or situation."

"The missile didn't almost kill us," she says. "It wasn't real."

"That's what you got from what I just said?"

"Don't you feel like it's getting harder to ignore the fact that you might not be a very good person? And that it's too late to change that? Like, what, if I volunteer weekly then start doing it daily, will that make me good? If you give away every last penny of your trust fund, will that be enough?"

"You're very into this idea that I must be stripped of my assets."

"I'm serious, though. Would that make you a good person? If we all quit our jobs this fall and go 'do the work,' will that make us good?"

"Clare, what is your point?"

"I don't know," she says bitterly. "I don't know. I just, I don't think I'm a very good person and I don't even know how to tell whether I can become one at this point."

"Remember when I said you race to the extremes? Is that possibly what is going on here? Like, you probably have a pretty good idea of when you are actively being kind of a bad person. Right?"

She heaves herself out of the water and lies flat on her back, her legs still in the hot tub.

"Okay," she says. "So you've all just known all week? Did Renzo already know before we got here? Is that why he convinced Liam to come?"

"No," he says. "I mean, I don't know. That sounded worse than I meant it, I just meant—we know when we're acting like bad people. I didn't mean that we *are* bad people."

There is a long silence.

"I just thought more would change," she says. "This past year. I thought we all were like, 'Okay, this is a wakeup call.' But it seems like we're all just kind of . . . doing our thing. Still. I don't think everything around us getting demonstrably worse has made us any better."

"So . . . this is the thing you decided to change?"

Another silence.

"I'm joking," he says. "Kind of. But, like, look. I think what I'm saying is that maybe telling the truth about whatever's going on right now doesn't make you a good person. But if you hold everything to that standard then you end up doing lots of shitty stuff, right? If we can only do things that will one hundred percent make us better, then whatever, fuck it all to hell, I guess. Don't even try."

"Okay, so what about your trust fund?"

"I mean, there's an argument to be made for investing it, to then think about the smartest way to really, philanthropically—"

She groans again.

"I'm sorry, did I miss it when you liquidated all of Jameson's accounts?"

"It's easier to know what to do with other people's money."

"Yes, duh."

"I'm just afraid, and he is too. Like, what if he loses his job? And we gave away the only money we'll ever make?"

"So, your fears are the ones that are justified, and the rest of us can fuck off?"

"You have zero sense of what that might feel like," she says softly.

"No, I know. I wasn't trying to be a dick. Sorry. I know that you two—I can imagine it must feel different."

He lies down beside her, their shoulders touching.

"Have you found it wild," she says, "how quickly we all reverted to our teenaged selves on this trip? Like, are we all trapped in amber this badly?"

"I don't know. Is that really true? I think it's just, like, we have these calcified stories about one another. Like, we decided something, and we tell the anecdotes enough, and then it becomes true. You always remember me nicer, when we talk about, you know. High school. You act like I was a lot less shitty to you than I was. And we all just act accordingly, when we see each other. But either way, would that be so awful? I liked you when you were fifteen. I like you now. I'll probably like you when you're forty-five."

She turns to him in the dark. He has said this in one steady stream, not rushing, not ponderous. She can't see his face, but she has it memorized. The lazy traces of a smile that never seems to fade; his willingness, always, to let her endlessly probe these tiny fissures in the façade that would never otherwise worry him. The slights from years ago that he happily forgets, rather than worry at them the way she does, until they weep and fester. It's easy to forget the times he was petulant, the flashes of ugly entitlement when he didn't get his way. She can choose to forget them whenever she wants, and she does. He's right.

"Do you really think you'll still want me in your life when I'm forty-five? Like, is there any awful comment one of us could have made on this trip that would have made you think, *Huh, maybe I'm done*? I want to know. I take for granted that you're easygoing, that it's mostly just path of least resistance, but I want to know."

He turns and puts one hand to either side of her face. He lets his thumbs trail the lines of her jaw, lets his fingers brush through her hair, and then he kisses her, once, on the forehead.

"You?" he says. "You'll never get rid of me, I don't think."

She waits, and then says it.

"I don't think I can stand to feel this horrible about myself and every single other thing for another thirty years. I feel like I have spent the last ten years, and especially the last year, imagining that I'm right on some precipice. That I will have the energy to change everything about my life, eventually, in the near future. When I actually grow up."

He chuckles, then stands up.

"You understand that you can do it, right? You can go back to Boston at the end of the week and change any part of this. I mean, that other situation, obviously. I don't know what's going on there. But it isn't all or nothing."

She sit up, cradles her knees in her arms.

"I don't think anything's too late, Clare Clare. It might be too late to feel, like, noble? I think the problem is you're so invested in this idea that we know for sure we're *good*, and maybe we're too late for that part. But you don't have to compare yourself to, like, me or Renzo, it's not about winning. You're not going to survive off that feeling of knowing you're superior to me, I guess."

"I don't," she says. "I do not feel superior to you."

"Clare, come on," he says, but his voice is soft and easy. "We both know that's a lie."

"But I love you," she says.

She looks at him and knows that it is true, that she is willing to excuse the fact that he really doesn't worry himself about any of it and probably never will. Because she loves him. She wants the people she loves to be somehow exempt from the series of judgments these past few years have undeniably, however they try to deny it, pushed them to make about themselves. She is, in the end, doing just what Geoff and Jessie were doing at dinner.

"I know that," he says simply. "Come on. Let's go back inside. They'll think we're just sitting around getting high out here."

"We did get high out here," she says, and that's how she realizes that the mints have taken hold, that what she says is true.

20

As soon as she's inside, her phone begins to jump. She carries it out the front door, putting the whole length of the house between her and everyone else.

"Short stuff," her husband sighs into the phone. "I miss you. I've been trying you all week but I can never remember what time it is there, I'm so sorry."

"Me too," she says, walking down the driveway in her towel. She climbs into the golf cart. "You're home?"

"Yep, finally." His voice is drifting already. She imagines him sprawled on their bed, his phone wedged between his ear and the pillow.

"I asked Madeline from the store to drop off some groceries yesterday. I didn't want you to come home to nothing."

"Thank you," he says. "Truly. It felt amazing to open the fridge and see actual food waiting for me."

"I asked her to go to the good bagel place, too. I remember I really missed bagels when we were in Shanghai. So weird."

"Yes," he says. "Definitely."

"But they'll be stale, I didn't think. But there should be cream cheese, anyway. If you can drag yourself out for bagels tomorrow."

"I don't like cream cheese," he says. "But bagels were a good idea."

"What are you talking about?"

"I don't eat cream cheese, you know that."

She feels the tears coming hot and jumbled, even though this is perhaps the one phone call of her life in which it is most important not to start crying without explanation. She thinks of Renzo, his seamless awareness that she doesn't eat eggs.

"I absolutely did not," she says. "How would I? You've never told me that."

"Hey, hey, I'm not trying to be a brat, I promise. You were sweet to buy your absentee husband some bagels."

"Not once have you ever told me you dislike cream cheese."

"Maybe not," he says, unruffled. She feels his certainty, his lack of doubt, like fingers on her neck, she can't breathe. *Not now*, she tells herself. She touches the key to the golf cart, left dangling in the ignition.

"Hey," he says again. "I'm sorry we didn't spend Christmas together, I'm sorry it's been so shitty all month. I know it's not great, being married to me right now."

She holds the phone away from her mouth so he won't hear her breathing.

"I just really miss you," he says. There's a scrape against a floorboard and she corrects her image of him. He's sitting at the kitchen bar, elbows on the countertop, exhausted. Wanting to hang up on his wife but not wanting to hurt her feelings.

"I miss you too," she whispers. "I really do."

"But I'm home now for, like, two straight months. I know that when it's like this you probably only remember all my bad qualities," he says. "My *alleged* bad qualities. But try to remember I can be lovable, too. We can stay in bed until noon next week. I'll go buy *you* the fancy cream cheese. Whatever you want."

She laughs, wipes at her nose.

"How's the trip been? Does Renzo miss me?"

"It's been kind of a shitshow," she says. "I feel like being around them again reminds me that maybe I'm a truly awful person, and Renzo weighed in tonight. Kyle did too, actually. In his way."

"Sounds like a fabulous use of everyone's leisure time," Jamie says, yawning.

She thinks of all the things she loves. His ability to make a goofy joke before he's fully awake, when she's still nonverbal, and the mornings he rolls toward her and falls asleep again with his face in her hair. That he knows all the crosscurrents in her family well enough to understand wordlessly why she needs to lie down sometimes after a phone call with her parents. That he treats her writing as something real and always did, even in college. The way he used to laugh when he was stoned, so hard he couldn't breathe, flailing his arms. That he stacks his leftovers neatly in the fridge, that he's always the one to cook and that there are always plenty of leftovers. The coffee table he built in his free time, during a stressful season at work, that his way to relax himself was to make her something beautiful for her home. His walk, the way he still moves like an athlete with perpetually swollen joints, and the way he smacks his stomach when he undresses at night, to reassure himself that there's no paunch yet. How quick he is to laugh at himself when he's said something tone-deaf or misinformed. How hard he's worked to get himself where he is, but how peaceful his love, his devotion, for the flawed mother he could so easily shun. How smoothly he has synthesized his two selves, the scrappy kid from rural Vermont raised by alcoholics and the polished Dartmouth graduate lunching with men who append Roman numerals after their names. His genuine belief that he will quit in five years so they can take stock and decide what to do next, that he will shake that job and its whole world from his shoulders without a backward glance.

They both do this. She pretends that the looming financial fears of her childhood, the resulting anxiety that's always muffled but never inactive, has left her with some deeper understanding of how this all works. That she will always understand better than Jessie or Kyle how corrosive it is to live this way. Because she and Jamie don't really need it. And when they give it up, then that will be exculpatory for whatever they've done up to this point. For ten years of adult life spent soaking in other people's hot tubs while the world around them rotted like abandoned fruit.

Jamie tells her that they're lucky, so lucky, so much more in love than most married couples will ever be. And that this luck charges them with the responsibility to do something incredible. That they're both capable of it, if only they are willing to try.

For ten years he has seen her this way, has made her the other half of his fundamental "we," but she knows what he doesn't: that his choice to see her that way doesn't make it the truth. That one day, tomorrow or in three decades, he will figure that out.

"When's your flight, again?" he asks.

The horrifying insult, the charge she's always trying to avoid, is that she's taken a situation and *made it about her*. Whatever you do, *don't make this all about you*. That's the spectral, looming horror: Whatever you do, don't be that girl. Don't be the girl feeding off someone else's pain, don't be a bummer when the boys just want to have a chill night.

But she's never understood how to avoid this. How to resist appropriating someone else's pain without somehow, on some level, ignoring that pain. If you're going to step in, take action, defend someone or help them or fight on their team, then—poof, you've made it about you. What are you supposed to do, exactly, to remove yourself from the equation entirely? Who among them has figured out how to do this? Or is it an essential marker of adulthood, the ability to do so unthinkingly?

"I really can't wait to see you, babe," he says.

If you're a selfish person, does it make any sense to trust that you'll one day be able to identify how it might feel, for once, to be unselfish?

She thinks again of that night in Los Angeles, of running into Liam. All her husband's generosity, all his kindness, and he could never honestly say that it is *virtually impossible* to imagine she might fail. How could he, living with her every day, seeing her? When Liam knew her, saw her each day, everything was still potential energy. Jamie knows her best. And that is maybe the worst part of what she's done to him this week: unless she tells him the most hurtful thing she can tell him, Renzo and Kyle, maybe Mac and Jessie and even Geoff, will now always know something more about her than he does.

She wants to stay out here on the phone, listening to the voice she loves most in the entire world. She wants to imagine burying her face in his neck, the smell of his skin more familiar to her than her own. Then she wants to go inside, find Liam, and kiss his ribs through his worn T-shirt, press her fingertips to the frayed holes in the shirt's wasted collar. Watch his eyes cloud over as she climbs on top of him.

She wants to do both, and it doesn't feel fair that this makes her a monster. Who, if given this choice, wouldn't want both? If you could figure out a way to do it without hurting anyone but yourself, who would ever refuse?

For the first time this week, she permits herself to think about going home. Because she knows that she will. All week, she has tried to protect some idea in the back of her mind, that this isn't nothing, that she could change her ticket, go to LA for a few weeks. But she knows that she will fly to Boston. That she won't be able to walk past a mirror for a while. That, whatever happens, it will get worse before it gets better. That she'll never tell anyone, because no one who knows her husband will comprehend it, let alone forgive it. The only people who could learn this about her and express disapproval but not utter horror, not shock, are the people in this house.

"Are you still there? I should get some sleep," he says.

"I can let you go, then."

She tells her husband that she loves him. She ends the call.

Los Angeles

Clare stopped moving halfway up the walk to the Harmon front door. She stood, holding her car keys in one hand. It should have occurred to her sooner, she thought, that Kyle might not want her to ring the bell. She wasn't clear on whether Mrs. Harmon was aware of whatever was going on. She wasn't clear on what *was* going on.

When Kyle opened the door she was still hovering undecided at the bottom of his front steps, just beyond the penumbra of the porch light. He peered down at her.

"What are you doing? Come here."

She darted up the steps and they collided almost violently. She hadn't realized he was moving toward her for a hug. She squeezed his shoulders, tried to move away again, and was surprised to feel resistance. She realized, her chin wedged against his shoulder, that he was inhaling slowly, taking a deep breath like he was preparing to hold it underwater for a punishing length of time. Then his shoulders heaved, once. He tightened his grip on her waist.

"Ky," she whispered.

She rubbed his back. He took another shuddering breath and squeezed her hips, let her go. He stared past her, at the street, the palm trees.

"It's okay," she said. "What's wrong? What happened?"

"I'm really glad you're here," he said. "I held it together pretty well, I think, but—I'm really glad you're here."

"Me too. You're scaring me, though."

"No," he said, clearing his throat and straightening up again. He took her hand and pulled her past him, into the house. "No, everything's okay. I'm glad he came over, and my mom has—well, I mean, she's honestly been great."

On cue, Sherry Harmon emerged from the dark living room off the foyer, a room in which Clare had never spent any time or even seen anyone else sit down.

"Oh, honey," she said, "I'm so glad it's you. I didn't know if—I mean, it would be lovely to see Jessie as well, I just—Everyone's very worked up tonight. I'm glad, you know. We need a level head to calm us all down."

Clare looked at Kyle, wordless. Since when was he not the level head?

"Sure," she said. "Well, thank you for having me."

Clare tried to peer into the living room without being rude, but Sherry caught her eye.

"Mr. Harmon is actually in New York for the week," she said. "He's, well. I'll catch him up tomorrow, I suppose, on all of this. But, in the meantime. Anything you guys need. The fridge should be well stocked, and I'm—Well, I guess, Kyle, is anyone else coming? I'll just, I'll leave my credit card. You can order something."

"He said he's not hungry," Kyle said.

"Well, your other guests might be."

"Mom, it's like, one a.m. in Los Angeles. Where am I going to order from?"

"And do you think, maybe, I should just try calling—"

"No."

"Just once, Kyle, just to see."

"Mom," he said firmly. "Please do not do that."

"Take the damn credit card," she said then, dropping the softened edges of each word that had clearly been for Clare's benefit. He took it, and she turned back to Clare.

"Let me know if you need anything, okay? Anything at all."

She walked upstairs, still somewhat dazed.

"I think she took something," Kyle said. "Which is fine."

He moved closer, put an arm around Clare's shoulders, and led her to the kitchen. He cracked two beers, produced an enormous bowl of green grapes from the fridge and several boxes of crackers and Cheez-Its and pretzels from cabinets.

"Kyle," Clare said. "What the fuck is going on?"

He braced himself against the kitchen sink with his back to her. When he turned around, he was pale.

"Okay," he said. "So, something happened with Renzo's parents. At least, his mom. I think both of them. But, he had AIM open on his computer, I think? And she walked in and saw it. He was, like, talking to some older guy."

She tried not to react, but he was watching her.

"So this is not a huge shock to you," he said. "This is something you've discussed?"

"Sort of," she said. "I mean, he—He hasn't, like, used the word? But yeah, we've talked about this. Were the IMs—Was he going to meet up with someone?"

Kyle's face slackened; he did the thing where he looked off to the side and for a second seemed bored and even irked by your conversation, and then snapped back to attention, and you realized he'd just been thinking about what to say next.

"What the fuck, Clare," he said. "I mean, he hasn't told me, either, we don't really talk about it. But I knew? I always figured he would tell me when he felt like telling me, it's not like I gave a shit either way. But he's been meeting these—I mean, he's met actual adult men a few times. And you knew about this? This isn't—I mean, this isn't his usual bullshit. This is potentially dangerous."

"I've tried," she said. "He knows how I feel about it."

"Okay, well, I guess we'll table that. That wasn't the issue tonight, technically. I think this was maybe just some guy from USC."

"But they saw," she said.

"Yes."

"And?"

"I honestly don't know completely, but. It seems like it was really bad."

"Okay, and then he called you?"

"No, he just showed up here. He took the bus and then walked. He showed up at the front door and my mom let him in. She said he can stay, you know. She said he can stay here for however long he needs."

"That's nice of her."

Kyle nodded.

"Anyway, I told him you were on your way, and Mac. He didn't want me to call Jess but I did, I just felt like getting Mac over here but not her, it seemed like . . ."

He trailed off.

"I couldn't figure everything out at once."

"No," Clare said, "she should be here. Maybe he won't want to deal with her, but we can deal with her."

"I don't think," Kyle said. "I'm not sure that she or Mac, have been, like, aware. Of any of this."

"That's okay," Clare told him again. She wanted to keep telling him that.

"He also mentioned Liam, so I called him too," Kyle said. Clare wrinkled her nose.

"Can we not, like, invite a dozen people, though?"

"Clare, I have literally called only the exact people he told me to call. And Jessie."

He started removing grapes from the bowl, lining them up on the countertop. She watched him for a moment, then walked over, put her hand on the back of his neck. He'd cut his hair so short that summer that it sprang back like cut grass at her touch. He softened his neck, leaned back into her hand. Then, in a motion so graceful it was hard to believe it was coming from Kyle, he put his hand on top of hers, circled her wrist with his fingers.

"You're a good friend," she said.

"Ugh," he said. "Stop it. I'm not joking."

"You're both wonderful friends," Mac said, appearing suddenly in the kitchen. "Is someone going to explain to me why I was summoned here under cover of night? Are we, like, getting the band together for one last heist? Because, I don't know, junior year starts next week, I've got a slammed schedule this year, I'm not really—"

He saw their faces, then, and trailed off.

"Clare," he said. "Is everyone okay?"

"Everyone's totally fine. I'm going to go find Ren, though. Kyle, you tell him, yeah?"

She stopped to hug Mac, who danced back from her touch at first. *I'm being Kyle*, she thought. *I'm holding him too tightly for too long. We're all passing the fear along the chain. Each one of us can stay calm for our exact prescribed amount of time and not one moment longer.*

"I'll be back down," she said. "I just want to go check on him."

"He's on the third floor," Kyle said. He started to say something else, stopped, picked up the grapes all at once and dumped them back into their bowl.

"What?"

"Nothing, but he might be trying to nap? Just, leave the lights off."

"Why are you being weird?"

"I'm not. I'm not! Go ahead."

"Can I have some of those grapes or have you fondled all of them already?" Mac asked.

She ran up the back staircase that led directly from the kitchen to the third-floor bedrooms, chose a door at random, and knocked.

"Who is it?"

"It's me," she said. "It's Clare."

The room was pitch black, a wedge of light from the hallway in sharp geometry on the floor. She fumbled for the bedside table, a lamp.

"Don't," Renzo hissed at her so loudly that she lost her balance, all but fell onto the bed.

"Okay! Okay."

"I don't wish to be seen," he said. "I've been crying my eyes out."

"That seems reasonable," she said. Even his voice sounded dry and swollen.

"Did he send you up here to scold me about my unsavory habits?"

"Renzo," she said. "Come on."

"No," he said. "He's right. I mean, part of him is just focusing on that because it's the acceptable part, he can't very well express any judgment about the general concept."

"I don't think he has any judgment about your sexual orientation, Ren."

"Charmingly naïve, Clare."

"Okay."

She slipped out of her flip-flops, kicked her legs up. Her eyes adjusted and she could sense him beside her, under the covers, lying on his side. She turned too and inched their bodies an exploratory inch closer together. He didn't balk.

"You know how I have felt about this whole 'meeting strangers in nonpublic places' thing," she said. "But that's not—We don't have to talk about what happened tonight, but that doesn't mean we need to talk about the rest of it, either. You don't have to talk to me about anything. We can just hang out. Come downstairs."

"No," he said. "I really do want to try to sleep."

"Okay."

He waited another few minutes, long enough that she thought he really might be asleep. But then he spoke.

"She was just so disgusted. They both were. It was . . . And then, poor Sherry. For me to just show up like this."

"I think she wants you to stay, though."

"She should be careful. I could live in that pool house without anyone even noticing! I might stay forever."

"Well," Clare said, "that way I'd always know you were safe."

"Don't be creepy," he said. He took his hands out from beneath his pillow and reached for hers, entwined their fingers. "Turns out we had no fucking idea where I'd be safe, did we?"

"Do you want to tell me about it?"

"Oh, Clare. Absolutely not."

A few minutes later she experimented with flexing her fingers, slowly slipping them out of his. He nestled his face more deeply into his pillow.

As she pulled the door closed, she heard someone clear his throat and nearly jumped out of her skin. Liam was standing at the top of the main staircase.

"Hey," he said. "Kyle sent me up to tag in, just in case."

"He's sleeping," Clare said. "Why is Kyle, like—He's acting like Ren's a Victorian invalid who can only receive guests from his four-poster bed, or something."

"Yeah, I don't know," Liam said. "He seems overwhelmed. Kyle."

They both stood there, uncertain who needed to move first. She was blocking the door to Renzo's room and Liam was blocking the stairs. Turning to walk in the other direction, to the back stairs, seemed somehow hostile. But there was always some part of her that wanted to be hostile to Liam. He was too fucking handsome. It was too much, like the most uninteresting possible preference. *Oh, my favorite movie is* Casablanca. *My favorite band is the Beatles. My high school crush is Liam.*

Of course, Renzo was obsessed with him. They had this weird, twisted routine, aggressive and posturing when they were in the same room and then glowing and affectionate behind each other's backs. It drove her nuts, but whenever she tried to complain to Mac or to Kyle, they were uninterested.

"It's nice that you came over," she said.

She could hear Jessie's voice, now, in the kitchen. She could hear Mac's, too, quieter, probably explaining to her why she shouldn't storm upstairs immediately.

"Of course," Liam said. "They're talking about a big party, this weekend. I think Kyle's mom is headed to Palm Desert or something and they're saying we can throw a big thing, to distract him. I don't, I mean—what exactly happened?"

"I don't think he really wants to say," she said. "I think he's just exhausted. I don't know if a Labor Day, like, rager? Is a good idea."

And then, of all the times for it to happen, she burst into tears. She was conscious only of the sobbing, of her throat surging and her eyes squeezing shut. She had no awareness of closing the space between her and Liam and collapsing, of the way he guided them both to sit on the very top step, of the way she was nearly in his lap.

"You have to breathe," he told her. "Count it in, and then count it out. It tricks your body into calming down." He put one hand to the back of her neck, brushing her ear with his thumb, and the other to her knee.

"You're okay," he said. "Renzo's okay, too. Even if he can't stay here he can come stay with me, and we love him. We'll take care of him. You know that. You'll be in his life forever. And you know he loves you. You're great. I mean, you know. You're a good friend."

She laughed.

"Why are you laughing?" he said. But she just shook her head.

"We should go back downstairs." A globe of snot ejected itself from her nose, and he pretended not to notice.

"We can take another minute," he said. "I mean, it's only two o'clock in the morning. We've got all the time in the world."

THURSDAY

21

Technically, they're trespassing.

They park along a winding road near a gate whose sign, hung from rusting chains, states clearly that they aren't permitted past that point. They climb over it and hike down a hillside path until the beach comes into view. A quiet inlet, white sand and abandoned driftwood and the perfect, gleaming water. There's no one there; no one else has ignored the rules.

They're being careful with one another. They brought two coolers, snacks and drinks and lots of bottled water. No alcohol, really, just a few six-packs. Geoff and Renzo carry one cooler, Kyle and Mac the other.

Everyone sets up on the beach. Renzo pairs his phone to a speaker and starts playing obscure tracks, waiting for someone to ask so he can express surprise that they don't already know the band. No one asks.

Liam spreads his towel next to Clare's. Renzo brings them two beers.

"My lieges," he says. "Drink to my good health."

After an hour Clare sits up, woozy.

"I'm going in," she announces. When she has swum out, she turns back and sees Liam diving under. The others are near the shore, throwing a ball back and forth. Liam surfaces right in front of her.

"Hi," she says. "I just wanted to—Kyle knows. I mean, he said something last night, sort of. You know Kyle."

"I love how you just assumed I'd follow you out," Liam says. He looks so unhappy.

"I wanted to apologize, too," she says. "I really am—"

"I didn't say anything to Kyle," he interrupts.

"No, I know that."

"But I'm guessing Renzo's aware, too."

"Believe it or not, I picked up on that at dinner."

They're drifting up and down, moving with the waves. Each one brings their bodies closer together, then farther apart.

He's waiting for her to say it. She wants to kiss him so badly that she could double right over, sink beneath the water and curl into a tight ball of frustration. She usually tries to avoid this, feeling so angry when there's no one else she can plausibly blame.

"I realize how crappy this looks," she tries. "But you're not married. And this whole year has felt so deeply awful, I can't really explain—"

"Oh!" he cries. "Let's not, Clare. I don't need to learn a valuable lesson. I'm not cheating on anyone. *I'm* not married. Thank you for reminding me. Just, stop."

There's nothing she can say. She stops.

"I haven't asked you for anything," he says. "I had the chance to be with the girl I was obsessively in love with in high school, so I took it. Anything else was, you know. Daydreaming. I was aware."

"It's not like that," she says.

"Right," he says. He swims close and takes her hand, interlaces their fingers. He brings her hand up out of the water and kisses her knuckles.

"I knew what this was," he says. "I told you to come back with me because, you know, why not? You seem like you aren't happy. It was worth a shot, no? But I didn't—I knew what this was."

Her back is to the shore now, but when he suddenly submerges their hands she knows why. She ducks under, letting the saltwater cleanse her face of tears. Ashes to ashes, salt to salt. Salt everywhere, crusted on their

skin, clearing their complexions. When they were children it was magical, how soft their cheeks felt after a long day at the beach.

"Who will race me back to shore?" Renzo calls out. Kyle, Jessie, and
Mac are close behind him. Geoff must have stayed on dry land.

"Oh, please," Clare says. Liam laughs, too, clears his throat.

Kyle swims to her side and furrows his brow gently. She shakes her
head once and he grabs her by the waist, tosses her over his shoulder. He's
tall enough that his feet still touch the sandy floor beneath them.

"Kyle, come on!" Renzo wheedles. "I need a real challenge."

He makes a great show of calling out their start, then immediately
doubles back. Kyle will be flopping onto sand before he realizes that he
hasn't actually bested Renzo at anything.

"You're awful," Jessie says.

"Serves Kyle right," Mac says. "For taking you seriously."

Renzo blows him a kiss, and Mac laughs, then turns to follow Kyle.
There is still, even with everything else flying around, that slight hesitance,
for Renzo, Mac, and Jessie to be in close proximity, to find themselves
alone together. Jessie watches him go, until Clare gets her attention. It's the
first time the two women have spoken directly since last night.

"The thing to do," Clare says, "is just cut him off. He'll have to learn
limits. We'll have to train him, to treat us better. We'll have to start from
scratch."

Renzo gathers them close and showers their cheeks with kisses.

"But you'd both miss me terribly," he says. "Once I was reliably
sweet, you'd be bored to death."

"You could get caught trying," Jessie says. "But I'm going back in. I
left my beer with Geoff."

Renzo stays, treading water, and looks at Clare and Liam.

"What are you two up to out here? Solving everything, I hope."

One of our, at this point, innumerable problems, Clare thinks, is that
we are a group of people sorely lacking in any sense of ceremony. The
only bald-faced emotion we're willing to show one another is anger. We
flew here to celebrate turning thirty, what could well end up being half

our lives, and on the first day we thought we might be about to die. And all week, even after that, all we could think to do was spend money and get drunk and bicker about all the same things that have caused us pain since we were fifteen.

She is already telling this week like a story, even in her own memory. She chooses the most evocative details: the breakfast sandwiches, the flower behind her ear, the yoga poses and the chopped shrimp and the sour wine on the deck of a fishing boat. And the imagined audience for this story, as with every story of hers, is Jamie. The one person she wants to tell about the explosive dinner and the conversation with Kyle and just the way it feels to stand on a lanai and look out at the sunset and recognize that, despite your best efforts to know better, you're really enjoying this place that people like you are doing everything they can to ruin—the one person she wants to tell is her husband.

They all missed an opportunity this week. They should have pushed for ceremony. They were here, after all, to celebrate the ends of things: a decade of youthful adulthood, a time in which they could rely on one another as travel partners. They shouldn't have let this occasion, like all the others, pass them by in an ambient, anxious haze. They should have written down intentions and thrown the scraps of paper into the firepit and then run naked along the nighttime beach. They should have sat in a circle and named the things they love about each other, maybe, instead of all the things they find so noxious. But of course, they would never do any of this. They would roll their eyes so hard in the first three seconds they'd pass out.

Maybe Renzo was right, in the end. Maybe they should have just all had sex.

She looks at Liam and Renzo, who are pretending to make conversation, pretending not to notice her silence. She imagines taking their hands in her own, the three of them breathing deep, and then plunging into the water, kicking down until they're on the shallow ocean floor. Watching one another's cheeks puff with effort until they couldn't bear it anymore and then launching up, up, bursting back through the water's surface and gulping air and feeling without a doubt that this was it, they were changed, they had seen something down there right before they lost consciousness from lack of oxygen and this was it, they would look and feel and act and sound like real, thoughtful, responsible, attentive adults from this point on. They had learned something from one another and from the water and from Hawai'i and from the fucking country that they were born into. They would go forward with this new knowledge.

Of course, she does none of this. And they will be leaving this island with only whatever wisdom they had when they got here.

"You know," she says. "I asked Kyle last night. If he thought he would still want me in his life when we were forty-five."

Liam, suddenly, becomes concerned with something Mac is miming from farther in, closer to shore. Maybe he's trying to get them to come join the game; it's not clear. Mac has been the most reserved all morning, not as punishment but seemingly out of genuine self-preservation, and she tells herself that this is why Liam immediately begins to swim back toward the group.

"Mac is being so antisocial. Should we go hassle him?"

"Ren," she says. "Leave it. If he wanted to talk about it, he would."

Renzo nods, turns back to her.

"You're right. I'm sure you're right. In any case, what did Kyle say?"

"He said of course," she said. "It's Kyle. I'm not sure what I expected."

"Ahh, but. You would never ask me such a question. You would never take the risk."

"Everyone seems to take great pleasure this week in explaining my own spinelessness to me."

"I didn't say you were risk-averse, per se. Just that you wouldn't ask me a question if there was a chance the answer might wound."

"Renzo, I present myself to you to be wounded all the fucking time."

"Oh, well. Maybe."

They continue treading water, watching one another.

"Do you think we'll ever talk to one another without being on guard like this? Trying to find the next sore subject?"

"Probably not. You know I'm always rooting for you, Clare. You know that I respect and admire the life you've built for yourself."

"Wow. Thanks."

"See, right there—why is that a bad thing? It's the truth!"

"But it's not the same, is it," she says. "It's not like it was when we were sixteen."

"No," he allows. "It is not like it was when we were sixteen. But then, we are thirty. So."

She looks at him and thinks, One day I will see him for the last time, but we won't know it then. We will nurture some flickering hope that next time it will be easy, fun, that we will hug each other carelessly and curl up together to sleep. And it will take years, decades, before we admit to ourselves that this friendship is officially a thing of the past.

They're never going to be any more similar, any closer, than they are right now. Never again will she and Jessie, for example, be forced into proximity the way they were in high school. But it's also true that they'll never know for sure that this is the last time; they'll never look at each other and think with any certainty, *I'll never see that woman again*. They've made it to thirty as steady, if niggling, presences in one another's lives. Some day they will think, *Jesus, it's been ten years since I saw her*, but they won't have had any advance warning. Until then, they're just stuck here. Unable to clear the air and yet still afraid to say anything that precludes the possibility of doing so in the future.

"Why can't this be enough?" Renzo says. "I love you and I've known you for so long. Why does it have to be that our lives knit together forever? Why is that the only way you'll feel it's been worth it?"

"I don't know," she says truthfully.

"Well, darling, this may be what you get for surrounding yourself with dudes your whole life. I mean, you're the one always watching us all so carefully. You should know this by now."

"I'm glad, that—I'm glad you said that, last night. About high school. I know we can't all just be constantly apologizing to you for things we said fifteen years ago. But I think it's good that you told us. And I am sorry. If that's worth anything."

"I'm sorry, too. For last night. It's none of my business and it's not—It's your life. Your *real* life. I shouldn't have been so flippant."

She stares at him.

"I don't think you've ever apologized to me before."

"Oh, come on," he says, drawing his arm quickly to splash her with a curtain of water. "That's not true and not fair. And certainly shan't encourage me to do it again in future!"

She waits and then says one more thing.

"You're the reason, Ren. That we've all stayed in touch. You're the central, like, centripetal force. You're the connector. You always were."

She can see that it's exactly what he wants to hear. He might have said more, something else to knock her breath from her stomach like a punch, but she'll never know, because Liam is back.

The three of them say nothing at first, treading water. Renzo's eyes move back and forth between Clare and Liam as if they might forget he's there, reveal something. They're all bobbing up and down in the warm water like champagne corks.

"I was serious, before," Renzo says finally. "I was hoping you two were out here dreaming up solutions to all my problems. Forget last night, obviously not our finest hour—but the missile, we got lucky. That was just a manufactured emergency. I'm counting on you two to fix everything else."

"Shit," Liam says. "I think we were counting on you."

The three of them wait for a moment, then another, suspended in the glittering water. They wait to see which of them will be the first one to make a joke, to say something that's actually funny. The first one to grow up, to let the other two off the hook.

Acknowledgments

The period of my life during which I wrote this book was an especially difficult one, and it's quite obvious to me that this novel would not exist without the kindness and care I was shown by the people named here (dating back to when I published my first book) and by so many others.

Thank you to Rumaan Alam, Deborah Antar, Ramona Ausubel, Jeff Bens of Manhattanville College, Julianne Carlson, Essie Chambers, Georgia Clark, Jenny Crapser, Emma Dries, David Dunning, James Faccinto, Jim Fuerst of the New School, Evan Gogel, Mark Iscoe, Emma Ledbetter, Clare Mao, Abra-Metz Dworkin, Stuart Nadler, Lilia Parker-Meyers, Mac Philips, Julia Pierpont, Dan Riley, John Rula, Tamar Schreibman, Lynn Steger Strong, Cynthia D'Aprix Sweeney, Chenault Taylor, and Monika Wasik.

Thank you to Jenny, Miles, Charlie, Katia, Reid, Norris, Elise, Soroko, Peter, Abram, Lubin, Jason, and all the other factual former teenagers who live in this fictional story in a million tiny ways. Thank you especially to Charlie and his parents, Alan and Cuchi, whose real-life home I borrowed for this imagined vacation, and to Miles Rutkowski, for his honesty, humor, and generosity.

Thank you to Christian Caminiti, Sam Graham-Felsen, Eli Hager,

Mandy Berman, and especially the incredible Essie Chambers for reading this book at different stages and for talking me down from various ledges.

Thank you to the women (and a few men) of the Child Care Center in Norwich, Springfield Learning Tree, and the Moss Street Children's Center, for taking such good care of my children while I worked. Thank you to Payton Sheridan, too.

Thank you to Michael Seidenberg. Life without you is unbelievably dull.

Thank you to Caryl Phillips, for striking the match all those years ago.

Thank you to David Burr Gerrard. I miss you. We all miss you terribly.

Thank you to Marya Spence for the steady hand and the clear-eyed intelligence, always. Thank you to Caroline Bleeke, who picked up this book when I was so sick of it that I could scream and then managed, against all odds, to show me with gentle wisdom that it could still be improved. Thank you to Megan Lynch for, even before that, seeing what was not quite there but could be. Thank you to Sydney Jeon, Mackenzie Williams, and everyone else at Flatiron and Janklow & Nesbit. And thank you to Emily Mahon and Katherine Corden for the gorgeous cover design.

Thank you to the extended Mills family. Keith, you are so feverishly missed that even mentioning your name is painful. The fact that we nevertheless talk about you all the time is an indication, I think, of how deeply you're adored.

Thank you to Tony, for sharing his wisdom with me every so often and for making me laugh when I really, really need it. And for allowing himself to be pressed into service so frequently when I moved to his coast in the middle of my final scramble to finish this book.

Thank you to my parents, who gave of themselves for a very long time so that I might grow up to be someone who had the ability (and the temerity) to write books. Theirs are the two voices always in my head—pushing me to do better, to work harder, to keep the faith.

Thank you to my children, both of whose arrivals delayed, thwarted, improved, and deepened key aspects of this book and of its author. You are both so fully your own people, and were from your very first moments, so my character is hardly your concern. But it must be said that becoming your mother has made me better, I think, in nearly every way possible.

Thank you to Connor, for sticking it out even though he'd already experienced this process once. These years were difficult in a way that, ultimately, only you can understand. Thank you for helping me to produce two other important things while I was writing this book, and for making our nomadic little life work for us. But above all, thank you for forcing me to shut the door, ignore the baby (eventually babies), sit down, and finish the goddamn book. I love you.

About the Author

Angelica Baker is the author of the novels *Our Little Racket* and *When We Grow Up*. Her writing has appeared in the *New York Times*, *Vogue*, the *Los Angeles Review of Books*, and *Literary Hub*. She lives in Eugene, Oregon, with her husband and two sons.